michele g.

AFTER THE FALL

A FROM THE WRECKAGE NOVEL

No one can run forever.
Falling may be the only escape.

After The Fall
Copyright © 2016 Michele G. Miller
Published by Enchanted Ink Press

All Rights Reserved.

No part of this book may be reproduced in any form or by any electronic or mechanical means, including information storage and retrieval systems, without written permission from the author, except for the use of brief quotations in a book review.
Copyright infringement is against the law.

This is a work of fiction. Names, characters, places and incidents are the product of the author's imagination or are used fictitiously, any resemblance to any actual persons, living or dead, events, or locales is purely coincidental and not intended by the author.

The author acknowledges the trademarked status and trademark owners of various products referenced in this work of fiction, which have been used without permission. The publication/use of these trademarks is not authorized, associated with, or sponsored by the trademark owner.

Cover by: Designed by Starla
Cover Photography by: Regina Wamba of Mae I Design
Edited by: Samantha Eaton-Roberts

ALSO BY MICHELE G. MILLER

Last Call

From The Wreckage Series
From The Wreckage
Out of Ruins
All That Remains

Standalone FTW spinoffs
West: A male POV Novel
Into the Fire - Dani's story
After The Fall - Austin's story (17+)
Until We Crash - Jess and Carter's story (17+)

The Prophecy of Tyalbrook
Never Let You Fall
Never Let You Go
Never Without You

Havenwood Falls Series
Awaken the Soul, Havenwood Falls High
Avenge the Heart, Havenwood Falls High
Co-written with R.K. Ryals:
Dark Seduction, Havenwood Falls Sin & Silk

CO-WRITTEN WITH MINDY HAYES AS MINDY MICHELE

Nothing Compares To You, a 90s novella

Paper Planes Series
Paper Planes and Other Things We Lost
Subway Stops and the Places We Meet
Chasing Cars and the Lessons We Learned

The Backroads Duet
Love in C Minor, Vol one
Loss in A Major, Vol two

Sign up for Michele's newsletter for exclusive first peeks and other perks.
http://bit.ly/MGMNews

Oh, love, let me see inside your heart
All the cracks and broken parts
The shadows in the light
There's no need to hide

—Hunger, Ross Copperman

THE ENDING

I blink, setting off a bomb of excruciating pain. A mirror has exploded within my head, the shards tearing fissures through my brain matter, chasing the lurking shadows from my mind.

"He's waking up. Tell them he's waking up."

A voice like a gunshot speaks from above me. Loud. Jolting. I turn away from the noise, and a click reverberates, filling my ears as a searing slice of pain screams up my neck, shooting into my jaw.

The shadows return, pressing me down, down, down. I gasp.

"Hey, dude, don't move." I feel a sudden pressure on my forehead. "We've called 9-1-1. Stay still."

My mouth fills with sour bile as I attempt blinking again. My eyes won't open, not completely. My vision is reduced to a slit of light. A glowing face. No. A face, lit by the glow of a cell phone and outlined by the night sky. My mouth opens and nothing comes out. My tongue is thick, coated with the tang of metal. I swallow. Blood?

"Is that—" A feminine voice joins the deeper one above me. She's further away. Standing, maybe? Her gasp is audible. "Ray, that's Austin Rutledge."

Ray's gunshot voice startles me, "Holy—"

Yes. Yes, I'm Austin. What happened? Why won't the words form?

"What about the other—?" the female's voice waivers. There's sniffling. A sharp intake of air. Is she crying? The pressure on my forehead lessens. What did she mean by "the other"? What is "the other"? Answer her question, Ray.

There's a faint whir of sirens in the distance.

"They're almost here. Hang in there, man."

I attempt drawing in a deep breath, wheezing at the pain and lack of oxygen. What is wrong with me? Think, man, think. Where are you?

A scream explodes in my head. A memory.

It's female and blood-curdling.

"Damn it," the words tumble from my lips, blood pooling in my mouth. I twist, spitting out the thick warmth, gagging on it, and on the fear in her scream. Dread coils within my gut.

"You shouldn't move. You could have a spine injury," the wavering female voice advises. Spinal injury?

My mind scrolls through sounds and images in an attempt at figuring things out. There was a scream—*she* screamed, didn't she?

Why can't I remember?

"What do you think happened?" the girl asks Ray. His reply is a low mumble, their voices fading as the sirens become louder as they come closer.

I blink. I have to concentrate to accomplish the simple movement—my forehead wrinkling, my teeth gritting. I have to force it. Each breath is an order, not an act of human nature.

Ray moves out of my line of sight and I focus on the sky. The night is black. No city lights or buildings. It's dark pillows of gray clouds painted against an inky sky with pin prick stars peeking in and out of view.

Red flashing lights break into the haze.

I grip at the cold grass beneath me, my fingers digging into the ground for leverage as I attempt sitting up. It's pointless. My entire left side throbs with pain. I vaguely remember something striking my arm. Do I even have an arm left? I can't feel it, but I'm pretty sure it's there. I hope. I know it was there because earlier she was holding onto it. I see it. I see her—laughing up at me, holding my arm, making a joke.

"C-c-c," the gurgled sound barely touches the air beyond my lips as fire and darkness press down me. Sirens fill the air, much louder now. Doors slam. New voices speak. My eyes slip closed as hands probe. I float between two worlds. Darkness and pain. Darkness fights harder, winning ... except—

Her scream ... her voice.

I jerk awake, but don't move. I'm tied down. Wincing, I force my head to clear. To see. To speak.

"Cassie." Her name is stronger this time. My chest tightens as though my air was cut off.

A face appears before me. "There you are. It's going to be okay, Austin. We're—"

"Cassie." Blood dances over my taste buds as I raise my voice. "Where's Cassie? Where is she?"

The face morphs into a frown, shaking back and forth.

No, don't shake your head at me. Where's Cassie?

My body goes weightless. A gurney. An ambulance. The pieces of the puzzle sort themselves, understanding sinking in. I've woken to a nightmare. I'm being loaded into an ambulance. I'm broken. The police are here. The medics are here.

Cassie?

She's not here.

I blink, forcing my eyes wider—and I vomit as the ambulance doors slam closed. A medic tilts the board I'm attached to sideways as the feeling of movement sets in. The ambulance drives away from the wooded field where my body was found, leaving behind the couple who found me. Leaving behind strobes of red and blue lights.

Leaving behind a black body bag.

BEFORE THE FALL

♥

Four months earlier...

AUSTIN

*Every story has a beginning,
But most of us walk in at the middle…*

What a shitty day. Those legs, though. They have the potential to turn it all around. I lean my shoulder against the cool metal shelving to my right and stare, blatantly. This is the best damn view I've had all day.

The legs aren't long and lean so much as shapely and—thanks to the position of their owner—shown to perfection. She's balancing atop a black stool, her body stretched from her toes to her fingertips as she reaches for the top of a ten-foot shelving unit. Her skirt—probably an acceptable length when standing flat—lifts dangerously high, allowing a glimpse of smooth thighs nearly up to where they meet her ass.

Hell yeah, the legs are worth the stop.

I'm on a quick library run. Grab a book for class and head to dinner. Fifteen minutes, tops. I'm exhausted. My plan for tonight is to grab dinner, knock out my assignments, and throw my ass in bed. But, like everything else about this day, I have no luck. Apparently finding a simple book requires the freaking FBI. I searched row after row for fifteen minutes before giving up and heading to the student desk for assistance. Or I was seeking assistance before I passed the higher reference stacks near the back of the building and caught this pair of smooth legs near the end of the aisle I'm currently standing in. The angel on my shoulder—and I'm surprised he's still there—reminds me of my original intent for being here. *Go find your book, Austin.* But the devil—oh yeah, he's a sneaky son of a bitch—has me admiring the view with the appreciative eye of a connoisseur.

The object of my attention, and a whole lot of lust, drops to the flats of her feet with a heavy exhale. She shakes her arms at her sides before stretching up once again. The girl is determined, and I'm transfixed. She can't be more than five feet tall. Her body, like her legs, is shapely. All of her curves are in all the right places. A curtain of long hair conceals everything else, the dark curls bouncing side-to-side as she struggles. She grunts once more, flipping her head back, and the curtain parts. The strands slide behind her shoulder—a shampoo commercial couldn't have caught the motion any better—and my breath catches.

I know this girl.

Neither her legs nor her ass hold my attention anymore. No, I'm caught by everything about her. I don't know her name, but she intrigued me the moment I spied her reading at a corner table a few nights ago. Her focus is commendable. She sat entranced by her books for hours, never noticing the people around her. Four days into classes and I've seen her here three times. Always at the same table. Always focused. Always alone.

"Excuse me," I call down the aisle before thinking better of it. "I'm looking for a book."

Twisting my way, she braces her palms against the shelving unit, and my breathing becomes difficult as her eyes meet mine. "I'm sorry?"

Damn, I'm turned on by the mere sound of her husky, irritated voice. This girl could wrap me around her finger with one lusty sigh. I have no sense of self-preservation, so I move deeper into the aisle and close the space between us.

"The system says it's in, but I can't locate it." I hold out the slip of paper with the shelving location.

Dark brows lift under black-framed glasses as she studies me. I've seen

her with and without those glasses. Either way, she's adorable. It's not the way I typically describe a girl I'm interested in, but that's her to a T. Adorable.

"And?"

"And I was hoping you could check behind the circulation desk. You work here don't you?"

Her cheeks puff, a disgruntled breath blowing from her mouth as her eyes roll heavenward and she lowers from her toes. "Actually, I don't." From the look on her face, I can tell she's restraining herself from calling me an idiot, or worse. Her irritation with my interruption is palatable, and I grin.

"Oh, my bad." I cock my head to the side. "I see you here all the time. I thought you must—"

"Of course," she nods, her lips twisting as she returns her attention to the shelves before her. "A girl can't possibly be at the library to study?"

A witty retort slips through my mind as my hungry gaze locks on her stretched calves once again. The way her muscles bunch and lengthen, pure lust shoots through me as my mouth goes dry.

"Here, let me give you a hand." It's either that or I grab some popcorn and enjoy the show. Moving toward her is a win-win option.

The heel of her blue flat pops off her right foot as she teeters on the stool. Her shield of hair flips over her shoulder. "You work here?" The sarcasm in her voice is thick as her brown eyes meet mine. "I mean, you're here all the time."

I halt mid-step. Well, hell.

"Touché," I drawl, biting the edge of my tongue as she resumes her search. Stepping back, I linger, watching her. I swear she squares her shoulders as her head tilts sideways and she struggles, reading the titles inches above her eyeline. Okay, I'll make her sweat. Make her ask for help. She can pull books down one by one until she finds what she needs, or she can ask me.

"Do you mind?"

Her frustration propels me forward. "Not at all." I reach up without permission, my fingers skimming the book spines on the top shelf as I move closer, brushing her back lightly with my free hand. "Which do you need?"

Wobbling, she stumbles to the ground as though my touch repulses her. "I wasn't asking for help."

"Which do you need?" I repeat.

"None, thank you." She inches back, her tone formal. I grin, but my boyish smile doesn't dent her facade.

"Oh, c'mon, I'm a foot taller than you. Let me help find your book." The words chase after her as she turns, hurrying down the aisle and out of sight.

Well, that's an ego crusher.

Shoving my hands in my pockets, I return to the main aisle and glance around the nearby stacks. There's no one around. No witnesses to my humiliating rejection. My phone vibrates in my pocket and I fish it out to find Jules's face glowing up at me. For the first time since we ran into each other in July, I don't answer her call. When she shoots me a text a moment later asking about dinner, I ignore it. All I can think of is the tiny little spitfire who blew me off moments ago, and it makes me question what I've been doing with Jules.

CASSIE

The panic is irrational.
He's a college guy hitting on you.
It's nothing…

Moving slowly as to not draw unwanted attention, I return to my things and immediately pack up. My fingers tremble as I stuff my open notebooks into my backpack, and I make a fist, shaking it off. My eyes search my surroundings. *Stop shaking.* I blink rapidly, taking deep breaths and willing the waterworks away. *Stop, Cassie. Just stop.*

"Hey, you weren't gone long. How was the library?" my roommate, Jess, asks when I enter our dorm. She's sitting in lotus position on her bed, her laptop in front of her. A canned laugh track plays from her speakers. I smile after a moment, recognizing the dialogue of a classic comedy.

"I thought you were going to study," I point out, dropping my bag on my desk chair.

"I was. I got distracted."

Don't I know the feeling? I head for the restroom, shaking my head with a half-hearted laugh at her feeble excuse as I close the door. We live in a two-room, shared suite dorm; the two bedrooms are connected by one bathroom in the middle. It's preferable to a community bathroom and more affordable than a private suite. Our other suitemates, Jules and Katie, are from the same small Texas town as Jess. The three of them were friends before coming to A&M; it makes me feel like a bit of an interloper at times. That's my own deal, though; they've been nothing but nice and welcoming from day one. The bathroom door leading to their room is open, so I peek in and wave hello.

Katie's head pops up. "Wanna do dinner?" She's exactly what one pictures a Texas girl to be. Blonde, bubbly, and always put together. Pageant girl, comes to mind, or Dallas Cowboy cheerleader. She's even dating a player on our football team. I like her, despite these things.

"Sure," I agree "Give me a sec."

Pulling the door closed, I lock it and nearly collapse to the floor. Squatting, I hold my hands out. They're shaking. Nervous energy has my leg bouncing.

Stop.

I alternate between flexing my hands and balling my fingers into fists as I press them against my bouncing knee. Coffee-colored eyes under the black bill of a baseball cap flash before me. I was fine, until he brushed up against me.

"Damn it." I stand, shaking out my hands and arms as though I can rid myself of this anxiety. I don't look in the mirror as I splash my face with cold water. I don't have the strength. Fear can't be an option. "You're not afraid." The words are barely a whisper so my roommates don't hear. Taking control is my only option. *I* control my life.

"Okay," I shout, opening Jules and Katie's door, then my own. "Who's ready for dinner?" It's easy to put on an act with people who don't know you.

"Me!" Katie sings as Jess nods, closing her laptop and scrambling from her bed. "I'll message Jules to meet us."

"Would y'all mind if we go to the MSC? I want Panda Express."

"Sounds good to me," Jess nods, and Katie agrees.

We walk the ten minutes to the Memorial Student Center while dripping sweat thanks to the late August heat. There are other dining options closer to Ward Hall, but the MSC is my favorite so far. Completely renovated a few years ago, the school touts it as the 'living room' of A&M. I've been dying to spend more time hanging out in the galleries since arriving on campus five days ago. Katie messages with Jeff Parker, her longtime boyfriend, and Jess goes on and on about the people in her classes and the crazy art professor she has.

"He has this bleach blond goatee, and then no hair on top of his head, with a long ponytail down his back. He's totally the textbook definition of an art professor." Jess trails off, slowing her steps as we pass a few guys walking the other way.

I smirk. Four days with Jess, and I know two things about her for sure—she's boy crazy and she doesn't stop talking. After exchanging a few words and flirtatious smiles, she skips to my side, weaving her arm through mine. "Man, college is going to be so great." Jess grins, glancing back once more as we enter the MSC.

"Are you two driving to Tyler tomorrow night or Saturday morning for the vigil?" Jess asks Katie and Jules once we locate Jules in the crowded dining hall and take our seats.

"Saturday." Katie rips open a soy sauce packet before pouring it over her noodles.

"Are Jeff and Austin bummed they can't go?"

"Sure, he's sad he'll miss out on seeing everyone, but you know him, he's so pumped for the game."

This is our second meal out together and I find myself sitting on the outside of the conversation, chowing on my chicken and broccoli as they discuss the one-year memorial of the Tyler tornado. They told me all about it on move-in day. The storm made state and national news last year. It was devastating. Their lives, an entire town, changed forever by one storm. It's why they're so close; they've been through something major together. Will I ever fit in with them? They finish each other's sentences; I've never had that.

"Cassie, you should come to the DZ mixer tonight."

"Hmm?" I glance at Jess. I heard my name, but I have no idea what else came from her lips. Certainly, she didn't ask me to a sorority event?

"Don't 'hmm' me," Jess frowns as Katie chuckles. "You could try one house. You never know, you might like it."

"Yeah. No." It's sweet of her to include me, but I'm not even open to the possibility.

"Jules is going," Katie hints, as though I'll cave to roommate pressure.

My eyes land on Jules. The girl is as into sorority life as I am, which is funny because, from everything I've heard about her life prior to the tornado, she would be the first girl signed up for Greek life. The Jules I've gotten to know this week is nothing like that Jules. While Jess and Katie went to a mixer last night, Jules ate cereal for dinner and studied in her room with me. I imagine her complicated love life throws her off. Last night she explained her soap opera love story involving West Rutledge and his brother, Austin, and the absolute turmoil it's putting her through. Of the three, I feel closest to her so far. I think she understands that there's more going on with me than the smile on my lips, and she doesn't push me to explain myself.

"Really, you're going?"

"I'm legacy," she shrugs. "Plus, I promised Katie I would." Katie pats her on the head and grins. "You will owe me something huge at a later date though, Luther."

"Ohhh, using the last name. Yes, Mom."

"Oh. My. Gosh, Becky would you look at those chests." Jess's jaw drops as she swivels in her chair, her eyes following a broad-chested, tank-wearing group of guys as they pass near our table. "Excuse me, ladies."

Jules captures her wrist before she causes a scene. "No stalking hot guys across campus tonight, girlfriend."

Pouting, Jess sinks into her chair.

"That one in the middle though," says Katie appreciatively. Jess wipes pretend drool from her chin as Jules nods.

"Y'all are boy crazy."

"Give us time to work our magic, sweet Cassie, and you'll be as crazy as us." Jess winks.

"There was this guy at the library tonight—" Crap. Why did I say that?

Three sets of eyes zero in. "Do tell. Was he hot?"

I downplay the moment. "We bumped into each other, that's all." His eyes flash through my head again. "But, yeah. He was easy on the eyes." I fan myself, playfully living up to my roommates' expectations. Sometimes it's easier to go along with the crowd.

"Maybe I should go with you next time you decide to study at Evans."

That makes me laugh. "What, and miss out on watching Netflix and doing yoga?"

Katie and Jules join in, teasing Jess about her habit of always getting distracted when it comes to doing her work.

"Look who's talking, Kay. You spend more time texting Jeff at night than studying," Jess shoots back.

We take turns pointing out each other's habits as we laugh and eat, and I grin at these three girls I've known less than a week. In one hour they've taken my anxiety from nuclear warning level red to somewhere between code orange and yellow.

"Alright, it's getting late." Katie stacks her dinner trash into a neat pile. "If we want to look our best for the mixer we better haul butt back to the dorm and clean up."

Walking to the first floor of the MSC, I consider my options. Go back to Ward and watch my roommates get ready for a party I don't want to attend, or stay, explore, and find chocolate?

"You know what, you girls have fun. I'll hang here for a bit."

"You sure?" Jess hugs me loosely. It's awkward, but I'm getting used to their hugs.

"Yeah, I want to check out Forsyth. I'll see you later tonight or in the morning."

I wave them off with a 'be safe' and find myself alone. Or as alone as I can be in a sea of people. The student center is huge. I make my way to the Forsyth Gallery on the first floor, eager to see the English Cameo glass on permanent display. I'm strolling through the exhibit in awe when an employee alerts me to the gallery's closing.

"These pieces are beautiful," I sigh, more to myself, but the student employee nods next to me.

"They are. My grandmother had a cameo brooch. I always loved it. These remind me of her."

"How are they made? They're stone engravings, right?"

"Yes, engraving and carving. The artist uses chisels and acid, and a multitude of tools. Once the larger picture is complete, they refine the piece, adding all the minute details. Look at this one for instance—" she leads me toward a plate I admired earlier.

The piece is blue and white and depicts a woman painting a picture in a Greek setting. *On The Terrace* by Thomas and George Woodall.

"See the detail? The buildings in the background at her feet, the canvas she is painting."

I lean closer to the plate—it's not much larger than a dinner plate—just skinnier and a bit longer—and she's right. The Parthenon is in the background, and there are detailed lines in the landscape portrait the woman is painting. "I didn't notice them," I breathe, studying the piece closer now.

"Most people don't. Most people see the beauty on the surface, the obvious, but so often in art the beauty is deeper. You have to take the time to stare, to get to know it, to find it."

Acutely aware I'm holding her up, I thank her. "Are you an art student?" I ask politely as we head for the exit.

"Ha, no. Humanities major. I just love art. I think they're still looking for volunteers if you're interested in being a docent."

"Oh?" It's not something I've considered before. "Thanks, I need to get my schedule under control, but I'll think about it."

"Freshman?" Am I that obvious? I nod. "Don't overwhelm yourself with too much. You'll get the hang of it. Oh, and have some fun, but not too much." Her eyes widen meaningfully. "See ya."

Leaving the gallery, I make a beeline for chocolate and then rush outside. It's a little after 8:00 PM; I have roughly ten to fifteen minutes of sunlight left, so I head for Ward. With the girls at a party, I can study in relative peace, as long as the room next to us keeps their music down. I pass groups of students hanging out, couples holding hands, and friends cutting up.

Where did Jess's group of hot-chested men go? She'd die if I stalked them for her. Granted, pigs'll fly before I do that.

The girl's words in the museum come back to me, "Have some fun, but not too much." I spend the night reading ahead in my sociology text and working on college algebra. Who says I don't know how to have fun?

AUSTIN

Labels.
Football star. Rutledge Boy. Fixer.
Stalker.
If the shoe fits…

"Hey, man, what happened between you and Jules Saturday night?"

I'm tying my shoes in the mostly empty locker room after practice Wednesday when Jeff walks up. Jeff—West's best friend since childhood, and my teammate.

"Isn't this conversation considered a conflict of interest, Parker?"

"Don't give me that shit. I walked with you to her dorm. Katie and I left you there with a sleeping Jules." He sits beside me, lowering his voice. "I told West you two are friends and that's all, but he thinks it's a whole lot more than that."

"He told you about the call?" Jeff nods in response. "Shit."

When I ran into my younger brother's ex over summer semester it didn't seem like a big deal. She rescued me from a bad date at a party. End of story. Except that wasn't the end. I sought her out. I enjoyed her company. I should have known better. West wasn't talking to our family, and Jules was a mess after everything they went through. I thought I was helping. I thought I could fix things.

"Look, man, I don't have to tell you what they've been through. Are you sure you're making the right choice getting between them?"

"You changing your major to psych?" I frown. The truth hurts.

Jeff shakes his head and laughs. "Your head isn't in the game. I saw Coach come down on you out there, and since I know what's going on in your personal life, I thought I'd ask. Katie and I swore we'd stay out of it, but don't let it affect your game, man. We need your best."

"Nothing happened. We fell asleep, West called me, she answered. End of story." I don't have to explain my relationship with Jules to anyone, and certainly not Jeff, but I'm not an asshole who sleeps with his brother's ex. I won't have people thinking that.

"He flipped his lid, man."

"And yet he hasn't called me," I point out. "Or Jules."

"Look, I get it. You're pissed at him for what he did to her. I'm pissed for how he walked away. She's pissed. We're all pissed. At some point someone needs to fix things." He slaps me on the shoulder and walks away. His words—*we need your best*—ringing in my ear.

He's right; my focus sucked today. We're barely two weeks into the season and I'm already exhausted. Personal drama drains the life right out of me. Grabbing my backpack, I slam my locker shut and head out. I'm halfway across campus when my cell vibrates.

Jules: Chicken?

'Chicken' as in Dixie's Chicken. Jules has thanked me a thousand times for introducing her to the place back in July. She's addicted to it, as is most of the student body. A cold beer, some greasy food, and a game of pool might be the thing to snap me out of this funk. Plus, it would give us some time to chat. We've ignored the elephant in the room for days now. I return her text, letting her know I'll meet her there. I have one thing I need to do first.

Cutting across Academic Plaza, I head toward the library. I stalk the building these days. It's not something I'm particularly proud of, my hunting down a girl. Especially one who ran like a scared rabbit the first time we spoke, but after that encounter I can't stop thinking about her and wanting to see her again.

She's in Evans all the time. Sitting in the quiet corners and pouring over textbooks, scribbling notes, typing away on a turquoise laptop. Always alone. She rarely speaks—not in person and not on her cell.

She likes to ignore me. Our eyes have met a few times, and each time hers flick away, as though she has no memory of our run-in a week ago. She doesn't bother smiling at me. I should be turned off, but I'm not. This girl is different. Everything about the way she carries herself tells me so. So I'm waiting. My life is screwed up enough right now. Football, West, Jules. I'll wait for her to look up and give me something, for her to make a move if she wants to.

I tug my ball cap lower over my face, as if that somehow makes me anonymous as I head into Evans. My unnamed girl with the legs is right where she always is, studying in the back corner, with her long, dark hair piled into a messy bun on top of her head, trendy black-framed glasses perched on her pert little nose, and a pen clenched between her teeth. What is it about her that continues bringing me back here night after night?

It's obvious that chasing her will take work. Is that it? I'd like to think I'm not so shallow that it's merely her great ass and legs I'm after. Maybe it is the chase. She keeps ignoring me and I'm not used to that.

Then there's Jules.

"Well if it isn't a few of my favorite ladies," I grin at Jules, Jess, and Katie sitting at the large wooden table when I walk into Dixie's, blinking and transitioning my eyes from the blinding sunlight to the dark bar.

"And yet you didn't bring friends." Jess pouts as I drop my bag and slide in next to Jules. I consider kissing her temple or squeezing her hand, but it doesn't feel right. When did it stop feeling right?

"Sorry, I didn't know I was supposed to provide you with entertainment."

"What good is it to have all of these football connections if I don't get to share in the spoils," Jess asks, scraping her hair up and piling in atop her head. Jules exhales deeply.

I bump Jules's shoulder with my own. "Hi."

"Hey," she offers with a lopsided grin. "How was your day?"

"Long." I pop a fry into my mouth from the pile of food already sitting in the middle of the table. "You ordered for me?"

"I didn't know how much time you had."

I check my cell. "About an hour. I'm on study duty tonight."

"Study duty?" Jess mumbles, her mouth full of chicken.

"That's code for babysitting the rookies," Katie clarifies.

"It's not babysitting, it's accountability. Gotta keep your boy in line."

Katie gives me a dirty look. "And here I thought you guys didn't care about anything but football."

We settle into a comfortable silence as we eat. Except for Jules, who's just silent. When Katie and Jess get lost in something on their phones, I lean into her side.

"You okay?"

"I'm tired."

I study her. There are dark smudges under her blue eyes today. Her face is pale and her hair is back in a messy braid, as though she jumped out of bed late for classes and threw herself together. It reminds me of how she looked back in July when I first bumped into her. Broken, sad, lost.

"Jules?"

Katie and Jess's conversation fades out. My eyes flick to theirs. Katie shakes her head almost imperceptibly; obviously I'm not supposed to push her today. I get it, the phone call with West early Sunday morning sucked. Jules answered my phone at 6AM, and of course he leapt to conclusions, especially after I didn't set him straight when he caught us together at the party the week before.

I exhale and change the subject, for Jules's sake.

"So, where's your fourth, anyway?" I straighten on the bench and look across the table. "Did you scare her off yet, Jess?"

"Nope, she loves me." Jess gives me a saucy look of superiority. "I imagine she's studying. The girl is always studying."

"How have I not met her yet?" I knock Jules with my shoulder once again. "Are you ashamed of me?"

"Well, obviously." She smiles back, returning the shoulder knock. "But Cassie has no interest in dating, so don't worry about impressing her."

Dinner continues on that way. Random conversations about nothing in particular until it's time for me to leave. Jules remains quiet, indifferent. The elephant in the room is not discussed, and I don't get a beer or a game of pool, but I do get two minutes alone with Jules in the corner by the restroom.

"I'm sorry about Saturday, Jules." I stand over her, my body hiding hers from view.

"Don't apologize again, seriously, Austin." Her fingers graze my forearm. "Thanks for meeting me."

"Anytime, candy girl," I assure her, playfully using the nickname I saddled her with at the first party we hung out at.

"Ugh, I can't with that ridiculous nickname," she laughs.

"You love it," I grin, kissing her cheek. "I'll call you tomorrow."

My days settle into the same rhythm they've always had at A&M: wake, eat, class, eat, football, eat, study, sleep, do it all again. I fit one coffee and two lunches with Jules in over the course of two weeks, and I continue to fit strolls through the third floor of Sterling Evans Library into my study routine as much as possible.

CASSIE

*Makeovers. Football. Wingman.
These are normal college experiences...*

"I hear Jules talked you into going to the game tomorrow."

Jess and I are spending a night in. Bonding. That's what she said anyway. Bonding currently looks like me sitting in a chair while she takes her curling wand to my long hair and I paint my nails A&M Maroon, per her request.

I attempt to contain my groan. "Yeah, I'm not sure how I let that happen, honestly."

"It'll be fun."

"I know nothing about sports, Jess."

"It's a good thing your roomies are all ex-cheerleaders in love with football players then."

"In love, huh? Which one have you decided on this week?"

Her knee bumps the back of the chair. "You're lucky my hands are full of your hair right now," she points out. "Anyway, maybe love is too strong a word for me at this point, but Jeff introduced me to Shane the other day, and be still my heart, he is the sweetest thing ever."

I placate her. "I'm sure he is." Last week, Darren, who we met our first night on campus, was the best, and before that one of the Sigma Chi brothers rocked her world. "How do you keep them all straight?"

"Would you believe that most of high school I was shy? I mean, I moved to Rossview at the beginning of freshman year, so even though I made cheerleading, I felt like an outsider. It took me three years to stop letting the queen of the school terrify me into being a pushover—"

"Wait, you were a pushover?" I'm so startled by that I jerk around, Jess's wand burning my scalp. "Crap."

"Hello, hot stick in hair. Don't move." She rushes, releasing my hair as my hand presses to the sore spot.

Setting the wand down, Jess takes a seat on the floor in front of my feet. "I wanted to fit in so I went with the crowd, you know? Aubrey was the crowd." The disgust in her voice is palpable. "She was horrible, but she liked me. So we became best friends. It took me a while to realize she sabotaged everything I went after to keep me under her. She flirted with guys who showed interest in me, she scheduled a mandatory practice during tryouts for a community theatre show I wanted to do. She ruled my life. I was kind of pathetic. Hard to believe, right?"

"Jess, you are one of the most outgoing people I've ever met. I seriously have a hard time picturing you as the type of girl to take a backseat."

"Want to know what changed me?" She leans back and stretches her legs wide into a straddle. "The tornado. I know you've heard all about the changes that occurred in Jules's and Katie's lives. Those of us in the surrounding area were hurt by it too. I mean, I didn't get stuck like they did, and I didn't lose my school."

Twisting her back to the left, then right, Jess clears her throat. I wait for her to finish. "So many things changed for a lot of people. I decided to stop letting Aubrey walk over me all the time, and I met Jules and Katie when they ended up at my school." She pops up from the floor, her cheeks flushed, and I get the feeling maybe she is leaving things out, but who am I to dig for secrets?

"Gosh, I'm restless," she laughs, picking up the curling wand once again. "Your turn. Tell me something about yourself that no one here knows."

"What?"

"We're roommates, we're supposed to share all of our deep, dark secrets."

"I hate nail polish." I hold my finished hand up for her inspection. My fingers look like a kid who can't color inside the lines. "That's my secret."

Jess snickers. "You suck at that."

"I know." A waterfall of hair covers my face.

"Fine, I'll confess first," she sighs as she twirls another section around the wand. "In high school I had a crazy crush on this guy and I never did anything about it."

"That's your deep dark secret?"

"No one knows." Her hand tugs and plays around with each piece of hair she unwinds before another piece is pulled tight. "Not even Katie and Jules."

Since I can't nod with my hair clamped in a hot iron, I give her a thumbs up. "Why didn't you speak up?"

"Like I said, I was a shy pushover."

"Let me guess, the Queen Bee chick stole the guy away, didn't she?"

"Yep, on and off all through high school. They were the cliché prom king and queen type, except she didn't win." Jess cackles, a bit evilly. "To give him credit, he wasn't really into her. He dated around a lot, everybody wanted a piece."

"I've never had a crush on a guy." Other than the one from the library, but that's not truly a crush. Is it?

"I'm sorry, say what now? You've never crushed on a guy?"

Open yourself up, Cassie. Baby steps. "I grew up with a single mother, and not a very great one. She liked men." Jess's face remains passive, so I go on. "A lot of crappy men. It didn't take long for me to know I didn't want to be her."

"Which is why I can't get you to say hi to a single guy." Jess nods, the lightbulb turning on in her head. "So do you judge me for being all boy crazy, then?"

"What? No." I hadn't considered that this is where her mind might go at my statement. "Jess, I had a lot of bad experiences with guys in my life and lived through a lot of crap with my mom. I wouldn't judge you for dating a million guys—as long as they're good to you," I point out purposefully. "I hope one day I'll want to find a nice guy and settle down, but right now I'm okay with being alone."

She leans over me, hugging my neck with one arm. "I'm sorry."

It takes all I have not to tell her more. I finally want to tell someone my whole truth, but I suck the urge back in. College is a new beginning. I tug her arm away. "Enough of this sappy stuff, finish my hair would you?"

"Fine." She goes back to work. Wind, unwind. Wind, unwind. Over and over Jess twirls and primps around my head until my butt is numb and my back stiff.

"So tell me more about this crush you had. Maybe it's time to make a move. Is he here at A&M?"

"Nah, he got a scholarship to Oregon. We haven't spoken since graduation."

"He's a football player, too?" Not like this surprises me. I scoop my phone from my lap and search for Oregon's team. "What's his name? You know I need to see this guy."

"Oh gosh," Jess moans. "You can't tell Katie or Jules. Carter Cooper."

"Carter. Cooper." I repeat as the roster pops on my screen. "Why don't they know about him?"

"Oh they do. I mean, they don't know I liked him, but they know Carter. He dated their best friend Tanya right before senior year. Actually, he was there with them the night of the tornado." She trails off.

My eyes settle on Carter. "Wow." Tan skin, dark hair, light eyes. He has this exotic look about him. I understand the appeal. Jess steals the phone from my hands.

"Yep, that's him. My lady parts just cried a little," she whines, handing my cell back.

"Let's go to the MSC," I suggest after as she finishes my hair. "I can get something chocolatey, and you can stalk hot guys."

"It's nearly ten."

I shrug. "So, your lady parts cannot end the night crying over some guy who wasn't smart enough to see what a catch you were. One night only, I'll be your wingman—woman—sidekick—whatever."

"Eee, I love you."

Twenty minutes later, we're heading out the door to find Jess a cute guy to flirt with. This is the college experience, right?

AUSTIN

I play my ass off. It's what I do.
Football.
Especially when I know she's watching.
I saw her during the spirit walk.
Hell yeah, I play my ass off...

Jules and I sit on my bed, sharing Chinese food and talking. It's our first time hanging out alone in two weeks—since the night of the vigil and the morning of 'the call'—and it's awkward as hell. Her feet are tucked under my calf gathering warmth after being soaked by the steady drizzle of rain that fell during the entire second half of our game this afternoon. I'm pumped after our win, riding the high and enjoying Jules's company, but a dark haired girl surrounded by books won't stop flitting around my mind like a moth floating around a light bulb. She keeps coming back. That had to be her I saw on the walk to the stadium today.

I look at Jules. I keep watching her, waiting for her to say something about us. A few weeks ago I was confused about my feelings for her, now I'm just worried about hurting her.

"I ran into Mindy this morning."

"Yeah?" I ask tentatively, unsure of what my future sister-in-law may have said to her.

"She had some interesting things to say." We both reach for the broccoli chicken in tandem. Jules narrows her eyes, tugging on the box, and I give it up. "You haven't talked to West about us, have you? Or Carson either?"

Are we going to finally do this? Have it out? Is it time?

"Well?" she asks expectantly.

"Well, what?" I play dumb, and she tips her head. Shit, it's time. "No, okay? No, I haven't talked to them. I've been busy, and I was waiting to have something to tell them."

"So, he still thinks we spent the night together?"

"We did spend the night together," I point out.

Jules shoves the broccoli chicken at me in anger. "Not what I meant, and you know it."

"What else did she say?" I clear the bed of our Chinese smorgasbord, and Jules stretches her legs over the edge of the bed.

"That's the interesting part, actually. She said that my dad and West had some fight. That that's why she and Carson didn't come see me."

I school my features. That's not my story to tell. She loves West still, doesn't she? She's sad all the time, and tired. She doesn't have feelings for me. I'm a replacement for West; I'm the brother who was there when he wasn't.

Time to go all in. "Come here," I crook my finger at her.

"Why?" she asks as she moves closer.

Here it goes. "Kiss me."

"What!" She shrinks back incredulously.

"You heard me. Kiss me. Let's figure this out."

She's horrified.

At the prospect of kissing me.

Well, if that doesn't answer our questions about feelings, what will? In my mind I see black glasses and a pair of brown eyes. Her face is all the proof I need about me and Jules. There's nothing here.

"Let's figure this out?" she repeats, her hand smoothing her hair. "Do you hear yourself? If that's how we are approaching this, then I think we've already figured it out, Austin."

My point exactly. Why have we tortured ourselves for so long over this? Releasing a long sigh, I fall onto my pillow. "Damn it."

A strange reaction, considering. I'm not upset by the situation with Jules. I'm frustrated by it, but not hurt or angry. I cover my face, thinking of the right words.

The bed shifts as Jules moves closer into my side, and I cave. "I met this girl."

"You what?"

"There's this girl ... I don't even know her name, but she's different and she seems to hate me, which is—"

"A first for you."

"Different, frustrating," I admit, dropping my hands and rolling to my side. "I didn't want to hurt you."

"You're not hurting me. Oh, Austin, this is our problem. We've both danced around the truth for two months now because we're too damn scared to admit our feelings."

She's right. We play the blame game. She's guilty, I'm guilty, West is absolutely guilty, but in the end we agree we're all a mess, and it's time to deal with it head on.

"I don't know how to forget the hurt he caused," she whispers brokenly, her head resting against my shoulder.

"I know," I pat her thigh. I love this girl, like a sister. In the months since we ran into each other at that frat party, I've opened myself up to her in ways I never thought I would. "No one said love is easy, huh? It confuses the hell out of me."

We sit that way silently for a few minutes.

"So this girl, why does she hate you?"

I sit up, gently shoving her head away. "She doesn't hate me. I mean, I don't think she does. I don't think she knows who I am." Mock horror flashes across Jules's features. "Shut up."

"I can't believe there is a girl on campus who doesn't know the legendary Austin Rutledge." She fans herself, her words coming out breathlessly like an old-time movie actress about to swoon. If she were a guy I'd punch her.

"Don't be a brat," I frown as she bites down her laughter. "She won't smile at me and looks away every time our eyes meet."

"Well, what did you say to her?"

"Nothing."

"Nothing?"

"Not since the first time we met. I mean, I don't know her name, so I use 'met' in the loosest of forms."

"You've only spoken to her once? You? The guy who walks around frat parties like an Adonis and simply snaps his fingers to pick up girls?"

"I haven't picked up any girls in months."

"That's because I've been keeping you busy, my friend. I should feel guilty for throwing you off your game." She digs around the piles of blankets on the bed in search of something. "Tell me about her."

Without Jules's full attention on me I'm able to lean against the wall and consider her request. What do I know about my unnamed prey? She likes to hang out in the library. She's got killer concentration skills, killer legs, a killer ass—

I shift uncomfortably—I doubt these are the attributes Jules is asking about—and my pants are a little bit tighter thanks to the visual.

"She's short."

Jules lifts her head, a bemused grin on her lips. "She's ... short?"

You're an idiot, Austin.

"Ha," Jules jumps, scaring the shit out of me. "Here they are!"

In her hand are two fortune cookies that somehow found their way beneath the tangle of blankets, pillows, and napkins on the bed. "Pick one. Maybe they'll have some sage advice on how to proceed with your short conquest."

"You think you're so cute, don't you?" I pluck the half-crushed cookie from her palm. She nods, popping the wrapper on her fortune as I tear into mine. "Be unconventional, even visionary." I chuckle, reading the words aloud.

"Well, that's so not helpful," she frowns and unfolds hers. Her blue eyes go wide as she stares at the slip of paper between her fingers. "Follow your heart's desire," she reads softly. "This should have been yours."

"Nope." My thumb and finger lift her chin. "That is most definitely yours, Jules Blacklin, and you know it."

Her lip trembles, and I curse my brother for the pain he's caused her, the pain he's caused himself.

"You know, stalking a girl in the library is definitely considered unconventional. Now we need to come up with something visionary to win her over," Jules changes the subject.

"Damn straight. I'm up to the challenge of being a visionary."

A weight lifts after my talk with Jules, and I spend the next week inventing a million reasons to walk through the library, simply to catch a glimpse of my nameless girl. Before practice, after practice. After dinner, instead of dinner. It's absurd, and I'm not sure how much longer I can stand being around myself. I'm a football star; there's no shortage of willing girls in my corner, so why do I troll the library throwing puppy eyes at the one female who doesn't bother looking at me?

CASSIE

He thinks I don't see him. I do.
It's been two weeks since our one conversation, and he keeps showing up.
My hands no longer shake with fear at the sight of him.
No, he seems harmless.
He's only a guy.
Gorgeous with a million-dollar smile...
But still, a guy.
I can ignore the unfamiliar softness of his brown eyes.
I can ignore the way he walks, stops, and stares as though he's waiting for something.
He'll lose interest. They always do once they know they'll get nothing from me...

AUSTIN

Visionary?
Screw that, I can barely find time to tie my shoes.

I feel a bout of depression over the 'loss' of Jules. Which is complete bullshit because we were never going anywhere, and there's a girl in the library who's occupied my thoughts for way too long for me to not have done anything about it. It's time to make a move, but I need to fix things with my brother first.

Since it's our bi-week, I choose to wait until Saturday so I can drive over to Freemont, watch West's game, and have it out with him. And have it out we do; in the damn parking lot. It's probably a good thing for him that I watched him play his heart out beforehand—I was too proud of him to kick his ass. As it is we tussle enough to cause a scene in front of his teammates.

I know West well enough to know I have to push his buttons to get through to him. He's a stubborn jackass.

"You need to make a decision," I tell him as we're about to part, trying to push him to either go after Jules or walk away for good.

"I know," he sighs. "You're right. I'm scared."

"You're a Rutledge. We're not scared of anything."

"Not until her, man. Not until her."

I drive away knowing I did everything I could to help Jules and West. He drives away knowing she was never mine in any way but friendship. The ball's in their court now; I'm out of the game.

A week later, I finally have the time to fix things for me. I'm walking into Sterling Evans when I receive a text.

West: I screwed up again. I let her walk away.

I hadn't heard from him all weekend, and I haven't seen Jules. What's going on with them now? Cursing, I dial him. "What happened?"

"I went to the house party Saturday night. She was hanging with Toby and teasing all the lovesick asshats that were drooling over her. I tried, Austin, I did, but then I saw her tattoo, and it all came rushing back ... the shit I put her through ... I left."

My irritation with his hang ups about does me in. He continues, "She followed me outside." West chuckles softly. "She got pissed at me, and we fought about it all. About me walking away, about the wreck. I thought—" he releases a deep exhale and I hold my breath. "It felt like we were crossing a bridge, and then some douchewad guy showed up."

"Please tell me you told him to get lost." I know that's not what he's about to tell me.

"I'm a fucking idiot."

"You've got to stop doing this, bro. It wasn't your fault. Stop running away, and tell her the whole story." He's quiet. "West?"

"I know. You better not tell Carson I called you crying like a wuss, man."

I laugh. "Don't you remember that one time he and Mindy had that huge fight and broke up? Dude was a wreck. It happens, bro. That's love for you."

West's low chuckle greets me. I'm glad I can make him laugh. "Thanks for talking me off the ledge."

"Anytime."

Crisis semi-averted, I head to the third floor of the library. She's not in any of her usual spots. Damn it. Throwing my books down on a table, I take a seat and set about studying. It's been two hours when I take a break, and for once I run into her unexpectedly. Well, sort of unexpectedly, since I wasn't actually looking for her this time. And I'm legitimately studying. I'm merely taking the long route to the restrooms, just in case. It's completely innocent.

Her eyes are fixated on the blue carpet beneath her feet when I spot her walking my way down an aisle while lugging three thick books. There's no need to debate what I want to do—I step before her, causing a near collision.

"Excuse me, can you help me find a book?" I ask as innocently as possible. Of course, my inquiry for help is fabricated. A guy has to do what a guy has to do.

"Sorry, I don't work here." Her reply is a distracted mumble as she side-steps me without glancing my way. We're so close her flowery scent sets my pulse racing. Damn, it's like I'm an amateur at this.

"So you've told me before."

She pauses. The evil voice in my head whispers a menacing "gotcha" as she moves in slow motion. Her moves are so reluctant; I doubt she wants to look at me. Her movement is fluid, graceful, the way one moves underwater. It's ridiculous, but I have no other way to explain it. Her chin skims her shoulder as her eyes meet mine, and instant recognition flares within the deep brown orbs. My confirmation that she hasn't been clueless to all of my smiles over the last few weeks.

"Then why'd you ask?" The outer edges of her eyes crinkle with a spark of humor, though her lips remain straight.

I'm not as good at denying my smile as she is. My mouth twists as I fabricate an answer, "I can never find help when I need it."

I search the stacks we're standing between, grasping for a title I can ask her about. Shit! What could I possible need in the Women and Gender Studies section?

Her body turns, facing me fully now, as though she senses my panic. A lioness smelling the fear of her prey. I thought I was the lion here! What the hell, man? One dark brow cocks. "Perhaps you're looking in the wrong section?"

Damn, she's perceptive.

"Is this not the Western European Studies section?"

"Western European Studies?" Her cheek muscle flinches, the corner of her mouth tugging up. The change is so fleeting I wonder if I imagined it. "Afraid not." She clears her throat, her eyes bouncing around the area as much as mine were a moment go. "To be honest, I have no clue what section we're in. I was cutting through on my way back to my things."

Her feet shift as she redistributes the heavy books between her arms. I'm an ass for stopping her, but I can't offer to carry her books. Not while we're standing in a section of titles written about women's equality. "The reference desk is over there." Her chin juts toward the clearly marked desk in the center of this floor—a desk I'm well acquainted with. "I'm sure they can help you find the—What was it again?"

"Western European Studies."

"Ahhh, yes." She nods, pursing her lips. She's forcing herself not to laugh at me. This isn't what I had planned for our second meeting, but at least she's speaking to me. "Do you mind if I ask what type of books you're hoping to find there?"

"Incredibly deep and meaningful volumes for the gifted mind."

"Dr. Seuss, then?"

My shout of laughter fills the stacks at her quick wit, and I shake my head with shame. Damn, I walked into that one. I grin, my mind formulating witty comebacks 'Do you like green eggs and ham?' Hell, if the guys on the team could read my thoughts.

We're shushed from someone nearby, and the amazingly sharp-witted, beautiful girl in front of me steps back, effectively putting extra space between us. The humor slips from her features as she bites her lip. I don't think she likes the attention I've amassed with my laughter.

"I need to go, good luck with finding your book." Her head sinks forward on her shoulders in a duck, cover, and run move. She's around the corner of the shelves before I can blink.

I follow after her. "Hey, you don't have to—" My words cut off as I run into two blondes.

Worst timing ever.

"Hey." The girls smile wide. They bounce on their toes, their arms jauntily weaved together. Their heads nearly touch as they eye me like the main dish at their next dinner party. I can't recall their names, but I've seen them at various parties. "Do you know Riley?" Blonde number one asks. Apparently I should know her name. "Riley's Kappa, too. Are you coming to the party this weekend?"

Ah, Kappa, right. Shay? Cher? "Hey, yeah. Um, maybe," I force myself to acknowledge them. My gaze slides over their platinum heads, verifying my prey has disappeared. Again.

Damn it. I still don't know her name.

I AM a stalker. It's the only explanation for what I'm doing. This is damn creepy. I'm creepy. I push open the doors to Evans the following day, ready to make another move. She's bested me twice; today I'm not giving her the chance. I head toward her usual corner. She's slouched over the table reading from a notebook as I approach. With a deep breath, I drop a brand new copy of Dr. Seuss' *Oh, the Places You'll Go* in front of her. "I'm done with this one and thought you might like it," I offer as I pass.

Her musical laughter provides the soundtrack to my walking away.

CASSIE

Isn't the saying "Admitting defeat is half the battle?"
Fine, I admit it.
I'm sitting in my usual spot, pretending to do work,
because yesterday he made me laugh.

This is stupid. I told myself I wasn't going to let him get to me. Pack up, Cassie. Stop waiting on—

A colorful book falls onto my open Sociology notebook.

"I'm done with this one and thought you might like it." *His* voice—there's no need to look up, I recognize the sexy timbre—says over my shoulder.

A brand new copy of *Oh, the Places You'll Go* lies before me. I laugh. Loudly. So loud my throat aches as I spin in my seat. He's walking away. Why is he walking away? I fight the urge to chase him. I should return the book, tell him thanks but no thanks. Growing up with my mother taught me men don't give gifts for free. Yes, I should refuse it. My brain demands I follow him as my fingers pet the bright swirls on the cover. The swirls win. Tucking the book into my lap, I open the cover carefully. The perfect spine crackles as it stretches open. Stuck between the cartoon drawing of a maze path in grass is a yellow sticky note. Bold capital letters spell out:

READ ME

I do as I'm told.

How have I made it through nineteen years without reading this book? I smile at the fantastical illustrations. Joy at the artist's creations fills me. I mouth the words, allowing them to flow in rhythmic cadence, the way they were meant to be. A story of going places and making choices. Getting stuck and finding your way. Unshed tears sting my eyes. My chest aches, my heart beating frantically as the end nears. This children's book is my life. The bleak despair of my past and the bright expectations for my future. My fingers carry the weight of the words with each page they turn. At the end there is another sticky note:

"SEE—INCREDIBLY DEEP AND MEANINGFUL WORDS."

He's right. Does he have any idea exactly how deep and meaningful they are, though? Of course he doesn't, Cassie. He's a guy. He knows nothing about you. He doesn't care about you. I shove it into my backpack and head out. The girls are probably waiting on me for Tuesday Movie Night. I rush across campus, my mind constantly returning to the book lodged in between my homework.

"What are you making us watch?" Jess pounces on me the moment I step into our suite.

The room smells like a movie house. There are three huge bowls of buttered popcorn and several cereal bowls filled with various colorful candies. I pop a Skittle into my mouth and dig the movie out of my bag, tossing it toward Jess.

Her jaw drops.

"Oh, no," Katie groans from her seat on my bed. "Is it something black and white? Something bloody?"

"Wow, who do you people think I am?" I slide my shorts off and find my comfies.

Jules walks into our room from the bathroom as Jess holds the case up. *Ever After.*

Katie's jaw drops much like Jess's did. Jules frowns slightly. I doubt she knows I saw it, because as quickly as her lips sink, they curve back into a smile.

"I figured you two must love all this fairytale BS," I explain to Katie and Jess.

Katie claps. "Are you kidding? I love this movie."

Of course she does. Jess slips the movie in as I get comfortable. There's enough wit to get me through the sappy romance, but my heart catches. I want this. I want to trust someone. I want to love someone. My eyes burn. A book, a baseball cap, and dark eyes forever remaining at the forefront of my mind.

I need to thank him properly. I've read the book multiple times since he gave it to me the other day. Each reading is another slap in the face. The truth of life swimming in the stanzas of a children's book. Who knew?

I've spent the majority of my life hiding in the stacks of libraries—they're my quiet spot, my hiding place from home, from my mother. From her men. Since bumping into *him,* I've lived at the campus library merely in hopes of seeing him. I find him humorous. He shows up every few days and watches me. At first, I was tempted to ask about him, worried he was some crazy stalker, but he seems well-liked and known. There hasn't been one time when he's walked into the library that I haven't seen a bevy of girls stop him with their batting eyelashes and ample chests. When the girls aren't petting him, it's the guys. They fawn over him as though he's a rock-star or something. He must be someone on this campus, but I don't care. I'm not interested in getting to know him. I just want to see him. That's all. His beautiful smile and eyes, those wide shoulders and tall frame … my palms grow damp. It's the heat, it's not him.

No, I need to thank him and return the book. I'll do that and forget about him. It's that simple.

"Cassie?"

"Hmm?"

"I've said your name like three times. Are you okay?" asks Jess beside me, her narrowed eyes scouring my face.

"Sorry, I was thinking about an assignment."

"You're always thinking about schoolwork. You need to have some fun, roomie. Are you sure you don't want to grab a bite to eat with us?"

I sigh inwardly. Jess ambushed me after class, her perky, vibrant, ex-cheerleader self begging me to go with her, Katie, and Jules for lunch off campus. I'm a crappy roommate, and a horrible college freshman. I hide in my room or the library seventy-five percent of the time while my roommates go to parties and football games. I'm a loner. I prefer my own thoughts to those of others. I prefer to stay in the corner. My roommates, not so much. While I've always hated their type, I love them. I love that they give me my space while always letting me know I'm more than welcome to join them. One of these day maybe I'll have the guts to go out with them.

I shake my head, "Not today. Braswell dropped a crap ton of work on us this week." I finished the majority of that work already, but she doesn't know that.

Jess frowns, making me promise to eat dinner with her later as we go our separate ways.

The air conditioning shocks my skin as I enter Evans. It might be October, but the Texas heat hasn't let up. I make my way to my customary corner, lowering myself into the chair and dropping my backpack on the floor. Bending, I remove two notebooks from my bag before pulling out my laptop.

"Do you mind?"

I yelp, my body leaping from the seat—from being startled or from his presence, I couldn't say. "Sorry," he grimaces as my hand traps my racing heart in my chest. His broad frame blocks everything around him as he slips into the chair across the table from me. He's wearing another A&M ball cap today, the bill low, casting a shadow over his eyes. His jaw is covered with a day's worth of stubble. He smiles when my eyes meet his and my computer slides from my fingers to the table. It takes me a second to realize I'm staring.

"No, of course not." I recover my wits and square my shoulders. "Actually, I was hoping to see you—"

"You were, huh?" He leans forward, playfully resting his forearms on the table. A slow burn creeps into my cheeks.

"Uh, yeah. I wanted to thank you for the book," I clarify. "I'd never read it before. Here, I have it with me."

"It was a gift, keep it." His firm refusal stops my hand from reaching into my bag.

He lifts his left wrist, checking his watch. The muscle in his forearm flexes, or flinches, whatever it's called—it moves. His arms are strong. His hands are large. He has to be an athlete with that body and tan. He's tanned as though he spends a lot of time outdoors. He's too—

His hands push against the edge of the table, sliding the chair back as abruptly as he sat, and I gape at him. His mouth twists to the side. "I'm running late, but I saw you walking across campus and wanted to say hi. I'll see ya later."

He moves quickly, gracefully walking away as I stare after him. He turns when he's roughly twenty feet away and catches me staring after him. I suck at being subtle. He flashes a smile, and something oddly familiar rattles in my brain. Warning bells sound as my stomach flutters.

"Hey, you have a name?" he calls, turning heads.

Cassie. "I do," I nod, cool as a cucumber. How I ignore the mental outbreak screaming my name at him and remain unruffled is a mystery. I want to melt into the floor, a puddle of humiliation and nerves. His outburst earns me several dirty glances from the girls at a nearby table.

He grins, cocking his head to the side. His tongue clicks off the roof of his mouth. He must think my evasive answer is cute. I bite the inside of my lower lip hard enough to cause discomfort as he nods and rushes off with a wave.

"Oh. My. Gosh," I mutter to the empty table. He saw me walking across campus. And followed me. Holy cow. I'd assumed he was already here and stopped because he saw me. I close my eyes. He followed me so he could say hi.

A few hours later, I meet Jess for dinner in the commons.

"Any hot gossip from the library?" Jess asks, her brow arching up in excitement as we find a table and set our trays down. The girl could be a reporter for a gossip site; she's constantly poking into my business.

"Hot gossip, why would you ask that?" My neck heats up. Please don't let my cheeks be red.

Jess laughs, "Because I'm teasing you, silly. I have to assume there must be something major to keep you going there day after day."

Apparently my roommate can't grasp the concept of going to a library to study. "Yeah, it's called my grades."

"Psh, grades shmades."

I toy with telling her about the Dr. Seuss book, or about the guy in general, but she would have more questions than I have answers.

"Sorry to disappoint you, but I have nothing of interest to share unless you want to discuss my sociology work."

Jess shudders, "No thank you. I don't know how you can read those books without wanting to kill someone."

If only she knew how right she is.

AUSTIN

Football. School. Sex life.
Judging by my frustration, one of these things is lacking…

I growl, my chest burning as I push through my last eight reps. "Damn, you're powering through this workout, man. What's up? You got a hot piece of ass waiting for you back at your dorm?" Scott laughs, spotting me and steering the barbell back to the rack. Now that Jules isn't playing the role of eye candy for me, the guys have been relentless about hooking me up.

My arms fall dead once relieved of the weight. "Something like that."

"Something like that?"

I sit forward. "Are you that hard up you need details on my sex life?" He doesn't need to know the length of my current dry spell.

A towel slaps me in the face. "Not on your life, man. I'm doing just fine."

The locker talk continues as Scott and I alternate through our upper body workout. What would the girls on campus think if they knew most of the shit they hope we won't spill about them gets spilled? Not all guys talk, but most do. Scott was right, I do have someone to chase, but she won't be hanging out at the bars or diners around campus. I can't figure her out. On one hand, I think maybe she's an excellent actress, the way she teased me the other day about her name kind of shouts skilled flirt, but then I recall the look on her face every time we talk. She comes off as confused and timid. And innocent, I think as I picture those warm doe eyes of hers.

After my workout, I shower quickly, brushing off my teammates' offers of food so I can catch some much needed z's before my first class. Whose idea was it to throw in 6 AM upper body workouts three times a week? Oh yeah, mine. Damn sexual frustration.

I hate that my life is so busy right now. I haven't seen her since my two-minute pop in to say 'hi' last week. Games, practices, meetings, and workouts take up seventy-five percent of my time. Schoolwork to maintain eligibility take the other twenty-five. Anytime I do anything other than football or study, I'm dipping into the reserve of time I'll have to make up. Maybe I should let it go, focus on the game and school.

I toss the idea around for days, working my ass off in the gym and on the field, working extra late on labs and with classes, and ignoring the call of the library. I'm killing myself to keep up with school and football. The thought crosses my mind that one of these days I'm going to have to make a decision about the draft, too. Do I want to go pro early? Do I want to go pro at all? Do I want to keep pounding my body for football? It's all I've even known.

I'm passing the library after another engineering lab when my willpower fails. The thought hits me. I miss her. Her nameless face, the way she chews on her lips while reading, the quiet focus, and of course her great ass and toned legs. They're all I can see. I curse loudly. A girl walking my way on the sidewalk give me a wide berth.

"Sorry," I mumble with a wave.

How can I miss a girl I don't even know? What the hell is up with that? Pulling out my phone, I send a group text to my brothers.

Me: Is the first sign of being whipped not being able to think of anyone else?

Carson, who's two years older and firmly whipped, answers first.

C: Who is this?
Me: Your younger but larger brother, jackass!
C: West?
Me: Shut the hell up and answer the question.

West chimes in before Carson replies.

W: No, if you can think of nothing else it means you're hard up.
Me: You guys suck!!
C: who is this girl who has you texting us for advice?
Me: I don't even know her name. She won't tell me.
W: lost your touch then?
C: no way, you can't be whipped if you don't know her name.
W: Bull, sure he can.
C: Explain, A...

I consider my reply carefully. What in God's name was I thinking asking these two for advice?

Me: Okay, I met this girl in the library—no comments from the peanut gallery—and we've played this little cat and mouse thing. I think she's into me, but she's got no idea who I am. I don't know how to proceed here. I keep thinking about her, but my schedule sucks.
W: so this is the girl you told Jules about?
Me: for real? Jules told you?
W: shit, don't tell her I told you she spilled.
C: why haven't I heard about this chick before now?
Me: whatever, you're both hearing about it now. A little help, please

Their replies are the same. MAKE A MOVE.

Point taken. It's only 8:30 PM. I can head to my room and study more, or I can set up in the library. Yep, there's no real debate here. It's time to hunt down my prey and finally ask her out, or get her name. Hell, who am I kidding? I'll take simply seeing her after the long week I've had.

CASSIE

*Don't sneak up on me.
I don't like being scared,
and I don't like feeling small.*

"This is becoming a habit." His chest brushes against my side as he reaches over my head, his hand covering mine on the leather binding of the book I'm attempting to pull from the shelf. I haven't seen him in a week. I was wondering if he found someone else to bother. It takes all my energy to keep from flinching and pulling away. His presence swallows me whole.

"Well, if it isn't Dr. Seuss himself." I fall to the flats of my feet. He holds the book between us; my hand trembles as I reach for it. "Thank you."

"You're welcome." He grins.

Lord help me, his smile is mesmerizing.

"I feel as though I ought to give you my number."

Huh? Did I miss something? "Your number?"

With me standing on the library stool, we are face-to-face. I avert my focus from his smile to his eyes. Shoot, such a bad idea. They are chocolatey brown with thick, dark lashes any girl would envy. He chuckles softly, and I shift my gaze beyond him, studying the wall of books at his back.

"You seem to always be in need of a giant to help get books down for you."

"A giant, huh?" Stepping down from the stool, I size him up. He is a giant. His shirt stretches over his arms, dipping in the curves of his biceps and hugging his shoulders. He's too big, too strong. My pulse goes to town.

"Compared to you? I would say so," he grins. "Can I help you with anything else?"

"I'm good. Thanks, though."

"Are you sure? I'm here, please use me." He points his thumbs at himself. "My being blessed with all this height can't be for nothing."

I suck the corner of my mouth between my teeth, biting the flesh of my cheek, thoughts of using him flashing through my mind.

"And she smiles. Finally."

Holy cow, this isn't like me. I'm lulled into submission by his soft, playful tone. His smile and his golden eyes draw me closer. I consider laughing. I contemplate saying something brazen.

I come to my senses.

"This is all I need. Thanks again," I nod, indicating the heavy tome in my hand and backing away before returning to my corner table, hyper aware of his eyes following me as we both cross the floor. What is wrong with me? I drop my head to the tabletop when I sit, disgusted with myself. My boy crazy roommates are rubbing off on me. My pulse won't quiet. He's right there, three tables to the right of mine. Sitting with his own books spread before him. He pushes earbuds in as he fusses with his cell phone. After a moment, his head tilts down and he's absorbed by his work. I, on the other hand, can't think to save my life.

This is so not like me.

. . .

"Okay, I've re-read the same paragraph five times." He startles me as he slides out the chair across from mine and sits. "It's no use. I can't concentrate when you're sitting this close."

"You can't?" My little rabbit heart goes wild.

"Don't act as though you don't know what I'm talking about. We've been playing peek-a-boo for twenty minutes. I saw the way your hand popped up to rub your temple when I turned my head with my ever-so-casual eye scratch move."

My skin burns. My mouth is a dry, barren wasteland. No words form. What am I supposed to do here? Do I admit to admiring him? Why would I? Nothing will come of it.

His right brow arches as he studies me. "We both suck at casual stalking."

"I wasn't stalking you. I was doing my work, minding my own business—"

A shout of deep laughter pours from his lips, the sound echoing in the large room full of hushed tones. A group of students at a nearby table turn our way, their faces irked at the interruption.

"My bad," he waves. The girls' faces morph from angry to something else—awestruck? Their eyes bounce between the two of us. Low giggles follow as the nearest girl waves and apologizes to him. To HIM!

My jaw drops as the girl turns to her friends. "Seriously? I did not see her apologize for asking you to be quiet, did I?" His smile widens. A childish, guilt-admitting grin. My fingers itch to close my laptop. Why is he sitting with me, why is he smiling at me, and—I gaze up beneath my lashes—why is he staring at me?

"Don't you have studying to do?" I snap, uncomfortable under his gaze.

He sighs through his nose as his huge hand reaches across the table. "What are you working on that requires such large books?" He steals one of the many books I have stacked around me.

"A sociology paper."

"*Profiles of Child Maltreatment Perpetrators*—"

"Give me that."

"Wow, heavy reading." He angles his head sideways, reading the spines of the titles facing him. "Sex offenders, fatal assault—"

"I'm doing a sociological profile on child assault perpetrators. Yes, it's heavy reading. Life isn't always full of cute rhymes, Dr. Seuss." The words snap like a whip from my lips. What a bitchy thing for me to say.

He crosses his arms over his chest as he sinks back into his chair, his brown eyes thoughtful. So thoughtful I stare at my computer screen to keep from blushing. Why is he here still?

"You don't like me."

My head pops up. It was a statement, not a question. "I don't know you."

"I know, so why don't you like me?"

"I can't ... I don't." I grind my teeth in frustration. "Look, I come to the library to work. I'm not here for the pick-up hour or to parade myself around the meat market. I simply want to write my paper. In peace."

His shoulders lift as he inhales deeply, pushing back his chair. "Okay, then."

He doesn't bother with goodbye, he merely walks away.

I feel horribly rude.

And sad he's gone.

"Oh good! Does this make me look too slutty?" Our door doesn't have time to shut before Jess hits me with her question.

"I was a complete bitch to this guy at the library tonight." I throw my bag on the bed, taking in her outfit. "And no, you look just slutty enough. Another party?"

Jess twists and turns in front of the mirror hanging on the back of our bathroom door. A peppy country anthem blares from Jules and Katie's room through our shared bathroom.

"Five minutes," warns Katie, her head popping out of the bathroom. "Oh, hey." She smiles, waving a black mascara wand in her grip before disappearing again.

"Another night, another party. I'd complain, but the guys ... there are just so many of them." Jess winks, adjusting 'the girls' to their best advantage in her tight tank top. I shake my head. I need more Jess in my life.

"Okay," she settles her full attention on me. "Why were you a bitch to some guy?"

Because guys scare me. "Because he spoke to me," I admit with a shrug.

Jess inhales. It's not subtle, she's done it on several occasions when the subject of guys comes up with me. "Cassie, one of these days you're going to have to tell me what's going on in that head of yours."

Again, this isn't a new conversation. What happened? Less than two months ago I stepped onto campus primed for a fresh start, prepared to put my past—my mother's past—behind me. I was prepared to change.

"Your mother is a loose woman." The words never leave me. As a child, they were whispered in my ear on a weekly, if not daily, basis. It's no wonder they're on perpetual repeat. The older I became the more elaborate the names became—harlot, slut, whore—until the day Molly Green knocked on my door. I was in the fifth grade, still a child, when she appeared at my house and slapped me across the face. I hadn't even stepped a foot onto the brick stoop outside the small home I shared with my mother before her hand whipped across my cheek.

That day, Molly threw out a new name, a name evidently overheard from her mother. *"Homewrecker."* That day, while the neighborhood girls I played with the day before stomped away from my house, I sank to the ground and cried. That day, Mr. Green, Molly's father, carried a suitcase to his car and drove away. From my vantage point across the street, I spied her mother leaning in the doorway watching her husband go, her hands pressed against her face. Most children my age would assume the woman was sad her husband was leaving. I knew better. At the tender age of eleven, I'd learned the signs.

I sigh, looking at my roommate wistfully. "I know."

AUSTIN

Anonymity.
College football stars know no such thing.
But she has no idea who I am.
And for once, I think I've met a girl who might hate me more if she did...

♥

"I owe you an apology."

The last voice I expect to hear this evening startles me. She's standing a few steps outside the doorway to the private study room I booked so I could get some work done. Her bag is slung over her shoulder; her ripped jeans hide her shapely legs today. It doesn't matter. She's as compelling to look at in her hipster-styled t-shirt and jeans combo as she is in her little skirt.

"Are you stalking me?"

"What?" Her fist tightens around the strap over her shoulder, and she takes a step back. "No, of course not. I just got here and I saw you walking—"

I chuckle at her confused vehemence. "You don't have to apologize. You didn't do anything wrong."

Her head swings back and forth. "I was rude."

"So?" I shrug. I want to absolve her of the thought that she somehow owes me an apology. "I was bothering you while you were trying to work. I should be the one apologizing. You were right, this is a library not a—what did you call it? Meat market."

Her cheeks flush. The deep pink against her dark hair and eyes stirs the lust lying dormant in my veins. My attraction to this girl is undeniable, but I won't push myself on her if she isn't interested.

She looks around before stepping closer. "I was hungry and tired."

"Ah, say no more. That explains it. I'm an ass when I'm hangry myself." I tease, and her lips curve up. "Not that you were an ass."

"Well, thanks, I think."

Silence hangs between us for a beat longer than is comfortable. I study her fresh, clean face and damp hair pulled high on her head. She's the complete opposite of every sorority girl I've hooked up with over the last few years.

"Did you finish your paper?"

"Not yet, I'm on my way to work on it now." Her fingers tap the black strap of her bag. I'd like to question her further, keep her standing here talking to me until I can get her name and learn all about her.

"I won't keep you then, good luck," I smile, dismissing her.

She nods, turning and walking away without looking back. I was hoping she'd say something more. I'm too used to girls wanting to be by my side, hounding me for drinks and attention. I have no idea how to play this game when I'm the one doing the chasing.

I close the door to the study room and force myself to work. This week's rivalry game has the guys in my building blowing off a bit too much steam for me. I need peace to finish a paper for my faculty advisor. I need to work, not fret over a nameless girl. Two hours fly by. One more read through and I'll be done. My eyes heavy, I close my laptop and call it a night. The next two days leading up to Saturday's game will be exhausting. The pressure to win rides my shoulders. We all feel it. Get by this one and we're home free until Thanksgiving and rivalry weekend, hopefully.

I walk through the nearly empty third floor, waving to the student assistant at the check-out desk. I love the library at this time of night. It's late enough that it's mostly die hard workers in here. The tapping of keys on laptops, swishing of turning book pages, and buzzing of florescent lights above are the only sounds.

I might have missed her if I hadn't been looking. She's laying across her table, her hand propping her head up. I move closer and find her eyes closed. There are two students nearby, but neither pay me any attention as I sneak up to her. Her books are spread across the table. I lean closer.

"Are you spying on me now, Seuss?" She sits up. Her palm has left a red mark across her cheek. Is it as smooth as it looks?

"Busted." I kneel at the edge of her table, dying to be eye level with her. Her dark eyes are veined with red. She yawns. "I thought you were asleep."

"And you were watching me?" Her lip curls into a cute snarl. "That's not creepy at all."

Shit. That look, the half-smile—I shift, instantly turned on by her voice, by her lips.

"What's your name?" I need to know.

Her brows connect, furrowed in a frown as her face scrunches and we stare at each other. My pulse quickens in anticipation. This nameless girl twists me into a jumbled mess. Wires and cords tangled behind a television. Yarn in a knitters overturned basket. A mangled mess. That's what I am. That's what she makes me.

"C'mon, how long are you going to make me wait?"

Her hands turn busily, closing books, pushing her notes and pens into her backpack. "Why do you want to know?"

"Uh, well—"

"What's a name? Just something your parents saddle you with when you're born, right? I don't need to know your name to talk to you. You're Seuss. That works for me." Shrugging, she zips her bag.

"Seuss, huh? So you don't care to know me?"

"I know you. You're the guy who conveniently bumps into me three times a week in this library. You're the guy who gave a stranger a book" Her tired eyes soften. "Your name isn't going to tell me who you are."

But it will. My name would be instantly recognizable to her. Maybe that would be a bad thing. Maybe she's right, my name doesn't tell anyone who I am. It tells them what I do—Austin Rutledge, football star. I'm more than that. Aren't I?

She pushes her chair back, interrupting my thoughts, and I stand as she does. "Can I walk you out?" Indecision flickers across her face. "To the door. I won't follow you or anything, I swear, I'm as innocent as a lamb."

She harrumphs. "Somehow I doubt that."

"You are making this extremely difficult, Annie."

Her face goes blank. "Annie?"

I attempt to quell my smile, but it doesn't work. "Anonymous Annie. If you get to name me, I get to name you."

The expression on her face tells me she doesn't like the name. Good. Maybe she'll give in and give me her real one.

"Fine."

Or not. "Fine?"

"Yep. I'm heading out the main doors. You coming?"

We take the staircase. Three flights down. Her steps are fast, like a skip. I get the feeling she wants to leave my presence as quickly as possible. When we push out into the crisp night air, she breathes deeply, smelling the early October scent.

"I'm that way," she points toward the right, away from the parking lot.

"Are you walking?" It's a quarter to midnight. She nods, her feet inching further away with each second. "I could give you a ride? Or walk you. You shouldn't walk alone this late."

She shakes her head, as though my suggestion amuses her. "I'm not that far. I'll be fine."

"Please."

Her lips purse as she dangles her keys before me. Hooked on the ring is a small can of mace and a sharp keychain. "I've taken self-defense. I may be small, but I'm not helpless."

I can't argue with her.

"Goodnight." She waves, backing up a few more steps and turning away.

"Goodnight," I whisper to her back. I'm contemplating following her anyway when she spins around, continuing to walk backward.

"See, now I know you're the type of guy to worry about a girl's safety, and I don't even know your name."

"I'm going to wear you down eventually, Annie," I laugh softly.

She twirls back around, waving a hand in the air. "Not likely," she returns, her tone playful despite her words.

Oh, yes I will. I like a good challenge.

CASSIE

His ability to disarm me is disconcerting.
Seuss.
A master of prose.
A fitting name.

"Annie!"

The late-October air holds less humidity today. Fall is upon us, finally. I sniff, searching for the aroma of dying leaves and bonfires. It's silly. It's ten in the morning on a college campus, why would I smell fire of any kind? But I try anyway. The scent of burning leaves is my trigger. My proof of autumn.

"Hey, Annie!"

I pause near a copse of trees at the shout. Annie? Turning, it's him—Seuss—hurrying my way. He's wearing his usual baseball cap with sunglasses, but I would know that huge frame anywhere.

"Hey. I've been yelling for you," he huffs, reaching my side and tugging earbuds from his ears. "What good does it do me to call you a name you won't answer to?"

"You truly are stalking me, aren't you, Seuss?"

"Not today I'm not. My second class got cancelled so I'm meeting some buddies at Rev's. Have you eaten there? Best breakfast taco's around."

"Really?" My stomach growls. The last bit of cereal Jess and I shared this morning isn't cutting it. I'm starving. "I'll have to try it sometime."

"Try it now. My treat." He tugs his sunglasses off with a smile, and my stomach flutters.

"You can't flash those gorgeous eyes at me and expect me to do your bidding. That doesn't work with me," I lie, schooling my features into perfect indifference.

"So you're saying you like my eyes?" His grin holds, widening as he hangs his glasses from his collar. His left brow lifts in challenge to my statement.

"I'm saying it's not going to happen."

"Breakfast? Why not?" He shoves his hands into his pockets.

"Are you this stubborn with everyone, or am I the only one who gets this special treatment?"

He moves in, his large frame towering over me. "I could ask the same question of you, Annie." I swallow hard at his deep tone. I should be scared of him. He's too sure of himself, too cocky. But there's something honest about him. Something—

"You're staring," he whispers huskily as his knuckle skims my cheek.

I jump back, my pulse short circuiting. How did we get so close? I scan our surroundings, verifying there are plenty of students nearby.

He frowns, clearing his throat. "To answer your question, I'm only difficult when I know what I want. I don't like losing." He grins, but his words spoil the affect.

My heart clenches. "Most guys don't." I roll of my eyes. "I have to go."

"Wait, you're leaving?" Disappointment colors his words.

"I've got class. Sorry."

"Let me walk you then."

My head shakes. "That's sweet, really, but not today. Besides, you're meeting friends."

"Tomorrow?"

"Tomorrow, what?"

"I'll walk you to class, your car, your dorm—coffee. Hell, I don't care, but you need to give me something here."

He's pleading. Why does he bother? This guy could probably have any girl on this campus; I notice the looks he gets, he's getting them right now. Whispers and stares follow him. I ignored it at first, but the more I'm around him, the more I notice them. I don't know why he garners attention, but I know I want no part of it.

"I don't like to lose either, Seuss."

His shoulders straighten, his head cocking to the side. "And saying yes to me means you would lose?"

"I think it might."

He nods. His lips releasing a sigh. His hand moves up, as though he intends to run his hands through his hair, but he encounters his ball cap and palms it, pushing the bill lower over his eyes.

"I thought you were gorgeous the first time I saw you in the library—"

"I'm sorry."

"No, let me finish." His hand releases his hat and he leans in without stepping closer. "I thought you were gorgeous, but if I had wanted another gorgeous girl I could have found plenty without nearly half the fight. You're more. I don't have to know your name to know that." He shrugs, a somber smile curling the corner of his mouth.

I hold my breath for a beat longer than necessary. "What do you want with me?" I ask on the exhale.

His head tips lower, his deep brown eyes searching my face. "I told you, I want to get to know you. One coffee. Nothing more."

I can't fight him. I don't want to. "Sorry." But I have to. "I can't."

I can't walk away fast enough. I leave him standing there staring after me, his face twisted in disbelief. I highly doubt he's heard the word 'no' very often. He's smooth, using my words against me. Complimenting me and teasing me.

Coffee and nothing more? Yeah, right.

"Coffee." His hand pops out holding a dark coffee with whipped cream and chocolate shavings on it an hour and a half later as I leave the humanities building. "No strings attached."

I should be completely spooked, but his low voice doesn't scare me. The baritone vibrates in my chest, like a humming. "Fine, I'll give you fifteen minutes."

"It's the chocolate, isn't it? My mom always said chocolate is the way to a woman's heart." His smile transforms him. Even with half his face covered by sunglasses and a hat, the change takes my breath away. It's sincere, honest, and oh so hot.

"Smart woman."

"She was," he nods.

Was? "I'm sorry."

He waves my apology off. "It's been a few years, it's okay."

He nods at everyone we pass as I follow him to a nearby bench. Two guys walk by giving him high-fives and offering good luck for tomorrow.

I take a seat. "What's tomorrow?"

"Eh, nothing," he shrugs. "You're a freshman, right?"

He's totally lying, but I let it slide and nod.

"Where you from?"

"All over. You?"

"Texas boy, born and raised." He tips his head, gripping the bill of his baseball cap as though it's a cowboy hat. I almost expect him to call me 'ma'am'. "Where's all over?"

"It's exactly what it sounds like. You name a state on this side of the Mississippi, and I've lived there."

He turns on the bench, facing me more directly. "You don't like to share much about yourself, do you?"

There are two answers to that question. I give him the one I can. "I'm not being cute, I'm honestly from every state you can think of. I moved around a lot, and before you ask, no I'm not a military kid."

"Do you have a favorite one?"

I don't have to think about that one. "Here."

"Here? As in A&M?"

"Yeah. It's freedom." I don't mean to add the last two words, not out loud.

"Hey, asshole, fifteen minutes!" A shout reaches us from across the quad, and Seuss throws a wave up. Muttering, he pulls his phone from his pocket.

"Friends of yours?"

"Shoot," he mumbles, checking the screen then glancing at me. "Sorry. Yeah, I didn't realize it was so late." He stands and I crane my neck to look up at him. He is ridiculously tall. "Annie, I have to run. Can I have a rain check?"

"It's not raining," I joke, holding my hand out and looking to the sky.

"Don't make me beg. I will, you know."

I stand, too, gathering my courage. "You know where to find me."

That glowing smile hits me again as he nods. "That I do." He leans down, and I hold my breath as his hot breath caresses my face. "Thank you for giving in." His lips brush my cheek lightly. It's not a kiss, it's more like he got closer than he expected, or that's what I'm telling myself as I frown at his words.

"I haven't given in, Seuss."

He's walking backward, laughter playing on his lips. "You have, you just don't know it."

"You're way too cocky for your own good." I laugh in spite of myself as I watch him leave. He bows. I expected no less. I don't stop staring until he jogs out of sight. He's right; I have given in.

Well, fabulous.

There's no reason for me to keep playing this game, right? I've put over 1,000 miles between myself and my past. I like this guy, I can let my guard down. I tell myself these things over and over as I sit in the library that night and wait for Seuss. He always shows up on Thursday nights, and after our coffee break this afternoon, I expect him to be here. My eyes connect with a table of guys I recognize from my Monday public speaking class. They smile, heads nodding, voices carrying when they spot me.

I grin and look at my laptop. I'm cleaning out my e-mail, which has somehow landed in the unmanageable realm in the two months since college started, while I wait. My brain doesn't want to concentrate on assignments. Nope, all I can think about is a pair of dark eyes, muscular arms, and a persistent smile. After I clean up my school account, I bring up my old e-mail, the one I haven't used since leaving home, just to check—

"Hey, you're in our public speaking class, aren't you?" The chair across from me moves as I'm joined by one of the guys from the table. "I'm Drew."

"Drew." I nod, my eyes searching the floor. The other three are packing their bags. The tables in our direct vicinity are mostly empty.

"We're going to get some drinks, want to join us?" He flicks his eyes to his buddies and back to me—no, to my chest.

My fingers adjust my shirt. "Thanks for the offer, but I'm good."

"Awe, c'mon, it's Thursday night. You know you want to let off a little steam."

It's an effort not to roll my eyes. "Really, does that work on the girls around here? Come out drinking with my four buddies, you know you need to let off steam?"

Drew looks taken aback.

"Drew, she's not all that. If she's a bitch, she's not worth it," one of his buddies says, loud enough for us to hear, and I go hot, flushing with embarrassment. To his credit, Drew frowns and waves his friend off.

"Hey, asshole, you want to say that again?"

Drew's buddies straighten, mumbling and taking off toward the stairs as Seuss comes around a stack as though appearing out of thin air. My hand flies to my chest as he strolls to the table, his face a mask. My teeth bite the corner of my lip as I smile and he flicks his eyes toward me with a wink. He freakin' winks.

"You're in my seat." He stands over Drew.

Drew's eyes are bugged. His face wiped clean of the confident swagger he wore moments ago. "Yeah. Hey, man, sorry. My friends are asses. I was asking her if she wanted to get a drink. We're in a class together." His mouth won't stop as he stands and backs away from the chair.

"Drinks, huh?" Seuss looks at me with raised brows. I purse my lips together to keep from laughing. "Let me guess, she said no?"

Drew shrugs and Seuss steps in; their stances remind me of lions fighting over a female during mating season. I expect them to circle each other next, but Drew gives in. "Look, she's with you, I've got it. I didn't know." His hands go up in surrender as he backs away.

"Tell your buddy that she is all that, she's not a bitch, and she is most definitely worth it," he calls out. "Not that he'll ever find out."

"Charming," I gasp as Drew disappears and my personal hero slides into the chair he vacated.

"You okay?" he asks, his eyes finally coming back to me.

"I'm fine. I don't understand why some guys don't know how to take no for an answer. Why do we have to get creative? I mean is it so hard to comprehend? No. Two letters, one word."

"You are talking about that joker and not me, right?"

I relax back into my chair, my hand slapping my forehead. "Sorry, yes," I giggle and he joins in.

"Wow, you laugh? I'm seeing a whole new Annie tonight."

I exhale slowly. He's wearing his trademark ball cap, some gym shorts, and a ripped up A&M Athletics shirt. His arms have definition for days, and my mouth goes dry. As if he realizes I'm staring at him he clears his throat.

"I came from the gym. Sorry, I'm a bit of a mess."

A mess isn't the word I would use. "Uh, you don't have a bag. Did you come here strictly to see me?"

"I did."

"You did?" I shift in my seat.

"I did," he repeats seriously.

There's something so familiar about him. It's on the tip of my tongue, right there—

"That's some intense staring you've got going there. I feel like a mushroom."

"Oh, sorry. It's just that you look so ... wait, what? Mushroom?"

He chuckles under his breath, sitting forward and leaning his elbows on the table. "In my family we call that the mushroom stare. You looked as though you wanted to kill me."

Oh gosh, was I really staring that hard? Of course I was. Chill out, Cassie. He's the same guy who's been stalking you for weeks.

"Do I want to know?" I ask him, leaning in the way he is. I push my laptop to the side, linking my hands in front of me to keep from fiddling out of nervousness. He nods slowly, a grin—that damn sexy grin he's given me before—melting across his face.

"Oh, yeah you do," he murmurs low. "When I was six or seven, my mom tried this new stir-fry recipe. Everyone ate it up the moment the plates were on the table, everyone but me. I sat there, arms crossed until my mother realized her mistake." He sits back and crosses his arms, his face transforming into an angry stare.

"It had mushrooms," I guessed.

"Yep, I hate mushrooms. I refused to eat it until she picked them all out, and after that whenever anyone glared at something, they called it the mushroom glare. My dad thought there was a bug on my plate. He said I looked like I was going to scream, I was so angry. It's not like they didn't know I didn't like them. She'd merely forgotten."

I laugh. "I love mushrooms."

"What?" His arms fall back to the table. His fingertips inches from mine. "This isn't going to work at all, Annie. Mushrooms suck. They squeak."

"They squeak?" I break into laughter, my head falling onto my arm as he continues.

"Yes, don't tell me you've never noticed. And the consistency? Ugh, they're hard, but soft and squishy."

I tilt my head up, my eyes catching the grimace he's making, and holy cow, my stomach aches as I laugh some more.

"You should laugh more often."

I feel the warmth of his finger grazing my knuckles when he speaks, and my laughter dies. Keeping my head on the desk, I roll it sideways and look at him. He sinks forward, laying his chin on the table so we're eye-level.

"Go out with me."

I yank back, my arm hitting my laptop, the screen lighting up. Seuss—I should probably get his real name if he's asking me out—sits up too.

"Tell me your name and go out with me. We've been doing this for weeks now. You can't tell me you're not interested."

I'm two seconds from diving in. From saying yes and telling him my name when my eyes float to the email I'd opened up before Drew sat down. The email I'd made it a point to ignore. And there they are. Message after message …

Subj: Love, please come back
Subj: Where are you
Subj: COME HOME
Subj: I WILL FIND YOU
Subj: DON'T MAKE ME TRACK YOU DOWN

My head spins. Bracing my palms on the desk, I swallow the dinner urging its way up my throat.

"Hey," his hand covers mine as he half-stands from his seat and moves closer. "What's wrong, you look sick. Annie?"

"That's not my name," I slide my fingers from beneath his. "I have to go."

"You have to go?" He flings himself back into the chair so hard the front feet lift from the floor. "Did I do something? I thought we were—"

"Not everything is about you, you know." My numb fingers slap my laptop shut, and I slam everything into my bag. He steps in front of me at the edge of the table.

"Of course it isn't. Something's wrong, and I know it's not me. I'm sorry."

I sigh, forcing myself to breath and remain calm. "No, I'm sorry. It's not you at all. I like you, I do," I pause, the subjects in my email box flashing before me.

"But?"

"But, I—" I can't tell him no and I can't say yes, not right now. "I need to go. I'll see you around, okay."

He nods, his eyes washing over me—studying, searching for answers. "I want to offer to walk you to your dorm, but I already know your answer. Are you sure you'll be okay?"

"I'll be fine, thank you."

I turn at the staircase to find him watching me, hands in his pockets, his face grim. When I'm out of his sight I run. I run down the stairs, push out the doors, and run across the dark campus until I sink to the ground near some bushes and break down.

AUSTIN

I can sleep,
Or I can be a good brother and friend.
Damn, why can't I be an ass?

I've just logged a four-hour nap. It's the best part about early kick-offs and home games, besides the crowd and getting time with Dad. I could roll over and go back to sleep. I'm exhausted. The game was tougher than it should have been, which means practices this week are going to be a special kind of hell. I check my phone for messages and shuffle to the bathroom before throwing myself back under my pillow. My eyes are three seconds from closing when the memory hits me.

Shit.

I check my phone again, re-reading West's text from earlier today.

"I planned a surprise at Freemont for Jules. She'd want you to be there. Tonight at 10."

It's almost ten now. I could be at Freemont in thirty minutes. I should go. I already skipped his game and dinner, I can't continue ignoring them as a couple.

Why am I? There are no hard feelings between us. It was an error in judgement, my weakness for damsels in distress got the better of me. That's how Mindy described it. My macho need to fix things—to fix people—found its way into my relationship with Jules.

Mind made, I snatch my keys from my desk.

Freemont's football facilities pale in comparison to A&M. Of course they would. An SEC premier school versus community college. No contest. To West, though, football is football, at least this year it is. I turn into the parking lot, coming to a stop alongside my brother's black truck. There are other cars in the lot too—Jeff and Carson's included—and my guilt at skipping out on the earlier plans of the night doubles.

I pick up on their laughter the moment I open my door and exit the car. It echoes in the empty football stadium as I walk through the open gates and onto the field. It's aglow with lanterns marking each yard line along the center, and I shake my head impressed with West's skills. The boy would do anything for Jules.

I search them out. There are dark silhouettes milling around off to the side of the lanterns, and near the end zone is West. He's setting up the ball, taking slow precise steps back and then kicking a field goal. I spot Jules a few feet away. Cheers sound as the ball sails through the uprights and West's arms go up signaling the kick as good.

"Damn, you're such a show off, little brother," I call out as I cross the field. He meets me half-way, our eyes connecting before he throws himself at me. We hug, his palm slapping my back.

"All is right with the world again."

West steps back, a wide smile on his lips. "Yeah, it is."

It is. Or it will be once I speak with Jules. West knows me well. He steps back, allowing me to approach Jules on my own.

"Hey."

"Hey, yourself. I'm glad you're here." Her eyes search my face, looking me over. "I've missed you."

"Hey, man." Jeff walks up, breaking the awkwardness between Jules and I. "Dude," he laughs at West, "the ball sailed. Maybe you should walk on as special teams?"

"Are you crazy? They are going to be begging him to play QB." Jules gives Jeff a dirty look.

"That's my cheerleader," West grins as he joins us.

Carson follows. "Rutledge boys at A&M, it's tradition," he says, punching me in the arm. "Sup, brah?"

I punch Carson back as West knocks into my side and Jeff piles on. A full blown skirmish breaks out. We should have been wrestlers, we've had enough practice.

"I thought I was getting a lesson here?" Jules pushes her way into the melee. My head is under Carson's elbow when legs join the group. Female legs.

Carson releases me, and I straighten as he laughs and pushes West. "Well, West is the only one who can kick, so he can play tutor."

"Really? Baby, you can't make a field goal?"

I hold back my laughter as Mindy looks at Carson and he groans as though he hates disappointing her. "Baby, field goals are typically kicked from thirty yards or further. So, no. I can't. I don't even think West can make that distance. Extra-point kicks are easier—"

"And no, he can't make those kicks, either," I laugh, looking at my future sister-in-law for the first time.

Carson replies. I know he does because everyone laughs, but my laughter has died. I blink twice, sure I'm imagining things because—and I think my eyes may be playing tricks on me—Annie is here—in front of me with my best friends and brothers.

"Hey," I manage, staring, completely shell-shocked.

"Hi. What are you doing here?"

"What am *I* doing here? I'm West's brother. What are *you* doing here?"

Silence hangs in the air. I can't stop staring at her.

"Wait! Have you two not met? Seriously?" asks Jess.

Jules steps to my side. "I never introduced you two. You were never around—Cassie, this is Austin. Austin this is Cassie, Jess's roommate."

"Cassie," I repeat. It's all I heard. A name, her name. It's about damn time. I smile.

She returns the smile. "Yeah. Did you come to play ball?"

"Yeah, I did. I had some other things going on earlier, but I hated to miss West's big surprise for Jules, so I took a chance." I look at Jules. "Sorry I couldn't be here earlier."

Jules shakes her head, her face confused. "You two have obviously met before, you seem surprised to see each other."

"*Cassie*," I put emphasis on her name, "and I have met, at the library. Although I didn't know her name, so I had no idea she was your roommate. Small world."

The lightbulb goes off in Jules's brain. "That it is," she agrees.

"Yep." Cassie nods. "Excuse me, I'm going to go learn to kick that ball." I want to stop her, but the look she gives Jules makes me pause.

"What did you do to her?" Jules hisses the moment Cassie is a few feet away.

What did I do to her? The better question is what has she done to me. Shit, I can't force my eyes to leave her. "Nothing! I swear. I helped her at the library one day, and then—"

Jules gasps as the word *library* hits her. "She's the girl, the one you mentioned? How did you not know her name? It's been weeks! And she never mentioned you to me!"

Never mentioned me? That doesn't sting at all. Maybe she has a reason for keeping me to herself. I'm vague, just in case. "We haven't exchanged names. I got the feeling she hates jocks, so I never told her who I was, and she refused to tell me. She thinks I'm cocky."

"No kidding, you?"

"Ha, ha."

She looks across the way toward Cassie who's standing by Mindy and Jess now. "You're right, by the way, she doesn't like jocks. Actually she's not a big fan of guys in general."

This doesn't come as much of a surprise. "Why?"

"I don't really know," she shrugs.

"Jules, get yourself over here so I can show you how it's done."

Jules grabs my arm, dragging me after her. "You and I are going to talk about Cassie later," she promises.

I stop walking, tugging her back. "Hey, Jules, I need you to know one thing." I look at her upturned face, and relief washes over me at the lack of feelings she invokes in me. "I'm not upset about us. I am thrilled for both you and West, okay? You're meant to be together and I'm good with that."

"You're one of my best friends, Austin." Her arms wrap around my waist. "I was scared things would change. You stopped coming around and barely answered my messages."

"No, candy girl," I tease, using the nickname the guys on the team insist on using. "I love you, and I love West. Nothing is going to change. I just needed a few weeks."

"I get that." We part. "I bet I can get more goals than you."

"Ha! You're on."

My eyes linger on Cassie as the girls take turns kicking field goals and screwing around. She doesn't come near me, and every time I walk her way she hurries in the opposite direction.

When she walks to the water cooler, I follow.

"Is everything okay? You know, since Thursday?"

"I'm fine." She lifts her bottle to her lips and turns from me.

I drop it for now. I'm sure it's as much a shock to her, finding out who I am, as her identity is to me. Jules's roommate. I'm floored. I try to recall anything I've heard about her through the guys or Jules in the past few weeks, but nothing specific comes to mind. Jules mentioned her in passing, said she was quiet and she really liked her. That was it. The girl is a mystery to her own roommates.

Good thing I like a good mystery every now and again.

CASSIE

Austin Rutledge. Football star. Football legacy.
Dr. Seuss, my ass.
He's more 007.

I've heard enough about him in passing to know his reputation. How did I not know who he was? It all makes sense now. The intense familiarity I had to him Thursday at the library. The feeling of familiarity every time I looked at him. He's a lot like West. Jules has had West around enough for me to see the similarity, but not enough to put them together. I'm a freakin' idiot.

Gah! And the sweet way he smiled at me Thursday afternoon when he waited for me with coffee. The way his lips grazed my cheek as he thanked me for finally giving in to him. The soft worry he showed after I saw those emails. My body flushes as my pulse quickens.

No. I push thoughts of him away. No. No. No. I will not allow myself another moment of weakness with him. I will not become my mother's daughter. I promised myself.

"So, should I call you Annie or Cassie?"

I expected him to show, but his voice startles me anyway. I chose a seat in the corner today, knowing what I was going to have to do. I'm more than a bit surprised that he didn't show up at the dorm now that he knows where I live.

"Neither." I don't look up.

"Neither?" He slips into the chair next to me. His voice is playful, as though he's awaiting the punchline to my joke. Unfortunately, this isn't a joke.

"Please stop bothering me." My grip tightens on the pen I'm holding. "I'm not interested and I would like for you to leave me alone."

He clears his throat. Garbled words form and fall from his lips, as though he can't think of what to say. Not in a full sentence anyway.

"Cassie?" His chest moves closer. I force myself to continue staring at the paper in front of me. "I didn't know who you were. You believe that don't you?"

I swallow hard.

We sit in silence for fifteen minutes, maybe longer. I stare at the pen in my hand resting on a blank notebook as he sits beside me. His face isn't far from mine. I steal glances out of the corner of my eye, but I pretend to ignore him. I've conditioned myself to look straight ahead. I'm good at ignoring people near me when I need to. It's self-preservation.

"Okay," he says after a while. "Jules said—"

"Don't talk to Jules about me!" My concentration breaks at her name. Fear takes over as I look at him. "I have to live with her, she's my friend. Please."

"Hey," his hand touches mine. A mask of worry slips over his face as I yank away.

"I can't do this." My throat clogs. Standing, I swing my bag over my shoulder and grab my things from the table. I remind myself I'm not only doing this for me, but for him as tears fall before I've even exited the building.

He doesn't follow, so I stop going to the library.

AUSTIN

*It's not that I've never been rejected,
It has happened once, or twice.
It's that every instinct I have tells me she didn't* want *to say no, but that she had* to.

"Austin?" Jules lifts her sunglasses up as she walks across the parking lot.

"What can you tell me about her?"

"Her? Oh, Cassie," she sighs, sliding her glasses into her hair and joining me leaning against her car. "What's going on?"

"I was hoping you could tell me. She stopped going to the library. I haven't seen her there in weeks."

Jules's forehead wrinkles. "Weeks? I don't know. Jess mentioned she felt like Cassie was acting strange back at Halloween, but she hasn't said anything."

"Strange how?" I push away from the car, stuffing my hands into my pockets. "Don't try to spare my feelings, Jules. I'm going crazy here."

"Your feelings?" Her shoulders shake with sad laughter. "Austin, what feelings? I don't understand you two. You're asking me questions I can't answer when neither of you will explain your relationship."

I groan, pushing my fingers through my hair. "There isn't one. We flirted, that's all. I didn't even know her name until that night at Freemont. Then she told me to stop bothering her. Jules, she disappeared. You told me once she didn't seem to care for jocks. Is that really it? Could she hate me because I play football?"

"Hey—" her hand skims my back. "Cassie doesn't know you well enough to hate you."

Jules soft compassion is my breaking point. "That's what I'm saying. We were finally getting somewhere. She was coming around to me; I could see it. Then she found out who I was and—" I don't finish my thoughts. The parking lot is no longer mostly empty. Students loiter about, and I sense my outburst is being witnessed by prying eyes. "Forget it. I don't know why it bothers me so much."

Jules grins, bumping into my side. "Because Austin Rutledge can't stand being turned down."

She's teasing me, I understand it and play along, but as I leave her my mind laughs at me. At Jules. I wish it were that simple. I wish it were an ego issue. It's not though. It's more. It's Cassie. She didn't run away because she doesn't like me, she ran away because she does.

She ran away because she was scared. I saw it in her eyes every time she looked at me. She was scared, not of me, but of her feelings.

The problem with Cassie and I is she's Jules roommate. She's my brother's girlfriend's roommate. Katie and Jess's roommate. It's my own private hell on earth that the one girl I find myself wanting is the one girl who won't speak to me. The one girl I can't keep from seeing.

CASSIE

*The emails keep coming.
Angry, scary emails, warning me.
It's only a matter of time.*

I've managed to block Austin Rutledge from my mind. Okay, that's a complete and utter lie. I've thought about him many times. Too many to count, but I've blocked him from life. I go home to Tyler with Jess for Thanksgiving, and thankfully Austin and his family, along with Jules, celebrate here instead of in Tyler.

I change libraries for studying, I block private study rooms, or stay in the dorm to keep from running into him. I skip tailgating, football games, and parties—except for one. I couldn't help myself. I wanted to see him play once before the season was over. It was a mistake. I could barely follow the game, but my heart raced from the moment he ran onto the field until the moment he walked off.

I've done everything in my power to keep myself from thinking about this guy. Everything. Nothing works. It doesn't matter. I can think about him all I want. I just can't do anything with him. I'm not sure if I can even stay at A&M. I certainly can't allow myself to fall for a high profile football player.

♥

There were two strikes against him from day one. My mother's past, and mine. I thought maybe I'd outrun mine, but it's only a matter of time before I have to make a move. Which is why I follow Austin when I spot him walking across campus by himself a few days into winter break.

"Austin," I call when I'm a few yards behind him.

He pivots, steam rising from the coffee cup in his hand, twirling through the cool air and mingling with his breath. "Cassie." He nods and continues walking.

I shuffle to his side. "How are you?"

"Good, thanks. You?"

"I'm okay."

"I'm glad." He sips his coffee, his eyes remaining straight on. "Look, I'm heading to a team meeting and practice, so I need to hurry."

"Oh, okay ... sure." I stop. He walks a few more steps and pauses.

I should go. Walk away now. He shifts, slowly turning before I can get up the nerve to walk away.

"Did you need something?" he asks, his eyes finally latching onto mine.

My head shake on its own, and he nods. "No," I call as his eyes close and I walk the four steps it takes to be at his side. "I mean, I'm sorry."

"For what?" His face remains unemotional as he looks down toward me.

"I'm sorry for what I said. I'm sorry I told you to leave me alone."

The corner of his mouth twitches and my heart beats faster.

"Are you?" The corner tugs into a grin. "So, have you changed your mind?"

This was a mistake.

"I'm sorry," my head shakes as I make my excuse. His lips fall to a straight line. His eyes narrow. "I wish I could, but I can't."

"Then why in the hell are you apologizing, Cassie? I don't need to be jerked around. I've got to go."

"Austin." Grabbing his elbow, I tug him back. "I wish I could explain it to you, but I can't. You're better off, trust me on that."

He gives a disgusted laugh. "You're probably right. I'm sure I'll see you around."

My fingers drop from his sweatshirt. "Good luck in the bowl game. Oh, and have fun in St. Lucia for your brother's wedding. The Caribbean while the rest of us are freezing here, lucky you."

He pauses again. This conversation is like a game of tug of war—he pulls at my heart, I back up. He takes a step, I tug at him until he stops.

He checks his watch and frowns. "Why are you on campus still? Aren't you done with your finals?"

"I'm staying through break."

"Alone?"

The worry he's shown every time he offered to walk me to my dorm appears. I grin. If I run, I'd like for him to have a nice memory, not one of me forcing him out of my life.

"I'm a big girl, remember?"

His hand lifts, rubbing the back of his head. "Yeah, sure. I'll be back on campus after the first of the year. If you need anything, let me know."

"Get to your meeting," I offer when he checks his watch again. "And thanks."

There's a moment when I think he's going to say more, but he nods and turns, hurrying toward the athletic facilities and away from me. Jules said he was a good guy, a great guy. She begged me to give him a chance and I refused, but God knows I want to change my mind. There's something about Austin that speaks to me. Something about the way he's always looked at me, as though he's looking within me, going deeper than the beauty, than the exterior. He peers into the dirty parts of my life.

The dirty parts I refuse to let anyone see. The parts that will kill me if I have to go back.

THE FALL

January

CASSIE

Terror.
It's a visual word, conjuring up pictures of cowering, simpering, helpless people.
It rushes through me.
Fright. Horror. Terror.

Every descriptive word one might use for what I'm feeling rolls through my mind as my cell phone beeps. The words "Call Ended" greet me, and I drop the phone from my hand, the urge to smash it beneath my heel overtaking me. Opening my throat to the first breath of air I've taken since the phone rang, I move quickly.

Without thinking, I flip off my lights, plunging the dorm into darkness as my fingers wrap around my keys, stabbing my palm in my haste.

I shake my hand out as I grab my shoes, fumbling them on as my door clicks shut behind me.

Run.

That one word replaces the others. It's louder and more urgent than terror, fright, and horror.

Run.

I tense, ready to listen as another word sneaks in between my reminders to breath and the urgency to run.

A name shifts to the forefront of the chaos in my mind.

I slip out of Ward Hall through the side door, rain slapping my face as I run.

To him.

AUSTIN

Who leaves St. Lucia early?
That is what I ask myself during my eleven-hour travel day.
That is what I ask myself when my homeward-bound plane lands in a storm
And as I walk to long-term parking and find my car in the pouring rain.
I could be drinking rum and swinging in a hammock under the stars right now...

Frantic knocking at my door wakes me. I fell asleep within moments of sprawling across my bed in my dorm room mere hours ago. Damn, I should have gone to the house. The knocks turn to a thud, as if there's a palm slapping against it and I shove my head under my pillow. After a pause, two more thuds have me rolling from my bed still half-asleep.

A gust of rain assaults me as I open the door; the droplets are shards of ice against my warm skin. "Cassie?" I shake my head to clear the mirage, but she's still here. "What are—" Cassie shivers, her thin shirt and jeans no match for a dry January night, let alone tonight's squall. "You must be freezing, come in here."

I move aside, opening the door wider and steering her into my small room toward my unmade bed. Water rolls down her face as she silently greets me with her eyes; they scan my face and touch on my bare chest before averting to the floor.

"Um, I was asleep," I explain, snatching a shirt from the end of my bed and slipping it over my head. My fingers comb through my hair nervously. "Here, sit down."

I smooth my sheets and comforter into some semblance of order as Cassie toes off her wet shoes, leaving them at the door before walking toward the bed. She lowers herself to the edge of my mattress, folding her legs to her chest and hugging her shins tightly. Her brown eyes peek over her knees, taking in my room before she lowers her forehead and silently hides her face from view.

My mouth opens and closes a few times, unsure of what to say. Usually I'm much better with midnight visits from beautiful girls, but this one is different. This is Cassie.

The wavering rasp of long, deep inhales and exhales leaks out of from within the ball she's formed. I count them, breathing in sync with her as I do. Waiting. *One. Two. Three. Four.* The chatter of her teeth spark the first coherent thought I've had since she knocked on my door. "You must be soaked through. What were you doing out there?"

I retrieve a blanket from the chair in the corner, draping it across her back and shoulders. She flinches. I was merely trying to warm her, to help her, and she flinches? I step back, throwing my hands in the air in a state of surrender as I put space between us. There's something about her that never fails to make me feel guilty. A stiffening in her posture, the unsure wrinkling of her brow—it makes me second-guess my every move around her, as though I'm doing something wrong.

She sighs, her typically graceful fingers curling tightly along the blanket's edge, pulling it closer to her body. She grips the throw as though it's a life preserver. Maybe it is. I've never seen her like this. I've never seen anyone look like this. There's desperation in her wide brown eyes. Desperation and hopelessness. And fear. Yes, definitely fear. This is Cassie after all; she's always afraid.

Her blanket-covered shoulders twitch and shudder, snapping me out of my personal musings.

"Let me find you something dry to change into? Do you want a coffee?"

"I shouldn't have come here," she sniffs, tugging the blue blanket even tighter around her.

I put the length of the room between us after she flinched at me, afraid of getting too close, afraid of spooking her. God, we've played this game of chase for months. Cassie's an enigma. Four months, and she's resisted me at every turn. Regardless of how often we see each other, regardless of her being suitemates with one of my best friends, this girl sitting on my bed, soaked to the bone with tears streaming down her face, has wanted nothing to do with me.

Until tonight.

"Then why did you?"

She lifts her head higher, her chin coming to rest on her knees. Sad doe eyes find me over jean-clad knees. "I needed to feel safe." The words are muffled and meek, uttered into her legs and my blanket.

Needed to feel safe? I'm across the room and at her side in three steps. To hell with spooking her, I'm freaking Clark Kent ready to strip into my Superman suit and save this damsel in distress.

I set my hand on her shoulder carefully. "Cassie?"

Releasing the blanket, her hand shoves her wet hair out of her pale face. When she rubs her jaw and chin against her shoulder, I take the opportunity to study her profile. Water drips down her temple, a solitary drop meandering along her skin, curving toward her jawline and slipping down her neck. Following the movement lights a fire in my veins, heating my blood. I swallow, my eyes moving to her lips. They're rapidly taking on a blue hue. She presses them together, sucking her trembling bottom lip under the top as though she's trying to tamp down the quivering, but her chin continues its shaking. Her head dips lower again as she tugs the blanket up, hiding her face from my view.

A weight crushes my chest. When she apologized to me the day before break, I was relieved. I could move on. She made it clear her position hadn't changed, she isn't—or couldn't be—interested in going out with me. We parted ways, my brain telling me it's cool, I'll get over it.

Yeah, I was wrong.

Cassie turns her face, resting her cheek against her knees, and finally looks at me again. "Can I stay here? Just for tonight. Would you mind?"

"Would I mind?" I repeat her request out loud to be sure I'm not hearing things. A barrage of questions runs through my mind as my eyes scan hers, but the anxiety staring back at me keeps me from asking a single one. I force them to the back of my throat, shelving them. They're words best saved for another time.

"Sure."

The one-word answer acts like a switch, releasing the tightness in Cassie's face and smoothing her forehead. "Thank you," she utters on the softest of breaths.

Anytime.

The promise doesn't fall from my lips as tenderness builds within me. I felt it the first time I saw her, this longing to know her, to give her whatever she wanted. I stand, frustration tightening my jaw. *Damn these thoughts.* I need to calm the rage within me. I can't stand the defeated look in her eyes. My gut churns at her uneasy voice. My eyes reject the dullness in hers. They're usually full of anger or sass when she's around me, never this cold, lost look.

As though she read my mind, she sighs. "No questions asked, okay?"

"Let me get something for you to change into," I offer, avoiding her request for the time being.

"Austin?" I freeze as I'm opening my dresser drawer, keeping my back to her. "No questions." Her words have a little extra oomph behind them this time. A little more Cassie.

There's no doubt in my mind she'll walk out of this room if I refuse her terms. Locating a pair of sweats and sliding the dresser shut, I hold the outfit out to her as I make my decision. "Okay."

The steady beat of rain lashing against my window fills the space between us. Ten feet, if that, of tense, wordless conversation. Cassie studies me, her jaw shifting side to side as though she's grinding her teeth while thinking. I relax my muscles, letting go of some of my worry as she gets her fill. My mouth molds into a small grin as I stretch my arm out, holding the thick, dry sweats between my fingers like a white flag—my surrender to her demand.

She accepts it, dropping the blanket as she stands. With an inward sigh, I locate a clean towel and show her to my bathroom. My eyes scan the tile floor and counter, relieved to see it's relatively clean for three football players. Thank God Mom forced us to clean after ourselves as kids.

"I share the bathroom with two other players, but they're both home for break." I set the items on the toilet. "You can take your time."

She doesn't reply, just offers a small smile as I close the door behind me. The click of the lock is a fist of rejection to my gut.

Now that she's out of sight, I allow myself to ask silent questions.

It's midnight. What is she doing out in the rain at this time of night? Why did she cross the campus from Ward to my building? And what is she scared of? Because she sure as hell is scared; it doesn't take a genius to see that. She's so scared she came here, to me. Why?

Question after question piles up as the shower mixes with the rhythm of the rain pounding against the window.

I part the blinds, peering out into the bleak night. The windows of the adjacent residence halls are mostly black. It's winter break, the campus is relatively vacant. I shouldn't even be here. I wasn't supposed to be back for two more days, but St. Lucia held little appeal after a week. Especially when I knew Cassie would be here alone. I'd considered all the ways to approach her while flying home today. Ten hours of flights, layovers, driving, and no answers. I never dreamed she'd show up at my door instead of me at hers.

Scrubbing my hands over my face and through my disheveled hair, I throw myself into the chair opposite the bathroom and wait.

Finally, the bathroom door inches open.

"I didn't hear the water turn off." I straighten in my chair, longing to check out my clothing on her body, but my eyes remain above her shoulders. For now. "Better?"

She glances down. "You're a bit larger than me."

"You think?" I challenge with a grin. "I think they look better on you." I don't have to look to know that much is true.

"I think you're blind."

"Just honest."

We stare at each other in silence a beat longer than is comfortable.

"Well, they're warm," she says. "Thank you."

The long sleeves of my sweatshirt puddle in her palms as she checks out my room. I tear my eyes away from her, looking at what she sees. Four walls. One bed. A desk and chair. At the end of my bed is a bookshelf with a flat screen television sitting on top. Across from that is my papasan—more commonly referred to as the comfy chair by the guys on the team—the blue suede cushion visibly soft and worn from years of use. My walls are bare, with the exception of a poster of me in uniform and a string of beer can lights hanging along the ceiling line. There are no other posters, no half-naked girls, or traditionally obscene manly items. My dorm is clean and sparse, atypical of most college guys.

"How did you know where I live?" I ask as she looks around.

Her shoulders lift for a moment before dropping back down passively. "Doesn't everyone know where Austin Rutledge lives?" She looks over her shoulder and grins. "Actually, Jules told me a while back."

"Big man on campus ... How did I not know, before?" she asks in a low voice as she moves toward the poster, studying it up close.

"I have to admit, I asked myself that question many times." Uncomfortable with her studying the stupid poster, I clear my throat. "The poster's a joke. I'm not that self-centered."

She looks over her shoulder and my hand shoots up, rubbing the back of my neck. I probably look like an ego maniac to her.

"Are you cold still? Here—" I stand, grabbing the blue blanket she'd left on my bed and flipping it around so the dry side wraps around her. "Have a seat. You look nervous. I promise I won't bite."

Her fingers latch onto the blanket, and she drifts to my comfy chair, curling into the cushion and hiding there. My blanket conceals her from her toes to her nose. I wait for her to slip the rest of the way under, as though hiding will prevent my asking for answers.

Does she have any idea how much her disappearing act affected me? Did Jules tell her? Does she know the restraint it took for me to stay away when she asked me to? To pretend I didn't care?

She shifts in my chair, her blanket-covered hand swiping at her damp hair as her eyes focus on me.

Damn, I was delusional to think I could pretend not to care about Cassie.

CASSIE

Now that I'm here, where do I begin with my explanation?
I should leave. I shouldn't have bothered him with this.
I pushed away every attempt he made, and now when I'm scared, I run to him?
What is wrong with me?

Just honest. Confusion marred Austin's face when he said the words. Confusion and the barest hint of a grin.

I take him in, the dark brown bedhead, the shadow of growth on his chin. He's so tall, at least a head taller than my petite five-foot-two. I don't know why his height strikes me every time I'm near him. I picture myself wrapped in his strong arms, his body bending down over mine, like an umbrella protecting me from rain. I shouldn't think such thoughts. My eyes run over his body. His long legs are covered by a pair of loose athletic pants, similar to the ones he offered me, along with his threadbare A&M tee, complete with fraying holes around the neck, does a poor job of hiding the muscles in his torso and arms. His feet are bare. They calm me. They're normal, relaxed. From head to ankle he is every bit the athlete I know him to be. A man with power and strength, a man who could get whatever he wanted out of me. But those bare feet? They remind me of the guy I glimpsed during stolen moments in the campus library. They remind me of the times I let my guard down and let him in …

I huddle under the warmth of his sweats and blanket. And his gold-flecked, brown gaze.

"What happened?" he asks, settling on his bed and leaning back against the concrete block wall.

Shaking my head, I remind him, "No questions asked."

"No, I mean with us." He cocks his head to the side.

I know I need to push him away. Coming here is bad enough, but giving him hope? Telling him how I feel? I brace myself. "There wasn't an us, Austin."

To my surprise, he lifts his brows. "Wasn't there?" I shake my head again and he rolls his eyes. "There was most certainly an us. It was happening, you were letting me in in little by little … and then we met up at the game for Jules, and you brushed me off. Do you hate athletes that much? I play football, so you won't give me a chance?"

Jules told him that. I almost laugh out loud. I'd told her I didn't care for sports players when school first started because it seemed the easiest way to shun off all their guy friends. Living with roommates as entrenched in sports as they are, I was trying to buy myself an out for being set up with every guy they know.

"You won't give me an answer?" he asks when I remain silent.

The plush threads of his blanket tickle my lips as I swipe it back and forth over my mouth and chin. I inhale. Filling my nostrils with the scent of the forest after a rainstorm. Light with a touch of spice—it matches the soap in his shower. Masculine, strong, Austin. He wants to know what happened?

A deep rumble of thunder rattles his window.

"You gave me a book."

His brows sink together. "I gave you a book?"

I shift, tucking his blanket beneath my chin. "The book was the start of something, yes."

"The start of something? I gave you the book in September, Cassie. You seemed fine. You didn't turn cold until after the flag football game."

His choice of words stings. *Cold.*

Austin winces as though he realizes what he's said. "Sorry, I—"

"No. No, don't apologize. You're right, I was cold." I am cold. Emotionally distant. Closed off. I have to be. It's the only way I know how to live. "Why did you and Jules go out?" It's none of my business, and yet, it's one of the things I can't wrap my mind around. West and Austin, from what I've been told, were very close—until the situation with Jules.

"Uh..."

"Explain to me how you could start a relationship with your brother's girlfriend." I narrow my eyes. "You make me understand that, then maybe I can tell you why I was so cold."

He sits forward in protest. "It wasn't like that."

"Oh, please." I push myself higher in the chair, dropping the blanket as irrational ire eats away at me. "That's what all men like to say."

He exhales. It's as though I've slapped him. He's stunned. "Excuse me?"

"You guys are all the same. You don't care who you hurt as long as you get what you want. I've seen it my entire life—"

"Why in the hell did you come here then?" He curses as he slides to the edge of his bed. His bare feet slap against the floor. "What is wrong with you? I know you know the story behind Jules and I. I can't believe Jess or Katie wouldn't have told you if Jules herself didn't. What are you so angry about?"

"You gave me a book."

"I don't—"

"You gave me a damn book, Austin. I wanted you to be different. I thought you were. Then you walked onto the football field that night and I learned who you really are. Big shot football royalty. West's brother. The guy who tried to steal his brother's love. You gave me a book. Then your name broke my hopeful heart."

My chest explodes. Saying it out loud, giving a voice to my thoughts, strips me bare.

"Cassie." His eyes meet mine. "I didn't try to steal Jules from West. That was never my intention. We leaned on each other. She was in pain and I was there for her, because I understood how she felt. Sure, it got a bit tangled up, but nothing happened." Pushing his hair up, he continues, "Then I saw you studying one night and I became a bit obsessed."

My heart stutters. "I don't want that."

His smile wilts. "This isn't about Jules and I, and you know it." The challenge is clear. "I don't think this is about me at all, not about who I am or what I've done in the past. I think it's about the way I make you feel, and—"

I shake my head, cutting him off and fold myself into the blanket, sinking down into his chair again. I can't. I can't drown in the warmth of his voice. "What do you want, Austin?"

"I want you to give me a chance."

It seems so simple. "I can't," my throat closes as tears threaten to spill. I cover my head and wipe my them away.

"Don't hide under that blanket. Please." The chair shifts as his hand touches my covered foot. "I can't stop thinking about you. I don't want to hurt you. I know you've been hurt, you're scared all the time. I wish I knew why. I wish I could take that away."

My lungs refuse to gather oxygen as my mind focuses on the weight of his hand resting on my body. His touch, even through a blanket, causes both physical excitement and emotional panic.

"I'm not a bad guy. I know you know that. You wouldn't have come here if you didn't. Let me in. Let me know you. That's all I'm asking for, I swear."

I contemplate his request from beneath the blanket. Can I let him in? My heart wants me to. *Take a risk, Cassie.*

"Tell me who you are." My voice comes out so quiet and hoarse. I don't even know if he heard it.

"Emerge from your cocoon?"

Sucking in a deep breath, I lower the blanket to find him kneeling in front of the chair. "First, I need you to tell me you're okay. Right now, at this moment, are you safe? You ran here for a reason—"

My eyes water. I'm not used to people caring about my safety, but Austin was trying to protect me before he knew my name. That's why my instinct was to run to him. "I'm safe."

Those intense brown eyes of his flare for a moment. "You are safe."

It's a promise. In this moment, I truly want to believe I am safe here, in this room, with him. I want to trust him, but as we stare at each other my heart begs to differ. I may be in more danger with him than without. When I don't respond, he returns to the edge of his bed.

"I was born and raised in Tyler." Austin's voice reminds me of a voice-over on a documentary, solemn and dry, then he ruins the effect by waggling his brows. "That's what you want, right? The Austin Rutledge life story?"

The edge of the blanket covers my giggle. "I do."

Shrugging in resignation, he exhales. "Just so you know, it's a boring story with lots of football." He flashes another perfect grin.

"I can deal with that." I need him to talk to me, to allow me time to calm down.

"Well, alright then." He rolls his head from side to side. "You'd think I'd be better at talking about myself. I'm not sure where I should start."

"Tell me about your brothers." We can start simple.

"Oh, those guys? Well, that's easy. You've met them both. Carson's two years older, West two younger—my parents had their timing down." He winks flirtatiously and I bite my tongue. "I can't think of a moment when they haven't been there for me. I can't imagine life without them. When our mom got sick we became even closer."

"Cancer, right?" He nods. "How old were you?"

"I was almost fifteen. A freshman in high school." A shadow crosses over his features. "It was quick. We didn't have much time once she was diagnosed. She passed away before school started the following year."

"I'm so sorry."

"She was the best part of all of us, and man was she a force to be reckoned with. I guess she had to be with my dad and three boys. Our house was the epitome of masculine. I mean, we would actually bring her lizards and frogs on a daily basis." He shakes his head thoughtfully, a nostalgic smile on his lips.

I shudder, recoiling at the thought. "Ew."

"She loved it. The bloody knees, cracked lips, black eyes—she said she was born for it. For us." The happiness in his eyes is nearly eclipsed by sadness as he leans to the side and picks up a frame sitting on his desk, holding it up for me. "That's her."

I lean forward in the chair. She's beautiful, like her boys. Dark hair, warm smile, happy eyes. They're a picture perfect family. The beach sunset backdrop, the loving couple, their three young sons with matching shirts and shorts. The American family with a seemingly all-American storybook life.

"Are y'all as perfect as you look?"

He chuckles. "Perfect? Hell no. Who is? We're disgustingly close, though." He sets the picture next to him on the bed. "Are you as perfect as *you* look?"

Flattery. Empty praises from a man ... No. He's not like that, Cassie. I release my frustration through a long sigh.

"You want a funny story?" Austin slides back. He stuffs two pillows under his ribs, lying sideways on his bed as he props his head up with his hand. "I went through a phase where I swore I was a magician. I'd gone to a birthday party for a classmate and he had one. You know, one of those pull-the-rabbit-out-of-a-hat type of guys, black cape and all."

Even though I've never seen a live magic show, I nod. The imagery seems pretty universal throughout movies and television shows I've seen through the years.

"Leave it to Carson to burst my bubble. Older brothers like to do that. Do you have any brothers or sisters?"

"Only child."

He nods, his brows knitting together as though he's filing the information away in a little Cassie folder in his head. "Well, take it from me, a sibling's main goal in life is to antagonize the other. Carson took his big brother role seriously. So here I was thinking I'm going to be a magician, practicing my card tricks and waving a wand, pulling quarters out of everything, and Carson decides to screw with me by telling me that real magicians have the power to control things like fire and water."

"Oh no."

He laughs lightly. "Man, I stared at water for weeks willing it to move." He shakes his head, chuckling at the memory. "Carson loved it. He egged me on every day. He was relentless in pointing out my failure. So I switched to fire."

I cover my mouth, worried where this might go. "Oh gosh, what does that mean?"

"Well, I swore I could make a fireball. He stopped bugging me after that. The End." Austin shifts on his bed, punching and poking at his pillows. His busyness doesn't sway me.

"Oh, no you don't. I want the whole story."

He grins, tapping his temple with his index finger. "Okay, I'll make you a deal." I eye him warily. "I'll tell you my embarrassing story if you explain the significance of the book." I refuse, shaking my head immediately.

"You have to tell me. If my giving you that book hurt you in some way, I need to know." The vulnerability in his words, the fact that he truly cares about my feelings, propels me into easing his worry.

"It didn't hurt me." My words are barely a whisper.

"It didn't? Then why, Cass?"

His eyes are my undoing. His eyes and the sweet intimate sound of his low voice calling me Cass.

"It gave me hope," I admit, my heart thundering under his gaze. "You gave me hope, and no guy has ever given me reason to hope before."

AUSTIN

My next breath hurts, it literally pains me as I inhale deeply.
It's almost as though the oxygen from the room was depleted by her words.

Cassie hugs herself, her hand rubbing up to her neck as her eyes hold mine. She opened up to me, now I owe her the rest of the story.

"I put lighter fluid in my palm and lit it on fire." Her eyes go wide as her lips part and her breath catches. "Burned the shit out of my hand," I laugh, showing her my palm. The skin's barely marked now, just one darkened semi-circle at the base of my palm remains.

"Oh my gosh," Cassie snorts back a laugh, her fingers pressing to her mouth. "I bet it did. Did you impress your brother?"

"Ha, I scared the shit out of him. The moment the fire ignited I threw my hand his way," I sink further into the bed. "The fluid caught his shirt on fire. He jumped in the pool to save himself. They don't let me light the grill to this day. It wasn't all bad though, I learned a lot of cool science tricks and illusions. I had fun with it. Well, I mean, except for the whole burn thing."

Cassie's head falls back against the chair cushion, laughter erupting from her lips with machine gun speed. Spurts of deep, rumbling giggles. I'm in awe. It shouldn't sound so cute—it's freakin' Elmer Fudd—but my God, it's amazing the way the deep, husky giggles sound coming from her lips.

"Jesus, you need to laugh more." She slaps her palm over her lips. "No, really. You need to laugh more, Elmer."

She straightens. "Elmer?"

"Fudd. The cartoon." Her face remains blank. "No way. You've never heard of Elmer Fudd? Looney Tunes?" I stretch to the desk again, reaching for my laptop before she can answer. "You've been so deprived." Pulling it into my lap, I search for a clip online and hit play. Elmer Fudd's laugh fills the room. "Yep," I nod, proud of myself for making the connection. "I think I have a new name for you."

"Elmer?" she deadpans.

I hit play again. "Laugh for me, let me compare."

"No." The pillow behind her head shoots across the room, and I duck.

"You really never watched those cartoons as a kid?" She shakes her head. "We're going to fix that. Come here." I pat the bed, shifting over to make room for her.

She doesn't budge. I pat the bed again. "I don't bite."

"Jules did tell me that."

"Oh? So you asked her about me?" My brows lift. "Interesting."

"Don't get excited, Seuss."

"Too late," I wink. Her face wrinkles up, a kind of frustration clouding over her eyes. Shit. My flirtatious teasing tends to send her overboard, but it's who I am. "I'm sorry."

"It's fine." She climbs her way out of my oversized chair, pulling the blanket with her. "Show me this Elmer Fudd guy."

She climbs onto my bed, and for a moment I assume she's going to sit over me, her hips near my shoulders. Then she moves. She scoots down, resting her head against the remaining pillow at the head of my bed and twists to her side, curling into a ball. I shift toward the wall again, giving her plenty of space. She cuddles into the space, my blanket covering her up. I wish I were that blanket. Adjusting the laptop onto my abs, I press play. The classic rabbit hunting scene lights up my screen, and I look at

Cassie out of the corner of my eye. Her face holds no recognition. Have I ever met someone who doesn't know this clip?

She rolls her head to the side on the pillow next to me when the credits roll. "I remind you of this guy?"

"Well, he is rather short."

Cassie gasps, half sitting up, her hand pushing into my ribs and toppling my laptop onto the bed between us. "That's not nice."

I grab her wrist, twisting toward her. "He's not nearly as beautiful as you are, though."

"Austin."

"Cass."

My free hand closes the lid of my computer as I lean over Cassie. She falls back onto the pillow, her inhale ragged as her eyes close. I've never been this close to her face. Faint freckles dot the bridge of her nose. She has a small scar at the edge of her right brow. Her make-up probably covers it most of the time. I can't help myself.

"What happened here?" I ask, my thumb smoothing over her brow and touching the slightly raised skin.

Her eyes open. Warm puppy eyes looking at me in such a way I know my world will never be the same. It's as though she's opening a door into her dark, wounded soul.

"What happened to your eye, Cassie?"

"Nothing."

She's lying. Her forehead creases, and my thumb shifts from her scar to the indention. "You are Elmer, you even have the same wrinkles in your forehead," I tease.

Her lips part, a small crack, as though she's going to speak, and my resolve breaks. I lean down, my lips touching hers, my hand releasing her wrist.

Her palm slaps my cheek.

"Shit." The shout comes naturally, a reflex when someone hits you.

Cassie rolls herself off the bed, falling onto the floor with a loud thud. She scrambles to her knees, the hand she used to slap the hell out of me covering her mouth. Her eyes widen and immediately fill with tears. "Oh my gosh. I'm sorry, Austin. I'm so sorry."

I rub my cheek, dazed. Cassie's in a ball, huddled on the cold floor up against the side of my dresser. She's about as far as she can get from me without running out of my room. What in the hell happened to her?

"Cassie?" I slide to the edge of my bed slowly when she doesn't answer. "Cassie? I'm sorry. I shouldn't have kissed you like that."

Her dark curtain of hair shakes side to side as her arms tighten around her knees.

"You have some power in those tiny arms of yours," I say, opting for a tease when she remains head down. Nothing. "Have you had a lot of practice?"

I sink onto the floor, leaning my back against the side of my bed. I want to crawl over and lift her face from where she's hiding it. I want to look into her eyes and tell her I'm not upset with her. I should have known better than to kiss her. I should have—

"I've been hurt." Her voice is small.

There's so much more going on here than I know how to handle. "You can trust me."

She laughs. There's no humor in it. "No, I can't. I don't trust men; I don't know how." She looks up, her face blotted with new tears, her eyes red and puffy. "I'm so sorry for slapping you."

I force a smile. "I shouldn't have kissed you. It's fine."

"No, it's not fine," she sniffs. "I could have pushed you away, I could have—" she bangs her hand to her chest, the horror at what she did evident in her pale, frightened face.

We stay that way, sitting on the cold floor on opposite ends of my room while the rain pounds against the building.

I wake up on my floor with a stiff neck and a numb ass. My blue blanket covers my legs, and Cassie is gone.

CASSIE

When life gets hard, run.
That's been the theme of my life.
Why should now be any different?

Back on that day, when Molly Green slapped me, Momma didn't come home until well after dark, and when she did, she was fuming. She stomped around her room, drawers slamming, curses flying, as I lay in bed waiting for the moment I knew would come. It was inevitable. My door flew open, and the light flipped on, and I did what I'd done so many times before. I slipped out of my bed, pulled my old suitcase from the closet, and packed my belongings. All of them.

And just like that I said goodbye to Iowa. The same way I'd said goodbye to the Dakota's, Utah, and Arizona before that. Always on the move. A lifetime of decisions made by a woman who made her decisions based on how much she could milk out of a man.

The day I walked onto the A&M campus and saw Ward Hall for the first time was a game changer for me. My cheeks ached from my smile, and my eyes watered as I hoisted my duffle over my shoulder and followed the crowd of new students to the front entrance. I was but one of the new faces in a crowd, one of the many idealists ready to forge my own future. When I reached the second floor suite, I simply stood in the doorway and stared. My unopened boxes were piled on one side of the room thanks to the unnamed freshman welcoming committee member who helped me unload them when I pulled up to campus earlier that day. The opposite side of the small dorm was decked out in shades of purple and teal courtesy of my new roommate. I took it all in, appreciating the moment. The room was nothing more than white plaster and prison-sized windows. That's it. That's the make-up of my home for the next four years, and it was perfect. Simple, glorious, and permanent.

It was freedom.

I hadn't known how short-lived that freedom would be. Had I known, had I had any inclination—I would have run further. Last night, I considered running. Everything within me told me to go when his name popped into my mind.

Austin.

I'd like to kick my own ass for listening to the name. What was I thinking? I can't bring him into my mess. Zipping my bag, I grab the jacket hanging over my chair and leave my room.

The sky remains mostly dark, it's not even 7:00 AM on a January morning after a torrential rain storm.

"Cassie!" Austin's shadow appears from nowhere as I cross campus.

"Go away, Austin."

"Why did you leave like that?" He jogs, easily catching up with me.

"Go away."

"Where are you going?" His voice is even, not angry or short, just concerned.

"To my mom's." It seems like the most obvious of answers.

He steps in front of me, his arms folding across his chest. "Bullshit." His voice is still even, but if I thought that meant he wasn't angry, I was sorely mistaken. He's still wearing his sweats and tee from last night. No jacket or hat. It's freezing outside. "You hate your mother."

My stomach lurches. "Excuse me?"

"It's the one thing I've been able to get out of Jules. You hate your mother."

"She told you?" He nods. "How … why did she tell you?"

"When I left the island to come home early I asked her why you stayed here for break. She told me you don't see your mom and that, while you try to play it off, she could tell there were deep-seated issues there."

I step back, primed to run, but I don't want to. "Why would you do that?"

"Why would I do what?"

"Why would you ask her about me? After everything—"

"You really have no clue," Austin scoffs, shaking his head as though he can't believe I asked the question.

I think I shake my head, but I can't be sure because I'm too numb to think.

"You drive me crazy. I haven't stopped thinking about you since the first day we spoke. All I've wanted for the past four months was to get to know you. I came home early because I knew you were here alone. Jules told me you came to our last game. I wanted to talk to you. To work this out."

A droplet of water slaps my forehead from the wet branches overhead. "I have to go."

"Where?" he growls.

Scanning the campus, my mind lingers on the call from last night. "Anywhere but here."

"Okay." He digs his keys from his pocket and holds his hand out. "Come with me?"

"I can't."

"You can. Cassie, do you trust Jules? And Jess, and Katie? You know me by virtue of them. Come with me."

He doesn't get it. He doesn't realize this isn't really about him at all. I look around and sigh as I place my cold hand in his, letting him lead the way back to his dorm. "You walked over here?" I'd expected him to walk me to the parking lot behind Ward.

"No, I ran over here."

"Without a jacket? Why?"

"You forget who you're talking to. I'm well acquainted with playing ball in freezing temps with no sleeves, remember?" His hand squeezes mine. "Plus, I know you don't have a car. I didn't want to miss you running across campus by driving on the streets."

As though he senses my worry, he walks swiftly, bypassing his dorm and heading straight for his car. He takes my bag as I climb into his little sports car and hurries around to the driver's side. Throwing the bag in the backseat, he climbs in, fastens his seatbelt, and cranks the engine before my frozen fingers can properly buckle my own belt. Turning the radio down as music blares on, he peels out of the parking lot and away from the A&M campus without a word.

"Where are we going?" I ask after ten minutes.

"How far do you need to go?"

There's no way he has any idea what I'm running from, yet somehow he knows I'm running. "I don't know yet."

He nods, his brows lowering over his eyes. I've seen that face on television. After I found out who he was, I secretly watched him play a few games when the girls weren't around. I refused to go to any, except for the last one, but in my room I watched him. The face he's making now reminds me of the one I've seen him make before a big play. Even with his helmet on, I could see the way he narrowed his eyes and scrunched his face in concentration.

"I'll take you to the house then, for now. If you want to go somewhere else, you can tell me when."

"The house?"

"Don't worry, the newlyweds won't be back for a week, and Jules and West are going to Tyler when they come back."

"Weren't you supposed to go with them? Jules and West?"

"Concrete plans were never made. I came home from St. Lucia early, but I hadn't decided on going home to Tyler or not. Coffee?"

I glance away from his profile. He pulls into a strip mall and parks in front of a donut shop. "That would be fabulous." I unfasten my seatbelt.

"You stay here. I'll run in and out." He leaves the car running as he climbs out. "Lock the doors behind me."

I smile as he walks into the shop, looking back at me several times. I consider searching for my phone; I haven't checked it since I ran from my room last night and threw it in my bag this morning. Just as I'm unbuckling to turn around and pull the bag from the backseat, Austin returns with two coffees and a box of donuts in hand. I snap the buckle back in place and sit forward again, hitting the unlock button to let him in.

"Obviously I didn't know what you like, so I grabbed one of everything good." He hands me the large box and settles the coffees in the cup holders between us. "Did you need something from your bag?"

"Nah," I lie, popping the lid to the donuts, the scent of sugar and love filling the vehicle.

Austin inhales deeply. "Ahhh, that's the scent of pure happiness." I choke at his words, causing him to eye me suspiciously. "What?"

"I was thinking the same thing," I say.

"I'll be a gentlemen and let you choose first, but I highly suggest against the frosted marble chocolate ones."

"Oh yeah? Why's that?" I ask, eyeing the twelve donuts before me and weighing each one for its individual merits. The crullers are always light and fluffy, like little clouds in your mouth. Blueberry are a favorite, with their sweet fruit bits and glaze—a definite possibility. My eyes pass right over the jelly-stuffed one; it doesn't seem right to me, stuffing globs of jelly into donuts. There's also a chocolate with white flakes covering it that looks promising.

"Is this coconut?" I ask, pointing to the donut.

"Toasted coconut, to be exact. Smell it, they're heavenly."

Lifting the box to my face, I sniff the donut, salivating at the scent. "Sold." I pass Austin his marble frosted with a napkin and eagerly pluck the coconut from the box.

My first bite is embarrassing. I close my eyes and hum as though I'm starving and this is the first morsel to hit my lips in ages. "Holy cow, this is the best thing ever," I moan, promptly taking a second bite.

Beside me Austin groans, wiping his hand on his thigh. His face carries a pained expression.

"Uh, did you want this one?" I ask as his eyes follow my third bite. He shakes his head before taking a bite of his own.

"How was the wedding, anyway?"

"New Year's Eve wedding on a tropical island, how do you think it was?"

"Romantic." If I were Jess, Katie, or Jules, I imagine I'd sigh right now. It must be most girls fantasy to marry the man of their dreams in such a beautiful spot.

Austin nods, "Exactly."

"Ahhh, kinda sucked being the odd man out, huh?" I lick a piece of coconut from my finger.

Austin clears his throat, and I glance over, taking in his strange expression. He shakes his head as though clearing it of some thought. "Something like that. I mean, it was fine. My dad chartered us some fishing boats for this week and we went out for a day, but one day is enough. West's the fisherman, not me."

Taking another bite of my donut, I sigh, "Yum, where has this been all my life?" The chocolate is fabulously moist, especially where the frosting puddled in the middle, trapping extra coconut around the edges. I savor every last crumb and lick each fingertip.

"Hey, Cass?"

"Yeah?" I open my eyes and find him staring.

"Could you try not to eat the next one like that?" My mouth hangs open at the hungry look in his eyes. Oh my gosh, I just moaned my way through that donut like it was sex. Now I understand his throat clearing, head shaking misery. My face heats up as Austin nods at my revelation. "I mean, it was sexy as hell, but I'm a mere mortal. I don't think I can take that again."

Resisting the urge to cover my face and hide, I shrug instead. "It was delicious."

"I could tell."

Flipping the box open once more, I check the contents for my next victim. "Don't worry, you only bought one of that flavor, so there won't be a repeat performance."

He flicks his eyes from the road to my face and back to the road again. "Well, I can go back and buy more if you want." I laugh, unable to help myself. The solemn face he's making is just too much.

"And there's Elmer," he sighs, causing me to laugh harder. He's right, the giggles roll off my tongue in little stutters, just like Elmer Fudd. "You just let me know if you change your mind about the donut. I won't mind," he winks, pulling his keys from the ignition. *He's taking the keys?* My attention goes to our surroundings.

We've pulled into the driveway of a perfect little brick home. We're roughly twenty minutes from campus. Is it far enough?

AUSTIN

Most girls I go out with see what they want to see
Football, popularity, money.
How do I get Cassie to see the beneath that?

Cassie's mouth is a tool of perfection, capable of sinking the strongest of men. A mouth. I've been seduced into situations by breasts and legs, a round ass, and even some toned abs—thanks to body shots—but I have never found myself obsessed with a mouth. Until now.

She eats like a mouse, every bite a nibble, which only prolongs my misery over breakfast. Knowing donuts and coffee alone aren't going to sustain me until lunch, I pull her into the kitchen the moment we walk through the door, and we raid the fridge.

"You really didn't have to cook," she says for the fifth time as she stirs the frozen glob of orange juice I found in the freezer. "I can live off sugar quite well."

I scoop scrambled eggs onto two plates. "I can't."

Removing a plate of bacon from the microwave, we sit at the kitchen bar. She picks and nibbles while I shovel the food in until it's all gone. I thought she was eating slowly out of nervousness or to avoid a conversation, but that doesn't seem to be the case. She just eats slow. I can't complain; I love watching her mouth.

"What did you do for New Year's Eve?" I ask as I help myself to another piece of bacon.

"I was predictably boring. I watched the countdown on television and ate massive amounts of junk food. There were a few parties off campus, but that's not my scene, obviously."

"Eh, big parties are overrated." Her eyes narrow, calling me out on my bull. "No really, they are. You think I go to all those parties because I like to? You really don't know me, Elmer."

"I guess you're right, I don't know you. I know the myth, though."

"The myth isn't anything like the man," I mutter, frustration bubbling up. I'm curious where she's received her information and how much damage control I might have to do. "Would you like to know the real me?"

She inhales sharply through her nose. I'm serious and I hold her gaze to prove it. No smiles, no winks.

"So, what's the deal here?" She pushes her empty plate away, her eyes wandering around the room questioningly.

It's not an answer to my question, but I don't consider avoidance a definite rejection, so I take it for now. "Let me show you the house."

I give her the grand tour. "The master belongs to Mindy and Carson, but they'll be house hunting when they return. First bedroom is West's, second is mine. Mine is the least personalized. I tend to stay on campus during football season, so Dad uses it when he comes for games." I set her bag on my bed. With this season over and Mindy and Carson on their way out, I've contemplated moving in permanently for the remainder of this year and next.

"West is already arguing with me about who gets the master next. I think he's hoping Jules will move in with him."

"Oh? I bet her parents will love that."

"Yeah, I wouldn't hold my breath on it if I were him." My brother's relationship with Jules's parents is good, but not that good. "You can sleep in here, and I'll take West's room."

She hugs herself, looking around the room. She's wearing my sweatshirt; I haven't commented on it, but I sure as hell noticed. I'd be happy if she never took it off. Well, that's not true. I'd like to take it off for her.

"I can't stay here." Sadness clouds her features.

"Sure you can, I don't mind sleeping in West's room."

She stops studying my room and looks at me. "It's not that at all. You offer me your house as though it's a simple decision. You don't know what you're getting into—"

I force my feet to remain still when all I want to do is get closer to her. "Then tell me. Tell me what made you run to my door last night. What made you run this morning?"

She shakes her head slowly. Her dark hair is a mess; pieces have fallen from her bun and they float around her face making her look years younger. She's so vulnerable, so tiny. My protective instinct kicks into overdrive.

"One week." An idea takes shape. "Today is Sunday. The others won't be back until next Sunday. Stay with me for one week. Get to know me, the real me, and let me get to know you."

Cassie's shaking her head before I finish. "This isn't a good idea."

"One week. No strings attached. I'll be a perfect gentleman, I promise. Where else are you going to go? You have nowhere else to run, Cassie. You're safe here."

Indecision flickers in her eyes. "You don't know my story, Austin."

"Then tell me." She flinches at the strength of my request. "When you're ready," I add, softening my tone. I get the feeling I'm one wrong word away from running her out of town.

"One week?"

"That's all I'm asking for."

"Okay. I'll stay," she agrees reluctantly. "Thank you."

I step closer, finally unable to resist the pull. "You don't have to thank me, but I do have to warn you." She leans back inquisitively. "I plan on being my most charming self this week, Elmer."

She frowns, a brow arching. "Keep calling me Elmer and it won't matter how charming you are, Seuss."

"Ah, the gauntlet has been thrown. You don't know what you just walked into, little one." I push her wild flyaway strands behind her ear and force myself to step back. "You look like you're about to fall asleep standing. Take a nap, I'm going to make a grocery list, take a shower, and rest as well."

I grab a change of clothes from my closet as Cassie looks on. She sits on the edge of the bed, yawning as she slips off her shoes.

"Take as long as you need"

She's already crawled to the top of my bed and curled up onto her side before I close the door. "Hey, Austin."

"Yeah?"

"Can we keep this a secret? Us being here?" Her eyes are half-closed and she yawns once more. "It's safer if no one knows where I am right now."

"Yeah, sure." I pull the door closed, her ominous words lingering in my mind. What is she afraid of? Or perhaps the more accurate question is, who?

I'm still debating if agreeing to keeping her visit with me secret is the best plan when she drags herself out of my room around 3:00 PM.

"Hey," she says with half a smile, sleep lingering in her voice.

"Hi. Feel better?" I'm stretched out on the couch, the television on mute as I doze off and on.

"Much," she nods. "Do you have any water?" She points to the kitchen, already shuffling that way.

"Yeah, there's water in the door and bottles in the fridge. Help yourself to whatever. Mi casa es tu casa. Oh, the glasses are in the—"

"Cabinet to the right of the fridge. Found them." The cabinet closes, and ice and water spray into her glass. "You went to the store?"

"Yeah, I didn't want you to have to get out of bed, and we needed food. I put the cold stuff away, but I was worried I'd wake you. You were safe here, I wouldn't have left if I didn't think so."

The bags on the counter rustle, and I turn my head, watching her rifle through them. "I know. I'm not worried, just surprised."

"Surprised I know how to grocery shop? I'm a pretty smart guy, you know."

Cassie giggles. "So I've heard. Oh, Pringles!"

Bless Jules for giving me insider information. "I'm hoping you like all the normal foods. Tacos, burgers, spaghetti." I pull my legs up and sit upright as Cassie walks around the couch and takes a seat on the oversized chair to the right of me, Pringles in hand. The chair swallows her. It's perfectly sized for my brothers and I since we're all freaks of nature and over six feet tall, Mindy and Jules both fit in it comfortably with their small, but normal stature, but Cassie? Her pocket-sized body can't reach the ground in the deep seat. She pulls her feet beneath her and curls into a ball, leaning against the back and arm of the chair, facing me.

"Are you kidding? I'm happy with mac and cheese, or cereal. Speaking of," she waves the tube of cheddar chips in the air. "Do you mind?"

"Not as long as you share."

Her face lights up as she pulls the back the cover, dumping a handful into her palm before stretching my way.

"I'm not sure if I'll know what to do with real food," she crunches out.

"By the time this week is over you'll never want to go back to campus food and dorm living," I boast.

"Hold your horses, cowboy. Let me taste your cooking before you start making such lofty comments," Cassie grins playfully.

"I already cooked you eggs and bacon."

"Any idiot can cook eggs and bacon."

"Hold on, you haven't tasted Mindy's cooking yet." Cassie laughs. "The woman cannot make breakfast to save her life. She can bake, though, I'll give her that."

"Poor Carson."

"Nah, he'll take care of her. My mom taught him most of her skills before she got sick. He had the most time with her." I picture Mom standing over us in the kitchen supervising us chopping ingredients and stirring mixes. *'A woman wants a man who can cook,'* she told us growing up. Dad would always follow that up with *'But make sure you find a woman who knows her way around the kitchen.'* They were that couple. Always sharing everything they did. When Dad was around.

"You miss her, don't you?" The tenderness in her question stirs me from thoughts of the past.

"Sorry, I got caught up in a memory." I rub my eyes, standing. "Yeah, I miss her. We all do, of course. We were a really close family."

It's time for a subject change. Patting my stomach, I head toward the kitchen. "You slept through lunch, and it's too early to start dinner. Can I get you something more substantial than Pringles?"

"Bite your tongue, these are the chips of the Gods." She pops one in her mouth.

The nap did her good, she's more relaxed than she was a few hours ago. I dig in the bags and find a protein bar. She might live off sweets and junk, but my body—and my coaches—will kill me if I don't get sustenance. I put away the food while I eat, racking my brain for conversation topics and things to do for the next several hours. I pause, face-palming myself. We have the house all to ourselves, and I actually have to think up things to do? Well, this is a first for me.

Cassie offers to help, but I refuse, so she sits and watches the muted sports station. I check her out when I'm finished. She's sitting with a small pile on Pringles in her palm, her legs pulled to her chest and her hair up in one of those messy bun things on top of her head. My sweatshirt swallows her up, and I love it.

She catches me staring. "Wanna watch a movie?" I ask, swallowing down my attraction.

"Sure, my choice?"

"Yeah, the boxes under the cabinet there are sorted with a bunch of DVDs, or you can pull up whatever on the TV. The buttons are on the controller."

I'm not surprised when she chooses to raid our DVD collection. A movie collection tells a lot about a person—what they choose to spend their money on, what they want to own instead of stream. The Rutledge boys are heavy on the action, sports, and comedy. Mindy has worked in a few romances over the years, but she's outnumbered three to one here. Cassie laughs as she goes through the box and I put some nachos together.

"You know I was watching a Bourne movie the first time West dropped by the dorm," she calls from the other room.

"Really?" This is surprising.

"Yeah, he was shocked too. I was sitting alone in my room on a Friday night watching Bourne Identity. He and Jules were in quite the rush to get to her room, so much so they didn't have a key and ended up banging on my door to let them in."

I roll my eyes at my baby brother.

Cassie walks into the kitchen, two movies in her hands, but she must have caught my eye roll because concern slips over her features. "That doesn't upset you, does it?"

"What, a story about West and Jules? God, no. Cassie, I told you there was nothing between Jules and I. Really, I love them both, and I'm really happy they made things work the way they did. Jules and I are friends. Best friends, even. That's it."

"It's none of my business. I shouldn't have asked. Sorry."

"You can ask me anything you want, I'm an open book." I remove the platter of melted cheesy nachos from the microwave and see Cassie lick her lips. I'm dead now—that damn mouth of hers. "There are some Cokes in the fridge if you want to grab us two."

We walk into the living room together and I watch as she heads for the chair furthest from the couch. That's not at all where I want her. "If you sit way over there, I'll eat this entire plate within two minutes and you'll be out of luck."

I can see her mind calculating the length of the furniture. It's oversized, like the chairs, plenty of room for two without feeling too intimate. After a moment longer than I would have liked, she moves over and we settle on the couch, nachos between us, and Cassie's legs tucked under her.

"Alright, Mr. Open Book," she turns my way, "I heard a rumor that you're a lot smarter than you look."

I gasp, "Who would say such a rude thing?"

"I know, right? I'm sure you lose points with the girls every time word gets around." Cassie rolls her eyes as she stuffs a chip in her mouth. A bit of cheese lingers at the corner of her mouth, and I contain my urge to remove it with my tongue, handing her a napkin instead.

"Do I lose points in your eyes for having a brain?"

"I'm not keeping score."

"No? Well, be sure to let me know when you start so I can help you with the tallies."

"Austin—" She says my name with a sigh of frustration. I can guess the rest of the sentence before she says it. "I appreciate your help, but I still mean what I said back in October. Nothing is going to happen between us."

I lean back and take a long swig of my drink. She's not fooling me. Her words might say she isn't interested, but her eyes say differently. Just like in October, I can see the fear behind those brown eyes, I can see the confusion flicker across her features every time she tries to turn me off. The waver in her voice keeps me pressing forward—intent on breaking her walls down.

"Nothing, huh? So we can't get to know each other and be friends?"

She frowns. "Well, no. I mean, yes. Yeah, of course we can be friends."

"Okay then, friend. Give me your movie choice, sit back, and stop worrying so much."

She stares at me for a moment before holding up the movies. She's picked out two action thrillers. Either she didn't find Mindy's romance stash or she's the perfect woman. "I'm a sucker for chase scenes," she explains.

Aww shit, she is the perfect woman. "Then *The Italian Job* it is."

I grab a throw blanket and toss it to Cassie as she curls into the corner of the couch. Pulling the blinds to block the late afternoon light, I start the movie and take my seat. As old previews play, I sneak looks at Cassie. She's pulled her hair out of the bun now, her fingers combing through the ends absentmindedly. She catches me staring for the second time in thirty minutes, and I smile, returning my gaze to the screen. Twelve hours of travel on Saturday, followed by very little sleep thanks to Cassie showing up at my door last night, and then dealing with her today catches up with me a quarter of the way into the movie. Sinking down into the corner of the couch, I stretch my legs across the ottoman and stuff a pillow behind my head. I'm out within ten minutes.

CASSIE

Explosions, car chases, and gun shots shake the room, but Austin sleeps. Once I realize he's truly asleep, he receives as much attention as the movie. I can't help myself.

There's something about sleep that softens the hardest of faces. Not that Austin Rutledge has a hard face. For all the muscle his body has, his face is soft. Or softer. He doesn't possess the same chiseled jawline that Jules gushes on and on about of West's. No, Austin's face is—comfortable, like his bare feet in the dorm. When I look at him I feel at ease, normal, safe. How did that happen? I barely know him. Comfortable: a foreign word for me when it comes to men.

I clench my eyes tighter as the wind howls through every nook and cranny of our new little trailer. Will the walls fall down? It's blowing hard enough. At least the noise covers the ones coming from Momma's room. I hate those sounds.

A thud hits against the outside wall of my room and I leap from bed, scurrying to my door.

The hallway is pitch black, but there's a dim light shining in the living room. I move toward it.

"Well, hello, darlin'. You must be Gwen's daughter." A man in nothing but thin shorts sits on our couch.

"I'm Cassandra, who are you?" I ask as I walk closer.

He smiles, taking a drink from the can in his hand and waving me toward him. "Did the storm scare you?" I nod, and he smiles again. "I'm a special friend of your mom's. My name is Randy."

The trailer rocks as a gust of wind whistles under the front door. My legs tremble at the sound. Randy's hand, scratchy and moist, cups around my wrist pulling me in front of the chair.

"Sweetie, there's nothing to be scared of. Why don't you sit in my lap and I'll keep you safe." He leans forward and sets me on his lap easily. He smells dirty. My nose wrinkles as his arm wraps around my little waist and his fingers rub up and down my leg. "There, now isn't that comfortable."

The main title screen of the DVD pulls me from the memory. I shake my head. Randy. Why would that memory flit into my mind at this moment? Austin's head turns on the pillow, his lips parting into a sleepy grin, and I smile back as though he can see me. I smile because he doesn't scare me. It feels good to admit that to myself. Nothing about Austin is remotely like Randy, or any of the men I grew up around, but there is something out there I should be afraid of.

I crawl from the couch, turning off the television and walking into the kitchen, needing something to do.

Austin said he bought spaghetti stuff. I hunt it down knowing I can get dinner going while he rests a little longer. Rifling through cabinets and drawers, I find what I need to brown the meat. He made this job easy by grouping all the ingredients together when he unloaded the groceries. The noodles, a jar of sauce, and two cans of chopped tomatoes sit together in the pantry. Next to those items he's set beans, taco seasoning, taco shells, and sauce. I smile. He's an organizer. Ten points for Seuss.

The freezer reveals a loaf of pre-made garlic bread. This boy thinks of everything.

I slide the bread into the oven once its pre-heated and look toward the couch as I stand. Austin's gone. I turn, jumping when I see him standing behind me.

"Holy cow! You scared the crap out of me."

"Dang, you got some major air for such a little thing." He laughs, stepping back as I grip the edge of the kitchen counter and breathe. "Sorry, I was following my nose."

I look around the kitchen at my handiwork. "I hope you don't mind. I figured you needed the sleep."

Reaching around me, he pulls open a drawer and grabs a spoon. "Hell no, I don't mind. I'm starving. Although you're my guest, I should be cooking for you."

The spoon hovers over the sauce, his brows lifting, silently asking for permission to taste.

"By all means," I nod. "I don't cook much. It's probably missing something. I'm not good with spices." I located the cabinet full of different seasonings, but didn't use them, afraid I'd just muck it all up.

Austin blows on the sauce, tastes it, and reaches for the little jars I've lines up on the counter. He adds small dashes of several containers, never measuring or second guessing himself. "How was the movie?" he asks as he removes a jar of something yellow out of the refrigerator.

"Judging by the way you snored through it, I would say boring."

"I do not snore." The pungent aroma of garlic fills the kitchen as he spoons some from the jar. *Good thing we're just friends, or we'd need some dinner mints for later.* The moment the thought enters my mind my face goes hot and I spin around looking for something to do. I cannot think about kissing him. It's such a bad idea to allow my thoughts to wander down that path.

"I don't snore, do I?"

I pull out plates and two glasses. "Hmmm?" I fish out silverware. "What? Oh, no. I was kidding. You don't snore and the movie was fine. I've seen it before."

. . .

"Tell me something about yourself," Austin says as we sit down to dinner.

"There's nothing to tell," I shrug, spinning my fork in the middle of a pile of noodles.

Austin's fork stops midair to his mouth. "I have a feeling there are a millions things to tell. I'm only asking for one tonight."

"You're so frustrating." I slurp a wayward noodle into my mouth. "Fine. I don't like ice cream."

Austin's fork clatters to the plate. "You don't like ice cream?" His hand goes to his heart as though he's having chest pains, and I throw my last bite of garlic bread at his head. "Whoa. She doesn't eat ice cream and she throws food. You learn so much about people over spaghetti."

"Ha, ha, wise guy. I take it you like ice cream? I guess I lost points."

"I thought we weren't keeping score?" His eyes gleam with mischief. Oh my gosh, he's impossible.

"We're not. Now tell me something about yourself."

"Hmmm, where do I begin, there are so many good things to tell." He picks up his fork and eats another bite.

"Geez, you're full of yourself, Seuss."

"I like it when you call me that," he grins. "And when I was a kid I was obsessed with The Lion King."

Some innate part of my being dances at his words; he likes me calling him Seuss. I bite back a smile. "*The Lion King*, huh?"

"Yep. And I like when you call me, Seuss." He repeats as though he's making sure I know he said it. My stomach does another little dance.

I stand, clearing my dishes from the table. "Then by all means I'll stop."

His shout of laughter follows me. "You're so mean to me."

When the dishes are cleaned and leftovers put away, Austin disappears down the hall. It's only 8:00 PM, still too early for bed. I explore the living room while he's gone. It has exactly the right amount of feminine touches, probably thanks to Mindy, while maintaining the personalities of the men who live here. Pictures clutter the mantle underneath a white ceramic set of antlers tipped in gold—Austin and his brothers in football jerseys, their parents in a forest, Mindy sitting on Carson's lap with her hand flashing her engagement ring. I smile at a recent picture of Jules and West that I've seen in her room. No girls for Austin on the mantle; I mentally raise a fist of triumph in the air.

"I have a surprise for you." I jump at his voice once again and he laughs. "Do I need to wear a bell to warn you as I walk up?"

"The idea has merit," I nod thoughtfully. "Maybe some of those little bells parents put on their toddlers' shoes so they can hear them running around the house?"

"Well, now you know what to buy me for Christmas next year. Grab your jacket and come outside."

I barely have time to contemplate the fact that he assumes I'll be around in a year, because he's already opening the door to the backyard. "Outside?"

Hurrying to my—his—room, I grab my jacket and slip on my shoes. He's disappeared when I return to the living room and I push open the backdoor, the January evening air instantly making my nose run. "Shoot, it's cold. What kind of surpri—" my words cut off at the flames dancing in a fire pit. "How? When?" I fumble with my words.

"There's a patio door in the master suite," he grins, waving me over to the fire.

"What are in those?" I point to the bags stacked on a table as I stand as close as possible to the growing flames.

"Open them up." He watches me, his hands shoved in his pocket as I approach the bags with care. "Nothing in there is going to jump out at you, you know." His voice is laced with humor.

"I'm not used to surprises," I shrug, as though the five words tell him all he needs to know. They probably do. If I were thinking more clearly I wouldn't have said them at all.

Parting a plastic bag, I pull out a small box. "Fireworks?"

"I figured since neither of us had a very festive New Year's, why not celebrate in our own way. Even if it is four days late."

"I've never set off fireworks before."

"Don't worry, I'm a pro. I make fireballs with my bare hands, remember?"

"Ah yes, your magic."

"Don't you know it, little one," Austin teases from directly behind me. I don't jump this time.

"You're finally getting used to me." The words are a whisper in my ear as he reaches around and grabs one of the bags.

"Yeah, you're like a fly who just won't go away," I grumble as I follow him closer to the fire.

"Take a seat and watch the show." He grins, walking over to the boxes of fireworks he's already set up on the concrete patio opposite the fire pit. Glancing over his shoulder at me, he clicks the lighter. "You ready?"

I nod and he fires up box one and then runs over to stand next to me just as the first spark lights up the sky. I clap as green, orange, and red fire flies out of the center of the first set. "So pretty."

"Just wait." He's like a little boy, his face wreathed in excitement as he goes back to the boxes, ignites number two, and returns to my side for a second time.

This one crackles like rain, white spots flying down above us. Box three combines the first two, starting with brilliant shots of color in the shapes of stars and flowers, and ending with, what Austin calls, a willow that seems to go on and on.

"Like the tree? A weeping willow?" I ask as long trails of what look like sparkling fairy dust fall from the sky. I thought fireworks were fireworks. "That was my favorite, for sure," I breathe once the final blast echoes.

"There's one left. You want to light it?" He holds the long lighter out for me. "It's safe, I promise."

My hands shake as we near the largest box thus far. Austin stands beside me pointing out the fuse.

I read the box. "95 shot. What does that mean?"

"That there will be 95 individual fireworks. 95 shots."

"What were the others?"

"They were small, the last one was 38. Light it up." This one is twice as large as the last. My excitement grows as Austin steps back, leaving me with a box of explosives and a lighter. My heart races. It's kind of crazy the rush I'm getting knowing I'm about to ignite this fuse. Nervously, I inch closer and closer until the flame catches the fuse and Austin tells me to back up.

Dropping the lighter, I duck for cover. The fuse sizzles as it burns its way into the box and *rat-a-tat-tat* three machine gun shots ring through the night followed by willows of red, green, and blue.

"Holy crap." I jump at the unexpected sound, sidling up to Austin's side and covering my ears as more go off. "It's like a war zone," I shout over the noise as shot after shot of light streams from the box. A warm wall settles against my back. He doesn't touch me otherwise, he just stands so close that I lean into him as I crane my neck and watch the light show I set off.

When the last spark has died out, I spin around, bumping into his chest and looking up at his handsome face. "That was so fun."

The backyard is dark. The fire pit and moon are the only light around, but even so, I see the way Austin clenches his jaw as he peers down at me. His hands went to my biceps, steadying me when I spun into him; they remain there, and I swear I can feel their heat through my jacket and clothes. His eyes grow heavy. Is he going to kiss me? My skin warms, my nerves driving me to feel antsy. My eyes drop to his mouth, recalling their quick touch back in his dorm on Saturday night.

What would it be like to actually kiss him? I want to kiss him. I inhale sharply at the realization, and Austin's brows snap to his hairline as though he knows exactly what I'm thinking. For a moment, we simply regard each other, then Austin blinks and drops his hands.

"I'm glad you liked them. I bought some sparklers, too. They'll be a little anti-climactic after those, but I've always liked them."

"Bring on the sparklers," I shout, charging to the bags with excitement. Anything to chase away the need clawing at my body right now. And the disappointment that he didn't make a move.

Austin remains by the fire, his shoulders shaking with laughter as I bounce around. Sparklers I know how to do. We take turns lighting one or two and swirling them through the air spelling words and making shapes. I spin in circles, allowing the air to cool my flushed cheeks.

'By the way, I bought ice cream and I have no intention of missing out just because you're a freak who doesn't like it." He looks at me pointedly as my Elmer laugh rings out in response. "No judging me," he continues as he lights another sparkler.

"No judging here." I hold up three fingers as proof.

He stops swinging his sparkler. "Are you throwing me the *Hunger Games* salute?"

"No, that's the scout's honor."

"You were a Girl Scout?" I'm a little offended he finds that so unbelievable. Of course, I wasn't so he's right, but still, I could have been.

"Heck, no. Why? Is it sacrilegious to flash the Girl Scout sign if you weren't one?"

"We're not talking about gang signs, crazy. I think you're good."

"Alright then. You eat your ice cream. I will not judge you. Besides, it's too cold to eat ice cream. You're the freak."

His dark head shakes, tsking me. "You're judging." He bumps into my side, pushing me off balance as he walks by. "You really are mean."

I sit in a chair next to the bonfire while I wait, wrapping myself in the blanket he thoughtfully brought out. If I were assigning points—and I'm not—the boy would be piling them high tonight.

The door to the house shuts and I glance over my shoulder at the freak with a bowl of ice cream in forty-degree weather. His hands have got to be cold. He's not wearing gloves and he's holding a glass bowl. Of ice cream. In winter. Freak. Wait, a stream of steam rises from the bowl.

"Did you lie to me? I see steam." I stretch up as he sits in the chair beside mine. I can't see anything. He's too damn tall and he's holding his bowl away from me like he's hiding a secret.

"It's called hot fudge."

My mouth salivates. Hot fudge I like.

He licks the spoon, humming much the way I did over my donut this morning. And now I understand his pain and Jess's joke months ago. My lady parts sigh as I watch Austin take each bite. It's like foreplay. He's so sexy. *You can admit that and keep your distance, Cassie.* I groan inwardly. *It's allowed.*

Austin smirks as though he's reading my thoughts. "By the way, if you're interested there's a platter of s'mores stuff on the table inside the house."

"There's what?" I shoot up, rushing inside. Grabbing the little tray, complete with a marshmallow stick, I carry it to the bonfire grumbling, "You're an ass."

"My, Annie, you say the sweetest things."

. . .

The fire is nearly dead, my limbs won't stop shaking, and I'm in a chocolate coma. Life is decidedly good. We've been sitting here simply staring at the sky, watching as the stars and moon play peek-a-boo with the clouds. There's been but a handful of words said between us, and most of them were about constellations and UFOs.

"If there were a colony on the moon, would you want to live there?" he asks out of the blue.

I look at the moon. It's bright tonight, almost blue, when it's not hiding behind the heavy clouds moving in. "Like in a bubble city?"

"Yeah, why not? Surely they've figured out how to build some sort of bubble city on the moon by now. Would you move there?"

I roll my head to look at him. He's staring at the moon, too. He's slouched down in his seat, his foot propped up across one knee, his fingers tapping the armrests on his chair, as though he's drumming his own beat. "Would you?"

He smirks, his eyes not leaving the sky. "I asked you first."

Nodding, I turn away from him. "I think I would. Talk about a fresh start. Could you imagine standing up there, looking down at everyone here?"

"Do you think we'd be sitting up there, under our bubble yard looking at Earth?"

"Nah, the moon's romantic, Earth is just—"

"Just what?" He's watching me, half his face lit by the last flames from our fire.

"It's sad." I shiver. "You know what, I take it back. I don't want them to build a colony up there. It'll just get screwed up. We should leave the moon the way it is. A beautiful mystery with the power to steer the tides."

He watches me for too long and I shift in my seat. "I smell like smoke." I sniff my hair.

"And your teeth are chattering so hard I'm afraid you're going to break one. Go inside and take a hot shower. I'll put the fire out."

"Are you sure? I'll stay out here with you." It takes effort to say the words. My face may be frozen, but I don't want to leave.

"Go inside, Cass."

I grab his bowl and the plate from my s'mores, along with the blanket. "Thank you for a perfect night, Seuss."

He smiles. "You deserve it. Happy New Year."

"Happy New Year," I whisper back, his sad smile burned into my brain.

AUSTIN

*I lay in bed half the night thinking of Cassie.
She's across the hall, sleeping in my bed. This is painful
The more time I spend with her, the more I want to be with her.
Will she ever let that happen?*

I'm watching highlights from yesterday's games, my conversation with Cassie from last night lingering on my mind. She thinks the Earth is sad, messed up. When she said we should leave the moon alone, let it remain a mystery, I couldn't stop myself from wondering if it was a metaphor. Cassie's the proverbial moon to me. This crazy beautiful mystery pulling me closer and closer with every second, then pushing me away. Maybe I *should* leave her alone. Maybe I'll just screw her up more. Are all mysteries supposed to be solved? Have I gone crazy?

"I don't suppose there's a blow dryer in this house?" she asks, making her first appearance of the day.

I'm struck by how tiny she is. Every time I see her, it hits me like a punch in the gut. "Good morning."

She's wearing yoga pants, thick socks, and my sweatshirt again. It's long enough to be considered a dress on her. So long it hangs over her ass, which is unfortunate for me because now I can only imagine how those black cotton pants mold to her body. A towel is wrapped around her head like a turban.

"That's a good look on you."

Her hand yanks the towel away, her cheeks flushing as the wet mass of dark hair tumbles around her face and shoulders. Shit, that's an even better look. My body betrays me to the point of humiliation, so I shift in my seat and pull a pillow onto my lap casually.

"I had to wash it twice to get out the smoke smell." Her nose wrinkles as she sniffs the ends of her hair.

"Still lingering?" She shrugs halfheartedly in response. "It's probably my sweatshirt. You wore it outside last night, didn't you?"

She opens and closes her mouth as she looks down. One of the sleeves has swallowed her hand, and she settles the handless arm across her waist as her shoulders lift. "I like it," she admits, drawing her bottom lip between her teeth.

"I like you in it."

I told myself take it slow; she's a wild animal unsure of who and what she can trust, but I can't help it. I'm not used to censoring my feelings. I go after what I want. I like to win, but Cassie isn't a chick to bang after a night of partying and then forget when the sun comes up. Cassie is end game. She's my end game. I knew it the first time we spoke, maybe even before that. She drew me to her before I knew her voice. My quiet girl in the library.

"Shit," I mutter, dropping my head into my hands.

"Are you okay?"

I rub my forehead and peak through my fingers as I process this revelation. She's standing there still, a towel hanging from her fingertips. My sweatshirt dotted with droplets of water from her hair, and her eyes seeking answers from mine.

"Yeah. Yeah, sorry." I stand, walking past her and down the hall into Carson and Mindy's room. I search for Mindy's blow dryer. Nothing. She probably took it with her for the wedding and honeymoon. Cassie stands in the door, waiting. "So, we're a house of three guys. Mindy's the only one with the need for a blow dryer, and evidently she took it with her."

I allow my arm to brush hers as I slip between her and the door frame. "I can, however, help you with the smoke smell." I check my closet and meet her back in the hallway, holding out a new sweatshirt. "It's last years, but I have a feeling it'll fit."

She grins a small lopsided grin. "Yeah? What year would I have to go back to find one that wouldn't?"

"To be honest, I don't know if I was ever that small." I take the opportunity to scan her body from head to toe. "Fifth grade, maybe?"

Her grin turns into a full blown smile. "So you've always been a giant?"

"It's a curse," I nod ruefully.

She scans me, her smile still warm on her lips, her eyes taking their time as though she knows she's playing with fire. "I don't think it's a curse at all, Seuss."

She slips past me and walks back to my room, leaving me dumbfounded and turned on as hell.

"You missed the games yesterday," Cassie comments over my shoulder. I'm back on the couch, not really paying attention to the highlights.

"Yeah, but it's not a big deal. This was the last week of regular season; most of the games were throwaways."

"Throwaways?" Coming around the couch, she sits on the chair closest to me as her fingers braid her wet hair. My faded maroon sweatshirt looks every bit as good on her as the gray one did.

"Yeah, typically there are two types of teams by week seventeen: those that are in and those that aren't."

"In?"

I scratch my head. "I'm not used to having to explain football to anyone." I chuckle as Cassie curls her lips into a playful sneer.

"Okay, so the play-offs start next week. By this point most teams know if they've made it, but there's typically a team or two, sometimes more, vying for something in the last week. It could be home field advantage, a bi-week, a wild card spot." I'm tempted to grab a notebook and pencil to write it all out while I explain. "The reason I called it a throwaway week is because most teams that are in the playoffs don't bother with their starters for more than a few snaps. If that. They don't need to win, so they don't try very hard." I pause to see if she's following. "You have a glazed look. Too much?"

Her fingers lift, her thumb and index finger pinching the air with little space between them. With a nod, she admits, "Just a tad. You've played your whole life, I assume."

I swallow my desire to laugh. "You really don't know anything about football, do you? I mean, you didn't know who I was, so—" I pause. "Damn, that sounded conceited, didn't it?" She merely smirks as I sink back into the couch. "Sorry, I'm just so used to people knowing the name—Rutledge—especially around A&M."

She nods as though remembering something. "Legacy."

"Yep."

"So you, your older brother, your father. He played pro for a few years, too, right? Was he good?"

"Yeah, he was. He retired early because of Mom's illness."

"And West?" Flipping her hair behind her back, she pulls her legs to her chest.

"He actually quit when Mom died. Picked it back up after all the stuff with Jules, though. He's bound for greatness. He's got more talent than the three of us put together."

"Really?"

"Don't sound so shocked. I can admit when I've been defeated."

"I thought you don't like to lose?" She purses her lips as she raises a brow in question.

"I hate losing," I correct her. "You think I'm bad now, you should have seen us as kids. Competitiveness is in our blood, but I'm man enough to admit the truth."

"Good to know."

"What about you? Do you admit defeat easily?" I raise my eyebrows. I'm no longer talking about losing at sports.

"Not at all."

"And are you competitive?"

She lets out a long sigh, cocking her head to the side. "I don't really know," she says after a moment.

"You don't know?"

"No siblings, remember? I didn't play games or sports—I didn't have anyone—" she trails off. Her stocking feet hit the floor as she stands. "I'm starving."

I want to urge her to finish her sentence, but I don't. What she doesn't say tells me her story bit by bit. I'll wait. We've got nothing but time.

"Sorry, I should have offered." I push off the couch.

"Don't get up. I'm a big girl, you don't have to serve me."

But I want to. "Uh, I ate cereal. There are a few boxes in the pantry. All college-age appropriate."

She moves around my kitchen easily, as though she's at home raiding the pantry. "I'm not sure what to pick here. Obviously, marshmallows are a favorite in this house," she giggles.

"Well, duh," I reply over my shoulder as I turn the volume up on the television when they roll the plays of the week montage. "Ohhh, dang."

"Did she say one-handed?" A slurp follows Cassie's question. I wasn't aware she was paying attention.

"Sure did. One-handed catch, while falling to the ground, no less. Great play. Come eat in here." I hit the rewind button so she can see the play again. "Those are the plays that live with you. I mean, other than touchdowns. The highlight reel plays rock."

"Do you have sticky gloves or something? How did he hang on to the ball like that?"

I don't bother containing my laughter. "Your lack of knowledge is adorable. No, we don't have sticky gloves—that would be against league rules. As for keeping the ball, it's talent, good hands, and a bit of luck." She nods her understanding as she takes another spoonful of cereal.

The countdown continues, an amazing 102-yard touchback, an interception, a smackdown touchdown denied. It was a good week for great plays.

"Have you done that? Smacked a ball away from another guy?"

"Have I done that?" I balk, the urge to pump my chest strong. I'm about to let her in on my own personal highlight reel when I look over at her. Suddenly, my train of thought is completely lost.

She's watching me over the rim of her bowl as she drinks the milk from it. I totally stare. More proof she's the perfect girl.

"What?" She freezes, an odd grin plastering her face. "It's a waste to not finish the milk."

"I didn't say a thing. By all means, drink your milk from the bowl. No judgment here."

Elmer's giggle floats from her lips. "That's right, you come from a house of men. No fastidious manners here." She tips the bowl back one last time before setting in on the end table. "I'll probably regret this, but explain football to me."

There have been no shortage of girls asking me to teach them the rules of football in my life. Early on I discovered it was their way of getting my attention. I fell for it when I was younger; the football player, telling the pretty little girls in class all about how awesome I am. The older I get, the less patience I have for the ruse. Hell, only a few weeks ago I told a girl shamelessly fawning over me at a party that if she had any interest in football, she'd have learned it by now. It was rude, but I was frustrated with another girl, the one sitting near me now to be precise.

"Why the sudden interest?" I ask, probably a little too harshly.

Cassie fusses with the sleeves of my sweatshirt, looking down as she speaks. "Because you love it." Her eyes lift. "We made a deal. One week, and I get to know you, remember?"

The tenderness sparking within me sours. "You don't have to make it sound like a chore. I'm not holding you hostage."

Her thin brows snap together. "I didn't mean it that way at all."

"Then what did you mean?" The vitriol hidden in my tone surprises me.

"Never mind." She slides from her chair, carrying her cereal bowl to the kitchen, and I'm up behind her before she reaches the sink.

"No." I remove the bowl from her hand. "Say what you mean. Why do you care if I love football? You've made it clear nothing is going to happen between us."

She sinks back, the counter blocking her from putting more than a few inches between us, and I lean over her, bracing my hands on either side of her waist.

"Am I not allowed to be interested in what my friends are interested in?" Her emphasis on 'friends' doesn't go unnoticed.

Dipping down to get her attention, I nudge her leg with my knee when she looks at the floor. She doesn't budge, preferring to look at my chest instead of my face. "Is that all it is? Interest in the name of friendship?"

Her arms draw in, crossing over her chest tightly. She blinks, her eyes narrowing when she finally deigns to look at me. "Why the sudden crazy interrogation?"

"Because you weigh your words very carefully, Cassie. You don't think I notice, but I do. I'm curious, have you said anything to me without filtering yourself?"

She squares her shoulders, "Please let me by."

"Answer my question."

"Let. Me. By." She moves forward, using her arms as a bumper, her elbow poking my ribs with enough force to sting. I scoff at her feeble attempt to move me. Her teeth catch her bottom lip and she releases a quivering sigh, "Please."

Shit.

Hands up, I move back. Shit. "Cassie, I'm sorry."

She's ducking around me, putting a room full of space between us. "I asked you to tell me about football." Her voice rises.

"I know. I'm an ass. Really, I'm truly—" Her raised palm cuts me off.

"Stop." She spins, her socks slipping on the wooden floors in her haste to get away.

"Cass?"

Pausing at the door to my room, she turns. "For your information, everything I've said to you is unfiltered. I don't trust guys, Austin. I told you that. If I weigh my words carefully around you, it's because I'm terrified of what you might make me say. What I might want." Her hand covers her face, and the door closes a moment later.

She asks me about football, and I scare the shit out of her. What the hell is wrong with me?

CASSIE

*For the first time since I met him, Austin scares me.
Only, it's not just him I'm scared of.
It's me, too.*

I press the lock on his door and back away. I expect him to knock, or pound, on the door any moment now. I expect him to sweet-talk me through the three inches of wood separating us. Three inches. That is nothing to a man on a mission; I know this from experience. My eyes automatically flit to the hinges. They're solid, no rust.

"No," I remind myself quietly, staying focused on the door—on the sounds in the other room. "Stop, Cassie. He's not one of them. He's not *him*."

I flex my hands, growling at my predicament. This was a bad idea. One week with Austin will break me. Throwing myself on his bed, I tuck into a ball. His scent fills this room. It's probably because I'm using his soap and shampoo, but I swear it's more than that. Every move I make feels as though he's wrapped around me. He never leaves my senses. I wrench his sweatshirt over my head, hurling it across the room.

"Jerk."

I should leave, go back to campus. It was one call. I'm being paranoid. My frustration sends me rolling off the bed and dropping to my knees. Reaching underneath the bed frame, I pull my duffle out and rifle through the hastily packed clothing, finding my cell. It's dead. Of course it is, I haven't checked it since I ran to Austin's dorm Saturday night. With trembling fingers, I fish the charger out and plug it in. My heart works overtime, pounding with the precision of a drumline. Fifteen minutes and I should have a good charge.

Leaning against the edge of the bed, I wait.

The house is quiet; it's eerie after months of constant noise in the dorms. The fine hairs on my arms stand. Why did I say those things to Austin? Why did I admit anything to him? I rub my bare arms; the tank top I'm wearing offers substantially less warmth than his sweatshirt. My hand digs through my bag for a sweater as my eyes betray me, flicking to his maroon sweatshirt lying in a heap near the door. Dang it, I have no willpower.

I purposely chant "don't think, don't think" over and over as I crawl across the room. Don't think about what you're doing, Cassie. Don't think about why you'd rather wear his clothing than your own. Don't think, just pull it on. Don't sniff it as it brushes your face. Don't think of him as it falls over your breasts and across your waist.

Sinking forward, my fingers press to my lips as a heavy sigh releases from my lungs and out my mouth. "You're in trouble, girl." I tuck my chin and nose under the neckline and breathe. "So much trouble."

The electronic music from my cellphone powering up helps confirm it.

The lock snaps as I open the door. It's an echo in a cave; I want to shush it as I step into the hallway. Alone. If my history were to repeat itself, Austin would be waiting to pounce on me the moment the door cracks, but Austin's not my history. I take deep calming breaths. It's morning, but there's little light streaming into the house. He must have the blinds closed, or maybe it's overcast outside today. I have no idea. It's Monday, I know that. I was only in the room for thirty minutes, but it felt longer.

Like this one argument between us could have damaged this—whatever it is—beyond repair.

"I'm a tight end."

His voice, thick and low, startles me. I move toward the sound, stopping short of entering the living room. Austin's sitting on the edge of the couch—head down, arms resting across his thighs, hands clasped between his knees.

"That's the position I play on the field. So what that means is I'm on the field when the offense is on. The offense would be the side that is trying to score."

I say nothing, and he lifts his head, somber eyes looking my way. "Is this too dumbed down for you?"

Rooted to my spot, I press my lips together, fighting the twitch of a smile playing in my cheek. "Not at all."

"It gets complicated from here," he continues. "As a TE—tight end—I have several jobs. I can go out for a pass, I can block—it's a hybrid position."

"What do you like best?"

"Depends on the day and the team we're playing. I guess I'd have to say receiving—uh, that's going out for a pass. There's nothing like pulling a bullet out of the air and making a play." His eyes flash as though he's reliving a memory.

"I've never had anything I was passionate about." I lean my shoulder against the wall, keeping my escape route to the bedroom open, just in case. "You light up when you talk about football. The way you cheered at those highlight shots ... I've never felt that way. That's why I asked you about it." I'm acutely aware of the touch of jealousy running through my veins.

"You've never had something you were passionate about?"

"I never lived in one place long enough."

Pity rolls off him. I imagine he wants to ask why, or say he's sorry, as though his words can somehow fix my depraved childhood. If only he knew the truth of it all.

His mouth twists and I brace myself. "Did you know footballs were originally made out of animal bladders?"

I choke on the saliva in my throat. "Okay, that's gross."

"They were never made of pigskin, even though that's the common name we use. Just a fun fact for you." He grins, cocking his head back and signaling for me to come closer. "I recorded the Carolina game yesterday. I'll walk you through it, if you want. Teach you a few things."

The face from earlier, all tight lips and wrinkled forehead, has given way to a little boy's excitement. This is him lighting up. My emotions war within as he shifts on the couch, and I straighten, my eyes verifying the distance to his room—a reflex that doesn't go unnoticed.

"Cassie, I wasn't trying to intimidate you or scare you. I'm not one of those guys who feels the need to prove the size of his manhood by being an ass." He rubs the back of his neck, his worry written all over his face.

"I know you're not." I'm still working on convincing myself his words are true.

He calls me on it. "How do you know?"

Gut instinct, faith, fate. Something, or someone, wants me to trust him. I felt it from the beginning. Plus, I want to trust him. "I like to think I'm a pretty good judge of character. I'm taking a chance on Dr. Seuss."

"Thank you."

I shrug. "I owe you that much." I could have left that out of our conversation. It's not because I owe him, but my heart isn't ready to shed its protective barrier. Maybe he was right, maybe I do filter everything I say.

"You don't owe me anything." He rises from the couch. "I don't want you to feel as though you're at my mercy here. This is purely out of goodwill." His nose scrunches as his lips twist to the side, as though he's tasted something unpleasant. "Okay, that's a lie," he admits.

"So, I do owe you?"

"Ha, no." His brown eyes have this way of cutting across whatever space is between us and burrowing right into my soul. I'm caught in his intensity. "I've made no secret of my interest in you. I didn't stalk you in the library for my health, you know. I told you I'm competitive. I play to win, Cass." He shoves his hands into his pockets as he releases a deep breath. "But, you made in clear back in October you were off limits. Jules made it clear. Hell, Jess and Katie did, too. Until you showed up the other night I was willing to follow your lead—"

"And now?" I'm unsettled. And unsure what I want him to say.

"I don't know where you stand anymore. I don't know what you want, but it doesn't matter because something has you running scared. I don't know what's going on with you and I don't have to know. I'm here for you regardless."

A weight releases from my chest. "And now I have to thank you."

He shakes his head, apparently not wanting my appreciation. He's a freaking saint. If I don't interject some levity into this moment, I'm going to sink to the floor in a puddle of tears. I force a smile.

"You shake your head, telling me I owe you nothing, but you haven't started teaching me the rules of football yet." That perplexes him, and I explain, "You'll be singing a different tune once we get into all the traveling and goal tending explanations."

There are three beats of complete silence before he laughs. If my laugh is Elmer Fudd, his is thunder—a deep rumbling vibration in his chest that rolls out of his mouth and leaves me tingling like the aftershocks from the electricity in a storm.

He slaps his forehead, his shoulders shaking as his head swings from side to side. "Oh, Annie. We've got our work cut out for us."

I grin. Subject change accomplished. He doesn't need to know I was kidding. I know those aren't football terms. Or, I don't think they are.

AUSTIN

When she asks 'How many innings are there in a game?'
I know I haven't done my job.
Maybe I'm not cut out to be a football teacher,
but teaching Cassie is the most fun I've ever had.

"You lied to me," Cassie admonishes, stretching as she stands.

"Did I?"

"Yeah, you said I'm not a hostage here, yet we've been watching football for four hours." Her playful tone undermines her ire. "And you haven't fed me. You're a monster, Seuss."

"Whoa, weren't you the one who said you're a big girl and can get your own food? Don't blame me." I turn the television off, our tutorial session apparently over for today. "As for the game, you were totally into it."

She tugs at the hem of my sweatshirt, pulling it down from where it's bunched up around her hips. "I still don't understand half the penalties, but I finally get the whole downs thing, so that's a win, right?"

I follow her to the kitchen. She's removing lunch meat from my refrigerator, setting it on the counter, and moving to the pantry for the bread, like this is her house. Like she's comfortable.

Smiling inwardly, I tease her. "Four hours and that's all you picked up?"

"I guess you suck as a teacher," she shrugs, peeking over her shoulder.

"Or maybe the problem is the student."

"Impossible, I'm awesome."

She moves to the silverware drawer where I'm standing. Her brows lift as she looks up at me. Instead of stepping back, I move forward. My hands close around her biceps as I spin us around, switching places with her. Her chest grazes mine as I bend down, my face near the top of her head.

"You *are* awesome," I whisper into her hair before releasing her.

Cassie makes us sandwiches and we eat in silence, the teasing mood between us gone after my very serious compliment. "I skipped my workout this morning," I say after a while, more as an observation to myself than something I'm telling her.

She looks up from the moody contemplation of her half-eaten sandwich, her expression concerned.

"It's okay, it wasn't mandatory or anything. The team gets a small break since the season is over, but I told my strength coach I'd be in. It slipped my mind."

Her head lowers. "If you need to go back to campus, I'll understand."

"And what would you do?" I shouldn't have asked, but I wish she'd open up to me. "Would you come back with me?"

Instead of answering me, she slips off the barstool and throws her plate in the trash.

"It was just a question. I don't have to go back. We have the week off. But I am going to go for a run." Her back is to me, and maybe I'm crazy, but I swear she tenses. "I'll stay on the main street out front. I won't go far." Of course that means I'll be running paces back and forth, but if it makes her feel safe then that's what I'll do. We need a treadmill here.

"Do whatever you need to do, I'll be fine." Her overly bright smile doesn't fool me, but I don't push it.

I head to my room to grab workout clothing. Cassie's a neat person. The bed is made and her dirty clothing is folded in a small pile on the floor. The one bag she brought with her is on the floor by the nightstand. I pull the drawer to the stand open, intending to grab my extra set of wireless headphones when her phone lights up. It's on silent, the screen showing a call from an unknown number.

"Do you miss your room?" Cassie's voice startles me and I grab my headphones from the drawer, turning toward her.

"Hey, your phone was ringing—"

"Did you answer it?" She pales, rushing into the room and pushing into my side, yanking the phone from its charger.

"Answer it? Of course not. I noticed it while getting my headphones. Calm down."

Mindy once told me a guy should never tell a woman to calm down. I should have listened to her advice because Cassie's face turns a mottled purple.

"You did not just tell me to calm down." The words shoot through Cassie's gritted teeth. "If I had known I'd have no privacy I would've kept my things put away."

Whoa, did this just escalate with lightning speed?

"It's your phone. It rang. I told you. That's all." I give her pale face a once over and leave my room before things get any more out of hand. I'm out the door and pounding the pavement within five minutes. The cold air rushing through my lungs burns, but it's invigorating. I run a mile, then two. And then one more. Around and around, back and forth, up and down my street so I can keep an eye on the house. The curtains in the front window move each time I run by, but I force myself to ignore the movement and continue running.

More than once I mentally phrase questions, asking her what's going on. She's worried I'd answer her phone. She's worried about getting away from school. I replay moments from when we first met. I replay Jules's warnings. I recall the pure fear on Cassie's face Saturday night. How much longer will she maintain this charade?

Cassie's sitting on the front steps when I return to the house. "I'm sorry, I know you weren't snooping. I shouldn't have snapped at you."

I walk in circles across the front yard, hands on my hips as my breathing evens out.

"It's freezing out here. How can you run in this air?" she asks, and I pause long enough to throw a look her way. "I guess you're used to it," she mumbles, interpreting my lack of response in her own way.

Her hands rub along the length of her shins, and I realize she's not wearing a jacket or shoes. It's not supposed to break 50 degrees today, and while the sun is out in full force, there's a constant breeze rustling the branches of the trees. My body temperature settles as I pace, the air cooling the sweat, and my earlier frustration.

Fine. I snapped at her this morning about the football thing, she snapped at me about her phone. Maybe we're even. She rubs her legs again. She's probably determined to freeze until I say something.

Okay then. "I'm gonna shower," I say without looking her way. Instead, I walk into the house, leaving her on the porch.

CASSIE

*I should stay in the bedroom.
Stay away from Austin because this will get messy.
It's already messy—but I can't do it.*

Maybe it's the smell of tacos coaxing me out, or maybe it's his brown eyes and impish grin I'm missing. Either way I manage three hours locked away in his room before I bend.

Cantina music plays softly in the background as I leave my sanctuary and walk down the hall. I stop in the doorway to the living room and swallow a giggle when I spy Austin's head swaying to the beat. He's standing over the stovetop, stirring the contents of a large pan. Behind him, the island is covered with various items: chopped tomatoes, lettuce, sour cream, olives—it's a Mexican buffet. My mouth waters.

"Can I help?" I offer, walking further into the room.

If I expected him to be embarrassed at being caught dancing around the kitchen I am sorely mistaken. He turns my way, still shimmying, his eyes wide as they set on mine. "Por favor, señorita."

Scanning the preparations, I zero in on the olives and go to work slicing them. Austin opens some beans, mixing them and adding salsa and flavoring before pouring the contents into a dish and shoving them into the oven. He does a little turn as he closes the door.

I feel lighter after only two minutes in the same room with him. "Do you always dance while cooking?"

"Not really. I was looking for some music and thought it would be funny. It sets the tone, makes the meal more authentic, don't you think?"

"So if we were having steaks tonight?"

He grabs the remote from the table and changes the station. "Country," he says as a pop-country hit comes on. Bumping up the volume, he gives me a look. "We could do a line dance. How about it, pretty lady?" He bows at the waist, his eyes never leaving my face.

"No. No dancing for me."

"Not even at parties?" The station changes to another tune. This one has heavy bass and electronic notes.

"I don't do parties," I speak up over the thumping beat.

"I'm sorry, did you just say you don't do parties, Annie?" His hands go to his head as though his mind is blown.

"You are such a drama queen, for a guy," I laugh.

"You room with Katie, Jules, and Jess, and yet you've not been to a single party?" he asks, evidently fixated on this issue. It's as though I've broken some law, a college law. He shakes his head. "I'm a little shocked, and disappointed, in my girls."

"Let me remind you something about *your girls*," I flash him a pointed look as I say 'your' and set the knife I'm using down before scooping the sliced olives into a bowl on the counter. "Katie and Jules have Jeff and West, and Jess is a bit over the top when it comes to guys. That's not my thing. As you well know, I'm much happier with a good book."

"Yeah, we need to fix that." He leans back against the counter, crossing his ankles in front of him.

"You planning on dragging me to one of your many frat parties?" I snort at the prospect.

He scrutinizes me—his mouth twisting from side to side as his eyes cloud over thoughtfully. The urge to slink back to my room hits me; I can see the wheels spinning in his mind. I know exactly when his lightbulb moment hits him because it comes in the form of a wicked smile and wagging brows.

"What do you think about shots?"

"No way." I shake my head profusely as Austin chuckles, his nod matching that of my refusal. "Nope."

"Yep." He straightens. "We're having a little party, just me and you."

"I'm not 21," I say, grasping for the most logical issue with his plan.

"Good thing I'm the bartender then," he smirks. "Come on, we're not going anywhere. Let me throw you a little party right here."

"Why?"

"Because I want you to dance with me. I want you not to think." He closes the distance between us, standing over me in a way that's extremely disconcerting and sexy at the same time. The bass thumping in the background might as well be my heart; the heavy beats vibrate the room the way the pounding in my chest rattles my entire body. "You think too much."

"I bet you say that to all the girls."

Austin shoves his hands through his hair, a bitter laugh escaping his lips. "Nice." His frown lets me know he's not happy with my comment. "I'm not trying to get into your pants. I just thought some fun was in order. You're always stressed."

"And you recommend alcohol?" Sarcasm laces my tone. Why am I being so difficult?

"I recommend trusting me." Trust. My shoulders tense at the word; it's instinctual. "Don't give me that face," Austin warns as he looks over his shoulder at the oven. "Let's eat so we can get this party started." He winks before moving to the oven and removing the beans he made.

Mexican dinner a la Austin Rutledge has a chance at becoming my favorite meal ever. He flips the majority of the lights in the house off, leaving us with three lit candles in mason jars on the center of the table, before switching the music back to authentic mariachi style. I transfer chips and salsa to a decorative hat/bowl dip combo thing and set it on the table along with cactus-shaped plastic cups.

"Mindy's a bit of a party theme nut," his muffled voice explains as he digs in a cabinet. "Do you want the pepper or the Chihuahua?"

"The pepper or the—" I grab the top of the chair to my right. "Oh my gosh. That is the ugliest thing I've ever seen." He's holding two ceramic taco shell holders. The pepper I recognize, but the Chihuahua? "I'm not eating my tacos out of a dog." I laugh at the absurdity.

"Pepper for you then." Setting the holders on the counter, he nods to the food. "Help yourself."

With the exception of the taco-holding dog Austin has strategically placed so it stares at me as I eat, dinner is perfect. He pours beer in our cactuses and tops them with lime. It's not terrible, though I return to my water more than the beer.

"I think Mexican is my favorite food. Somehow it never gets old," he comments as he stuffs another chip in his mouth.

"Hmmm, I'd have to say Chinese."

"Sushi?"

"Eww, no. Chow mein noodles with veggies, and a little teriyaki chicken. Yum."

"Panda Express in the student center, huh?" Austin confirms, a knowing smile on his face.

"Maybe once or twice." His mention of the student center reminds me of the day he asked me to get breakfast tacos with him. "You know, I still haven't eaten at Rev's."

"Really? Well, I'll have to bring you to breakfast next week."

The invitation hangs between us. According to Jules, Austin rarely has dates on campus. She made that clear after I learned who he is. It was her attempt to convince me that his behavior toward me is proof I mean more to him than just another booty call. She assumed I pushed him away due to his reputation.

"When was the last time you had a girlfriend?"

He sputters on the sip of beer he just took. "Straight to the personal stuff. Okay then." He finishes off the last drop of beer in his glass and sits back in his chair. "Lauren, junior year in high school."

I do the math. "Four years?" I'm honestly a bit shocked.

"Does that bother you for some reason? When was the last time you had a boyfriend, Annie?"

I take a long sip of my beer.

"That long?"

This is one discussion I don't want to get further into. "Aren't we supposed to be having a party? Where are the shots?" I slap the table with my palms.

"Subject change, noted." He lifts his empty glass to me in a salute. "Drinking and debauchery, here we come."

"Let's stick with drinking, hot shot."

He stands, grabbing his dishes. "You clear the table; I'll get the cups."

I follow him with interest as he digs a bunch of plastic cups out, filling them with water and setting them on the table, six at each end. Next comes a bottle of alcohol, two shot glasses, and ping pong balls.

"Beer pong with shots," he explains, switching our music once again. "I assume you've never played."

"Nope."

"Okay, you stand here." He steers me to one end of the table, handing me a ball before he rounds to the opposite end. "I'll stand over here. The goal is to the land your ball in each of my cups by either throwing or bouncing it in."

I study the pyramid configuration of cups on his side. "Okay, and where do the shots come in?"

"You get in my cup—I drink. I get in yours—you drink." His upper lip curls into a smile. I can only imagine where his dirty mind just went.

"Make a shot, other person drinks. Got it. How do I win?"

"I win," his eyes shine with intent, "by landing my ball in each of your cups. Whenever someone lands a ball in a cup that cup is removed from play. You lose when all your cups are gone."

"Easy enough."

"I like the confidence." He pours two shots of golden liquid from a bottle with a red devil-like creature on it. I'm too afraid to ask what it is. "You can go first," he offers.

"Oh gosh," I exhale, tossing my little ball from hand to hand. What have I gotten myself into here? "Can I get a practice shot?"

"Heck no," he scoffs, and I frown at his lack of gentlemanly manners. "I told you I'm ultra-competitive."

The, sorry-not-sorry face he makes is so perfect, I can't even be mad at him. Exhaling, I try to focus on his cups across from mine, but his constant movement distracts me. His upper body moves to the beat of the music. It's just a bounce, a little up and down rhythm, but I stare for a second longer than necessary. His lips move almost imperceptibly as he raps along to whomever we're listening to. I'm so out of the music loop, I have no idea what the song is.

Here goes nothing. I take aim and toss, my little white ball flying across the table and toward Austin's chest. Mr. Competitive snatches it right out of the air. Stupid football star.

"A little less muscle on the next one," he suggests, rolling the ball across the table back to me. I resist the urge to throw it at his head.

"Okay," he says under his breath, rubbing his hands together. A calm washes over his features. Is this game face? It has to be. He crouches down, eying the cups, arching his hand and flicking his wrist like he's mentally measuring the force needed to land the ball into one of my cups. He isn't playing around.

Pulling his ping pong ball from where he's stashed it in his pocket, his eyes lift to my face. "Hope you like cinnamon, little one," he drawls as he tosses his ball. It cuts through the air in a high arc and lands in the second row with a quiet plunking sound.

I expect a whoop or some in-your-face type of boasting, but Austin Rutledge surprises me again. Sliding his hands into his pockets with careless ease, he sends me a simple smile and arched brow. "One shot."

I roll my eyes. "Yeah, I know, showoff." Obviously, I'm not as gracious at losing as he is at winning.

He cocks his head and slides a small shot glass my way. "No. One shot."

Oh, crap. "What is this?" I cringe as I reach for the cup, looking at the bottle.

"Fireball."

"As in the song?"

Austin laughs, his hands going up and linking on top of his head. "Yeah, like the song, or like the whiskey. Whatever makes you feel better."

Raising the glass, I sniff. My eyes water at the scent. It's liquid Red Hots.

"I can't believe I'm doing this."

Pressing the shot next to my lips, I close my eyes, count to three, and tip my head back. For one beautiful second there's nothing. Then there's fire and sugar burning down my throat and making a hot path through my chest. "Holy crap, that's awful," I breath, coughing and grabbing one of the cups with water in front of me. My stomach aches.

Austin's comical. He makes his best attempt to not laugh, but he's losing the battle. I finally give into my earlier urge and throw my ball at his head.

"Sorry," he bursts, ducking. "Your face, though. That was great."

"You are evil." I gulp more water.

"It's not that bad," he lifts the second shot glass in a salute and tips it back in one quick shot. He gives me a 'told you so' look as he smacks the glass down on the table. "See? You just have to get used to it."

"I'm not drinking anymore of that. If that's what it takes to go to frat parties, I guess I'm out of style."

His eyes scan over me with a marked intensity. I wish I knew what he was thinking sometimes when he looks at me that way. It makes my stomach burn, although tonight I'm not sure if the feeling comes from Austin's gaze or the alcohol.

"C'mon, put the water down and remove the cup my ball landed in. No more Fireball shots."

"No more?" I ask, doing as he says.

"Hell no, six shots of that stuff and I could do whatever I want with you."

Jokes on him, he doesn't need alcohol to do whatever he wants with me. Wow, is it hot in here? I didn't say that out loud, or I don't think I did, but his eyes sure are bright as he leans his palms into the table and looks at me.

"I told you I wasn't trying to get in your pants. We can do beer shots instead. It's all for fun anyway."

My hands go to my hips. "You just wanted to see me do my first shot, didn't you?"

"Possibly." He turns, searching for the ball I threw at his head as I gape at him.

Over the course of the next twenty or so minutes, I miss the next three cups and he lands two. "This game is grossly unfair," I whine as I take another shot of beer.

"I've had a bit more practice than you," he shrugs in agreement with my assessment.

"A bit? That's an understatement. And this music." I wave my hand in the general direction of the television. My limbs feel gloriously loose right about now. "How am I supposed to concentrate with this angry stuff on?"

"Change it," he tosses me the remote. "This is what I use to get fired up before games."

"It hurts my ears," I counter.

I find the indie station and Austin groans, "This is coffee shop music for yuppies and hipsters."

We plan two rounds of beer pong. I drink with every shot Austin makes, and he doesn't drink on any of mine. I suck, but I've had two beers and one Fireball shot, so I'm okay with it all.

A playful song with harmonies and peppy drumbeats plays, and I find myself bouncing around the room with my hips shaking and my head swinging. Austin leans his hip against the table where our beer pong turned into a game to see how many times he could throw and not miss a ball. The cups are stacked three high. He hit them all, even one was while backward. I'm damn impressed with him. I smile his way, crooking my finger at him as I shimmy into the open space in front of the fireplace.

He tips his beer up, sinking the liquid before joining me in the living room. "You're quite the dancer."

"Dance with me," I shout, a little louder than necessary considering he's standing right in front of me.

"How do I dance to this?" He's thoroughly disgusted with my music choice.

I take his hands in mine and lift his arms. "Like this." I shake my shoulders and bounce from foot to foot, shaking his arms around.

He laughs, his tongue shooting out and wetting his bottom lip as he shakes his head at me. Then his head moves from side to side, like a bobble head, and his shoulders move. We're dancing. He's jumping, I'm jumping. He's laughing, I'm laughing.

It's perfect. I'm giving myself a moment. One moment of liquid courage.

"This is a frat party, Cass," Austin whispers, pulling me into his chest as a slow song comes on. "You're not thinking."

"Not true. I am thinking." My voice is raw from all of the singing I've been doing.

We stop swaying. "What are you thinking?"

I tilt my head back, looking up into his face. He hasn't shaved for a few days now; the dark stubble gives him a mysterious, dangerous look. My eyes zero in on his lips and they twitch under my gaze. My buzz is wearing off, but my desire is just kicking in.

Desire or not, my head needs to remain in charge. "I should go to bed," I breathe, my forehead falling forward and resting on his chest.

His hands splay across my lower back and I feel his deep sigh against my forehead. "Yeah?" he asks, and for one moment I want to take it back. Why not give in? Don't I deserve a piece of happiness?

My fingers play over the taunt muscles of his waist as I push away from his body. "Yeah, I think it would be a good idea."

His lips part, indecision flickering in his eyes before he nods and drops his hands from my back. "Sure."

The music shuts off. The party is over.

"Drink some water before you lay down, though. It'll help with the headache in the morning." I nod at his directions and he waves me away. "Go on, I'll clean up."

Before he can turn away, I take hold of his arm, his skin warm beneath my fingers. Using the last bit of my liquid courage, I stretch up on my toes and tug him down, pressing a kiss to his cheek. "Thank you for tonight, it was pretty perfect."

His hand holds my head close as he places a tender kiss on my forehead. Man, he smells like cinnamon and beer. "You're giving in, aren't you?"

My lips are mere inches from his when I reply. "Not yet."

"But you're getting there," he smirks, the rich timbre of his voice stirring my passion as his breath washes over my face.

He releases me, and I sway in place as I admit the truth to him, and to myself. "I'm getting there."

AUSTIN

Falling for Cassie is like magic.
That's the only way I can explain it. Magic.
How else do I rationalize these sudden, overwhelming feelings?
She cast a spell on me.

"Austin! Austin!"

Cassie's shouting and pounding on the door jolts me from my sleep. My brain going from sweet dreams to panic mode in two seconds flat. I nearly fall on my face as I untangle myself from my sheets.

"Aus—"

I throw the door open, a baseball bat in one hand and nothing but boxer briefs on my body. Cassie gasps, her eyes round as she takes me in.

"What's that for?" she asks innocently. But my brain isn't thinking innocent thoughts this morning. I give her a pointed look.

Her lips press together, pink staining her cheeks as her eyes flick down.

"It's morning, sue me," I wink, and she breaks into laughter.

"I meant the bat," she clarifies, and I give her another pointed look. "In your hand, pervert. The baseball bat." This time I'm hit with her full

Elmer giggle. And there I go, getting a little harder. Pants would have been a great option before opening the door.

"You were screaming my name and pounding on my door." I lower the bat to my side. "I was sound asleep. You scared the crap out of me."

Her cheeks puff out as she slaps her hands over her mouth. "I'm so sorry, I didn't think about how that might sound. Everything's fine."

"Then why are you waking me up? I'll have you know, we were in the middle of a very happy dream." God, the pink in her cheeks is so damn enticing. She likes to pretend my little flirtations don't affect her, but I see her shiver.

Mischief lights up her face. "Come here, I'll show you."

"Can I put some clothes on first?"

Her brown eyes scan my body once again. "Well, if you must."

"I don't have to if you don't want me to." I lean my shoulder against the doorframe. Could I just pull her into this room and throw her on the bed?

"Fine," she sighs as though it's a huge imposition. I'm loving this playful side to her this morning. "Go put some pants on, hurry though."

"No shirt then? Your wish is my command." She rolls her eyes, unable to contain her smile.

Remaining in the doorway, she averts her gaze as I pull on a pair of sweats. "Okay, what's up?" I ask.

She groans as she looks my way. "Oh my gosh, put a shirt on, you exhibitionist. And shoes too."

For the first time since I opened my door I notice she's fully clothed. "Are we going somewhere?"

"Just the backyard," she grins. Her face is flushed, her eyes sparkling. I've never seen her excited like this.

I glance at the clock on West's dresser. Seven AM. No, that can't be right. "Why are you up so early?"

She doesn't reply, so I finish dressing. Once yesterday's sweatshirt is over my head and my shoes are slipped on, Cassie grabs my hand and tugs me down the hallway to the back door. Her fingers tighten around mine as she looks over her shoulder, a secretive smile on her face. She's obviously escaped any aftereffects of her one shot and beers. I, on the other hand, could use a few more hours of sleep.

"Ta-da," she sings, throwing open the back door. "It's snowing." Releasing my hand, she claps with excitement. "Come on."

"Oh wow." I squint, the early morning sun already abnormally bright thanks to the glittering white snow. I follow Cassie onto the back patio, watching as she holds her hands out wide and throws her head back, her tongue darting out catching the snow. The ground is barely tinted white, but the flakes are fat and falling quickly. They coat Cassie's dark hair within moments.

"We haven't had snow here since, I don't know, five or six years ago, I guess. This is crazy."

"It's so pretty, isn't it?" She studies the flakes melting in her palm. "It's as though everything has stopped. The world is peaceful. I've always loved watching the snow. I love the way the flakes float down in a million different patterns and shapes, and the way the white blankets the brown winter grass and naked trees. It's so pure and clean."

I hold my palms out like Cassie, catching ice crystals on my skin. "You said you lived everywhere. I take it you grew up with some white winters?"

"My mom hated the cold, but we spent some time in Utah."

Her smile drops as she talks about her mother, so I change subjects. "My mom's family lives in Wyoming. We spent our Christmas breaks there skiing. For a while I considered going to school up there, but—" I shrug.

"But the family legacy won out?" she finishes for me, nodding in understanding. How does she seem to understand my life without my having to explain it? She scoops a handful of snow off the glass tabletop, balling it up. "Look, the world's tiniest snowball."

I barely get a look before the puff of white pegs me in the shoulder, disintegrating on contact. Cassie giggles, scooping up more and trying again.

"Oh, really?" I grab my own handful, and Cassie yelps as I smash it over her head. Her hands, red from the cold and ice, grasp at my left hand while my right reaches for more. She lets go with a shriek, running into the backyard, her shoes slipping on the slick ground as I stalk her.

"I don't think this is a fair contest," she whines as my snowball whizzes by her face, barely missing.

"Because I play football? The quarterback throws the ball, not me," I tease, reminding her of our tutoring session as I form another snowball.

"No, because you're a boy and twice my size," she gasps as a snowball hits her cheek. "And you're mean," she pouts, wiping away the wet snow.

"You started it, Annie." She falters, her shoes slipping on the snow and I pounce, throwing myself onto the ground and dragging her with me. "You give in?" I ask, panting from exertion as I lean over her prone body.

Whack.

She shoves a fist full of snow up my nose and down my throat. "No," she giggles, scrambling away when my hands release her, but she's not quick enough and I grab the edge of her sweatshirt before she's able to scramble to her feet.

"I give in, I give in," she cries, falling hard onto her ass as I pull her backward. "Ouch," she moans.

"You give in?" I repeat, bracing for another attack.

"I might have just broken my ass, and you want to know if I give in?" She frowns.

"I'll check your ass for you," I offer, pushing at her hip to roll her over.

"You most certainly will not." Slapping at my hands, Cassie sits up. I'm laughing so hard my stomach hurts. "Jerk," she mumbles, her arm pushing at me. I grab it; my cold hand sliding down her damp sleeve to her hand. Her fingers are wet, red, and as cold as ice as I bring them to my mouth, blowing on the tips.

"We should probably put on proper winter clothing if we're going to play outside in the snow," she says her voice trembling as her eyes focus on my mouth.

"Are you giving in yet?"

We stare at one another as swirls of snow blow all around us. Her free hand touches my arm and I lower the fingers from my mouth and roll to my feet, pulling her with me in one swift movement. To my surprise, she leans into my body, her hands wrapping around my waist. Her forehead pressing against my chest as my hand presses against her back. The same as last night. There's something so incredibly amazing about standing with her this way. There are a few inches between our bodies, yet there's so much trust in the way she lowers her head against me. The way her hands grip the back of my shirt.

"I want to," she admits softly.

I hold my breath.

"I just don't know if I can."

And release it.

"So we keep going slow," I say, more to myself. A shiver runs up her spine and I pull back. "Starting with hot chocolate and dry clothes."

Her teeth rattle. "Good idea."

CASSIE

My duffle bag, hastily packed Sunday morning, brings back a memory. I'm no stranger to leaving...

The house is dark, not uncommon, but something about the darkness feels out of place after last night. Leaving my bike near the sidewalk, I pull my key from my backpack and walk inside. It's nearly 10PM, but there's no sign of life. I check the kitchen. No dinner dishes or trash. I peek out the blinds of the door leading to the garage and see no cars. They're not home. Again, not uncommon, so why does everything feel different?

Pushing my bedroom door open, I flip on the light. There's a suitcase on my bed, a pile of unfolded clothes toppling over the sides. Another move. Figures. I'd curse, but this is one place—one man—I'm more than happy to leave. I drop my bag from my shoulders. Might as well get packing now. Who knows when Momma will return ready to leave.

That's when I see it. A note perched on top of a plaid pair of pajama pants. The words, scratched in Momma's overly looping handwriting, don't come as a surprise, but that doesn't make them hurt any less.

Much like that day, when I grabbed my bag at the dorm Sunday morning, I packed a pair of jeans, two sweaters, yoga pants, leggings, some tees, and a handful of socks and underthings. The bare minimum so I could get out fast. I push the memory away as I pull my clean leggings and snoop in Austin's closet for another sweatshirt. It must be a perk of being a football star—all the team gear you can wear. Scooping up my pile of dirty clothes, I carry them into the living room.

"Can I wash these?"

"Sure. Through that door. The detergent is in the cabinet over the washer." He points me down the hall.

I start the small load and return to the kitchen. Austin is standing before two mugs, packets of hot chocolate, and spoons sitting on the counter. He changed into a pair of plaid flannel sleeping pants and a knit jersey tee. He reminds me of a Christmas ad for some department store.

"Very domestic."

He shrugs. "When we were kids, my mom always bought us matching pajama sets for Christmas. We take turns now, the four of us buying them each year. This was Carson's purchase last year. He's the most mature. Dad bought us pants with food this year."

I try to picture a young Austin in matching pajamas with his dad and brothers, but I can't see anything other than the tall, well-built man in front of me. Behind him and out the window a hurricane of white continues falling to the ground. "It's coming down harder out there." I nod to the window.

Austin turns to see what I see. "I checked the weather. It's supposed to come down for a couple more hours. Then we might get more tonight. It actually might stick around for a day or two, according to the forecast."

The thought of having a beautiful winter world for a few days makes me smile. "It's amazing how peaceful everything looks."

"Will you watch the milk in the kettle?" Austin asks, and I turn from the window to the stove.

"Kettle? Is the microwave broken?"

"No, I'm just a bit old-fashioned with some things." He brushes by me, his body purposely sliding closer than necessary considering the width between the two counters I'm standing between.

Without explanation, he pulls the curtains back from the doors leading outside. The winter white glow lights up the room without electricity. He shuffles around the room, shoving an end table and one chair to the side and pushing the coffee table to the other.

"What are you doing?" I ask when he lifts one side of the couch up.

He holds a finger up high, signaling me to hang on. The low whistle of the kettle stirs to life, and I turn my back to Austin as the sound of him pushing the couch across the floor fills the room. While he rearranges the furniture, I pour steaming milk into our mugs and dump in the chocolate powder.

"I'm giving us a front row seat to mother nature," Austin finally answers my question, coming around the kitchen island and picking up our mugs.

A front row seat? I follow him. He's pushed the couch all the way up against the glass doors looking out into the back yard. "Climb over," he says with a smile.

I want to cry at the gesture, but an idea takes shape. "It's missing something," I tell him, hurrying from the room. I grab two pillows from his bed and the faux fur blanket from the back of the corner chair in the living room and drop them onto the couch. Climbing over the arm rest, I settle the pillows on each end, one for him and one for me. Then I reach out, taking the mugs from his hands so he can climb in. He lifts his legs to climb over, but stops midway.

"Hold up," he says, his mouth twisting thoughtfully. I grin as he moves to my side of the couch and pulls an end table up to the back. "A table for your drinks, Madame," he teases with a bow. He pulls one to his side as well before standing behind the couch and staring at the set-up. "One last thing." He produces a box of cereal from the pantry. "We'll need sustenance."

I dissolve into laughter as he sets the box on the table on his side and then climbs onto the couch. Thanks to short legs and deep seats, I'm able to sit crossed-legged without a problem. Austin isn't as lucky. His long body stretches from one end of the couch to the other, and I all but fold myself into a ball as he shifts around, searching for a comfortable position.

With a sigh, he reaches for his mug in my hands and sets it on the table behind him as his feet kick at my legs.

"Uh, do you want me to move?" I chuckle as he shoves his legs on either side of my hips without my permission.

"Nope, I'm good." He sinks down, sliding lower in the seat and leaning against the arm rest. "Give me your legs."

I pull my knees to my chest, wrapping my arms around them protectively at his request.

"Your legs, Elmer." His fingers wiggle at me.

"You know that nickname isn't the most flattering, considering." I glare his way, but follow his instructions, extending one leg, then the other, in front of me until his hands take hold of my ankles and tug on them. "Hey." My hand slaps the cold glass to my right as I slide down into a reclined position.

"There." He sets my legs down, my calves and feet laying across his thigh and near his hips. "As long as you watch where your feet go—" His handsome face twists in a playful grimace as his index finger points down. "We'll be good."

"I can sit up." I wiggle backward, but his hands clamp on my feet.

"No. You're perfect right here, Cass. Now drink your cocoa and enjoy the view." He nods to the window. "Also, I only call you that when you make that face."

"What face," I ask, shifting—with Austin's hands holding my feet to keep me from removing them—into the corner of the couch.

"That one," he points out as I stuff the pillow I brought from his room behind my head. My brows snap together. Austin chuckles while I groan.

I suck in my cheeks, biting the inside flesh and forcing myself to stop making whatever strange face he's deemed the 'Elmer' face. His thumb rubs the bottom of my foot as he shakes his head, causing me to lose all thought. "I like the face, don't change it."

"Couldn't even if I wanted to," I say, reaching for my mug and raising it. "You boil good milk, Rutledge."

His free hand grabs his mug. "And you stir some mean chocolate. Cheers." He takes a few sips, his eyes on my face as his other hand continues to rub the arch of my foot. I could moan, it feels so fabulous. I turn from him, worried he can read my thoughts.

"Hungry?" he asks, setting his mug aside and opening the cereal box. He pours a handful into his palm.

"Starving." I stretch out my hand for my own pile only to be pegged in the face by a tiny purple ball.

"You're supposed to catch it in your mouth," Austin tsks, throwing another crunch berry at my face. It bounces off my cheek.

"I'm not opening my mouth—" a third piece flies at me and I yelp as I open wide, in an attempt to catch it. "Austin," I whine as I miss again.

"C'mon, underhand this time." He flips his hand over, attempting an underhand throw, but his space is limited. He reminds me of a T-Rex, his arm tucked in at his waist as he concentrates on making the toss. I bite my lip, laughter bubbling up at the obnoxious scene he's making.

"I've got this," he says confidently.

The piece shoots straight up and falls between our legs.

"Or not."

"And you want to be paid to play football?" Austin's face wipes clean and this time my giggles can't be contained.

"Funny," he deadpans. His free hand clamps on my ankle. "Hmmm, I wonder if you're ticklish."

I yelp as his hand attacks my foot, kicking at him and twisting. With his legs clamped on either side of my body he has me at a disadvantage. I gasp, begging him to stop, my free foot kicking at his hand filled with cereal.

"Say I'm awesome," he orders, his hands moving from my feet to behind my knees, squeezing them until I want to pee my pants and I can't breathe. "Say it. 'Austin's an awesome football player.'"

"Nooo," I gasp, trying to sit up and fight his arms off, but I'm laughing so hard I can't pull myself up.

"Girl." His feet cup under me, and in some Herculean show of strength he uses them and his legs to scoot me lower on the couch as he traps my legs with one arm and aims for my stomach with the other. "I will tickle you until you're blue in the face. Or bluer—" he chuckles.

"Okay," I manage between gasps of air and laughter. "Austin ... Is ... Awesome. You're awesome." I'm screaming, my stomach muscles and face aching from all the laughter.

His hands still. "That's what I thought," he nods.

I'm on my back. Somehow he managed to pull me all the way down on the couch, my legs up in the air. He releases hold of my legs and grips my waist, picking me up and helping me sit as though I'm nothing but a toy. He is way stronger than I gave him credit for.

There's a crunch under my legs as I shift.

"Man, there are crumbs all under us," I bend forward intending to fish the dropped pieces of cereal out. "If you're so awesome, why'd you fumble the cereal, big shot?"

Austin shakes his head, laughing at my impertinence. "There was a massive amount of interference with my play there. I blame the refs for not throwing a flag."

I nod. "Always blame the refs."

"See, my football tutoring session did teach you something."

We stare at each other, the room feeling abnormally quiet after all the laughter a moment ago. His lips form a huge smile, while I chew on mine as my heart rate comes down slowly. The feel of his hands on my waist lingers as I cross my legs and start scooping up the discarded cereal.

"The couch is a mess," I say, eager to dispel the strange hush that's come over us.

"Hey," his foot kicks lightly at my hip. "Don't worry about that, it's just crumbs." He holds a red crunch berry up, working on his aim. "Let me try again, you ready?"

I roll my eyes as I lift my face, my cheek muscles once again aching from the pressure to not laugh as I open my mouth. This time I don't move, I allow him to get the perfect aim and toss.

"He shoots, he scores!" Austin shouts, his hands shooting into the air as I crunch down on the berry-flavored bite.

"Keep 'em coming, I'm hungry."

He tosses a handful of cereal pieces into my mouth, hair, and the cushions of the couch before giving in to my hunger whines and tossing the box to me. We lapse into silence, crunching on cereal, drinking hot chocolate, and watching the snow fall two feet from our faces. A chill resonates from the glass window and I pull the blanket from the back of the couch and over my legs after swiping the cereal dust toward the crack between the couch and the window.

Without a word, Austin tugs at the blanket, covering my feet and himself in the process. At some point his hand returns to my foot. The urge to purr at the way his thumb massages my arch is overwhelming. His touch is strong and smooth, a powerful tool caressing my muscles. I close my eyes as he takes my other foot in his hand. No one has ever touched me the way he is.

"Mmm." The low sigh comes unbidden and I open one eye, gauging his reaction. His languorous gaze only adds fuel to the fire building within.

"Is this going to be a repeat of the donut situation?" He's leaning back, his head resting on the back pillow cushion as he watches me with narrowed eyes.

"If you keep rubbing me that way, it might be." I match his lazy tone, biting my lip and sinking lower into the couch as his grip tightens. Who needs sex scenes and shirtless men when you've got hands like these on your body?

"You're so beautiful."

I resist the urge to bury my head under the blanket.

"The last time I told you that, you slapped me," he reminds me needlessly, and I frown.

"I slapped you because you kissed me."

"It couldn't be helped."

"The slap or the kiss?"

"Both, I suppose." His lips twitch. I don't argue with him. I'm not sure he'd understand how mortified I am about that moment. The slap was a reflex. Automatic for the little girl who used to protect herself, and a long time coming for the young woman who never did.

Our voices are as soft as the snowflakes dancing to the ground. Everything about this moment is dreamlike. His strong legs nestled on either side of me, his large calloused hands on me, his eyes watching my every expression. We're encased in a fantasy world of snow and blankets. I twist toward the glass, pressing my palm to it and reminding myself this isn't real.

I take a deep breath. "I've never met my father." Austin's hands still, but I continue as though I didn't just drop a bomb. "I mean, I don't know who he is. I guess I should call him my sperm donor, instead of my father."

The massage starts back up again. "Is that why you don't trust guys, because you haven't had any in your life?"

If only. My palm slides from the glass and I look at him. "No, I've had way too many."

His features draw together tightly at my vague reply. He lifts my feet and legs to swap positions with his own legs, shifting himself for comfort.

"Not the right ones, then." Those five words hold a world of meaning. "Come here." He taps the space beside him now that he's shifted his back against the back cushions.

I hesitate.

"Cass, come here," he repeats on a ragged sigh.

My heart hammers against my chest. Is this what animals feel like when they're being caged? My eyes flick from Austin to the glass wall in front of us. Only two feet of space there and a million demons in my mind.

"Whoever those guys were, I'm not them," he says tenderly.

I push myself into a sitting position, curling my legs beneath me. "I don't trust easily."

He laughs softly. "You think I haven't noticed that? Please, lay here with me."

The offer is too good to pass up. I slide forward, and he releases a held breath as I wedge myself against the glass, lying on my side and facing him. He props his head in his palm, his face hovering over mine.

"I haven't told you how honored I am that you trust me." I must frown because a finger touches my forehead. "Don't bother denying it. You wouldn't have come here if you didn't." He pauses for a moment before finishing. "Thank you for trusting me."

I'm speechless as he leans down, causing my stomach to flutter. Is he going to kiss me? One strong arm wraps around my waist, his hand tucking under my side between my body and the couch and pulling me away from the cold glass and closer to his body. I anticipate the moment his lips will touch mine, I expect it. Instead, he smiles and jerks my body up from the couch.

"Now, let's shift around," he says.

Moving me down, he lifts my body and shifts me for the second time today. I'm a rag doll he poses as he makes himself comfortable. Between the tugging of his arm and the nudging of his legs, chest, and hips, I'm shifted into a spooning position with my head tucked under his chin while facing the window.

"Better?"

What? No, not better. I was expecting a kiss. I might have even wanted one. His arm slips over my side, his hand coming to a stop and resting low on my stomach.

"Better," I breathe as I tuck my own hands beneath my cheek to keep them for reaching for him.

"Does your mom know who your dad is?" he asks after a few minutes.

"She's always told me she didn't. There were a few prospects, all losers she met at bars, but she never bothered figuring out who." It's hard to keep the cynicism from my voice. I've never believed her story.

"Thank you for letting me in."

"Thank you for letting me stay here."

We lay that way in silence for a long while. The snow stops falling, leaving behind a landscape draped in white. Mere inches of accumulation coat the ground, but it's all the world needs to look pure and serene; a beautiful veil to hide the ugliness around the corner.

AUSTIN

*It's snowing in southern Texas. That's rare.
Cassie is in my arms? That might be rarer.*

Cassie's tiny fingers draw shapes in the clouded glass of the back doors. That's the first thing I see when my eyes open. I fell asleep. I guess getting only five hours the night before will do that. My gaze focuses past the top of her hair; the snow no longer falls, but the sky remains dark with heavy clouds. A sign of more to come?

Her hand slides from the glass, falling onto the blanket. Did she sleep at all? She has her body snug against mine. Her feet pressed to my shins, her hips aligned perfectly with mine, and my arm around her waist. I never want to move, I'm content to enjoy this moment for as long as she'll allow me to.

"I know you're awake."

I rub my chin along the top of her head, her silk hair snagging on the stubble I've let grow for two days. "What, are you psychic or something?"

"You gave yourself away."

The arm under my head is dead with sleep. "How did I do that," I ask, shifting my arm under Cassie's head and reaching for the glass to stretch it out. Cassie's hand follows my arm, her nail tracing the lines of my veins. Something's changed, the way she's touching me is intimate. All my blood surges to one spot and I shift my hips away from her backside. After all, there's no need to scare her.

Somehow she snuggles closer to me. "You held me tighter while you were sleeping."

Okay, I'm 100% awake now. I close my eyes, fighting the lust surging through me. "Should I go back to sleep then?" I'm gritting my teeth at this point, my arm tightening around Cassie.

She squeezes my forearm. "I'm not going to lie, it was really nice. But—" She wiggles to a sitting position, and I ease onto my back now that she's out of my arms. "I think we should go play in the snow while we can. And I need some food."

I study her flushed face. Her eyes are wide, hopeful. I don't want to press her too hard. She just admitted to liking being in my arms. I'm feeling like a god right now, so I'll quit while I'm ahead.

"Okay, let's go play," I agree, feeling even more powerful when she smiles at me like a little girl getting a pony.

We climb out of our hole and wash up. While Cassie throws together peanut butter and jelly sandwiches, I hunt down some of Mindy's winter gear for her to borrow. There's so much about her I still don't know. I planned on talking this afternoon, not sleeping. My brain pulls together a list of questions as I pull on an extra layer of clothing. It's time to get this girl to open up, because right now I'm in the dark and falling fast. And that's starting to scare the shit out of me.

Cassie suggests a walk once we're both wrapped in warm layers, so I give her a tour of the area. The house isn't in a traditional neighborhood setting. We're settled on a long stretch of road with nothing but farmland and two other homes in view. There's a larger subdivision just over a hill to the south, but it's out of site from our yard, making us feel as though we're away from civilization instead of twenty minutes from a college town.

"I like the feeling you get here. Like you're way out in the country by yourself, even though you're not." She crosses the road from our house and walks toward my neighbor's split wood fence. Their farmhouse sits back away from the road with smoke puffing from their fireplace. It's a postcard scene—snowy farm, beautiful home. "I want that." Cassie leans against the fence and props a booted foot on the bottom rail.

Digging my cell from my pocket, I pull up my camera. Her dark hair against Mindy's light blue ski jacket and hat, along with the winter background, provides a compelling shot. I take it. I want *that*.

"Hey," she turns, her arm waving me away. "No pictures."

I look at my screen zooming in on her face. Her profile holds such emotion. Her dreams appear to be sitting right there in her features on display for only me. "What do you want for your life?" I ask, walking to her side and ignoring her protest about the pictures as I snap another shot.

She frowns, looking at me from under angry lowered lashes. It's not a real angry look, it's her frustrated-with-Austin look. I've seen it a few times now. I hope it's only for me, because it's adorable as hell.

"That. The simple life." Her voice is wistful as she turns back to the house and farm.

"You want to live in the country?"

"Yeah, I think so." She kicks at the rail causing snow to slide off from the top. "I moved around so much growing up. I want some roots, and what better way to grow roots than out here?"

Her answer gives me the perfect opportunity to ask questions. With a deep breath, I dive in. "You have no family? Other than your mother, I mean?"

Her gloved hands wrap around the fence post. "Nope."

What would that be like? Moving all the time, no family, a mother who obviously isn't worth much. My own upbringing makes me feel guilty compared to hers. Why do some of us get so much and others so little?

"You know, West is the one who cursed life for taking away our mother. I've always been thankful that I had her as long I did. So much of who I am is because of her. I'm sorry you didn't have that growing up." It's an intimate thought, probably best left unsaid. I don't want to make her feel bad, but I can't help myself.

Cassie chews at her lip, something she does a lot when she's thinking, as her eyes remain on the farmhouse in the distance. A flurry floats down, and then another and another, this one landing on her red cheek. Finally, her tongue darts out to wet her lips as she says, "Thank you."

It's getting late; the sky is darkening by the minute as the flurries pick up speed and swirl around us. "For what?"

"For caring." She drops back from the fence and looks at me.

"Cass," I can barely say her name for all the feelings raging within me.

The right side of her mouth curves up. "Let me see those pictures you snapped illegally." She swipes the phone from my hand and takes a look. "My nose is all red."

Tamping down the urge to change the subject back to our previous conversation I bop the end of her still red nose with my finger. "Like a lightbulb," I wink.

Her smile grows. "Here, we need one together." She moves in front of me and holds the phone out and up. "Damn it, you're so freakishly tall I can't get you in the shot."

I take the phone from her. "You're the freakish one. I could carry you around in my pocket." I snap the picture as Cassie's head swings up at me. "Look at the camera," I say as I poke her side. It takes five shots before we have one where we're both smiling with eyes open and mouths half-closed.

I zip the phone in my jacket and take her hand in mine, pulling her back to the house where we build a tiny Cassie-sized snowman as the snow continues to fall.

"It sucks that this is all going to melt away in a day or two," I complain as Cassie roams around the yard in search of twigs and rocks for the snowman's body.

"Boo, don't tell Hugo that. He'll get scared."

"Hugo?"

She halts her search, plunking her hands on her hips. "Hugo, the snowman." My face must be a portrait of horror because she breaks into a fit of machine gun giggles.

"Elmer, that is the worst name for a snowman I have ever heard."

Cassie sends me a bratty look, sticking her tongue out before disappearing around the corner of the house to continue her search for body parts for our snowman. After a few minutes, she returns to Hugo's side with two dead branches in hand. "This'll only hurt for a minute, little guy," she says conspiratorially as she plunges each one into the small ball of snow making up the middle of his body. I play along, groaning and begging for mercy in a slightly French accent as she adjusts the sticks.

"Apparently Hugo is French, huh?" She rolls her eyes at me as I grin.

"Also, I don't think you're allowed to make fun of Hugo's name since you can't seem to recall my name half the time."

"I can't recall—? Oh, you mean you don't like it when I call you Elmer?"

She cocks her head, standing back and appreciating our creation. "You call me that whenever you want. It's cute, even though I'm a bit offended by your suggestion that I resemble a bald hunter."

I toss the snowball in my hand at her shoulder. "I said no such thing."

"You have a poor memory. You said my forehead wrinkles like his." My eyes flick to her forehead, but it's covered by the winter hat she's wearing low over her ears.

"Well then, you should also recall I said he's not nearly as beautiful as you are."

"I'm not even sure if that's a compliment. It's apples and oranges comparing me to a cartoon man."

I give Hugo a fist to branch bump as I confide in him. "The girl is crazy, Hugo." Cassie harrumphs, and I turn, nearly taking a snowball to the face. "Dude, she never learns."

Cassie screeches, running around the side of a bush as I bend down to form my own ammunition. A ball hits my back, breaking in a soft patter. "You throw like a girl," I call over my shoulder.

"No, you did not just say that," she shouts from behind her bush. Two more balls of snow fly my way, each one landing softly near me.

"Are you throwing bunny tails at me? They're so soft and fluffy."

She disappears from view, her small body easily ducking behind the hedges, and I laugh at the little growl she makes. Using Hugo as a shield, I pack a small pile of snowballs and wait for her next move. "Whatcha doin' over there, making weapons of mass destruction?" I call.

I'm hit in the leg, and this time there's a little more power behind her throw. I toss one back her way and she laughs. Apparently, I missed.

"Only cowards hide," I heckle. Between the lack of light, the falling snow, and the hedges, I can't see her at all.

"All's fair in snowball fights."

Oh, is that so? Piling the small stash of snowballs into one arm, I plan my attack. Crouching low behind Hugo, I wait until another one of her balls flies across the yard. The moment she gives her position away, I strike, charging the bushes. I come upon her crouched down on the ground forming a few more snowballs, but I'm too fast for her. One by one I drop my little bombs on her until she's balled up on her knees with her arms covering her head. Taking advantage of her cowering, I jump around the hedge wall—the advantage of being a giant—and push her over.

Her hands fly to her face as I straddle over her. "Surrender?" She shakes her head wildly. "You really should surren—" my words are cut off as Cassie leaps up, grabbing my biceps as she pulls my upper body down and bucks her hips, flipping me over like a wet cloth.

"Holy shit," I breathe when she pins my arms between us and sits on top of me.

"You ready to surrender?" She grins, looking so confident and excited by what she just did I don't have it in me to fight her. "Your ego is your downfall, Rutledge."

Well, hell, now she's baiting me into retaliation. I sit up easily, snatching my arms out from beneath hers and giving her a bear hug. With her legs bent underneath her while straddling me, and her arms pinned under mine, she's stuck. And damn, what a position to be stuck in. Her hips are right over me, our bodies separated by a few layers of clothing. I bend my knees up, cradling her frame between my chest and my thighs. There's so much about this position I'm digging right now.

"Your ego is your downfall, little one."

"I know," she admits breathlessly, her chest rising and falling rapidly. Snowflakes land on her lashes as she looks down. She bats her eyes, chuckling. "I'm being blinded here."

I have no intention of letting her go, so I lean over her, my head and shoulders providing her some shelter from the onslaught of snow. "You told me you knew self-defense; I didn't take you seriously. That was impressive."

"It would have been if you hadn't gotten out of it so easily." She's not looking at me, but I can hear the disappointment in her voice. "Granted, if you were a real attacker I would have jabbed you in the eyes or nailed you with my knee and run, so I guess it would have worked."

Don't piss Cassie off, got it.

"Well, thank you for being gentle," I whisper against her hair. She tilts her head up just enough for me to see her coy smile.

"When did you learn how to do that?" I ask. I'm not kidding, I'm truly impressed with her. Her upper body wiggles beneath my tight hold, so I loosen my grip, allowing her arms to slide forward.

"Uh, when I left home," she offers vaguely, her breathing evening out as her gloved fingers grip the edges of my jacket pockets.

"And when was that, Annie?"

"Why do you call me Annie still?"

I swallow. Every time we get close like this there's a fragility to the moment. I'm waiting for something I do or say to break her, because she's so damn breakable. I feel it. Instinct warned me from the beginning that Cassie is one wrong move away from crashing and splintering apart like the porcelain doll she resembles.

"You haven't figured it out?"

Her head shakes.

I release my hold on her completely, letting my hands fall to her hips, yet she remains on my lap. "I call you Annie in those moments when I don't know something about you. Like when I ask you a question about yourself. You're still very much 'Anonymous Annie' to me."

"And Elmer?"

I chuckle. "That's a tease for when you wrinkle that pretty face of yours or laugh in that way you do." Her lips purse, she's so dang self-conscious about something I'm completely enamored with. "Don't ever change that laugh, I think it's my new favorite sound."

"You call me Cass sometimes and Cassie others."

I only nod in response.

"You like nicknames, huh?"

"I guess I do. It's a habit. I'm not sure if I use the real name of most of the guys on the team. Growing up we were 'champ' or 'sport.' There's a method to my madness though, I promise you."

"What do you mean?"

"Most people get one nickname. You have a few."

"Why so many?"

"There's a difference in my feelings when I use them."

"Little one?" Her voice hitches when she repeats that nickname.

I lift a hand, toying with her hair. "That's an endearment. I can't help it, the words sort of fall from my lips when you make me think too much."

She releases my jacket, pressing her left hand below her chest.

"You jumble my thoughts until I can't think. Everything just goes until all I want to do is bury myself in you." Cassie gasps at my words and I lower my legs, putting more space between our chests when all I really want to do is swallow her up. "I'm just being honest."

She nods shakily, but without anger.

"Let's go in," I shiver. My jeans are soaked through and my face is numb as the wind picks up. "It's getting late, and cold."

CASSIE

All I want to do is bury myself in you ...
There isn't a spot on my body that doesn't surge to life at those words.
I'm reeling from his honesty, and a good dose of sexual desire, as he helps me up.

We enter the house, kicking off our boots and peeling off wet clothing in the foyer. Unlike Austin, who's soaked through from lying on the ground for so long, I wore yoga pants under my jeans, effectively keeping everything but my knees and rear protected. I shake out my wet jeans, laying them across the bench by the door along with our jackets and my gloves.

Austin's already pulling his sweatshirt over his head when he says, "I'll shower in the master, so you can take the hall."

I wait for him to grab clothes from his room and head down the hall before I move from the entryway, purposefully putting space between us. I need to clear my head. I need to shake the Austin Rutledge fog from my senses. My eyes water at the memory of the way he held me on the couch.

"Hey," his head ducks around the hallway corner. "You jumping in?"

I busy myself, picking up our wet boots. "Yeah, I'm going to set these on the porch so they don't leave puddles."

He nods. When the click of the bedroom door closing echoes through the house, I move. My face stings, it's so frozen; my cheeks are like ice. Already anticipating the warm shower, I peel off my yoga pants and two layers of shirts, leaving me in my underwear and a short-sleeved tee that barely covers my hips. It's at that moment I realize I'm standing in the middle of Austin's room half-naked. I have nothing clean or dry to put on. I threw everything else in the wash earlier and I still haven't put them in the dryer. Hearing the faint sound of water running from his shower, I dart across the hall to start my own. I return to his room while I wait for the water to warm, checking his closet one more time since he doesn't seem to mind my borrowing his sweats. I pull my last clean pair of underwear from my bag next to the bed.

My gaze crosses over the cellphone sitting face down on the nightstand, and I hesitate. Should I check it? I've shoved my problems aside over and over during the last few days I've been with Austin. He makes it so easy for me to pretend that I'm a college girl staying with a guy. He makes me feel so normal. Snow fights, winter walks, movies, and dancing. I want to be normal, forget my past, forget what's unforgettable.

But I can't forget.

Reaching for the phone, I turn it over, the missed call symbol unsurprisingly showing in the corner. There's no need to swipe to see who I missed because the screen comes to life with an incoming call as though he knew I was looking. My knees buckle.

The phone doesn't stop going off. Call after call from one number. I sink to the floor, leaning my back against the bed, the phone cradled in my lap as I watch the screen light up with each call. I answered Saturday because I didn't know who it was. Now I know. I won't answer it again, but I do need to make a call of my own.

God knows I shouldn't care. I should let him deal with it. Chewing on my nail, I listen for the sound of the shower water running. It is, so I dial. My hands shake with each number pressed, but there's no other way. I have to call; I need to check on her. The call connects, the ringing loud in the earpiece. My thumb hits the volume as the call rings twice, three times, then a fourth. The connection clicks; no answer only a beep.

"It's me. He's looking for you. You have my number now, so call me back." Vomit rises the moment I press end. I hadn't planned on making that call ever. I was done with her.

My phone lights up again, sending vomit burning up my throat as anger fuels me to answer. There's no logical thinking going on; two seconds ago I swore I wouldn't answer this number, now I press the green button yelling, "Leave me alone" as my salutation.

"Oh, come now, is that any way to talk to me, love?" His voice punches me in the stomach, the saccharine tone thickening his already heavy accent. It sends snakes slithering over my skin.

I shudder. "I don't know where she is, Emil."

"Then tell me where you ran off to. I shall take her ransom out on you." My grip slackens, the phone nearly dropping from my sweaty palm. "You're much sweeter—"

"Please, leave me alone," I gag, my eyes flooding.

"Hey, Cassie." *Oh no.* I register the quiet in the house; the shower water has stopped. I look over my shoulder—Austin is standing in the doorway.

Emil growls in my ear, "Cassandra, who the—" My finger moves quickly, ending the call.

Scrambling to my feet, I rush past Austin and into the bathroom where I lose the contents of my stomach.

"Cass?" Hands touch my back. Fingers sweep my hair from my face as I lean over the porcelain bowl on my knees. "Hey, are you okay?" The bathroom is damp with steam from the shower that I totally forgot I left running. Austin must have turned it off.

"Don't ... just go," I gasp through tears and saliva as I wait for another wave. My hand waves him away, slapping at his arm.

"If you think a little puke is going to run me off, you don't know me at all." His sturdy presence presses at my back as he kneels behind me. The warmth of his thighs wraps on either side of me and I fall from my knees, sitting back in defeat.

My hand reaches for toilet paper as Austin rubs my back. "Wait," he says, pulling the towel from the rack by our heads and handing it to me.

I wipe the mess from my nose and mouth and swipe the tears from my face. Closing the lid, I flush the toilet and lower my forehead to the cool lid.

"Who was on the phone?"

My blood pounds in my ears. Oh, God. He heard Austin. Emil heard him.

"I've got to go," I whisper, pushing myself away from the floor. "I need to leave."

My back pushes into Austin's chest. "Whoa, Cassie. What's going on?"

"I've got to—"

"—leave," he finishes for me as his hands take hold of my hips and pull me back into a sitting position. His arms wrap around me, hugging me from behind, and the last bit of my strength slips. His face moves next to mine, his mouth pressing against the edge of my ear as he speaks, and I close my eyes. "I know, I heard you. What the hell is going on, Cassie? Answer me, please."

"I can't. I ... you don't understand. I don't know what he'll do. He heard you."

"Who?"

His name, my past. I can't speak about it. I can't. A sob rushes from my lips.

"Cass, you're shaking." His heat leaves my back as rough hands twist me into his chest. "Whoever he is, he doesn't know you're here. He doesn't know me. You're safe. Okay?"

I shake my head, but he only shushes me and repeats himself. Over and over—he promises me that I'm okay. And over and over I hear Emil's voice: *I will own you.*

AUSTIN

*What has happened in her short life to scare her this completely?
What can I do to make sure it never happens again?*

We remain on the cool tile floor until the sun sets outside and we're enveloped in darkness. Until the humidity from the shower she never made it to has faded. Until her tears are long gone. But her fear isn't. I sense it in the way her fingers dig into the skin of my forearms. Her tension is noticeable in the rise and fall of her chest against my arms holding her as they wrap around her. What is she thinking?

"Cassie?"

"When I was five, my mother used me to get herself a diamond tennis bracelet." Her voice is robotic, and tiny. A little girl's confession.

"Her new boyfriend, a big shot lawyer, took us to dinner for my birthday. When we were done, we walked around the high-end mall where the restaurant was located. I still remember how excited I was." I can hear the smile in her voice. "It was a good night, of course he didn't know it was all planned by a master manipulator."

Disgust replaces her smile as she releases a long exhale. "The boyfriend, his name was Max, held my hand the entire time we walked around. He was a good guy. He wanted to buy me this fancy doll, but of course Mama had a better idea. We ended up in a jewelry store. When the night was over she received a bracelet and Max received a night he wouldn't forget."

Cassie removes herself from my arms and pushes herself off the floor.

"Wait." I stand, rolling the kink out of my neck. "How exactly did she use you?"

She turns on the faucet, splashing her face and rinsing her mouth with several palms of water. "I'm not proud of my past, Austin." She swishes another mouthful and walks from the bathroom. I follow.

"You were five. Whatever you did wasn't your fault."

She stops. The hallway is dark; the whole house is dark, and dread washes over me. I'm hit with the sinking suspicion that today was a dream. My one day with Cassie before she leaves me, before whatever has the chance to happen between us happens. Life is cruel.

"She trained me well. I was her puppet." I still don't understand as Cassie sighs, explaining. "I batted my little brown eyes and told her how pretty I thought the bracelet would look on her." She rubs her arms. "Subliminal messages, I guess. Max did buy me a pretty little necklace with a golden butterfly. Then he gushed over her, agreeing with me and buying the bracelet. He lasted a few months."

I can't discern the cause of her disappointed tone. Is she upset about what she did wrong, or thinks she did wrong? Or about the fact that Max wasn't around long?

I clear my throat, "A few months?"

"She uses men for what they give her. They never last long."

"And you grew up with that? A gold digging mother."

I'm not asking a question; I'm just trying to wrap my brain around what she's saying. She merely shrugs. Damn, it's maddening. Trying to pry information from Cassie is impossible. She offers me nothing, frustrating the hell out of me with her lack of explanation.

"Tell me about it, about your childhood," I request.

"There isn't much else to tell."

"Why do I get the feeling that's far from the truth? Good or bad, there's always a story."

She turns away, a mumbled, "Forget it" coming over her shoulder. I grasp at her hand, my fingers tightening around hers as I pull her back. Her head snaps my way, her dark eyes wide. We're standing in the hallway with barely any light, but I don't need light to see her anger.

"Cassie, I'm just trying to be here for you."

She looks away, her voice flat and even as she replies, "What do you want me to tell you, Austin? That I stopped counting the states I lived in by the time I was eight? That I quit trying to learn the men's names before I was a teenager? Do you want me to tell you about all the other times my mother used me as bait for asshole men? That the reason I fell for you was because you were the first guy to ever give me something without expecting something in return?" She twists her wrist, pulling free of my grip, and I lunge after her, grabbing her arms and spinning her to face me.

"Jesus, Cassie—"

"My *mother* kicked me out of her house when I was seventeen because she found her new, younger boyfriend standing over my bed one too many times. My *mother* allowed a parade of men throughout my life to look at me with their disgusting thoughts clearly written on their faces, using me as a means to pay the bills and win herself favors, but the moment one showed me preference to her—" her voice cracks, her fractured breath decimating me, "she threw me out like the trash I am."

"Hey, don't you dare say that. You are not trash, Cass."

"You don't know my past; you don't know my story."

I gulp for air, grasping for words. I have no clue what to say, so I let my heart lead the way. "Then tell me." I release her arms, shoving my hands through my hair as she stares at me. My stomach recoils at the picture Cassie painted. The thought of her as a little girl with men twice her age—what did she mean by what she said? What happened to her? "I didn't know. I wouldn't have pressured you to go out with me. I wouldn't have—" I lose my words, thinking of how jumpy she was when we first met, how against guys she's been.

Her palms press against my ribs. "Other than being a bit full of yourself, you've done nothing wrong, Austin. You came to my rescue, remember?"

Shit. I crush her against me, my arms wrapping around her back and pressing her face to my chest, my fingers winding in her hair.

"You're trembling," she says, her arms wrapping around my waist.

"I'm angry."

"I'm okay."

"No, you're not." My gut says there's more to her story, more she isn't telling me. The stiffening of her arms confirms it.

"I will be," she says.

"Who are you running from?"

She sighs, her hands slipping to grip my shirt at my sides as she rests her forehead against my stomach before pushing away. I remain in the hall, watching her silhouette move into the living room. After a moment, a lamp clicks on and I force myself to count to ten, taking deep breaths and shaking the anger at her mother away as much as I can.

She stands at the fireplace, her arms over her chest.

"Why do you push me away?" It's a crappy thing to ask her considering what she's just revealed to me about her upbringing, but I can't help the words from spewing from my mouth.

"I've involved you too much already. I need you to stay out of this."

"Stay out of it?" I scoff. "Shit, Cassie, you brought me into it." Whatever *it* is.

"And now I'm removing you. I'm going to leave in the morning."

"Like hell you are."

"You don't know the whole story."

"It doesn't matter. Nothing you tell me will change how I feel. Nothing will change who you are."

"How you feel?" She laughs bitterly. "Are you having trouble distinguishing the difference between lust and feelings?"

"Nowhere near as much trouble as you're having distinguishing the difference between me and all the men from your past," I spit back.

"Your life's been lived within the protective barrier of wealth and love. You have no idea what reality is, what life outside your walls is like." She flicks her hand at the pictures adorning the mantle, the still frames of a happy life, and my anger fades to sadness. Sadness for what she has done to herself. Sadness for a little girl who deserved better, a woman who deserves more.

"No, Cass. You're the one who lives life between walls. You live in a jar, afraid to open the lid and see what your world could become if you'd only allow others inside."

I move closer, taking small, slow steps so she won't retreat.

"I let people in, I've let you in. You know more about me than anyone ever has," she says defensively.

"Thank you." I smile sadly. "Thank you for telling me about your life, trusting me with things that I know must have hurt you deeply. But you're not letting me in. You're right, I've been lucky. I had everything you didn't, but I still see the real world. I see it in you, in your pain. In the pain of losing my mother, the pain of seeing what my brother went through last year. I see reality in those I love every day—because I love them and I let them share their lives with me. But you," my fingers sink into her hair, cradling her head and forcing her to look at me. "You choose to close yourself off from people, never sharing yourself. You only see your pain. You deny your feelings and so you've never given yourself up to the chance of happiness."

"I'm not denying my feelings."

I want to laugh. "Remember when I said you hadn't had the right guys in your life?" Her eyes close briefly before she nods. "Let me be the right guy, Cass. Let me show you what you've been missing. Let me show you what love is."

"You don't—"

My mouth descends, my lips covering hers and quieting her words. She whimpers against my lips, her hands grasping my shirt for support as she kisses me back. When her mouth molds to mine, my fingers release their hold on her head, allowing her the freedom to pull away if she wants. She doesn't.

"Don't think I didn't hear you say you fell for me," I say against her lips between devouring kisses. "Tell me you don't have feelings for me."

Her teeth tug on my lip as her fingers slide around my neck effectively pulling me closer. Bending down, my hands grip her bare hips, my fingers digging into her flesh as she jumps up and wraps her legs around me. Her hands hold my face as our mouths fight a battle for dominance. I shift, bumping her into the wall next to the fireplace, my hips grinding between her legs. She pulls my face from hers. Her lips and chin are red and splotchy from the stubble on my face. Her eyes sparkle with unshed tears.

"Tell me you don't have feelings for me, little one," I repeat, the words barely audible, my tone a raspy plea I've never used before.

"I can't."

My heart stops, anticipating those same words she spoke back in October when she walked away from me. *"I can't do this."*

Tears roll from her eyes. "I can't tell you I don't have feelings for you because I do. I'm tired of fighting them, Austin. I'm tired of fighting for my life. I don't want to be scared anymore."

"Then don't be. I won't let anyone hurt you." I kiss one cheek and then the other.

Holding her like this, we're face to face. I can't stop looking into her eyes, into her soul, searching for what it is I can be for her. Can I be what she needs?

CASSIE

I want to remember his eyes locked on mine forever.
I've never believed a promise more than the one he just made.
"I won't let anyone hurt you." His eyes don't lie.

Reasonable thinking flies out the window when Austin's hands slide over my bare thighs and dig into my rear. For the love of Pete, his touch rocks my world. He drops his forehead, his eyes holding mine, until we both move forward—our mouths reconnecting in a kiss that won't stop.

"You didn't think it might be appropriate to remind me I wasn't wearing pants?" I manage between kisses.

"I didn't think it gentlemanly, no," he teases as my spine thumps against the wall again. Oh, Lord. With nothing but his shirt between us, my thighs feel every flex his stomach muscles make. "I mean, who am I to tell you what you should or shouldn't wear?"

"Good thinking." I catch a breath before he dives back in. My hands shift down his back, pulling at his shirt until my fingers are under the hem and touching his warm skin. "Maybe if you were pantless too it wouldn't be so awkward."

His low growl shoots liquid fire between my legs. I'm jostled upward, my arms and legs clutching his torso for dear life as his lips slide down my throat. Have mercy, his mouth is on fire. Pressing me into the wall, one hand leaves my behind as his tongue swirls along the base of my jaw. His teeth nip once and I throw my head back, smacking the picture hanging above me and causing the frame to clack against the wall.

"Ouch." My hand flies up as Austin smiles against my skin.

"Sorry," he murmurs, his lips and tongue applying pressure where he bit. I swear I'm going to die from the touch of his mouth. His hand returns to my thigh as he backs away from the wall, lowering my body, until—I gasp audibly. My thighs slide down, making contact with his bare waist. His pants are gone; only his boxers remain low on his hips, and his skin is a hot skillet burning my flesh.

"Your room," I order, although sex against this wall would work too.

"Yes, ma'am," he breathes, his fingers flexing against my skin.

He moves awkwardly as he kicks his athletic pants the rest of the way off and turns, carrying me toward his room. I bear hug him—legs wrapped tightly, my fingers rubbing over his back muscles, my head nestled between his shoulder and lips. Those lips that haven't stopped planting fire bomb kisses along my neck.

He's not even winded as he walks to the edge of his bed and slides me down his length—his erection making itself known as he stands me on his mattress.

"Now you're taller than me." His voice is thick as he buries his face in my stomach, kissing me through the fabric of my t-shirt. He slips his hands under my shirt and up my ribcage, stopping short of touching my bra. "Tell me to stop."

My fingers dig into his hair as the words fall from his lips. The heat of his breath through my shirt elicits chills along my spine. Leaning back from my body, he looks up. "Tell me to stop," he repeats.

I shake my head in response. No, I don't want him to stop. I want to lose myself in his mouth, his touch, his body. I want to allow myself to feel what I've never allowed myself to feel. Intimacy. Want. Need. It's not a bad thing. It's not what I grew up with. It's not …

"Don't stop," I plead, discarding my thoughts. I lean down and tug at his shirt, balling the fabric in my fists until he releases me and finishes dragging it over his head. I do the same with mine.

He inhales sharply, his hands hovering inches from my body as he takes me in. "You are so damn gorgeous."

I'm not tall and skinny. I'm not blonde. I'm not a sorority girl, cheerleader, groupie, or overly made-up co-ed. I'm not anything like the girls I've heard Austin's hooked up with in the past. But the way he's looking at me, the way his hands skim over the curves of my waist and hips—

My hands run down his muscular forearms, my fingers lacing with his. Carefully, I sink down to my knees and fall backward, bouncing onto the bed and pulling him with me. He wastes no time, grabbing me and rolling us to our sides, his mouth finding mine again. This time he's slower, more deliberate. His tongue traces my lips as his hands explore my nearly naked body.

"Cass, are you sure? I know what I said outside about wanting to be with you, but I can wait. I don't want you to do anything you don't want to do."

I kiss him deeper, my hand pressing against the back of his head. The more we kiss, the more we touch, the more I discover I do want this. I'm not afraid of sex. For the longest time I thought I was. I've had three kinds of experiences. There are the nights I fell asleep to the melody of strange men grunting and screaming from Momma's room. That terrified me, until I understood what was happening—then it disgusted me. There are the men who took my innocence without taking my virtue, and the man who took my virtue long after my innocence was gone. Men with lust in their eyes and nothing else. Men who used me, and hurt me, and obsessed over me—I squeeze my eyes shut at the memories, a choked gasp escaping my lips.

"What? Shit, I'm sorry." Austin's hand is under the cup of my bra. I hadn't even noticed. He jerks back as though I've burned him with my cry.

"I'm fine." I slap my palm over my lips to keep a sob from releasing as I reach for his arm. "I'm fine." Why? Why would my mind go there when Austin is so different?

"No, no you're not." The warmth of his skin disappears as he untangles himself from my limbs and rolls off the bed.

Suddenly, I'm a young girl exposed and trembling, and alone. I curl into a ball, staring straight ahead, blocking out everything around me.

"Cass? Sit up, sweetie," a voice, Austin's voice, whispers against my cheek. "Little one, sit up." He tugs at my body, pulling me into a sitting position and yanking a shirt on over my head. It smells like him. I inhale deeply before my head goes through the hole. "Stick your arms in. That's right." The cool fabric tickles my skin as he pulls it over my chest and down my stomach. It puddles at the hips, more proof of how much larger he is than me.

I blink, clearing my brain of the fog, the nothingness. Turning, I see Austin again. Actually see him. His face and body are flushed with desire; he didn't leave my side for more than a few seconds, but where I went it could have been hours. I study him.

His face is clouded with worry as he taps at my knee. "Let me fold the covers down."

I help him, maneuvering myself under the comforter and sheet, sinking down against the pillows. I worry he's going to leave me, that I screwed this all up royally, but as he slides in next to me I don't give him time to wonder what to do next. I butt up next to him, wrapping my arms around his waist and pressing my cheek into his chest.

"I'm so sorry. I thought ... I wanted to." What am I supposed to say in this situation? Sorry I just led you to the point of a massive erection before hitting the emergency off switch?

"You have nothing to be sorry about." His voice matches mine, hoarse and strained as he shakes his head. "I don't know what got into me. I shouldn't have taken things so far. I should be able to control myself around you, but the moment my lips touched yours—"

"You lost all thought?" I interrupt.

"God, yes." His palm rubs my shoulder.

Perhaps it wasn't the right moment for us to start ripping clothes off each other considering what I'd admitted to him moments beforehand, but I know why it happened. Or maybe 'know' is the wrong word. I can't understand why anything that's happened with Austin has happened the way it has, but I know that since that first day in the library I've had to fight myself from thinking about him.

"I don't think you understand how you've changed me," I confess as his low laughter vibrates his chest beneath my cheek. "No, seriously."

"I'm not laughing at you, Cass. I'm laughing because you're speaking my mind. Do you have any idea how crazy you make me?"

"I changed my entire day-to-day schedule so I wouldn't run into you and give in to my feelings," I point out, as though this is a game.

"Yeah, and I'm still pissed about that," his hand pinches my shoulder lightly. "I wasn't looking for you. I wasn't expecting to fall for anyone, let alone the girl who kept ignoring me."

I press against his chest, sitting up. "Fall?"

A slow, sexy smile appears as he leans forward. "Yes, fall." His lips brush against my forehead as he speaks.

No, this isn't what I wanted.

That's a lie. I close my eyes. In a perfect world this is exactly what I wanted. When we stood outside yesterday and I told him I wanted a quiet life in the country, I pictured him beside me. My dream life would be with this man, loving me the way I'm falling in love with him. The way he is right now ... But he can't, I can't let him.

"It's not smart," I try to tell him, but he merely lifts his brows.

"I don't think I had much of a choice in the matter."

I fall back to his chest, savoring the warmth of his skin against my cheek. He's right. I'm starting to believe our hearts overpower our brains. If my brain were more powerful, I would have run and saved him, but my heart ... Damn, my heart wanted nothing more than to be with him the other night. And every night since.

"Can you tell me the truth now?"

There are so many truths to tell him. Which one do I start with?

AUSTIN

*Be careful when you ask for the truth.
You might not like what you hear.*

"I've never told anyone," Cassie whispers against my chest.

I'm being careful not to touch her too much. I still my hand on her shoulder as the other combs through her hair. I don't have the words for this. There was a moment earlier when I turned around to get her a shirt and came back where she looked like she was gone. Her eyes dead, her body rigid.

"If I'd grown up with a mother who simply used men for money in exchange for sex, I suppose I'd be okay right now, right? I mean, maybe I'd be a slut or an opportunist like she was, but I'd be okay."

"But it wasn't just about her, was it?" My stomach rolls as I put two and two together. "She used you."

Cassie nods. "I don't know when it started. Like, why she did it. I guess she realized I could be a powerful tool, just like her body. She dated influential, rich men when I was young. Many were married, of course. So

I was locked in my room while she entertained. It wasn't that bad when she was happy. It was when she was dumped that things became ugly."

She sits up, tugging the sheet over her lap. Blowing out a long exhale, she fidgets with the cloth. "This isn't easy."

I want to encourage her, to tell her it's okay, but that's not something I can do. I highly doubt anything she's thinking of telling me is okay. She wouldn't be so terrified of talking about it if it were easy. One thing I learned from our family grief counseling, and the sessions about West, was to listen. So I do. I wait for her to speak, and when she does, I listen.

"The first one was Randy. He—he sat me on his lap during a wind storm in the middle of the night. Then there was the pirate. I didn't know his name, but he had a scruffy face and earring, so I called him the pirate." I clench my jaw, forcing myself to remain quiet. "I don't think she knew about them, I never told her. I was too terrified, and they were one-nighters. So was Hector. Simon was the worst. Simon hung around." Her eyes lift to mine. "He had money," she says with a shrug, as though that explains everything—which I guess in her mother's world it did. I want to throw up.

"She knew about Simon. She caught him in my room. Yet she kept him around. I didn't understand it, Austin. I never had a father, I didn't know what was right and wrong when I was that young. I was four when Randy touched me. He rubbed my thighs, and while I sat on his lap he got an erection. I was a baby for crying out loud."

"No, don't," Cassie waves me away as I sit up and reach for her. "Just let me get it all out." I make fists as my heart races. An angry fire like none I've ever felt before rips through me. I want to tear someone apart. The meaning of the word 'revenge' has never been so clear to me. I want revenge for Cassie's sake, and I want it *now*.

"Simon took things farther; he was a sick man. An upstanding citizen of our town who everybody knew and loved." She sneers, rolling her eyes. "Little did they know he was a womanizing child molester. He took his own life when he was caught raping a young daughter of one of his conquests. That mother wasn't bought off by money and looks."

Nausea sweeps over me and I close my eyes, leaning my head against the headboard. Cassie's cold fingers touch my knee. "Austin, I wasn't raped by him."

I snap my eyes open, relief washing over me. "I was touched, fondled, and made to do ... things. But, I was never raped by any of those men."

"How—" I don't have the right words to ask any questions. "How did your mother allow that to happen to you? You said she didn't know."

"The bad ones were the in-between guys. Except for Simon. She had a problem with being alone. When one of her sugar daddies would leave her, she would usually find a one-night stand at a dive bar to bring home for the night. Those were the ones I'd have to watch out for."

"At some point, there were a string of men who got their jollies off while gaping at me. It started simple enough. 'Cassandra, put on your little white nightie for Mr. Perv,'" Cassie mimics in what I suppose is her mother's voice. I concentrate on taking slow, even breaths to remain calm as she continues.

"I'd stand in a short, white lace girls' nightgown while some child predator stuck his hands in his shorts. My mother would leave the room, as though she couldn't bear to watch what she was allowing these men to do."

"They stared at you? Like you were some type of porn?"

Cassie rubs her arms absentmindedly. "It was better than what Simon did. It was sick, but at least they didn't touch me. As I, uh, developed, the outfits became smaller. Eventually, there were pictures."

"Pictures?" I snap, and she flinches. "Cassie, that's child pornography. You didn't tell anyone?" If she'd hit puberty she was old enough to speak up. I can't understand how this happened.

"I wasn't naked," her hand brushes over her face. "They were overtly sexual, but not illegal. Honestly, they probably saved me.

"I'd gotten so used to standing like a statue while a man jerked off right before me. I had to force myself to block it out. I would go to this empty place where nothing could touch me. After she did the photos, I'd just get creepy eyes watching me, but I guess they used the pics for foreplay instead of me."

I grit my teeth so hard, my jaw hurts.

"I know it sounds crazy, but I was happy they left me alone, Austin. As I settled into my teens things went better for a while. That's when I started spending all my time in libraries. I stayed away from home as much as I could. The few boyfriends she had around me made comments, telling her how pretty I was and commenting that I was going to grow up to be beautiful like her." She snorts. "It made me sick. Even as a child, I knew I didn't want to be like her. It made her livid.

"There was a bad stretch of men, low income rentals, and four cities in one year. Then she met Emil."

The way she says his name sets off warning bells.

"I was nearly sixteen. He was younger than her. European and rich. Tall, dark, and handsome. My mother would sing as she got ready for date after date. She was on cloud nine. We lived in Vegas. Our third time, if I'm counting correctly. Emil was a professional gambler—a VIP from what Momma said. After a few months of seeing each other Emil invited us to a private pool party. We'd never met. Momma was sleeping at his place more and more, and he always sent a car service for her."

"What a nice guy," I drawl, hating Emil before knowing why I should.

"She bought me a new little bikini for the party. She said she didn't want us to look like trash to the rest of the crowd there. So there I was in a skimpy bikini with kitten heels and a see-through cover up, and in walks Emil."

She pauses, her eyes far off. I reach for the hand she's wrapped around her stomach, rubbing my fingers along hers.

"Let me guess. He fell for you at first sight."

She plays my comment off. "That's what he said later."

"We became friends, though, sort of. It's hard to explain."

For the first time since Cassie began explaining her past, I see the confusion on her face. The other men she mentioned garnered complete disgust from her. She feels differently about Emil, whether she knows it or not.

I doubt their relationship is hard to explain at all. Not really. I can picture some slick dude working his charms on a young, beautiful girl merely to get a piece of her. I imagine he buttered her up, made her mom happy, bought them both things they needed, all the while waiting to make his move.

"After the pool party, Emil went from never coming to our house to sleeping over a few times a week. He became suggestive. I walked into the kitchen one evening and he was hugging my mother from behind. I apologized, trying to back out gracefully, and he winked while staring me directly in the eyes as his hand slipped into my mother's shirt. One time he walked into my room with only a towel wrapped around his waist—said he wasn't paying attention to the doors."

The more she explains, the heavier the dread becomes in my stomach because I know I'm right. Cassie doesn't speak of Emil as though she hates him, or like he's someone who did something wrong. She says his name with a touch of reverence.

"He was grooming you." My fingers toy with hers, rubbing her palm as they memorize every inch of her hand.

"Yeah, he was." A tear escapes her eye and she swipes at her cheek. "Damn it." Pushing herself from the bed, she shakes her head while blinking rapidly. "I was a stupid girl who never knew love."

Throwing my legs off the side of the bed, I lean forward. My pulse quickens. Damn, I'm scared. I asked her about her past and now I'm scared shitless by what she might divulge.

"She flaunted him, flaunted his presents and his money." Acute anger colors her words now. "She told me I'd never be able to attract a man like him. She said none of the men who looked at me ever wanted to touch me because they knew I wasn't good enough. They knew she was better."

Mother or not, I'm pretty sure I'll kill the woman if I ever meet her.

A low moan forces its way from Cassie's lips as she sinks to the floor, her face covered by her curtain of hair. "She'd point out all of my flaws. My legs were too short, my ass too round, my waist too thick." Cassie's hand pushes through her hair as she looks up at me with dark eyes dipped in anger. "I was nothing, and she was flawless. And I hated her."

CASSIE

*He says he's falling for me.
Will he still want me when he knows about my past?*

Leaning his elbows on his knees Austin's hands curl into fists and release. Over and over, fists clench and release as he stares at me. His lips draw a tight, white line as the muscle in his jaw flexes. He's livid. Everything about him is angry, except his eyes. They're ... I don't know a word to describe what they are. Powerful? They bore into my soul, speaking silent words that have never been spoken to me. They connect with—and soften—the heart I locked up years ago. They're freakin' eyes, but they watch, and they listen, and they care. I have to be honest with him.

Tucking my hair behind my ears, I swallow hard. "I hated her more and more every day." I give the words the opportunity to sink in before admitting the truth. "So, I sought revenge."

"No wonder your mother is jealous."

I spin at Emil's voice. I'd just returned home and was in the middle of changing, my discarded shirt falls to the floor as I raise my arms to cover my chest. "I thought I was home alone."

"No, love, it's just us." He leans on my doorway as though he owns the place. His hip resting against the frame, his right ankle crossing his left as he slips his hands into his pockets.

"Where's my mother?"

He ignores my question. "Were you at the library again?"

I nod, my throat too dry to form a response. He straightens, crossing my small room in four strides, his dark eyes pinned on mine. The heavy cologne he wears tickles my nose. He's not a tall man, nor is he muscular, but his presence —his presence overwhelms me. He wears all black, all the time. Slim black slacks, crisply pressed black dress shirts, and black shiny loafers. If I had to describe him in one word it would be dark. The thought lifts goosebumps across my skin.

"Are you cold?" Of course he notices. The back of his hand brushes my shoulder. I don't flinch. "Uncover yourself, Cassandra." It's an order, said in a low, intimate way. My hands comply, falling to my sides.

It's been over two years since one of Momma's men forced me to stand half-naked before him. I'd become good at hiding. My eyes flick to a poster on the wall behind Emil's head, my mind already clearing of all thoughts—finding the nothingness.

"I want to touch you." His low confession reins me back to him.

"No touching."

Emil chuckles, his white teeth gleaming against his tan skin. "That, love, is Gwen's rule, not mine." His use of her name is jarring.

"What are your rules?"

His hands rest on my shoulders, his index fingers looping under the straps of my bra, running up and down lazily. "My rule is pleasure."

My eyes flutter closed at the deep timbre of his voice, the soft caress of his fingers playing over my skin. His hands sink lower and lower along my bra until his palms falls over the cups. He squeezes once, his thumbs edging their way under the thin fabric. I inhale sharply.

"So soft," he hisses, the pads of his thumbs circling my nipples. Emil leans *in, his face hovering inches from mine.* "So sweet." *His tongue darts out, wetting his full lips.*

Butterflies flutter low in my stomach.

"Emil! I saw your car outside, what are you doing here?" Momma's voice echoes through our small apartment as the front door slams shut.

His hand drops as my eyes go wide and he turns, leaving my room without a word, pulling the door behind him. "I wanted to surprise you." His mumbled voice bleeds through the door as I sink to the edge of my bed with his touch seared into my breast.

And a knowing smile on my lips.

"It was easy once I knew he found me attractive. I made myself available to him. I let him touch me, kiss me." Austin's entire countenance changes, and he's green. "I'm sorry. I'll spare you the details, but you have to know. I can't allow you to look at me the way you do. You can't say you're falling for me when you don't know me."

His face twists. "I have to know what?"

"I seduced him. I stole him from my mother's bed." His head drops to his hands and I rush my explanation, as though anything I say could absolve myself. "I never meant for it to go that far. I just wanted to prove her wrong. I wanted her to lose him because I had lost so much, thanks to her."

"Shit," he mutters, scrubbing his forehead, his fingers pushing his hair back. "Shit. How old was he?"

"Twenty-seven."

"And you were sixteen?"

"The first time, yes."

"The first time? Damn, Cassie, how many times were there?"

Stepping around me, he walks to his dresser and removes a pair of sweats, pulling them on. The action makes me feel trashy. As though he had to cover himself from my eyes, as though he needed to erase the reminder of how close we just came to having sex. Like I'm not good enough for him. Which I'm not.

"I'm sorry. I should have told you before." My eyes search for the pants

I'd pulled out to put on after my shower. "I shouldn't have let things go so far between us, considering."

"Considering what? That you're not a virgin?" I stop searching as he faces me from the other side of the room. Emotions fly across his features like ads on an electronic billboard. Switching from anger to shock to hurt so quickly I can barely decipher one emotion before it changes to the next. He's all over the place. His eyes flick to my bare legs and clench closed. Disgust or lust? What is it he feels when he looks at me now?

"Here," he opens his dresser once more and throws a pair of plaid pants at me. "I can't keep looking at you." The edge is gone from his tone, yet I cringe at the words.

"I'm sorry," my voice cracks. My heart feels like it's breaking into pieces. Turning, I slide into his flannel pajama pants—my mind stupidly wondering what novelty shirt went with these as I roll the waist a few times and tighten the drawstring.

His chest bumps into my back, his arms coming around me and trapping my hands at my waist. "Why do you keep apologizing, Cass?" he whispers against my ear.

"You just said—"

I'm spun around so quickly I see stars as his hands take a hold of my face. "I told you to put pants on because I can't keep looking at you. I can barely think when you're clothed, let alone half-naked."

My damn eyes betray me by watering.

"You think I'm mad at you?" he asks incredulously, and I nod. He kisses me. It's simple, and soft, and by most people's standards nothing special. Just a peck, but to me it's a pardon. "Are you kidding me? I feel like the most disgusting man in the world right now because I'm having trouble controlling my lust even after everything you just told me."

And the tears fall, my chest burning as Austin's face transforms once again.

"I'm not a hypocrite. I can't judge you for what you've done in your past. I'm not angry, I have no right to be. Not at you." His eyes narrow. "I'm mad at your whore mother who exploited you, and the man who took advantage of you." His anger on my behalf shocks me. "Sorry if you think I'm being harsh."

It's taking all I have to not break down. "He didn't force me." He needs to understand that. I need him to know my part in this all.

"It doesn't matter, Cassie. He shouldn't have touched you."

"I know." Or I'm trying to. It's taken a long time for me to see my innocence.

"Do you? You understand what he did is illegal, no matter how you provoked him?"

"Sociological profiles on child assault perpetrators," I offer.

The muscles in his face relax as understanding dawns. "Your paper," he nods.

"My major."

He's still holding me close, his hands shaking as they hold my face. His emotions are still so tangible and close to the surface. "I don't know what to say," he admits.

"You don't have to say anything, Austin. You're not obligated."

"Like hell, I'm not. Has anyone ever stuck up for you? Has anyone ever loved and protected you?" His thumb strokes across my forehead. "I don't know what's happening between us, Elmer, but I'm not finished just because you have a little baggage."

The use of Elmer and the insinuation that my shit storm of a background is merely a little baggage puts a smile on my face. I'm having a hard time comprehending the notion that he cares that much. That anyone cares that much.

"I understand now how hard it must be for you to trust me, but I'm going to ask you to anyway. I have questions, but I don't want to overwhelm you with them." He steps back, taking my hands in his. "How about we eat something and take a break?"

I agree easily, hoping he'll let the rest of my explanations go. A bit far-fetched on my part, I suppose. We take an hour-long reprieve—enough time for soup and sandwiches and general conversation about everything and nothing at all. I should commend his patience; he's absorbed a great deal in the last few days where I'm concerned.

♥

"Cass?"

"Hmmm?"

"Is Emil the one who called you? Saturday?"

We've moved back to the couch. The moonlight glistens on the winter landscape outside the window, casting an unnatural glow to the world. Stray flakes flutter to the ground every now and then. I wish it would stay, the snow, the peace. I sigh. Austin's holding me as we lay on the couch, my head tucked under his chin so I can't look at him as I answer. "He was."

"And you ran to me. Why?"

"I had two thoughts that night. *Run* and *Austin*. I chose you."

There's a long pause.

He inhales deeply, then exhales, his warm breath blowing across the top of my head when he speaks. "I need to go home, will you come with me?"

Prying myself from his arms, I prop myself up. "To Tyler?"

He merely nods.

"I don't know if that's a good idea."

"You're scared of him, why? What are you worried he'll do? He's in Vegas, right?"

I have no idea where he is or what he'll do. No, that's not true. He'll come after me. Once he figures out where I am, he'll come. He made that clear. How much longer can I press my luck? And now that he knows I'm with a guy ...

"Yeah, sure," I agree. What else can I say? Austin grins, grabbing my wrist and pulling me back into his arms. I fall asleep this way—safe, but sad. I can't continue letting my heart make these choices. At some point I have to use my head. I have to run.

AUSTIN

*Cassie's background doesn't scare me.
I'm not turned off by the things she's endured.
But I'm angry as hell at the people who took advantage of her.*

I wake before the sun rises, climbing off the couch without waking her, eager to head for Tyler. I'm man enough to admit when I need some sage advice, and right now I need my dad. What do I say? How do I treat her? And how do I protect her, because contrary to what she says, I know damn well she's lying to me. Her phone's lit up with missed calls, all from one number. I don't want to push her away by prying.

The sky is clear this morning. I check the weather. Sunny skies. The snow should melt here, and in Tyler there was only a dusting that will most likely be gone before we arrive. Letting Cassie sleep, I head outside to check the driveway and street. The street's already plowed, and I clear off my car, scraping the windows and removing snow from around the tires. The accumulation wasn't more than a few inches, so we should be fine.

I pack a bag, clean up, and get dressed all while Cass sleeps on. When I'm ready I lean against the wall and watch her sleep. She's turned away from the window and into the spot I occupied last night. The throw we used is tangled around her legs, her face buried beneath it. How does she breathe like that?

Before I wake her, I think about last night, about everything she said. Reconciling what I knew about her before with what I know now. She was sexually abused as a child by at least three men. She was mentally abused by her mother. She's never known one home for very long. She was used over and over. She's scared to let people in. She slept with her mother's lover to prove her worth. She was kicked out of her home after her mother found one of her boyfriends in her room. Was it Emil? She never told me who it was. How long was she with Emil? When was she kicked out? And why is Emil is calling her now?

And most importantly why does she feel the need to run?

"You look deep in thought." Cassie's sleepy voice startles me.

"Hey," I move closer, propping myself against the arm of the couch. "I didn't want to wake you."

She stretches, her back arching as she makes a little humming sound. I reach out and tug on her stockinged foot because I can't not touch her.

"I'm guessing you're ready to go?" She sits up, combing her hair back. "Can I take a shower first?"

After a shower, a selfie with Hugo, a run for toasted coconut donuts, and some gas, we're on the road.

"It's Wednesday, right?" she asks after her second donut-gasm. This girl will be the death of me.

"Yep. I get you through Saturday, don't try to get out of it."

Elmer attempts to hi-jack her giggles into full blown laughter, but she manages to keep him at bay. Reaching across the console, I wrap her hand in mine.

"I'm not trying to get out of it." She squeezes my fingers. "I've lost track of time, that's all."

"I have that affect," I wink. She rolls her eyes, so I kiss the back of her hand.

"So tell me about your life in the spring. Do you guys still have a million practices and workouts a week?"

"Yep, same schedule. No pain, no gain and all that shit."

"Ahhh, so you're excited then."

"I don't know what I am," I admit, releasing her hand. "Truth is I'd planned on entering the draft this year. That was the goal, as long as I played well. Now, I'm not so sure. I'm leaning toward finishing out my eligibility."

Cassie shifts in the seat, tucking a leg beneath her and turning sideways so she's facing me. "Eligibility?"

"*Football for Dummies,* sorry I forgot." She sticks her tongue out. "We get four years of play. That's our eligibility. Many players get five years with the team because they redshirt their freshman year. That means they're on the team, but don't play their first year. Which is why you might see guys their senior year playing ball who have already graduated."

"And why would you want to come back next year instead of doing the draft?"

I don't correct her 'do the draft' statement. "Well, I'd like to win a National Championship and I'd like to play ball with my brother again. That might be the biggest selling point, right there. Then there's the reality that I'm not entirely sure I want to play pro."

"Wait, I know I'm the football dummy here, but you're saying you have the chance to get paid to play football and you might not want it?"

Those exact words have driven through my own mind a million times. I imagine Dad saying the same thing before he slaps me upside the head and tells me to snap out of it. "Stupid right?"

"No, not stupid at all. It's admirable."

God, this girl gets me.

"The sport hurts, Cassie. Our bodies take a beating, and our brains—"

"The concussion stuff? That I do know."

I arch a brow, impressed.

"I watch the news."

"Right. Well, yeah, the concussion stuff scares me, if I'm being honest. And knee pains, and broken bones, and surgeries. I love the sport, but I don't think I want to sacrifice my body up to it. Plus, as close as my family was, when my dad played he wasn't around a whole lot. I kind of want to sleep with my wife every night and raise a family with her." My eyes slide to her face. Are her cheeks pink? Shit, did I seriously just picture her as the wife in my fantasy?

"Geez, where did the genes come from that made you Rutledge boys such saints?" she asks in faux disgust. I nearly drive off the road choking on my laugh.

"What the hell?" I wheeze, taking a sip of the water I grabbed for the road.

"Jules is my roommate. You don't think I haven't heard enough sappy love stories to last me a lifetime? From everything I've heard, it's like you guys have some special programming that prevents you from being assholes."

"Ha, I can assure you that is far from the case. Family is important to us though. We were raised that way, and love—" I pause, not wanting to freak her out. "Well, we love deep."

She clears her throat lightly. "Did you just admit to being an asshole?"

"Should I go into my sordid dating life? I suppose it's only fair that I give you any information you want, considering."

"I thought you don't date."

I smile. "That's right, you already checked me out. You can ask me anything you want. I told you my last girlfriend was Lauren back in high school. I spent my freshman year sowing my wild oats. Last year I calmed down a bit, hung out with a few KD's after games or parties, that type of thing. And this year I've been celibate."

The traffic is heavy, but I quickly slide my eyes to Cassie so I can gauge her reaction to that news. Her face is blank.

"Celibate?" You'd think I told her I knocked off a bank, she sounds so doubtful.

"It's rather embarrassing for me, so I'd appreciate it if you'd not use the word more than once."

"What, *celibate*?" I flinch as though she's stabbed me, and she chuckles softly. "Austin Rutledge hasn't had sex. In how long?" She holds her fingers out, ticking off the months.

"Hey, that's uncalled for and personal." I feign my aggravation. I'm not embarrassed at all.

"I've seen the way girls look at you. Geez, I was there when they apologized to you for getting mad at you in the library that night, when you were the one making the noise. All you have to do is trip and you could land on a naked girl—"

"Are you serious? Why didn't anyone tell me about that trick?"

"Austin," Cassie laughs, shaking her head. "You know damn well you have no shortage of girls to choose from, how is it that you've been sexless for what, five months?"

Sexless. It's damn depressing when she says it.

"Six months," I correct her. "And it's because none of those naked girls falling on the ground before me were the one I wanted."

"Really?" There's so much doubt in her voice.

"Look, I've told you, I'm not a saint. I've slept around. It was partying and fun and pretty meaningless. I met you and I didn't want meaningless anymore. That's just the way it is."

She doesn't reply and we lapse into silence, the radio filling the air between us. I check her out several times, my eyes flicking from the road to her face covertly—she's wearing a small smile each time.

When we hit the town lines it hits me, I'm bringing Cassie home to meet my dad, to see my town. This feels monumental. Even if I'm not introducing her as my girlfriend—I think she'd run out the nearest door if I tried—she's still the first girl I've invited to my childhood home since Lauren.

"I forgot how cute Tyler is. I love it," she smiles as we drive through mid-town passing the main street shops and offices still wearing their Christmas decorations from the holiday season.

"Oh, that's right you went home with Jess over Thanksgiving, didn't you?"

"Yeah, we spent Black Friday shopping the little boutiques on Main Street, and she gave me a tour of Rossview."

"So I owe you the full Tyler tour then." I roll my window down as we hit a light across from the newly rebuilt Remington's and tap my horn twice. "Hey, Darcee, happy new year."

"Hey, sugar. How was the wedding?"

The light turns green before I can reply. I wave, "I'll fill you in soon."

I wave to no less than five people on the ten-minute drive to the house while Cassie gapes out the window and points out buildings she says she didn't see on her last visit.

She's still babbling on when I pull into the drive and park around back of the house. I glance at her casually trying to figure out what she thinks. She stares. I catch the way she sucks her bottom lip under her front teeth, but that's the only betrayal of her thoughts. Climbing from the car, I walk around and open her door.

"This mansion is yours?"

"Dad's, technically." It's not a mansion, but I imagine compared to the nicest place she lived in growing up, it is. "Come on."

Leaving the bags for later, I give her the grand tour, allowing plenty of time for her to study the many pictures adorning the walls throughout the house.

"And this is my room, much like it was throughout my high school years." I wave my arm, inviting her to enter first.

It's a basic guy's bedroom. I've never been much for clutter and collections. The media room holds all of my football accolades, my bedroom holds the rest of me.

"I'm digging these little guys," she smiles at the stuffed animals I've kept.

"Oh, Troy and Steve. I've had them forever." Of course she has no idea they're named after two of the greatest football players of my lifetime.

She removes the worn dog from the edge of the bookshelf hanging over my computer desk. "Hotshot football player kept his childhood friends, be still my heart." Her fingers rub along his little head. Damn, I've never wanted to be a stuffed toy so bad. "And the books. You keep surprising me, Seuss."

"Good."

"*The Outsiders, Tale of Two Cities, Lord of the Flies*," she taps the spines as she reads them off. "Required reading?"

"Yep, AP English."

"AP. Impressive." Her brows lift in acknowledgment. "Which was your favorite?"

"Hmmm, *Lord of the Flies* for sure." I step behind Cassie, reaching over her and pulling a title from the shelf. "And this."

"*The Things They Carried?*" She flips the paperback over, her eyes scanning the back.

"It's not a war story, not really. His writing style is unique, it blurs fact and fiction—our class discussion was amazing after reading it. Borrow it if you want."

Placing Troy back on his perch, she smiles. "Thanks."

A heavy roll of thunder comes out of nowhere, darkening the room as clouds cover the sun. "Is it supposed to rain? I better grab our bags from the car. I'll be right back."

My pocket vibrates halfway there. Jeff.

"Hey, man. What's up?" I answer the phone, grabbing my keys from the counter.

"You're in town?"

Good news travels fast. "Yeah, Dad gets in late tonight. Thought I better spend a day or two with him before we get back to the grind."

"Good deal. Want to catch up with us for pizza later?"

Shit. I didn't think things through before answering his call. Does Cassie want anyone to know she's here? "Uh, can I get back to you on that?"

"You have a better offer?" Jeff chuckles.

"I'll call you back." I'm starving. Just the idea of pizza spurs my stomach to growl. Another wave of thunders echoes through the sky as I return to the house and drop our bags by the door.

I find Cassie in the media room, her fingers touching over the golden busts of years' worth of trophies. She threw on her ripped jeans with an electric blue sweater this morning. I miss seeing her in my sweatshirts. I miss her lips too, but after everything that went on yesterday, I'm giving her the choice on what our next move is.

"You played t-ball?" She picks up one of the few non-football trophies in the room. "This poor guy must feel like a loner among the rest of these."

"There's a soccer guy on the end there," I point toward Carson's statues. "Maybe they can form a club."

"The random whims of the Rutledge brothers club?" she murmurs, setting the t-ball guy down.

"Random whims, blatant rebellion—same thing right?"

"Playing t-ball was rebellion?"

"To Weston Rutledge, yeah. My poor mom took a shitload of slack for signing me up without telling him"

"Weston? Ahhh, West is named after your dad?" I nod, forgetting how little she knows about my family. "What happened to t-ball? Did he make you quit?"

"Nah. My dad is nothing but supportive of everything we do. My mom went through a protective phase. She started suggesting all the safer sports we could try instead of football, and of course Dad called her crazy. So she signed me up for t-ball and Carson up for soccer. I think we had three or four practices before Dad found out about it." Cassie laughs.

"He was doing some spring camp for local kids or something, I can't remember, but that's the only reason she got away with the secret for so long."

Cassie nods, returning to her perusal of the Rutledge museum. Nestled among trophies, jerseys, and more pictures than necessary are school art projects. Clay pots and animals, a few framed drawings, even a macramé dreamcatcher Mom and Carson made when he had a severe case of strep and missed several days of school. My stomach growls again. Dang Jeff for putting pizza on my mind.

"You hungry?" I finally ask when I can't take the rumbling in my stomach any longer. Cassie shrugs. "Well, I'm starving. I really can't live off donuts like you seem able to. I doubt we have much here, since Dad's been out of town. Want to raid the freezer?"

"Sure." She's a bit withdrawn suddenly, but I let her sudden moodiness go as she follows me downstairs where we scrounge up some frozen mac n' cheese and a few frozen dinners.

Cassie chooses an oriental meal, she loves her noodles, and I decide on the Salisbury steak. The rain moves in halfway through lunch, lightning streaking the sky like crazy as we watch out the kitchen window. The trees sway, groaning as the wind picks up. I pull up my phone to check the weather report, wondering if dad's flight will end up delayed.

"So, two things," I say nonchalantly, confirming the storms are expected to move through relatively quickly. "First, Jeff called earlier." Cassie lowers her fork mid-bite. "He heard I was in town and asked if I wanted to meet up for pizza later."

The color drains from her face. "Does he know I'm with you?"

"I doubt it. He didn't mention you, and he absolutely would have had he known."

She relaxes. "I don't want anyone to know I'm here. How could I not have thought of him? And Jess and Katie?" She slaps her forehead. "God, that was stupid of me."

"Well, that leads me to issue two. My dad's flying in tonight."

"Your dad? I thought he was spending the week in St. Lucia." She pushes away from the table, her hands rubbing her thighs. She's freaked and I feel like shit for not being honest.

"I'm sorry."

"Are Jules and West coming home too? I would have gone back to school if I'd known, you should have told me." She turns toward the window, closing her body off from me as she stares out at the rain and trees and sighs deeply over and over.

I slide from the table, walking around it and standing before her, blocking her view. She averts her gaze. "I don't want them to know," she says faintly.

A surge of protectiveness builds within me. I squat, my hands touching her knees to help me keep my balance. "Cassie, your story isn't mine to tell. Jules and West aren't coming home until tomorrow night. We can head back tomorrow afternoon if you don't want to see them."

"It's not that I don't want to see them, it's just—"

"You don't want them to know you're with me, do you?" I assumed she was worried I'd spill her past, but maybe that's not it at all.

"That's ridiculous." She touches my cheek, a smile twisting on her lips. "I want to protect them. I want to protect you," she says meaningfully.

There it is again, her saying she wants to protect us. Why?

"You know what?" I cover her hand, removing it from my face and pulling her up from her chair. "I'm done with this cryptic shit, Cass. It's time for you to come clean."

Dragging her behind me, I walk her into the living room and set her on the couch. I pull an ottoman over, sitting myself in front of her the way Dad did when he interrogated us as teens and bracing my arms on my thighs. My legs trap hers between my knees as I school my features into a calm mask and wait.

CASSIE

I can't protect him without telling him the truth.
And I can't tell him the truth without risking losing him.

♥

"I want the truth."

I bite the inside of my cheek at Austin's grim parental expression. My mouth gapes, a fish gasping for air, as words formulate in my head.

"The truth, Annie." His eyes narrow, as though he knows I plan on deferring.

Annie. It's a kick to the gut, the insinuation his calling me Annie implies. He's making it clear that he doesn't feel as though he knows me. Anonymous Annie.

But where do I begin?

"Can I tell you something?" He exhales through his nose.

"Of course." Especially if it puts off my explanation.

"I have zero patience for lies."

Well, okay then.

He continues, "I've been screwed over once, and once was enough. I also have zero patience for games. Life is too damn short to play games."

His brown eyes are intense. They're angry, but soft. Full of something more profound than the evil I always saw in Emil's dark eyes. "I'm here. Period. God, you scare the hell out of me." He rubs the back of his neck, a small smile playing at his lips. "That's how I know."

I'm barely breathing. "How you know what?"

"This," his finger waves between the two of us, "is the real thing. From the first time we met, I knew it. I'm here, tell me the truth, tell me what I need to know, Cass. Tell me what's really going on."

Why is he so amazing? I want to scream because I know I don't deserve someone like him. "You keep saying all these wonderful things. You keep professing feelings for me, but you barely know me, Austin. How can you think such things?"

"Don't pretend that you don't." He shakes his head with a smile. "You said you fell for me because I gave you a book. You said you heard two words after Emil called you Saturday—run and—"

"Austin," I breathe. His shoulders lift as he nods.

"Look, I'm not one of those guys who wants to add notches to my bedpost and never have something real. I know that must be hard for you to believe, given your history and what you know about me. I'm not saying I don't like sex and hooking up, cause I sure as hell do, but if any of those girls had sparked something in my soul, I would have committed. I'm not afraid of relationships, Cass. I just never found the right girl. Until now."

His honesty cuts straight to my soul. I haven't had much honesty in my life. It's refreshing. Tears spring to my eyes and sweat forms along my hairline as heat rushes through me. My palm covers my mouth as the tears slip down my face. "I don't know if I've ever been loved."

Saying the words out loud hurts. They turn me into the little girl who was slapped by Molly, they turn me into the girl who was told she was no good, who was used by a woman who should have loved her, who was used by sick men, used by Emil.

Austin inches closer, his knees touching the couch as his hands cradle my face, drawing me up so I'm looking at him. "Not true. Jules, Katie, and Jess love you."

I draw a shaking breath, my chin trembling.

"And I love you."

I refuse his words.

"Don't you shake your head at me." He inhales, a light sparking behind his eyes as his fingers tighten along my jaw. His mouth curves into a smile as he shakes his head. "Fuck. I'm in love with you." I flinch and his eyes flare. "Yeah, I said it."

He stands, shoving the ottoman back in his haste. His hands clasp on top of his head as he turns his back, laughing softly and muttering words I can't make out. He's in love with me? That's impossible.

"I haven't given you anything."

Austin spins. "What?"

"I haven't given you anything."

Confusion, then understanding flash across his face and he drops his hands from his head with a groan. Grabbing the ottoman once again, he slides himself back in front of me.

"That's not how this works. People don't fall in love because you buy them off. Shit, Cass," he snorts. "If my little freak-out there didn't prove that, nothing will. I didn't even know I loved you until I said it. You stole my heart and you did nothing but be yourself."

"You don't love me, you can't." I don't know how I'm smiling at him at this moment, except—except I want to breakdown and beg him to love me. I want to beg him to need me like I think I might need him.

Oh, God.

My chest hurts. I need him. I love him. No.

No, no, no. I can't.

His lips touch mine. "I can and I do. Like it or not."

"Austin." My hands cover his, pushing him away as I sink back on the couch. He flips his hands, his fingers grabbing mine and holding them.

"Push me away, it won't change a thing, little one."

"You're crazy."

"For you," he counters.

"Stop it."

"I can't, done deal."

"I don't want you to love me."

His eyes narrow again, although a smile lingers as he calls my bluff. "Liar."

Okay, the truth.

"My mother is missing." I relay that little nugget of information with all the emotion I feel. Which is none. She means nothing to me, but the consequences— "It would mean nothing to me if she didn't run with a lot of money. Emil's money."

Austin sniffs, his chin lifting as though he understands already.

"He's a dangerous man. Drugs, racketeering, illegal fights—I don't know, you name it and apparently he's involved. I didn't know. Not until she kicked me out." My foot bounces, my nerves breaking. "I had nowhere to go, I was scared. I—"

Austin leans closer, his hands squeezing mine tightly. His eyes urging me to continue. *I'm here. Period.*

"I didn't sleep with him before she kicked me out."

"But, I thought—" He shuts his mouth, his brows knitting together.

Closing my eyes, I attempt to explain the past. "I teased him. I played this game with him because I knew he liked it. He liked excusing himself to use the restroom to find me purposefully half-naked in my room. He liked cornering me in the hallway and grabbing me. It was a game to me, but to him ... I don't know. I guess it was exciting. The longer I held out the more desperate he became. When she found him in my room the first time it was easy to explain, he said he thought he heard a noise."

"The next time he snuck in," I swallow hard. The shame of my past isn't an easy thing for me to keep down. "I woke with his hand under my shirt and his tongue on my lips. I didn't push him away." The tears fall. "I was a teenage girl; he was a handsome older man who wanted me. More than he wanted her." I point out. "That part's important, but as far as I knew they hadn't been having sex. I would have heard it. She never kept it secret."

Austin releases my hands, crossing his arms across his chest as I wipe at my face.

"I know how demented this must sound."

"Just tell me everything, Cassie." There's a bit of defeat in his tone. He told me he loves me and I'm about to throw that all away with my truths. I shake my emotions away, determined to relay the facts with as little emotion as I can.

"Fine. Nothing more than that happened that night, but he came back. There were a few close calls, my mother waking up calling his name, finding him outside my door. When she caught him in my room again, she pulled him out without a word to me, but the next evening I came home to a suitcase and a note. I didn't get a goodbye. I called Emil and he put me up in a room at the hotel where he lived."

"He told me he would take care of me, he even let me finish out the school year. Of course there was a price." I let the obvious hang in the air before I continued. "I was stupid and trusted him. It didn't take me long to see reality. I thought he'd stopped seeing her once he had me. I was wrong, he didn't leave her, and he wouldn't let me go. He said we needed to hide out until my eighteenth birthday. Too many people had met me as Gwen's daughter, they would recognize me and question him. He just wanted to keep me locked up for his amusement—he wasn't gentle."

"You smell like her," I complain, stepping out of his embrace with a frown. I haven't seen him in two days. His employees, two men who leer at me, brought me meals but no information as I waited.

"Her?" His heavy accent makes the word sound like 'hair' as he raises a brow.

"Gwen." I will not call her 'Momma' ever again.

His palm cracks across my cheek, snapping my head sideways. I stumble back, hot tears springing to my eyes.

"Do not question me, love." He slides his black jacket from his lithe body. "Now, how much did you miss me?" His fingers pop the buttons from his shirt. "As much as I missed you?"

"Not if you were with her," I challenge, my fingers tightening around the closure of the silk robe he bought me. Everything I wear is from Emil. Everything I own—his.

Tsk, tsk, tsk. Emil's lips form the sound, his head swinging side to side. I expect his anger; I expect him to walk out of the room at my defiance. I've witnessed fights between Momma and her men many times. They always ended with us in a vehicle, bags packed, new city on the horizon. Emil doesn't play by those rules though. I should have known.

He undresses, his black eyes holding mine the entire time, and when he's naked before me he finally speaks again. "Drop your robe and show me how much you missed me, Cassandra."

There's a hidden anger in his voice. My shoulders curl in protectively at the sound. "No."

"No?"

"Were you with her?" Try as I might, I can't hide the hurt in my voice. I don't love him. I never did, I only wanted to prove to her that she was wrong about me. That I was worthy of love, of a man.

He moves like a snake, striking out and ripping my arms from my robe with such power and quickness I'm tripping over a coffee table before I can think. I land hard on my hip, Emil's naked form over me, his face leering down at me.

"You will do as I say, love." He lowers himself. His hand shoving under the slip of a nightgown I'm wearing under the now twisted robe, and between my legs. "You will never question me." His right hand presses to my collar bone, splayed across my chest, his thumb so near my windpipe I feel slight pressure. "You," a finger shoves at my underwear, "will give me what I want, when I want it." I cry out as his fingers slide between my legs forcefully.

"Show me how you missed me," he says once more.

I lift my fingers to his erection, stroking him, pulling him down toward me. My mind going to the past, to the nothingness, as I allow him to take me there on the floor.

"I learned to keep my mouth shut." I touch the small scar at my brow—the one Austin asked about—absently. "After six months I ran."

With the exception of the angry twitch of his clenched jaw Austin reveals nothing as he asks, "How?"

"He had a habit of carrying cash. After we ... when he fell asleep, I would steal enough to stash away without him knowing. It took a few weeks. When I couldn't take another day, I lied to him. I told him I could be pregnant. He was insanely careful in that regard. Of course he flipped out. He ordered his driver to take me to a clinic and made me promise to get an IUD or some other long-term birth control. He gave me money, just in case."

"How nice of him," Austin scoffs. "And if you were pregnant? What was his plan for that?"

"What do you think?" I ask blandly. Austin's fury makes the hair on my arms stand.

"I knew I wasn't; it was just a ploy to get out of the building. I walked into that clinic and out the back door. I've been hiding ever since."

"How did he find you?"

"I don't know. I hopped towns for a good six months before settling in Dallas last year. I wanted to finish high school, and I wanted to go to college. I didn't want to let them win."

His brows lift as though he's had a revelation. "You're nineteen then, aren't you?"

Such a minor question. "Yeah, sorry if that disappoints you." His answer is a kiss on my palm, the heat of his lips making me shiver.

"He's looking for me, Austin," I say after a moment. "His exact words were that he'd 'happily take my mother's ransom out of me.' "

"Let him try. I'll kill the son of a bitch." The challenge is clear in Austin's voice. He isn't joking, he's out for blood.

"No." I slide forward on the couch, shaking my head wildly. "It's best he doesn't know about you. Any of you. I don't trust him. I think he'd use my feelings to get back at me. He's obsessed with me. I could tell you stories ... this is why I wanted to leave, why I should run."

"Run where?"

"Away, anywhere."

"Are you serious? Cassie, you can't spend your life on the run. That's crazy."

"I have nothing else."

"You have me." His feet lock around mine, his knees sandwiching mine as we face each other. We've eaten up all the space between us until we're wrapped up—hands, legs, feet—together with our faces inches from one another. "You have Jess, and Katie, and Jules. You have my brothers and dad. Cass, you've spent nineteen years alone. Not anymore."

AUSTIN

I hold her until she pulls away.
She assures me she's fine,
then I excuse myself to the bathroom...

I'm a selfish son of a bitch, hiding here after everything she told me. I just can't ... I need a moment. The water from the faucet isn't cold enough as I splash my face. I could use an ice bath to numb these feelings, and still I'd be fuming.

I pull out my phone and shoot off a text:

Dad, I brought Cassie (one of Jules's roommates) home with me.
Just an FYI

He won't answer, he's mid-air at this point, but a warning's nice.

"Would you like to hear the rest of the Austin Rutledge life story? I never got to finish it, and I think we could both use a break," I offer when I return to the couch, sitting beside her.

She nods. "A change would be good."

I launch into tale after tale of my childhood. We sit for hours, her curled into the corner of the couch and me stretched out on the opposite end. I talk about Mom's cancer, football, my brothers. With the exception of a few monosyllabic words, she doesn't speak. We don't talk about her life. We don't talk about my confession of love. I simply try my best to introduce her to the boy I was and the man I am. I want her to know everything about me so she can see I'm not someone to be afraid of. It's all I've got right now, all I know how to do. My voice is hoarse and the room is dark, the sun having long set when I run out of words.

Cassie's been fingering her lips, staring across the dark room for five minutes. I can't take it anymore.

"How about I order pizza?" I move to the edge of the couch, a smile plastered on my face for her benefit.

She nods.

I pat my pockets. No cell. "I think I left my phone in the kitchen. I'll be right back. Can I get you a drink?"

Her eyes finally lift to mine, a sweet smile touching her lips. "Please," she says softly.

My hands itch to pull her up and into my arms, and I force myself to leave the room without another word. God, she's all-consuming.

I have missed calls from Jeff and Dad. Grabbing drinks from the fridge, I ignore Jeff's dinner invite and hit the call button for Dad. I flip on a few lights as the line rings.

"Hey, son," he answers, the music in the background lowering.

"Hey, you almost here?"

"Twenty minutes. Want to tell me about your house guest?"

He has no idea. "I do actually, but later. I was going to order pizza. You want to grab it on the way home?"

"I can do that. Do we need anything else at the house while I'm out?"

"Nope, we're good for tonight." I pause and he closes our conversation, telling me he'll be home soon. Before he can hang up, I jump in quickly. "Hey, Dad? Just be cool with Cassie, okay? There's some stuff going on."

"Some stuff? What kind of stuff are we talking about, Austin?" His voice flips from light to concerned.

"The kind I need you for."

"I thought the days of you needing your old man were long gone."

I murmur a humorless "me too" as he reiterates he'll be here soon. Turning, I find Cassie standing in the opening between the kitchen and living room.

"Hey, my dad's picking up the pizza. He'll be here in twenty to thirty."

She chews on the corner of her bottom lip, sucking it in between her teeth as her eyes flick toward our bags still sitting on the floor near the back door.

"You okay?"

A flicker of a smile crosses her face. "Better than okay," she replies as her head bobs.

My body tingles at the lightness surrounding her. There's something different, a release all of her past? With drinks in hand, I walk up to her, a million words swirling around my mind. A million feelings about this girl ravaging through my formerly cool and collected interior. This is the gooey emotional shit West went through when he fell for Jules. The stuff I gave him crap for. Who's the idiot now?

Cassie inches forward, her hands straying to the pockets of my jeans. Fingers tugging the edges as she leans in, landing her forehead against my chest, as she's done several times in the past few days.

"This may be my favorite spot ever," she breathes as my arms cross behind her shoulders.

It's in this moment that everything I am changes. Everything I've been changes. Strange that I can pinpoint it. I told her I loved her, I promised to protect her, but this ... this moment when her face has lost its tension. When her breath against my chest makes me tremble. I'm done. No hesitation, I'm all in.

I rest my chin on top of her head. "You're welcome to it for as long as you want."

Her fingers tug on my pants. "You're very accommodating, thank you." Her musical giggles shake her shoulders. "I have one thing I need to do before your dad gets here, though."

"Yeah, what's that?" I tighten my arms.

"Not that," she lifts away, regarding me with a wry smile upon her perfect lips. I school my face into a perfect schoolboy innocence as her brown eyes roll. Then she says, "I'm going to call her."

The gooey emotional shit turns to abject misery. "Wait. What?" We scoot left as one with her hands still holding my pockets, my arms still wrapped around her shoulders so I can deposit our drinks on the kitchen table. Once relieved of their burden, my hands grasp Cassie's biceps, moving her back so I can get a good look at her features. "Cass, is that a good idea? When did you last speak to her?"

"I left her a message yesterday." I imagine I'm doing a piss poor job of hiding my shock right now. Cassie's rush to explain confirms that. "It was stupid. I had all these missed calls from him, and I just wanted her to know he was looking. I thought maybe she'd answer or call back and give me some explanation ... I don't know why I even cared."

This is her mother. Even after everything she put her through growing up, of course some small part of Cassie would still care.

"Honestly, I'm not even sure if I can believe Emil, maybe he's lying to get to me. Maybe she left him a long time ago." Her fingers drop from my pants. "Or maybe she's still there."

She needs to do her own thing. I don't want to say anything to deter her, so my hands slip from her arms and into my pockets as she steps away. Her phone's in her bag, tucked away as though she's saying if she doesn't see it she doesn't have to deal with it.

I stand back in silence, watching her pace the room and bite at her thumb nail as she dials the number.

"It's me again. Emil has been emailing me since I left. He never stopped, did you know that? Now he knows my number and he's been calling and texting. I'm not going back. I'm in school, and I want nothing to do with him, or you. Wherever you are, I hope it was worth it. I hope the money was worth it. I know I said call me, but don't. I'm starting over and I'm good. I don't need you. No," she turns, her eyes tear-brightened but resolute. "I don't want you."

Her thumb slides over the screen, ending the call, and Cassie lowers her head and nods slowly as she blows out her cheeks.

"When I arrived on campus back in August I thought I'd outrun them, the past." She draws nearer. "I'd been here all of five days when you offered your help in the library. Five days, and I freaked. I kept reminding myself you were just a college guy hitting on me, or being helpful." She gives a half shrug. "It didn't matter what you wanted, my first instinct was to be afraid. To get away. I don't want to expect an ulterior motive of every man I meet, Austin."

"Then we'll work on that." I step forward, thrusting out my hand. "Hi, I'm Austin Rutledge, and for the record I was totally hitting on you back in August when we first met, and I'm totally hitting on you now."

She places her hand in mine, shaking it. My fingers tighten around hers, and I tug, pulling her toward me. Slipping my free hand around her waist, I smile down at her.

"I'm putting my motives out there right now, I want you."

"And it only took us six months to get here." Her hand winds around my neck, bringing me down until our lips touch. "Thank you," she whispers against my mouth.

She's thanking me? Her lips spread into a grin as she backs down, leaving her hand on my shoulder.

"So, I'm Cassie. I'm a bit skittish, I'm a sports dummy, and I have two tons of baggage you may not want to deal with." Her face smooths, the muscles around her lips tightening. "And if it's too much, I'll understand." She pauses for a beat. "But, for the first time ever there's this guy who's caught my eye and captured my heart."

"Really? Your heart?"

"I do have one. I know, it's shocking, isn't it?"

"Not what I meant at all," I assure her, touching the very spot where her heart is. I tap, as though verifying a piece of electronic equipment is working.

If it wasn't for the whirring of the garage door opening, I'd pick her up and devour her. Instead I groan as she jumps back nervously at the sound.

"I'll follow your lead, say as much or as little as you want about yourself," I tell her as her eyes go wide. "He's easy, don't be nervous."

There's no time for more as the back door opens.

"Welcome back to dreary winter," I laugh, removing the pizza boxes from Dad's hands and taking in his golden tan. My skin got a touch of color while I was there for the wedding, but he looks like an island native.

"Thanks, I considered turning right back around the moment I stepped out of the airport." His eyes flick toward Cassie, his smile remaining as he bobs his head and looks back to me for introductions.

"Dad, this is Cassie. Cassie, this is my dad."

"Cassie," he nods again, reaching out a hand. "It's a pleasure."

"It's nice to meet you. Austin speaks very highly of you. I'm sorry I'm crashing your homecoming. I'm sure you weren't expecting company after a long day of travel." She shakes his hand, but I notice the uncertainty in her voice. Her shoulder curves under just enough to let me know she's not one hundred percent comfortable.

Dad scoffs. "Any girl who gets my son home to Tyler is family." He winks. "Now who's hungry?"

That was easy. Pizza, soda, and a shit ton of questions from me to Dad about his deep sea fishing in the Caribbean—that's all it takes to for Cassie's body to unbend. With Cassie looking over my shoulder we scan through the pictures on Dad's phone. She owes me big time because I truly find fishing to be one of the most boring things in the world, and we've been talking about it for what seems like hours.

"I can't believe you left early," she admonishes me, her hand touching my forearm as each shot of paradise slides by. The green coastline, the blue sea, the clear skies.

"Can't you?" I ask purposefully.

Pink tints her cheeks, her fingers tightening reflexively. I catch Dad's eyes flickering between Cassie and I, putting two and two together. Cassie squeals as a school of dolphins pops up from the water, effectively stopping him before he can say anything.

"Oh, my gosh. Look at them all," she coos. Dad chuckles as Cassie slaps at my hand to slow my scrolling. "Did they follow you?"

"Every day. They love the wake, and played along on and off for hours. Jules begged us to stop so she could swim with them."

"In the middle of the ocean? Sounds like Jules." I hand the phone to Cassie so she can get a better look at the shots. "Dolphins, huh?" I ask, surprised at her excitement over them.

"They're so carefree."

Carefree. Freedom. A reoccurring theme with Cassie.

"Have you ever seen them up close?" Dad asks when she finally hands his phone back.

"I haven't. I've never even been on a boat. I went on a field trip in elementary school to an aquarium, but that and pet stores are about the closest I've been to sea life."

It makes sense considering her childhood. I flash a discreet look at Dad when he appears ready to probe further. We're a little over four hours from the beach so it's safe to assume that most people here have been once in their life.

"Austin's not much of a boat fan himself." Dad's eyes gleam and I just know a story is coming.

Cassie shifts on the couch, curling a leg up under her. "Really? You mentioned you weren't the fisherman in the family. Why not?"

"It's okay, I just prefer keeping my feet on the shore."

She regards me with doubt and turns to my dad.

"There might have been an incident once," Dad offers.

"An incident? You dumped me in the ocean thirty miles from shore."

Cassie gasps, her fingers pressing to her lips.

Dad shakes his head and clarifies, "He had a life jacket on and we turned right around." Ten years and he still has no shame.

"I was standing on the back of the boat, relieving myself, and someone thought it would be funny to knock me on my ass, but when my dad there floored it, I flew off the back instead."

She laughs, her deep Elmer giggles making my dad laugh too.

"It wasn't funny." I frown.

"No, of course it wasn't." Her hand touches my thigh lightly and I'm instantly hard. "You had a life jacket, and you knew they'd pick you up. Why did that turn you from boating?"

Dad's brow lifts, challenging me. I'm gonna have to talk with Cassie about taking my side in all family matters in the future.

"It was Shark Week," I admit reluctantly.

Cassie's giggles continue with a gasping 'Oh, no' pouring out between the chatter. "Dude, I was terrified a Great White was going to pop up and eat me. Those were the freakiest three minutes of my life."

"His mother threatened my life in those three minutes," Dad chuckles at the memories.

"Your life and your body parts, if I recall correctly," I laugh. "Then she had Brown and Clint toss you into the ocean." Cassie's eyes volley between us as we fill in bits of the story. God, the memories are sweet now, but back then ...

Cassie nods when we stop talking. "No boats or sharks? Any other fears I should know about?"

"Wait, I didn't say I was afraid—"

"Oh, no, of course not."

"What about you? What are you afraid of, Annie?"

"All the obvious things: snakes, spiders, clowns." I spider my fingers across her knee and thigh, and she swats at me. "Small locked spaces."

Her small voice wipes the smiles from our faces and my hand finds hers, giving her a gentle squeeze.

Cassie and Dad head upstairs an hour later for showers, so I sit alone, allowing myself time to think. She handled meeting Dad better than I expected. I suppose if I have to be the butt of a million jokes and old stories to make her feel at home, then I'm okay with it. He shot me questioning looks throughout the night, his watchful eyes taking note of each touch Cassie and I shared, each delicately phrased answer she gave, each change of subject I conveniently made.

"You're not making me a grandpa, are you?"

"Shit," I choke, glancing around the kitchen to verify Cassie isn't near. I should have known by the look he shot me when he told us goodnight that he'd be back to talk. "Geez, Dad."

"It's a valid question."

"Considering I haven't slept with her, it's not."

I flip the light over the sink off and grab a bottle of water knowing Cassie goes to bed with a glass every night.

"What's going on?" he asks, and I pause to listen to the house, checking on her whereabouts. He sighs through his nose. "The shower was still running when I walked by."

"Dad, she came out of nowhere," I admit as he grins, resting his hip against the counter. "I wasn't looking for anything serious. You know me, I barely have time for myself."

"So, what's the problem?"

"What's the problem? She drives me crazy. I fell for her months ago and I didn't even know her name. She wouldn't give me the time of day and I had to fight for every word."

His head bobs as he waits for me to get to my point.

"She's been through a lot, Dad." I pause. "A lot." I won't give him her story, I wouldn't betray her like that, but— "It scares me. I don't want to do or say the wrong thing."

"Are we talking bad relationships? Or something else?" he asks and I hesitate.

"You're my kid, no matter how old you are, son. You tell me there's stuff going on and that you need me. Here I am. Tell me what's happening."

"She had a pretty skewed representation of relationships growing up. Her mom wasn't a great role model." I cross the kitchen and lower my voice. "Let's just say I'm not surprised she wanted nothing to do with me, or any guys for that matter."

His eyes—replicas of my own—give me an idea of what I must have looked like when Cassie spilled her past to me. There's the frustration any decent person would have as he draws conclusions from what I've said. There's sadness on Cassie's behalf, and there's something else. Anger? At me? His mouth tenses.

"You don't screw with her heart, Austin." Yep, it's anger. "You don't mess around with a girl who's been hurt like that. She's not fair game."

"No kidding, that's why I brought her here. I'm not talking about screwing around. I'm talking about love." The click of a door upstairs tells us Cassie is out of the shower. "You fell for Mom pretty quickly, didn't you? I mean West was in love with Jules forever, Cars and Mindy were friends for a while, but you and Mom—"

"Enamored the first time I saw her. Sometimes love really is like an arrow to the heart."

This is why I needed him. I needed confirmation and wisdom. "So, I'm not crazy?"

He chuckles at that. His large hand clasping my shoulder and pulling me into a loose hug. "Not at all, son. If you love her you'll say and do the right things. Your parents raised a good man."

"You think?"

"I know."

Slapping his back, I slide away. "I'm going up. Thanks, Dad."

"I'm always here."

CASSIE

Austin's father called me family.
I might have felt like crying at that.
Then I saw the light blinking on my phone...

"Cassandra, I miss you, love. I'm not looking for your mother, I just want you to come home. Come back to Vegas and we can work things out. I'm sorry I hurt you, I was wrong. I didn't—"

Three taps at the bedroom door have me ending the voicemail prematurely. The door slips open a notch.

"Cass?"

"Hey, come in," I call, the phone still in hand as his dark head and eyes peer into the room.

"I brought a water."

I remain standing, my pulse racing at Emil, and at Austin.

"I may have noticed the way you took a glass of water to my room the past two nights," he admits.

"He keeps calling."

Austin falters in the doorway and I lift my palm, the cellphone clutched between my fingers.

His eyes go cold. "Emil?"

I nod and he crosses the room.

"Then we get you a new phone." He removes the cell from my hand, tossing it on the bed, along with the water, before wrapping me in a hug. "I can set you up in the guest room, but I would prefer it if you slept in here with me. I mean, if you want."

"With you?" I attempt pulling back, but Austin's hand stops me. "What about your dad?"

"He won't be scandalized, if that's what you're worried about. Besides, I already told him we're not having sex."

"You what?" No amount of pressure he exerts can keep me tied to his body this time. "How does something like that even come up?"

A wicked gleam crosses his features and I sigh at his twelve-year-old maturity level.

"I sort of had to tell him something. He asked if he was going to be a grandpa." My knees go weak. Not the first impression I was hoping to make on his father.

Austin kisses my temple. "Obviously, I don't ever bring girls home."

I suppose that's his version of an explanation. "So you bring home a girl and your father's first assumption is you got her pregnant? What does that say about you?" I have a difficult time keeping a straight face.

"Nothing you didn't already know," he drawls before turning away. "I'm washing up."

When he returns I've already climbed into his bed, settled into his soft sheets and fluffy pillows, and turned out the light. He moves around the dark room for a minute, unzipping his duffle and using his cell to light his way as he plugs in his charger. The screen glows as he slips out of his sleeping pants and slides next to me, rolling to his side and propping his head on his palm as the light cuts off.

"You're in my bed." His statement comes out hoarse.

"I am."

"I'm glad."

"Me too."

"Sooo—" There's mischief in the way he drags out those two letters. "Does this mean you've decided to give in?"

Oh. My. God. I'm tempted to push him right onto the floor. "Considering I'm sleeping in your bed. I would say so."

"That means I can kiss you without fear?"

I push up on my side, a mirror image of his pose, though he can't see me. "Try me."

I wish we'd left a light on. I wish I could see the shape of his wicked smile as he leans in, see the heat in his brown eyes, see the way he looks at me before his lips collide with mine and I lose all thought. The moment I taste the minty toothpaste on his tongue I'm falling onto the pillow beneath me and Austin is following me down. The bed shifts as his body inches closer to me, his muscles pressing against mine.

My breath catches as his tongue strokes mine, as his hand cups my face, and his fingers dig into the hair near my temple.

"Does this scare you?" His lips tease mine when he speaks above my mouth.

"Not at all." I'm listening to my body, waiting for the panic, but it doesn't come. "Why? Does it scare you?"

"Sure as hell does," he breathes and my cheeks twitch, a smile playing on my lips as my hands flex against his skin. "Go ahead and laugh, little one. It's humorous."

I'm unsure of his tone. I haven't learned all the nuances yet; is he joking, making fun of himself? Frustrated?

"You know you have the potential to hurt me a whole lot more than I can hurt you."

He falls next to me, taking his hands and mouth with him. "That's why I'm scared," he whispers, releasing a harsh breath. "I don't ever want to hurt you."

"You know what," I say as I move closer. "Let's not get all serious again. Let's take it day by day." I kiss the corner of his mouth thanks to bad aim in the dark. "Let's kiss until we can't stand it, go to bed, and then do it all again tomorrow."

"You're saying you want to make out with me, in my bed, in my parents' house?" Austin whispers playfully, and I laugh against his shoulder as he pulls me partially on top of him. "It's like I'm back in high school."

♥

I fall asleep kissing Austin Rutledge. I wake up kissing Austin Rutledge. I eat breakfast between Austin kisses. My lips are chapped and my mouth gloriously exhausted by the time Jules and West pull up to the house late Thursday.

"What the—?" Their faces say everything they're thinking the moment the garage door goes up and the headlights of West's truck flash across Austin and I standing in the opening. We didn't tell them we would be here, and of course, they wouldn't expect me here for anything in the world.

The driver side door opens, and West jumps out of his truck. "I knew something was up when Dad asked us to stop by before I brought Jules home."

Austin winks over his shoulder as he meets his brother by the hood of his truck, they do some brotherly handshake ritual, West mumbling something low and Austin chuckling his hushed reply as I watch.

Their reunion is replaced with a vision of my suitemate with a ridiculously happy smile on her face, as she heads my way. She throws her arms around me, nearly knocking me over. "What are you doing here?" She smells like coconuts and sunshine. I'm jealous. "Am I allowed to ask?"

"It's a long story. How was St. Lucia?"

"Ha, that is not going to work tonight." Jules's arm weaves through mine as she drags me toward the house. "Cassie, you're in Tyler. With Austin." She studies my profile. "And you look happy."

I bite my lip, almost afraid to jinx it. We'd spent the day relaxing. Austin and his dad went for a long run—something he said they always do when they're together—while I read a book. We ate lunch and dinner together, we watched a movie, and I fell asleep with my head on a pillow in his lap. It was a lazy day. So lazy and easy that when he suggested we needed to get going if I didn't want Jules and West to know I was here, I had no trouble making the decision to stay.

♥

"You want to stay? You were so worried—" his knuckle brushes across my cheekbone as I look up at him from his lap.

Hearing his father in the kitchen I respond quietly. "I told you I don't want to run and be scared anymore."

His upside down face glows with excitement. "Did I bring you home because you were alone, or because there's more?"

He's asking for a status. Friends or relationship? My skin heats up merely thinking of all the kissing and grazing we've endured in the last eighteen or so hours. I doubt either of us can keep our hands, or mouths, to ourselves for very long—with or without Jules and West's presence.

"Who would have thought Austin Rutledge was the type to have to define his relationships."

"Relationship. You said it, not me." He taps my forehead. "I'll tell them whatever you want, but if we stay you'll be staying in my room, and I have a feeling West will be able to read into that pretty quickly. We could maybe bribe him to keep Jules in the dark, if you insisted."

I'm laughing at the suggestion as he leans down. And I'm kissing Austin Rutledge once more.

♥

"I am happy," I finally respond to Jules.

Jules nearly knocks me over a second time as she bounces on her toes, clapping her hands before turning and hugging Austin. Little shrieks of "I knew it" giving dog whistles a run for their money.

"That is the most cheerleader-like I have seen you in the six months I've known you," I say.

"I'm just … Ugh, so excited you two finally did something about all that damn sexual tension you had." West snorts and Jules hugs me once again. "Boo, my parents and Jase are waiting for me to get home. I could call, but they're anxious to see us."

I nod. "No way, of course you should go. I get you at school every day."

"Why don't you come with me? I know they'd love to see you."

Thankfully, Austin shoves Jules and steps to my side. "Yeah, not happening," he says without a smile.

"I didn't think so." Jules wags her brows, obviously she only made the suggestion to unsettle Austin. I smile inwardly, happy to know where he stands.

When West returns from dropping Jules off he joins Austin and I in the media room upstairs. Throwing himself on the chaise and stretching out with an exhausted groan.

"I'm under strict orders to not talk about this." His hand waves around as though he's motioning between us even though his eyes are closed. "Until Jules is in the same room."

I'm lying on the couch, a blanket over my legs, my feet across Austin's lap, and a book in hand while he watches the sports channel. His hands massage my feet, occasionally veering up and rubbing my calves or shins. I could get used to this, this peaceful existence we have together. I'm still thinking about that when we climb into bed together for the second time.

"You're not what I expected," I whisper after kissing him goodnight.

"How do you mean?"

"Television and foot rubs. Taco dinners and dance parties. The two of us sitting together quietly."

He frowns. "Obviously, what you're getting now, here, is different from what you will get back on campus, Cassie. That is, if you choose to be with me."

"So parties and girls hitting on you all the time?" Does he know how much the thought of my having to compete with girls like Katie and Jess for his attention bothers me? They are bubbly and fun, and Texas princesses born for the college politics of dating, sororities, and party life. I'm a hides-behind-books-and-keeps-to-self-in-the-library kind of girl. I can work on pulling myself out of my past, but it will take time. Crowds scare me. Trying to pretend I grew up with a normal life scares me.

"I can't change who I am, Cass. I can skip the parties if you want to. I would be happy to spend my free time with you at the house or in my dorm, but I can't stop the girls and fans from popping up. You crave anonymity, and I can't be anonymous."

My hand slides up his chest. "I just want you to be you. I'll figure the rest out."

"I can be the guy who is in love with you. What do you think about that?"

I slip my free arm around his waist, tucking my head into the space between his shoulder and chest. "I think you're crazy and that I have you fooled somehow."

His hand teases the back of my shirt up, his warm fingers skimming over the small of my back. "You're right, I can't possibly fall in love with you until I take you out on a real date." The tips of his fingers play beneath the waist of my leggings. My breathing is shaky at the heat of his skin dipping up and down my sensitive backbone.

"Tomorrow I'm taking you out and then tomorrow night I'll be the guy who tells you he's in love with you."

His words are solemn and true and I hold him tighter.

Tomorrow can't come soon enough.

AUSTIN

The winter sun warms our skin,
but my lungs still burn as the cold air I gasp in and out freezes my airways.
Winter workouts suck, no matter how used to them I think I am.

"I did something stupid," I breathe, swerving around a car parked at the curb, West keeping pace beside me as we jog through the neighborhood early Friday morning.

"And this is a shock?" West teases, pushing the sleeves of his long shirt over his forearms.

I slow enough to regulate my breathing so I can speak in complete sentences. "I'm going to tell you something you can't repeat." West's eyes flash my way. "That means no telling Jules," I clarify.

Our pace slows more as West nods.

"Cassie has an ex who's been harassing her," I lie. I don't want to call Emil her ex; from all indications on her end it wasn't a relationship. It was revenge, it was desperation, and now it's over—at least that's what I'm working on. "It's been over for a while, but the guy calls and emails her. He's threatened her."

West's face darkens. "Is he dangerous, or all talk?"

We're going around the final bend back toward the house so I slow to a walk. Blowing puffs of steam into the air as I cool off. "Honestly, I don't know." My hands go over my head as I stretch out a stitch in my side. Since our Bowl Game before Christmas I've gotten in very few workouts. The coaches are going to give me hell next week when I check in. "That's where the stupid comes in."

West looks less winded, the little shit, as he waits for me to explain.

"I stole her phone last night."

He swears under his breath. "What did you do?"

"He left her a message yesterday. She told me about it. I just wanted to see how many times he's been calling. I checked her texts." My heart rate picks up at the memory of the words I read. "I couldn't stop myself, man."

Cassie shifts next to me, her head turning on her pillow, a heavy sigh leaving her lips as she sleeps. I've been watching her sleep for an hour, unable to relinquish the look on her face when I caught her listening to Emil's voicemail. The fear. The same fear she had six days ago at my door. I hate that fear.

I slip from underneath the covers twenty minutes later, my hand swiping her phone from the floor where it had slipped off the bed earlier after I'd taken it from her hand and tossed it. The house is quiet as I make my way downstairs. I'm just checking the amount of missed calls and texts. Nothing more. For her own safety, that's all.

His number isn't saved in her phone, but the missed calls from one number are a clear indication it's him. Ten calls. Yesterday.

More the day before, and the day before that. I can't check her voicemail; I don't know her password. I click on her messages app and find a litany of texts. I scroll back to the first. To Monday morning. That was the same morning we fought when she asked me to teach her football. Christ, has it really only been four days since then? Did she lock herself in my room and read this message? Alone, scared, and hurt by me? I want to do physical harm to anything or anyone as I read the note:

Cassandra, you have hurt me deeply. Running away, when I only wanted to care for you, my love. I now know I was too hard, I worried about your age, about what the others thought so I hid you away. We can start anew now. Don't keep hurting me this way. Gwen is gone. I only want you. Come back.

I scroll on.

Answer me, Cassandra.
Come home.
Where are you?
I will find you.
It will not be pretty for you if you do not talk to me.
WHO IS HE?? DO NOT PUSH ME. REMEMBER WHAT HAPPENED TO BRIAN.

Shit. It's nearly three in the morning, but I dial anyway as I close myself up in the garage.

"My Cassandra."

His voice is thick with sleep and is heavily accented. The 'r' of Cassandra rolling on his tongue. The tongue I would like to rip out with my bare hands.

"Not likely, asshole. You need to forget this number and leave her alone," I growl, my body coiling tightly, a snake waiting to pounce.

Silence.

"Did you hear me? Leave her alone, she's through with you."

He breathes deeply through his nose. "And who are you?"

"I'm the guy who's going to make sure people like you, like her mother, don't hurt her again."

A breathy chuckle causes me to cringe. "No, I do not think so," *Emil hisses.*

My calm snaps. "She's not alone anymore. You want to play big man and hurt and destroy a tiny girl. You're a fucking sociopath, man. You want a fight, fight me. I'll take you on, leave Cassie out of it."

"A protector? How noble. You will not keep her. She will come back to me. I own Cassandra and I will punish her—"

"Austin Rutledge, asshole. You find me before I find you because if you lay a hand on her, I'll kill you." The phone flies through the air and bounces off a box and crashes to the concrete floor before I realize what I've done.

I gave him my name. My legs give out. Squatting down, I shove my hands through my hair and take deep breaths.

West grabs my elbow, pulling us to a stop. His nose and cheeks are pink, but beneath that flush from the running and cold, he pales. "Austin."

It's a whispered sort of plea, and I feel it. His fear that I've opened a can of worms bigger than I know. I nearly froze my balls off in the garage waiting for my pulse to stop racing before I returned to Cassie. I never slept. This morning she rolled over and touched my back lightly, as though testing if I would wake before she pressed her lips to my shoulder. When I felt the touch I yanked her into my arms, breathing her in, stroking her hair—telling myself it would be fine.

I tug my arm from West's grip. "What's done is done."

"What's done is," he repeats.

I turn to the house and West follows.

"Who the hell is this guy? You goaded him into coming after you."

I keep walking.

"Austin." His yell is loud enough to be heard inside and stops me in my tracks.

"I don't know," I admit. My hands fist at my sides. "I don't know, West. That's why I'm telling you."

"Okay." My little brother walks up the lawn and stands before me. Hell, I've run to my dad and my brother in the span of a week. His palm scrubs over his face before he speaks. "I'm sure it'll be fine. He's probably some riled up douche who gets his jollies off by scaring his ex."

I slap him on the back, giving him a tentative smile as I attempt to agree, and he slings his arm around my shoulders locking my head under his arm. "I've got your back, bro," he teases as we tussle, his fist lightly punching my stomach. I'd laugh, but I keep seeing that one message from Emil—WHO IS HE?? DO NOT PUSH ME. REMEMBER WHAT HAPPENED TO BRIAN.

♥

"This is where West and I had our first date," Jules says over her shoulder as we climb up the narrow staircase of The Coffeehouse.

"Different," Cassie replies.

I smile at her tone. I've been coming here for years. Study nights in high school, before parties, date nights; the place is a staple. Cassie pauses at the top of the stairs and I step up against her back, holding our drinks up. "You gonna clear the steps and let the rest of us up?"

She jolts. "Oh, sorry."

I attempt to see the place with her eyes. Two dimly lit, rustically furnished rooms with some chairs, small end tables, and two threadbare couches scattered about. It is different. No frills or fancy high-tech art and lights.

Jules is already pulling a chair closer to the couch in the room on the right as I nudge Cassie forward.

"You okay?" I ask as she moves with some reluctance.

She looks over her shoulder, her smile bright even though her eyes are clouded over. Her eyelids flutter. "Yes. Yeah, I'm sorry." She looks behind me. "For a moment there, I thought ... that guy in the other room reminded me of him." She lowers her voice.

I tense, my steps slowing as I contemplate backing up and getting a glimpse of someone who had obviously spooked her for a moment. Her hand tugging at my jacket stops me. "I'm fine," she assures me, holding my gaze.

And I'm not. I haven't told her about the call. I'm not sure if I'm going to.

"What else did you two do on your first date?" Cassie asks Jules as I hand her the hot chocolate from my hand once she's settled on the couch.

Jules happily launches into her and West's story. I watch the two talking, taking in the ease in Cassie's body, not for the first time today. She's comfortable with Jules, and that makes me happy. I knew they got along as roommates, Jules had told me as much, but after Cassie blew me off I made it a point to not hang around if we showed at the same place so I haven't seen them together much. Seeing her with a friend, a good friend, gives me a different perspective of her.

She spent the morning in the house with three men, something she told me she's never done. To me it was simple—my brother, my father, and myself. To her it was an act of trust. I move my leg, my thigh touching hers, as I think of the way she opened up as the day went on. By the time Jules arrived after lunch, Cassie was relaxed as we pulled out video games and spent the day having an old school tournament. I shoved the idea of having our first official date tonight on a back shelf when the hunger pains ended our gaming and a trip for burgers was suggested.

West arrives a few minutes later, sitting on the edge of the seat Jules pulled up and leaning over his knees. Cassie and Jules barely break their conversation to acknowledge him.

"Girl chat?" He tips his head toward the girls.

"It would seem so. I tuned them out. What took you so long downstairs?"

"Some kids from school came in," he kicks at my foot. "I told them the famous Austin Rutledge was upstairs so they should be up soon."

"What the hell, man?" I'm straightening and checking over my shoulder before I catch West's chuckle.

"I'm just kidding. They wanted to know about college and asked about you, but I didn't say anything. They play for Rossview."

"Is that strange for you?"

"What?" West asks.

"Having people ask you about football after all these years?" He avoided involvement with the sport for so long after our mother died.

"No, it's the opposite really."

Like Cassie, West has the same happiness about him. After everything over the last year with Jules and the last five with our family, West is back to himself.

"I feel as though people are finally waking up and seeing me. I never stopped being about football, not inside you know?"

I can't stop my frown.

"I guess you do know," West says, keeping his voice low. He has my full attention now. "You don't feel it anymore, do you?"

I look at the girls, still talking animatedly. They're the only two people I've had this discussion with. "Not the way you do, no."

"When are you going to talk with Dad?" That's the million-dollar question. West's eyes go wide. "Dude, you have to declare in what, ten days? I can't believe he hasn't been hitting you up for information already."

"I've been busy," I say as I give Cassie a side glance. "We talked about it while in St. Lucia. I'm not declaring early. I want to finish school."

"And he knows this?"

"He knows it's where I'm leaning. Especially after you signed." I slap his knee. "My baby brother, the JUCO star turned A&M signee. The last few weeks have been a zoo with our bowl game, the wedding, me coming home early—we've hardly talked about you. Are you ready to pull on your jock strap and play with the big boys?"

West laughs as Jules and Cassie's heads snap our way at the word jock strap. "I'm more than ready. You and I, man, one last year on the field together."

"One last year." It feels right when I say it. One last year. Yeah, I'm pretty sure I'll be done with football after that.

"I can't believe I agreed to go for a walk with you, it's freezing out here." Cassie huddles next to me as we walk down the street toward Center City Park, her hands curling around my arm as though she can soak up whatever warmth I have.

"I'm going to tell my dad I'm not entering the draft. I want to finish out senior year."

She slows, and by proximity I do to. "Are you sure? That's a huge decision."

"It's really not. The degree was always supposed to come first. I don't want to play pro."

"Ever?"

I move, tugging my shoulder, and we walk again. "Nope. I'm done."

"Can I ask when this revelation hit you?" She sounds nervous.

"About five minutes ago in the coffee shop. Right after I said jock strap."

She giggles, her hip bumping against my thigh.

"This doesn't have to be my final decision, I could change my mind, but I don't think I will. I really think I'm done playing."

"So you'll become an engineer of something, somewhere?"

"Ha, sure."

She stops again. We're at the intersection across from the park. The green traffic light along with the taillights and headlights of traffic glow in the windows of the shop beside us. The sidewalk is empty, save for us and a few people dashing into a shop a few storefronts back.

"I'm glad you're staying," Cassie says as she stands in front of me. "Is that selfish?"

"It depends." Looking right, I take her shoulders in my hands and angle her toward the buildings next to us. "Why are you glad?" I ask, walking us over until her back hits the brick.

"I just found you."

Jesus, my entire being goes haywire. My heart explodes with feelings I can't contain as I look down at her beautiful face and delicate features. My muscles tense out of desire to protect her. I smell her scent, and my blood rushes, my body wanting to possess her. Her eyes flash as though she reads my mind, *I love you,* she seems to say.

I love you, too.

I brace one arm against the wall over her head and move in. "Cassie, are you ready for this?"

Her lips part. "Are you?"

Her hands grab the lapels of my jacket, pulling me to her mouth as my free hand takes hold of the back of her neck. She tastes like chocolate and snow. Her lips freeze at first touch, then melt beneath mine. Our noses skim, icicles thanks to the brisk air.

Just like that, we've both fallen.

AFTER THE FALL

February

CASSIE

The girls at the table in front of me alert me of his presence before he does.
They love staring at Austin Rutledge.
Too bad for them, he's mine.

"Excuse me, I'm looking for my girlfriend." As usual, his presence swallows me whole as he sneaks up from behind, looming over my chair while I'm studying in the library.

He hovers over me as I tip my head back. "Yeah? Too bad for her you found me instead."

"Too bad, indeed." He cocks a brow, his eyes twinkling. Strong hands shift from the back of my chair to my shoulders as he squats. "I had grand plans for her back in my room, but I guess you'll do."

Warmth spreads throughout my limbs at the suggestive timbre of his words. "I'm a lucky girl."

"Yeah you are, so let's go get lucky." His brows wag suggestively.

Our gazes hold, my face schooled in contemplative flirtation—eyes narrowed, lip between teeth. Lord, he's sexy. I have to remind myself he's mine every time I see him. A thumb presses into the muscle along my neck and shoulder causing me to break into a smile. Austin follows, popping up and pressing a kiss to my lips before sitting next to me and dropping his bag to the floor.

"Hey," he whispers, inching the chair closer.

Shifting back to the open notebook in front of me, I finish the sentence I was writing when he showed up before asking about his day.

"Same as usual. I missed you." I feel the warmth of his hand on the side of my neck where wisps of hair hang loose from my messy braid.

"Our schedules suck this semester."

"Yeah, they do." His chair creaks as he leans closer, his eyes scanning my notebook. "Are you done yet?"

"Do I need to be done, Mr. Rutledge?" I ask, mentally adding the hours of schoolwork I have left. I'm nowhere near done.

"Well," his nose skims my jaw as his lips slide up to my ear, "I wasn't kidding about grand plans." His hot whisper sends shivers over my skin.

Hours with Austin or hours of schoolwork? It should be a no brainer, but ... my hand goes to his chest. "Don't you have a paper due tomorrow?"

He huffs, sinking back in his chair. "I just came out of a study session, Cass. My brain is mush."

"Two hours, then I'm all yours."

"Two?" he repeats, and I flash a coy smile his way. His sigh is audible as he shakes his head and swings his bag up onto the table. "You're such a good girl."

I smirk as he mutters and pulls out work of his own, but I can't help but wonder if it bothers him. Surely he's just playing. He likes my focus and my no partying rule, doesn't he? In the three weeks since we've been back at school and gone public with our relationship we've kept to ourselves.

He turns down invitations to parties, he rarely goes out with the guys, we eat dinner with West, Jeff, and the girls or alone. He's not the Austin Rutledge of six months ago, and judging by the looks I get from some of the sorority girls in my dorm, people have noticed. We've settled into a pattern, similar to Jules and West or Katie and Jeff. A relationship pattern.

Maybe, that's not a good thing. Maybe that's boring.

"You know what?" I slam my book closed, startling him with the sudden movement. "Forget studying, let's go to your dorm."

"Don't have to tell me twice," he winks, helping me stack my notebooks and folders together and loading them in my bag.

Austin's fingers wrap around mine as we leave the warmth of Evans for the frosty air outside. It takes only moments for the wind to steal my breath, and I tug the hood of my jacket over my head. "I'm so ready for spring," I complain, sidling up to his side.

He immediately wraps me under his arm, shielding my left side from the wind. "Me too. We'll go to the beach."

"The beach, really?"

"Spring break, if you want." We pick up the pace as a bitter cold gust howls its way between the buildings. "We could go to the beach house. I might even let you convince me to go out on the boat for a day."

"And what about *Jaws*?"

His arm tightens around my shoulders. "They killed her, remember? I think we're safe."

"Wait, *Jaws* was a her?"

"Seriously, Cass?"

"Like I'm supposed to know that? How can you even tell?"

Austin laughs, mumbling about my lack of cinematic knowledge as all around us trees crack and sway in the wind. A gust swirls between two buildings as we take a shortcut and my hood slips off, exposing me to the elements and causing my eyes to water in the brisk air.

"Wow! It's freezing," I gasp, bending at the waist as I reach back for my hood.

"Let's run." Austin grabs my hand, and we take off.

We sprint the remainder of the way to his door, my ears stinging and my nose running as we enter his room. He keeps his dorm cooler than I prefer, but it's still warmer than the freezer outside. The moment he locks the door behind me he's cranking the heat on for me.

"I hope those plans you have call for us snuggling up in bed, because I'm frozen," I laugh, already throwing myself into his unmade bed after shrugging out of my jacket and boots. "Where's my blanket?"

"You mean *my* blanket?" He eyes me, kicking his shoes off. "It's in my chair where it belongs."

Dang it. I'd jumped in bed without grabbing my—his—favorite blue fuzzy. I wiggle my fingers, reaching for it silently even as I continue to fix his sheet and thin comforter over my body.

"Are you asking for this?" Austin asks, flinging the blanket around his shoulders.

I plaster a puppy dog pout on him.

"Oh, you *are* asking for this," he grins, pulling the blanket tighter. "So, we seem to find ourselves in a little situation I like to call 'supply and demand.' How badly do you need this blanket, Elmer?"

I smooth the frown wrinkling my forehead. Damn him and his Elmer jokes. "I need it. Your bed is always so cold."

Austin's face withdraws. "Like hell it is."

Twisting to my side, I prop my head up. "It is when you're not in it."

The tip of his tongue darts out and runs across his lips quickly. "And now I have more supplies to offer you. How badly do you want them?" The honey dripping from his voice curls my toes.

"How bad do you want what's in your bed, hotshot?" The subtle twitch in his pants answers my question, and my lips stretch ever so slowly into a smile as I point out the obvious. "Now it seems as though we have ourselves a problem."

He cocks his head.

"You have the ability to slide up in here and warm me up." My brows lift as I drop my tone deeper. "Something I want really, really badly. And once warm, I have something I assume you want pretty badly yourself. Or maybe not," I shrug, my head falling onto the pillow as I pout.

Blue fuzzy wings attack me as Austin's heavy body jumps onto the bed and smothers me. Our heads end up beneath the blanket, his face nudging my chin out of his way.

"Or maybe not, my ass." His breath blows across my neck as his lips kiss the exact spot where my pulse is surely leaping beneath my skin.

"Get under here then."

He strips the sheets and comforter down, crawling back on top of me before my body has time to register the loss of his weight. We tilt sideways, as we always do when we're lying in bed together—thanks to his fear of crushing me. If only he knew how steadying his body feels against mine. How his weight holds the demons of my past back. His slow tenderness—

"I want you so much, Cass." Warm lips tickle the hollow of my throat. "So, so much."

The affectionate words blot out all other thoughts. We've played this game for weeks now. Frantic kissing, frenzied touching, fractured breathing. Our bodies writhing against one another, begging for a release that neither of us has given into. Yet.

My fingers grasp at the back of his head, tugging him away from my skin. "Are you happy?" I ask.

His thumb runs across my bottom lip, the salty taste of his skin lingering along the trail his touch leaves. "Are you serious?" he counters, his eyes scanning my face. My eyes are very serious.

"Cass," he groans as my fingers release his hair and he presses himself up and away from me on one arm. "Am I happy? What do you mean? With you? With life?"

I try to maintain eye contact, but suddenly the question feels stupid and fear creeps in.

"Don't," he says roughly, his palm sliding tenderly over my jaw and turning my face toward his. "Ask whatever you want. Don't let the past belittle your feelings. Remember?"

"I never should have told you about my counseling sessions," I jest as I blink away the murky shadows of fear, but Austin doesn't grin back.

"Yes, you should have. Now tell me what's wrong. Do you really have to ask how I feel? I'm doing a terrible job at being your boyfriend if you don't know."

"No." I push myself into a sitting position. I'd hate for him to think I'm unhappy with him in any way. "I let my stupid thoughts run wild. I just—sometimes I have a hard time believing you are happy to be with me."

He scowls. "You say that like there's something wrong with you. How could I not be happy with you? I think the better question is how could you be happy with me."

I roll my eyes at the absurdity. "Now you're just humoring me."

"Am I?" He sits up and faces me, slipping one leg between my hip and the wall, scissoring our legs so I'm nearly straddling his lap. "Cassie, you are smart, and funny, and beautiful. You are a survivor, a strong woman who can do anything. You know what you want and you're focused on it one hundred percent." His mouth twists into a grin. "Well, you were until I forced my way into your life.

"Who am I? A football player. The son of a football player. You look at me and wonder how I can choose to be with you? I look at you and think how can I ever live up to what you deserve?"

"That is absurd," I say slowly, punctuating each word as I wiggle my way closer to him. My hands move to his sides, my fingers prying up the thermal shirt he's wearing so my eyes can feast upon his muscled abs. His skin leaps at my touch, goosebumps breaking out as his arms lift and I pull the shirt over his head. My breath catches, as it always does when I see him shirtless. "Everything you are is perfect for me," I assure him.

His hands climb up my thighs, gripping my hips and hauling me even closer until I'm wrapping my legs around his back and my chest is touching his. Kissing his shoulder, I slip my hands up his neck and press my forehead to his.

"Football is what you do, not who you are, Austin."

His mouth crushes down on mine as his hand splays over my backside. I squeeze my thighs around his waist in an attempt to get closer. I need to be closer. Our mouths play, tongues teasing, teeth tugging. *Closer,* my body screams. My nails dig into his shoulders, his skin warm under my assault. His scent fills my nostrils; the hungry little sounds he makes in the back of his throat tickle my ears.

"I want you," I groan against his lips. "Please."

The air is sucked from my mouth as he inhales sharply. His right hand bunches the back of my shirt and pulls it up. His arms go behind his back, his hands unclasping my legs and pitching me backward as he shifts. My head hits the pillow, the loss of his heat instantly chilling my skin. When I open my eyes I find him on his knees between my thighs, his brown eyes staring. Burning.

I'm burning.

"Tell me to stop at any time."

I feel my head shake, as if on reflex. "We're not stopping," my voice trembles. "Not this time."

He gives a half smile, his brows rising as my finger catches a belt loop and wrenches him forward. His arms brace on either side of my head as he swoops down, kissing me. The position allows me to explore his naked torso, my fingers playing along the hard muscles built by years of football. He presses himself against me, my hips rising up to meet his every time he pulls back. I lift a leg over the back of his thigh, attempting to pull him down to close the distance between our skin, but he doesn't relent. I raise my head, lifting to meet his kisses again and again, my skin searching for his.

"Austin," I beg, licking his lips as they tease mine.

"I love your mouth," he breathes. "I could kiss you forever. These lips —" he sucks my bottom lip into his mouth. "You win so many points for these lips."

I turn my head, laughter bubbling up. He simply redirects his mouth to my jaw, sucking at my skin as he continues down my neck. "Are we keeping score now?" I ask on a moan as he sucks the skin below my chin.

"I've been keeping score for a while." He lifts one arm and rolls off me, sinking down by my side. "This," he says as his pointer finger traces over my collarbone, "is an extra point. And down here? Another one." He trails over my breastbone, over the peaks and valleys of my chest, and down my stomach, playfully adding points for each spot he deems worthy. My neck, he says, dipping low and breathing in against my skin before pressing his lips and tongue below my ear, earns a field goal.

"Three points, really?" My fingers curl into the sheets at the suction his mouth creates.

"Oh yeah, I feel the surge of your pulse when I kiss you there, and your scent," he growls, his gaze sticking on me, "I get hard thinking about it."

I shift slightly, my thigh slipping between his legs. "You were already hard," I remind him, my thigh rubbing the proof gently. "Is this the touchdown?" My fingers snap the button of his jeans, tugging at the zipper. His eyelids flutter as I work the opening of his pants.

"No, little one," his hand touches over the heat between my legs. "This is the Super Bowl. Calling you mine was the touchdown."

"The Super Bowl, huh?" My palm touches his flesh. Hard, ready. His breath catches. "Are you ready to play?"

"Hell yeah, I'm ready." His mouth descends to my chest, his teeth grazing my breast through my thin bra as my back arches. My stomach twists as his hand matches mine, delving beneath my clothing.

I close my eyes at the touch. And I wait. I wait for Randy's voice, for the gleam of the pirate's earring, the husky scent of Hector, the forcefulness of Simon, the lies of Emil—I wait for the splash of cold water to freeze me and send me to where nothing matters.

But it doesn't come.

My body remains present. My mind remains present. My heart remains present—pounding beneath the skin Austin's lips are so very skillfully tasting.

I'm free. Every touch, every thrust, every claim his hands, mouth, and body make upon me, I surrender willingly. Happily. With complete and total trust. And love.

When the fire we've built consumes me whole, tearing through my veins until I'm shaking and biting my lip to keep from screaming, I cry.

AUSTIN

I can't breathe.
Haven't been able to since the moment her hand palmed me.
I've claimed to love a handful of girls in my life, but only one slept with me.
Well, two now.
As I hover over Cassie, our bodies still joined, I'm certain I've only truly loved one girl.

And she's crying beneath me, her red, sweat-dampened face turned away from mine. My first instinct is to jump off her, to ask her what's wrong. Then I remember my father's words. *You'll say and do the right thing.*

My body, nowhere near finished with her yet, remains buried within as I push my chest a few inches off hers. I press a kiss over her heart, then move to her face, kissing her jaw. "Cass?"

Nails dig into my ass. Her thighs, slick with sweat and us, lift an inch—bringing me deeper—reflex or want? She inhales deeply, her bottom lip trembling as she turns her head back to face me.

The fine baby hairs around her forehead are soaked, plastered to her flushed skin. Her dark hair is a fan of silk spread over my pillows. My hips press closer—instinct, lust, and pure need coursing through me, even after one climax.

"I've never—that was—" she fumbles her words, a wide smile on her face as tears sparkle in her eyes.

"Amazing? Earth shattering? Incomparable?" I supply the synonyms for her.

"Perfection," she whispers, brushing her hair back.

The vise holding my heart hostage loosens at her smile and words. I lower back to my elbows, happy to have her satiny skin warming mine once more. Our mouths are inches apart, the little puffs of air she breathes as she attempts to calm her lungs flowing over my face. "Perfection makes you cry?"

"Apparently," she snorts.

I kiss her, dropping from my elbows and allowing my full weight to press her body into my bed, then rolling us onto our sides, arms adjusting, her leg going over mine.

"Well, hello," she chuckles as we shift. Proof that I'm ready for round two springs to life as my hips rock against hers.

"Can I give you perfection again?" I ask, my body already moving within hers.

"And again, and again."

"That was some Super Bowl," Cassie giggles, closing and locking my shared bathroom door. She's pulled on my football tee and nothing else. Her hair is a sex goddess mess, and my boxers grow tight again as I look at her. Damn, my desire for her is insatiable.

"What do we do for halftime?" I ask, my eyes staring at her shapely legs as she returns to my bed.

Climbing beneath the blankets, she snuggles up next to me. "Sleep?"

"Not as exciting as the televised ones, but I guess it'll do." I settle my arms around her shoulders as she nestles her head against my side.

We lapse into silence with only a desk lamp for light and the muffled sounds of the occupants on either side of my dorm. Cassie's restless, some part of her—her fingers or hand—moving in circles over my abs, ribs, and chest constantly.

"I don't know how to do this part."

Her hand stills. "This part?"

I probably should have kept my mouth closed. I'm exhausted as hell and could be asleep in less than a minute, but her hand fidgeting over my skin makes me think there's something on her mind.

"The after part." This kiss-and-cuddle, whispering-sweet-nothings, declarations-of-love part. I've never done this part. Not in that way.

She rolls her head on my chest, her chin jabbing me as she looks up. "Are you saying you want me to leave?"

"What? God, no. You're not going anywhere. I just don't know what to do now." I laugh at my stupidity. I feel like it's my first time. This is awkward as shit. "I don't want to fall asleep and have you angry at me, and I don't want to launch into some dissertation about how amazing and wonderful you are like some chick flick—not that you're not wonderful."

"Austin." Cassie sits up. "Quit digging yourself a hole."

"Who the hell am I right now?" I groan, slapping my forehead in utter disgust.

Her famous Elmer giggle rolls from her lips, so I attack. My arm shoots out, grabbing her shirt and pulling her back to the bed as I flip from my back to my knees. Once I'm straddling her hips with her arms pinned over her head, I study her glowing face.

From the fair freckles sprinkling over her nose, to the tiny crease along her cheek to the right of her mouth, this girl is perfection. The scar at the edge of her dark brow, the curling of the fine hairs at her temple, the minuscule flecks of gold in the eyes staring back at me, the way her body feels beneath mine, the soft curves of her breasts, the warmth of her bare thigh pressed against mine …

Jesus.

"I love you, Cass," I blurt out, my fingers weaving in-between hers. "I'm in love with you."

"Is this the post-climax satisfaction talking?" There's a spark of humor in her eyes and a tad of curiosity in her tone.

I should have said it before sex. I haven't told her how I feel since I learned the truth about her past. She shouldn't have to wonder. She shouldn't have to ask me if I'm happy. I imagine her childhood keeps her doubts at the forefront of her mind, no matter what I do. I'll try harder.

"No, this is the guy who's madly in love with his girlfriend talking. The dip shit who should have made sure you knew before now."

She breathes through her nose, so deeply I feel her chest rise beneath me as her left hand loosens from mine and goes to my ribcage. The soft touch of her fingertips tickling my skin.

"So, this is what it feels like?" She speaks softly. "I have to admit, I was trying my hardest not to fall, to not want this—you—so much."

I get it, I get her. "I didn't know I could want you like this. I didn't know I could want anything like this," I tell her, worried about sounding like a lovesick lead from a romantic movie.

"I'm scared," she breathes her confession. "You know all my sad stories. You have the ability to destroy me."

"Cass—" I release her right hand, moving to cup her face.

Her arms wind around my back. "I'm not saying you will, I'm just saying you could."

"I won't," I promise.

"I lied before," her voice full of apprehension. "I think this is my favorite place. Here in this room with you."

My eyes flick to my alarm clock. "It won't be your favorite in a few hours when my alarm's going off," I point out, pressing a kiss to her lips.

"Five, right?" she asks, all but groaning.

"Yep." Winter conditioning. The football equivalent of hell week, only it's a month. Early morning work outs on a frozen field with the entire team. The fact that I'm still awake and coherent testifies to Cassie's appeal. Tomorrow, though, I'll be hurting.

As though she can read my mind, her hands run up my spine, pressing my shoulders down toward her body and kissing me. "Enough talking. You need sleep."

"I won't argue with that," I agree. "Think we could pick this up tomorrow? Same place, earlier time?" I ask as I slide off her.

"I think I could be persuaded." Her lips touch the tip of my nose before she turns and snuggles her backside into my chest.

"I will be happy to work on that," I yawn, falling asleep with a smile on my face and my girl in my arms.

CASSIE

I'm happily exhausted.
So happy, even Austin's 5 AM alarm couldn't dampen my spirits.

"What's your favorite flower?" Jules drops her backpack at her feet and takes the seat across from me.

"Who's asking?" I smile over my soup as she shrugs with a knowing grin.

My mind goes to this morning. To the light kiss pressed against my forehead as Austin snuck out of his room for practice before dawn. To the note he left me.

If I spent the rest of my nights like last night, I could die a happy man.
Stay as long as you want. I'll text you later.

I've been floating through my day. His short and sweet between-class texts fueling me through my grueling schedule. "Tell him I don't need flowers."

Jules laughs as though I've said the stupidest thing ever. "Cassie, he's a Rutledge, they excel at romance."

"So I'm learning." My cheeks flame.

"Learning, learning?" Jules probes, a knowing gleam in her light eyes.

I'm not answering that question. I'm sure she'll figure out the answer without my confirmation quickly enough.

"Let him spoil you, it's what he wants."

I sigh a hefty sigh. Favorite flower? I have no idea. No, that's not true. "Snapdragons."

"Snapdragons?"

"Yeah," I grab my cell from the table and pull up an image. "The botanical garden in Dallas has them. They're cool. See the little face?"

Recognition dawns on Jules's face. "They look like little fairies."

"Right? I could totally see them sprouting wings and granting wishes."

"Snapdragons, it is," she says, handing my cell back. "So, how's it going with you two?"

"How long have you been wanting to ask me that?" I can't stop myself from chuckling at her eager eyes.

"Since the day we came home from St. Lucia and found you two at the house."

"Impressive." I check my phone for the time. My break's about over; time to head to my third class of the day. "Thanks for not prying, Jules. I know how much you care about him. I appreciate it."

"About him? About you both," she says meaningfully, her hand reaching across the table as I pile my trash on my lunch tray. The sentiment causes me to pause.

"I know I'm not the most open person in the world. You, Katie, and Jess have made me feel like family from day one. You don't know how much that means to me."

"Hey, you listened to me more than once when I was a mess. No thanks necessary, it's what friends do."

She walks with me to drop off my trash, and her comment spurs me to admit the one thing bothering me about last night. "He told me he loves me."

Jules's eyes light up. "Then he does, trust me."

"I feel like such an idiot."

"Why?"

I freeze at the question. Jules doesn't know about my background; she doesn't understand what a big step being with Austin is. I watch as the protective sister comes alive in Jules. The happy light from a moment ago turning darker. She grips my arm, pulling me to the side out of the flow of students entering and exiting the commons.

"You don't doubt his feelings do you? I promise you he wouldn't say it if he didn't mean it." The suspicious way she's studying me tells me where I stand if I hurt Austin. I should be angry at her lack of confidence in me, but how can I be? She's protecting someone special to her. Who would protect me if he did something to hurt me? The thought scares me. I've been broken too many times. I've been hurt, but my heart was never in the game. Until now.

"No, of course I believe him." I reply, and Jules releases a held breath. "I was merely going to say that when he told me he loved me, I didn't say it back. I hate that I didn't. Only two other people have claimed to love me in my life, and neither meant it. Not the way Austin does. It's not hard to tell the difference between a person using you for sport and a person who doesn't have a choice in the matter."

Jules eyes soften at my explanation. "Cassie."

I shrug, pushing away the sympathy in her voice as she says my name. "He loves me," I smile. "And I love him. I've never loved anyone. Ever."

"It's scary isn't it?" Her shoulder knocks into mine. "I dated my last boyfriend for almost two years before West and I were thrown together. I thought I knew what love was, but I was clueless."

"Can I tell you something?" Jules nods and I lead us out of the building into the wintery sunlight. "Something you won't tell Austin. Or West."

Her tapered nail draws a cross over her heart.

"There's a very small part of me that understands my mother now." Jules's expression is confused. "She did a lot of things through the years to keep certain men in her life. I kind of get that. Not that I would stoop to the levels she did, but the way I feel when I'm with Austin—" I let the thought linger between us. I'm relatively sure Jules knows what I mean. She's been through hell and back with West, and I'm imagine she would do just about anything for him.

"You know that's the great thing about love though, don't you?"

"What?"

"You love him enough to do anything for him, and he loves you enough right back to make sure you don't have to." Her stare is pointed as she teaches me a well-deserved lesson. "True love is give and take on both sides."

"Do you think it's too soon?" The question has plagued me since the day he gave me the Dr. Seuss book. The day he broke the glass case around my heart.

She shakes her head. "To be in love with him? I don't think so, but then again you're talking to a girl who fell in love in a week."

"Jules, it's a feeling deep within my gut. The realization that I've found something—someone I never want to let go of. You know I wasn't looking for it, yet it found me."

"I think you two are perfect together. He really needed someone to knock him off his football star pedestal and challenge him. You do that."

I check the time again. "Shoot, I'm going to be late if I don't hurry." I wrap her in a tight hug, something I'm getting better at the more I do it. Falling in love, finding good friends, learning to trust others—my life has changed so much in six months. "Thanks for listening."

"Of course," she waves my thanks away, as though I'm silly for offering it. "The boy adores you, Cassie. West and Carson are having a field day giving him hell about it. I don't think anyone expected it to happen anytime soon. I'm just happy you're both happy."

I can't tame the smile on my face for the remainder of the day. Everything Jules said, the things Austin did the night before, the way my heart leaps in my chest each time I see a tall frame across campus—I'm on cloud nine.

When I find an arrangement of snapdragons waiting outside the door to our dorm a few hours later, I'm floored. There's no card attached to the vase overflowing with pink and red flowers, though, which feels odd. I would expect Austin to leave a note, like the one he left me in his room this morning.

"Hey, beautiful," he answers his phone when I call him after entering my room and setting the flowers on my desk.

The sound of his voice automatically sets a grin on my face. "Hi."

"I've only got a sec; we're heading into a positions meeting with Coach. What's up?"

"I just got back to my room," I hint, but he doesn't take the bait. "Would you believe I found a flower-filled vase at my door with no card? You wouldn't know anything about that, would you?"

"Flowers?" he asks, his voice muffled by the noise around him. "Wait, are they for you? Did—" he cuts off and I hear a mumble through the line. "Hold on," he says after a second.

"Austin?"

There's an echoing click of a heavy door, and I picture Austin stepping outside in an attempt to get away from his teammates. "Cass, I didn't send you flowers."

Of course he did. "They're snapdragons."

"Snapdragons?" he repeats. The tone of his voice sets off warning bells and I wish I could see his face.

"Austin, you had Jules ask me my favorite flowers at lunch. I told her snapdragons."

A deep inhale reaches me. "I asked her to find out, discretely I might add, but I haven't spoken to her yet this afternoon. You told her snapdragons?"

"Yeah."

"And now you have snapdragons at your door?"

"Yeah," I sigh. What type of game is he playing? "You're joking, right? Just tell me you sent them. They're beautiful."

Silence hangs between us for a beat too long. "Fine. I sent them. I guess it was pretty obvious, huh?" His voice sounds forced. Why would he tease me about sending them when it's clear it was him? He clears his throat. "I was going to wait and surprise you, but I couldn't help myself."

"They're gorgeous, Austin. Thank you."

"Thank me in person?" He lowers his voice suggestively, and every place he touched me last night tingles.

"Over dinner?" I clarify.

"Over dinner, over studying, all night?" It's my turn to inhale deeply. I have to study and work on a paper tonight. He is well aware of this.

"Come to my room, please? I've got a shit load of reading to do."

"Then let's go to the library after dinner and study together, like we always do," I suggest in an attempt to remain the responsible student I've always been.

"My room."

"Austin."

"Elmer." He duplicates my warning tone. Out of habit, my fingers touch my forehead. Each time he calls me Elmer I can't help but feel for the wrinkles he swears I make, and I'll be damned if he's always right. I smooth my features as though he can see me through the phone.

"If I come to your room we won't get work done," I point out the obvious.

"Sure we will. I'll be on my best behavior." I picture him making a sweet begging face on the other end of the line. "C'mon, Cass. I want you to myself tonight."

"I can't say no to that voice," I admit, my body sparking to life. I want to grab him and kiss him right now. His scent fills my nostrils by memory and my hands itch to hold him close.

"I'll stop by your room to pick you up in two hours?" I swear he's smiling.

"Why don't I meet you at your dorm? I can get some work done in the library—"

"No. Stay there, I want to see the flowers," he interrupts. "I'll take you to dinner, then back to my dorm. Okay?"

"Okay. Two hours."

"Hey, Cass," he says as I'm about to hang up. "Plan on spending the night."

"Oh, you better believe it," I agree as we end the call.

Two hours. Time to kick my studies into high gear. The more work I do now, the more time I have to play I have later. And I need me some play time.

AUSTIN

Snapdragons.
I've spend the last month thinking her past is behind us.
One mention of flowers reminds me it might not be.

I text Jules. Who would have sent Cassie the exact flowers she said were her favorites not two hours after she said it? In the month since we've been an official couple and I spoke to Emil, things have been quiet. We traded out her phone for a new one. She promised to never check or respond to her old email account, and we've moved forward. I didn't tell her about my call with him; there was no need to worry her.

When Jules replies, swearing she didn't say anything to anyone about the flower and that they had the conversation in the commons, I'm not sure what to think. I pull West to the side after our meetings.

"They were surrounded by students in the commons. Maybe someone thought it would be funny to screw with you, or her," West offers, attempting some explanation to ease my worry.

"You realize that's a lame ass excuse, right?"

"Yeah, but the only explanation isn't one you want to consider, Austin."

I pull my hoodie over my head, more than eager to get to Cassie's side. "Do you think he's been searching for her all this time?"

West's face says he does even as his words try to tone down my worry. "We don't know what he is capable of. From what you've said, and haven't said, he isn't a good man. He was obsessed with her, right?" I nod, and West continues. "Let's figure out where the flowers came from and see if we can find out who sent them then."

"I don't want her to know." I agree with doing some investigating, but I don't want Cassie frightened. Not now when she's finally feeling safe and opening up to people.

"Austin?"

"I don't want her to know. Not yet, it could be nothing." I'm not arguing this point.

"And if it's not?"

"Then we'll deal with it."

West and I make a few inquiries as we enter Ward Hall, checking with some of the students hanging in the commons and the RA for both floors. No one noticed Cassie's flowers delivered. Nor have they noticed anyone suspicious or unusual hanging around. Certainly not an older guy. West says he'll talk with Jules about keeping an eye open while I head to Cassie's room.

"You're late," Cassie says the moment she opens the door with her hand plopped at her hip, her glasses sliding down the bridge of her perfect little nose.

"I know, I'm sorry." I swoop in, my hands sinking into her hair and my mouth covering hers before her smile can fade. "Let me make it up to you," I offer against her lips, my tongue getting a taste of the Skittles she's been eating.

Her fingers splay across my back, holding me close. This is heaven. Being in her arms, kissing her, loving her. How in the hell did I end up winning her trust? How did I end up this lucky? My tongue rubs against her and I hum in approval before pulling back. "Taste the rainbow, huh?"

She moves away, grinning up at me like the cat who ate the canary. "You were late, I was hungry."

I press a kiss to her forehead and step further into her room. "So, dinner then studying. Got it. Did you pack something to spend the night?"

She bites her lip. "You were serious?"

"Are you really asking me that?" I study the flowers I supposedly sent from across her room.

Cassie lifts her shoulders. "I wasn't sure if you wanted me to actually pack anything. I didn't know it was a full-fledged sleepover."

"You sound unsure. You don't have to stay the night if you don't want." I study her. She's come such a long way from the girl who jumped and ran from me the first time we spoke. Right now, though, she reminds me a bit of that girl. Like she's questioning my intentions or her place. "Cass?"

"You're asking me to stay the night with you. To pack clothing and sleep at your place." She says the words slowly, as though she's giving me time to rethink the request.

"It wouldn't be the first time."

"I know, but the other times were unplanned. We fell asleep watching movies or cuddling. You didn't ask me to stay with you."

I turn from the flowers, giving her my full attention. "Let me clarify this right now. You are more than welcome to stay with me every night. I don't have to ask, okay? Hell, I'll give you a drawer and buy you a toothbrush."

She shakes her head, laughing. "I'm sure Trent and Brice will love that. Having a girl hog their bathroom each morning."

I could care less what my suitemates think, but she has a point. Plus, I'd rather they not get the chance to ogle my girlfriend every morning. "So, let's stay at the house."

Her brown eyes go wide. *Too soon?*

She turns her back to me, running her fingers through her hair as she begins rummaging through her closet. *Yep, too soon.*

"Hey, remember how I told you I wanted to move into the house full time once Mindy and Carson found a place? Nothing's changed with that plan, Cass. Except for you." I shove my hands into my pockets. "I love being with you whenever I can be. I'd love for you to stay with me whenever you choose, that's all. No pressure."

"No pressure," she nods, speaking over her shoulder as she folds some clothing into a small bag.

I take the opportunity to check over the flower arrangement when she goes into her bathroom to grab her essentials. Plain vase, no markings or stickers anywhere to be found. No way to track where the flowers came from.

Arms slip around my waist from behind, her hands sliding into the pocket of my hoodie. "You didn't send them, did you?"

I weigh my answer carefully. "I didn't."

Cassie releases a deep breath, her face pressing against my back as she strengthens her hold around me. "There's a guy," she starts, and I stiffen. "He's been hanging around me a lot lately. In the library, the commons, I've seen him around here."

"Wait. What?" I pull her hands from my pockets and unwrap her from my middle, turning to face with her.

"He seemed innocent enough. We've exchanged smiles, or a passing hello."

"How long?" I ask.

"How long?" she repeats slowly.

"Yes, how long. How long has this guy been hanging around you?" The words come out more forceful than intended and Cassie frowns.

"Maybe three weeks. I didn't think anything of it, but…"

But, if she's getting flowers from a stranger … "Was he there today, do you remember seeing him?"

"He was." I'm not sure if I should be relieved that Emil is most likely not behind the flowers or jealous that some random guy is. She touches her fingertips to my jaw, her eyes softening. "You acted so strange on the phone earlier, telling me it wasn't you then admitting it was. It didn't add up. Then I remembered him. He sat at the table next to us. He doesn't particularly try to hide his interest in me when I see him. Like I said, he smiles and nods. We've never spoken though, not more than a hi."

"And you didn't think to tell me about some dude stalking you?" I'm dumbstruck at her comfort level now.

"Considering it wasn't that long ago when you were doing the same thing?" she chuckles, but I'm not amused. Do I need to worry about Emil and this mysterious guy, too?

Her smile fades, "He's not stalking me."

"No? Three weeks and he's following you around campus? He's obviously decided to step things up if he's sending you flowers. I want to talk to him." I step back, picking up the bag Cassie placed on the floor when she hugged me.

"You're not talking to him." She shakes her head firmly.

"Like hell I'm not. I'll be nice, I just want to make sure he takes a step back. No one should send you flowers but me." I hold her bag up for her in an attempt to end the discussion. "Are you ready to go?"

"You're so bossy, you know that?" She takes the bag, pushing at me with a smile. "I might point the guy out next time we go to the library. If you promise to behave yourself."

"I make no promises," I reply, only half joking, and she groans. "Let's eat, I'm starving for dessert."

"You mean for dinner," she clarifies, locking the door as we exit.

Leaning over her back, I burying my face in the hair by her neck. "Nope, I mean dessert. I'll bend to your request for dinner and studying time first, but at some point tonight, this man is getting some dessert."

"Really, Rutledge? What type of dessert would you say I am?"

I weave my fingers between hers, bypassing the elevators for the stairs. "That is a very good question. I think I'd have to say apple pie. You're sweet and classic with just the right zing of tart to make my mouth sing."

Cassie stops mid-step and melts into loud giggles. They echo off the walls and up and down the staircase, filling the well with her musical Elmer laughter and making my smile twice as large. "You've rehearsed that, haven't you?"

"Rehearsed? No, are you accusing me of using lines on you?" I ask in disgust. Of course I'm not about to tell her I spent months wishing she were mine, dreaming about her, and comparing her to all manners of things. She's my apple pie, my velvet blanket, and my catchy one-hit wonder pop song all rolled into one. I could probably write a few country hits about her at this point.

"What am I going to do with you?" she asks with a shake of her head, turning and taking a step before my hand tugs her back.

"Love me?" I shouldn't have said it, but I want so badly to hear the words come from her lips. To know I'm not the only one so far gone.

She takes a step up. And then another one and another until she's almost eye to eye with me. "As we've said, I don't think I have much of a choice in the matter."

It's almost an admission. It's good enough for now. Pressing a quick kiss to her lips, I take her hand once more and we hurry down the stairs to the parking lot where my car is.

♥

"No one has ever touched me the way you do," she sighs, flexing her foot as my thumbs stoke the arch.

Her confession isn't meant to be sad, but I cringe anyway as my hand runs under the hem of her pant leg, kneading her calf as far as I can reach then returning back to her heel and her toes. Up and down, up and down, anything to touch her. After dinner she made me promise to be on my best behavior so she could work on an assignment. It's proving to be a difficult promise to keep. Especially when she releases those little purrs of hers. My blood sings as she groans. I lift her leg from my lap, raising her ankle to my lips and pressing a kiss to it. "He didn't show you affection?"

I want to cut my tongue off for asking such a ridiculous and prying question. For her part, Cassie merely lifts her eyes, holding my gaze as she slowly closes the lid to her laptop. Her lips thin out, her throat bobbing as she swallows.

"No."

Her tone unreadable, I press for more. The constant memory of my conversation with Emil making my curiosity bloom.

"You lived with him for, what, six months? He chose to let you stay with him, and yet he was—" I don't have a word to describe him because she hasn't given me enough information about their relationship to form an opinion. Unless 'sadistic asshole' suffices.

"Possessive," she supplies. That makes sense. Memories come back. The words she cried into my arms the night she answered his call at the house, *"... I don't know what he'll do. He heard you."*

She bristles, shaking off whatever shadow speaking of the man casts over her, rallying her emotions before sending me a smile. "My point is, I like the way you touch me." She winks and I grin in return.

My hands tighten around her ankles and I yank, pulling her from where she's leaning her back against the wall to having her back flat on my bed. It takes me only a moment to crawl between her legs and up over her body. Carefully, I remove her laptop from where she's gripping it to her lap and set it on the floor next to the bed. Sitting on my haunches, my fingers go to the buttons on her shirt.

"Do you?" I ask. She nods, excitement lighting up those eyes of hers. "It must be your lucky day then, because I'm going to touch you right now." Cassie's tongue peeks out, wetting her bottom lip, and the little devil inside me grins at the wickedness in the curve of the smile she wears.

Popping button after button of her shirt, I spread the fabric wide, my eyes feasting on her creamy skin, and the lace edging of a bra I can barely see as I lean down and kiss her abs. She sucks in a breath.

"I'm going to worship you, Cass." I unbutton more. "I'm going to love your body the way you deserve."

My tongue traces her clavicle before I nip at her warm skin, while my fingers push her shirt open and over her shoulders. She shifts, lifting her back from the bed as I remove the shirt and throw it on the floor. Her hands reach for me, but I press them back to the bed, my fingers encircling her wrists—placing them on either side of her head. "No touching."

Cassie grumbles.

I put myself to work. My mouth, tongue, and teeth nipping, licking, or sucking their way along the exposed skin of her neck and arms. My nose teases across the swells of her breasts, inhaling her warm skin.

Everything about this moment with Cassie is different. With Lauren I was young and horny; foreplay wasn't in my playbook. With the other girls I've been with—the one-night stands brought back to my room after a party—they were used to scratch itches. Sex. Nothing more.

With Cassie, I want to memorize everything.

I roll her over, straddling her hips and releasing her arms so I can massage her back.

"That is perfection," she moans as my hands rub circles along her shoulders and neck.

"Your neck is knotted." My thumb digs into the lump of tense muscles along her trapezius muscle.

"Those are some sexy foreplay words you've got there," she jests before moaning as I apply more pressure. Her head turns on my pillow. "If engineering doesn't work out for you, rest assured you can totally be a massage therapist."

"Good to know." Sliding lower over her body, I lean down, kissing her shoulder and brushing my lips against her ear. "By the way, we need to hit up a party Friday."

"We?" she asks as my lips close on her ear lobe.

"Yes, we." I press my chest against her back, dragging my mouth from her ear, across her cheek to the edge of her lips. She turns her face my way to kiss me back. "It's just one little party."

"You're trying to seduce me into saying yes, aren't you?" she asks as my fingers unhook her bra.

"Is it working?"

She wiggles, turning her body underneath mine as her hands go to my shirt. "I'll let you know when we're finished," she smiles.

All intentions of going slow walk out the door, and when we collapse in a sweaty mess, both of us gasping for air, our hearts racing, she agrees to the party.

CASSIE

*I swore I'd never let a guy dictate my life.
So why can I not get through one day without Austin Rutledge?*

Austin: Are you sure you don't want help studying?

How many messages can one guy send? Digging in my backpack for some study snacks, I tap out a quick reply.

Cassie: We had a deal, Seuss.
Austin: What if I show up unexpectedly?
Cassie: Well now it wouldn't be unexpectedly would it? One Austin free night. You promised.
Austin: I underestimated how much I need to see you.
Cassie: You're laying it on thick tonight. I need to study. I'll call you later?

I set my phone upside down on the table, feeling horrible for blowing him off, but if I don't nip the conversation in the bud, I'll give in. When given the choice between studying in the student-filled library or laying in Austin's arms, I'm going to choose him, every time. Admittedly, that's not the best way to earn my college degree.

I feel the same way he does. I want to be near him all the time. I love his smile, his hair, his voice. I love the way he makes me feel safe.

I think about the flower delivery yesterday. The guy I told Austin about, my 'stalker' as he called him, sits two tables over right now. He's a well-built brunette wearing jeans and a college sweatshirt. From the closer run-ins we've had I can tell he's a few inches shorter than Austin. He's cute. Sort of unassuming. Which is why I don't think he's the one interested in me. I know exactly why he's following me and who he's here for, I just don't know what to do about it. Or how long I have.

"*Will you stay with me?*"

Brian's eyes cloud over as his gaze flicks toward the hotel door. He checks his watch, rolling his neck side to side as though he's working out the kinks.

"Just to watch television. I'm tired of being alone. I feel like a prisoner in here. You guys drop off food three times a day, then walk out. I need someone to talk to before I go insane," I beg from my spot on the couch.

He's unsure. Over the past few weeks I've broken down his wall bit by bit. The stone-faced bodyguard who keeps watch outside my room each night has gone from stoic to a little less than that. He's not exactly warm and friendly, but he's taken to leaving me candy as he walks from my room for the evening. Tonight I've decided to take that as a sign. A sign that maybe I can get him to open up. I need details about Emil. How long is he planning on keeping me locked in this room? It's been a month since he last let me out. A month since school ended, since we fought about him seeing my mother, since I had hope for my future. One month is a long time to feel hopeless.

"Is he coming home tonight then?" I ask when Brian finally deigns to answer me with a firm shake of his head.

Emil coming home means sex. Plain and simple. That's all I am to him. A sex toy. Something to be used for pleasure and then locked away when he's done.

I see the muscle in Brian's jaw tick. "His plans were unclear, but no. I don't believe he will be back tonight."

"Wow, an entire sentence." My brows lift in amazement and his mouth twists up slightly. "You have the same accent as Emil, though not as strong."

"I've been in the States longer."

Like Emil, Brian is dark. He's larger, though. Beefed up under his button up dress shirt and dark slacks. I wonder if they're family. Maybe distant relatives, as they do bear a slight resemblance. So I ask about it.

He moves closer, taking a seat on the arm of the chair nearest me. "Cassandra, we aren't supposed to talk to you."

His eyes soften as mine water. "I see."

He stands, pulling a bag of Skittles from his pocket and tossing them in my lap. "I heard they're your favorite." I nod, swiping at the moisture pooling under my eyes. He holds my gaze before turning to leave the room. When he reaches the door, he stops. There's a stillness in the air. I recognize his intention to speak before he does. I wait for his words, knowing they'll be something unexpected. And they are.

"You shouldn't be here." He turns the handle and steps outside without another word.

I look back at my shadow. He reminds me of Brian. Beefy, dark, stoic. A hired man to watch Emil Cermak's possession. There's one way to be sure, but if I speak to him it might tip him off. Do I dare let on that I know? If Emil's watching how long will it be before he becomes impatient?

Brian's hand grazes my fingers as he removes the remote from my grasp. He turns up the volume on the television until the commercials blare before he leans closer. "You need to get away from him," he whispers into my ear, the television nearly drowning him out.

I shake my head, fear blooming within my chest at the thought. "He's threatened me. More than once. I can't."

"Cassandra, you have to. He suspects something." His large hand wraps around my wrist.

"Suspects what? I've done nothing." My eyes scan his face. He's barely older

than me, but the faint scar near his mouth and his crooked nose make him seem worldly. They add character to an otherwise unremarkable face.

"I can't keep talking to you," he warns. Talking. That's all we've done. Since the night three weeks ago when I asked him to stay in my room and keep me company he's lingered longer and longer. He's become somewhat of a friend, all things considered.

"Will he let me go?" What a stupid question. I know the answer before I ask it, and his expression tells me so.

The door to the room beeps, swinging open suddenly and sending Brian to his feet, but not before Emil sees the haste in which he moves. My palms press into my stomach, feigning sickness as Emil's fury springs to life.

"What is going on here?" His question asked with deadly calm.

"I'm feeling sick. He was checking on me."

"Was he?"

I nod.

Brian shifts back, half shielding me from Emil. That's a mistake.

"Perhaps it's from all of the treats he brings you?" Emil's dark eyes narrow.

My stomach sinks. "Emil—"

"Leave us." The order is clear, but Brian wavers. He dares a glance my way, and I see the desire to defy Emil written all over his face. I nod as discreetly as possible, warning him to remain quiet and leave us before things get worse. Although I'm not sure if they can.

My eyes follow Brian's back, worrying as he passes Emil a little too closely. I'm so fixated on his leaving that I don't pay attention to Emil until it's too late. His palm cracks across my face, pulling a cry from my lips before Brian disappears through the open doorway.

The rest happens in slow motion. Brian growls Emil's name. Emil snatches me from the couch, pulling me into his chest and fisting my hair, forcing me to watch as two men I recognize from my weeks in this room take hold of a fighting Brian. I catch two punches connect with his gut before I'm thrown toward the bed and the door closes, the sound of a fight fading away.

"You will not talk to my men, Cassandra."

"What are you going to do to him?"

"You are mine and mine alone. Do you understand me?" He stalks closer.

"Emil." I hate that his name is a plea. I hate that I'm scared of this man. Of course I have good reason to be, but I hate it.

"I own you."

My head shakes of its own volition. "You can't hold me hostage forever. He was just being nice. I asked him to keep me company."

His hands go to his belt, unbuckling and sliding the black leather from his waist slowly. Deliberately.

"I own you," he repeats. I fall back, my legs hitting the edge of the bed.

"Do you care about me?"

It happens so fast. His arm lifts up, the black strap slashes through the air, the metal buckle connecting with my brow so hard I see stars. And blood. The heat drips down the corner of my eye as I fall dizzily to the bed behind me.

"I own you," he says again, rushing me and pushing my body down to the mattress. "Until I am sick of you, I own you."

I'm too weak to fight him. I'm a homeless seventeen-year-old girl with nowhere to go. With no one to protect me. I'm helpless. Hopeless. So I give in. "Yes," I shout, my hands grabbing at his biceps while his hand rips at the shirt I'm wearing. "I'm yours, Emil. I'm sorry. Nothing happened, nothing at all."

I beg and plead, promising my devotion to the man who has spilled my blood more than once. He becomes my prisoner. I turn into a seductress, kissing and caressing his anger away. I allow him to find his release while my blood smears my temple, then I sleep next to him, letting him whisper his false words of endearment—all the while formulating a plan to get away as soon as possible.

I don't see Brian again, and I never ask about him.

♥

"Cassie?"

I look up.

"Are you okay, you look like you've seen a ghost or something." West's gaze darts around the immediate area as he slides into the chair beside mine. I shake off the past, running my hand through my hair, turning in my seat.

"I'm fine, just lost in thought." The table two over is empty now. "What are you doing here?"

West smirks. "What can I say that you'll believe?"

His answer throws me for a loop. I push myself to be present, to forget

Brian and his fate. I study West's overly concerned expression. What does he know? "Excuse me?"

"My brother is in love with you." The chair inches closer as West props his elbows on the table. He picks up a pen, twirling it in his fingers. "You know that right?"

"I think so."

The pen he's twirling clatters to the table top as his fingers grip my wrist lightly. "Don't think, Cassie. Know it," he says with determination. My mouth goes dry as I nod.

He releases a deep breath and returns to the pen. "He told me about your ex. Not all the details, just the basics." The blood drains from my face as he finishes. "He's worried about you."

I inch closer, closing off anyone who might be lingering nearby from hearing us. "So he sent you to check up on me?"

His shrug confirms it. "Tell me the truth. Is this guy looking for you?"

I nod.

"Is he dangerous?"

I nod again. West flinches, his nose scrunching as though he's in pain.

Closing his eyes, he inhales deeply and asks, "And the cops?"

This time I laugh under my breath. "Cops? What can they do? I have nothing to provide them with. How often do the cops protect people from stalkers? I don't think a protection order will keep me safe, West."

His hand touches my forearm. "That's not true. We know people. My dad has friends. You need to report this guy. You're putting everyone around you in danger."

Oh, God. What if he's right? The worry is so clear on his face. Austin's concern for me shows up differently. His is a jealousy, protection-based fear, but West's… West isn't thinking of only me. He's thinking of his brother, of the people—like Jules—who could be in danger if Emil comes after me.

"He thinks Emil sent the flowers, doesn't he?" I ask only because I need the confirmation. I need to know that Emil is as much on Austin's mind as he is on mine.

"Well, he sure doesn't buy your secret admirer story." West's face is so similar to his brother's that I nearly reach out. My fingers itching to graze the sardonic little smirk he wears. "But he's not going to say anything to you. He doesn't want to scare you."

My head drops.

West's fingers squeeze my forearm harder. "Don't run away, Cassie."

A scream burns deep within my chest. The moment I knew Austin didn't send the flowers my mind went into run mode. Run before he finds me. Run before he finds Austin. Run farther, faster. And just like in December my heart screamed Austin's name. If I run, I leave him, I lose him. I don't think I can do it, but what else can I do?

AUSTIN

*I'm in constant agony when we're apart,
but it's better than never having her at all.*

"Put your phone down before you get called out," West hisses, slapping my back as he passes me in the weight room.

"I'm checking on her."

"You've been checking on her every twenty minutes since you walked in here." He jerks his head to my left, a signal we're being watched, and I slide the phone into my waist band. Twisting around, I stretch out my back before moving to stack another plate on the bar I'm spotting for one of the rookies. I glance across the room to where West has moved and read his lips as he mouths, "She's fine."

She's fine. I repeat the two words with every lift, every count, every pound added to the reps. *She's fine.*

West walked her to her dorm last night with little fanfare. Maybe the flowers truly were from some guy following her around. Maybe I'm just crazy paranoid. But my gut tells me I'm not. My gut tells me something's about to happen.

♥

"Why are you dragging me out into the cold?" Cassie laughs as I tug on her hand, crossing the street and leaving the music and laughter of the party behind.

Damn her and her conditions; they've turned me into a lunatic. Thirty minutes. Thirty minutes of half-drunk frat boys and teammates hitting on her before I wanted to rip off a few arms and shove them down some throats, thanks to that bargain she made in bed with me. One night—that was the price I had to pay to get my girlfriend to a college party. Let her have a full day and night off from me and she'd come. It should have been easy, and it was until I picked her up for the party. I underestimated my feelings, my fear over the flowers and Emil. West helped sooth those when he made sure she returned to her room safely last night, but I'm still going crazy over it. Wondering when, not if, something is going to happen.

That's not the reason I'm pulling her from the party, though. Nope, the moment I saw her I wanted to ravage her. Forty hours of not touching her felt like a lifetime, so here we are.

"Because I want five minutes of you to myself," I answer, nodding to a few guys walking our way as I head for the park across the street from the party.

"I didn't peg you as the jealous type." She chuckles behind me, as if this is funny.

"I'm not," I lie, angling toward the trees and walking faster. She obviously thinks my urgency is due to the idiot she was dancing with. I wish it were that simple.

"No, of course not." She makes a mock serious face. "You're the one who made me come, I would have been happy to stay in tonight."

I bring her around, towing her to a stop under the dark branches of trees and pushing her back up against a trunk. My body immediately pressing into hers.

"Then I couldn't have done this," I say into her mouth as my lips descend. My hand slides under her sweater, moving up her ribcage until my thumb swipes at the silk of her bra.

Our tongues dance together as she grips my hips, bucking up against me, a satisfied sigh filling my ears. She shivers—at my touch or at the cold

—I'm unsure, and I move closer. My hand kneads her breast as the other grips her ass. Damn, I want her. Always. It won't matter how long it's been. The hunger is ever present, the taste of her tongue always on my lips, the feel of her body trembling beneath mine. A dance keeping my skin warm when we're apart.

"God, I missed you." It was forty hours; I'm so freakin' whipped.

"I missed you, too. You get me all weekend, though."

"So you're caught up on all your assignments?"

"It's amazing how much I can get done without you distracting me."

"I'm a pain in the ass, aren't I?"

She agrees with a giggle.

"Do I have your permission to distract you all weekend?"

"How about here?" she nibbles at my lip.

I think about it, calculating the risk of being caught. It's close to midnight by now, we're in a neighborhood park off a college campus with a party raging not twenty yards away. "Now?"

"Now," she nods, the urgency in her voice making the decision for me.

"Now, it is."

Hunger fuels us. Her body a chain, holding me hostage. I'm so damn lost in her all thoughts disappear. She hums, a low moan against my mouth as my hands release the button on her jeans. Falling to my knees, my tongue traces a circle around her navel. My hands slide her pants down her legs, my fingers remaining on her exposed skin as I push them down.

She grips my hair, holding my head against her stomach. I nuzzle my nose against the lace covering the spot I really want to taste. Cassie's body rolls into me. Lifting her left leg, I slide her boot off of her foot and pull one pant leg from her body. I repeat the process with her right leg, all the while tickling and teasing her center with my mouth and nose through her panties. Her heat, her scent, drives my fingers up her thighs.

"Austin," her voice is hoarse, her hand covering mine on her hip. There's a quiver in her voice not born of desire, and I still.

I look up at her from down on my knees. Her beautiful body shivering before me, her dark hair falling around her face as she stares down at me in the moonlight. I stretch up on my knees, pressing a kiss to her stomach and wrapping my arms around her backside.

"Don't run, Cass," I whisper against her skin. "Please don't run."

I feel her knees go weak, a tiny gasp leaving her lips. "If he knows I'm here—"

"Please." I scatter kisses across her skin, from hip to hip and down her thighs. "Stay and fight. I'll help you."

Her hands fall to her sides. Her breathing picking up as my mouth and hands continue to explore her. I use sex to break her down. To show her how badly I need her. When her hips thrust forward as though they're telling me to get a move on, I grin and give her what she needs. Pulling one leg over my shoulder I devour her. Candy. She's so damn sweet. So damn amazing.

She releases her grip on my hair and I glance up, my mouth still covering her. Her arms are over her head, her fingers gripping the tree behind her as though she's using it as an anchor to remain standing. Every whimper and moan pushes me deeper. My mouth and fingers forcing her body's crescendo.

The moment her thighs clench my head and her hips thrust forward I move. Yanking my pants down, I stand and enter her body in one swift move, lifting her feet from the ground and holding her against me. I can only hope her thick sweater protects her back from the rough bark of the tree behind her, because I'm too far gone to stop now. The bite of cold air licks against my feverish wanting skin.

My rhythm is steady. Her arms cling to me, her head tucks between my neck and shoulder. Her tongue licking at my skin. When her body spasms against mine, pulsing and pulling me deeper, I pour into her. Crashing our bodies together over and over and over. Waves of fire shooting through my veins as her name sings on my lips.

"I love you," Cassie breathes, one hand tugging on the back of my head, steering me to look at her. "I'm in love with you."

I can't speak with my body buried deep within her sheltering warmth. I rock my hips—out and back in, as though that's my answer to the words I've been longing to hear.

Leaves crunch and the sound of a twig snaps nearby. I still, my heart still pounding in my ears so hard I can barely hear.

Cassie's hand taps at my shoulder. "Someone's coming."

Another crunch of the underbrush. "Shit." Pulling out, I set her down, tossing her pants to her as I yank mine up.

Cassie giggles.

"Shhh," I chuckle under my breath as she grabs my arm, using me for balance as she slips her panties on. She doesn't stop laughing as she bounces up and down in her attempt to dress herself.

She's bent over at the waist, struggling to pull her jeans over her foot when she pauses, glancing up. Her eyes dance in the dark. "We should totally go to parties more often," she suggests playfully.

After what just occurred between us, it doesn't sound like such a bad idea.

"I love you too, by the way," I offer, earning another smile as I press a kiss to the top of her head before moving to intercept whomever is wandering our way.

"Hey, Austin?" Her hand grabs my elbow, her face serious. "I'm not leaving you."

I swing her back into my arms, holding her as close as possible as the meaning of her words hit me. "Let's go to Tyler in the morning and talk to my dad. He can help you. We'll go to the police and file reports. I'll be with you every step of the way. Okay?" Maybe I'm taking things too fast. Maybe I'm too paranoid. Cassie nods, though, so I take her face between my hands, promising, "I'm not letting anything happen to you."

She nods once more, mouthing "I know" before kissing me.

"Now finish getting your ass dressed before someone sees you." I smack her bare ass lightly.

She's snickering softly behind me as I button my jeans and step around a tangle of winter-stripped bushes and evergreens. And stop mid-step. The woman standing before me is vaguely familiar. Petite like Cassie, with her dark hair and the same standoffish expression of fear Cassie wore so often when we first met. Warning bells sound within my mind.

"I'm sorry," she says calmly.

Fuck.

I turn, terror stopping my heart, as a shadow appears. An arm lifts in the dark and pain cracks through my skull, rattling my brain and sending stars soaring around me. Stumbling forward, my arms reach for the menacing figure before me as Cassie's scream pierces the night and fire plunges into my shoulder as something rips through it and I'm thrown into darkness.

CASSIE

*I just had sex outside.
In public.*

My lips won't quit smiling as I tug on my boots and follow through the brush after Austin, the light stripe across his shirt my beacon in the dark. When he pulled me away from the party, I laughed. I saw the look he flashed my way from across the room. The hunger. The jealousy. We'd barely made one round through the house before he got caught up in a conversation about football. Jess rescued me, pulling me into the fray of people dancing in the middle of the living room. It took one chorus before bodies flocked around us, male and female, and we were swallowed up by the crowd. One more chorus before a chest, not belonging to Austin, pressed up against my back; a breath that wasn't his brushed across my cheek. And barely half of another chorus before a hand that was Austin's reached into the crowd and pulled me out. His face that of the focused football player intent on smashing heads, he led me out of the house, across the street, and into the park. Damn Neanderthal.

And to take me up against a tree. Lord, I want to laugh and dance and fall to the ground because my body was in heaven five minutes ago. My soul shattered as he drove into me, the bark biting into my spine and scalp. I'm tingling all over. ALL OVER.

"Austin?" I skirt around the bushes, the woods eerily quiet.

I catch sight of his head as a figure moves from the shadows of the trees to his right and a low voice reaches my ears.

"I'm sorry."

The world tilts. *Mom?*

A second shadowed figure, much closer to my position, steps from the copse of evergreens with an arm raised. The horrible thud of something connecting with Austin's skull flips a switch. It all happens too quickly, yet so slowly. I'm sure my spirit leaves my body so I can get the full view of what's going on.

Emil is here.

My mother is here.

She stands by while the man I hate attacks the man I love. The man I just made love to, against a nearby tree, in the open for them to hear and see.

Oh, God.

I scream.

Austin stumbles. There's a flash in the moonlight and Austin half-groans half-screams as he's pushed to the ground, his body bending in an unnatural way.

"No!" I think I shout the word as I throw myself on the ground next to his body. "Austin?" My hands come away wet as I touch his head.

Above me, Emil stands, a blade in his hand and a satisfied smile on his face. "What did you do?" I frantically search Austin's prone body with my eyes. There's darkness staining the length of his right arm from his shoulder all the way down. I swallow hard as my fingers touch the spot. Blood. Lots and lots of blood. "Austin, baby? Wake up."

I don't have my phone. Frantic, my hand moves to Austin's jeans pocket, searching for his when I take a blow to my ribs. I fall partially on top of Austin, pain shooting through my side and stealing my breath away as more sparks of pain bite at my scalp.

Emil's hand winds in my hair, yanking me off Austin and throwing me backward. I land, sprawled on my ass, hot tears blurring my vision as Emil nudges Austin's leg with the toe of his shoe.

"You little whore." His face is evil incarnate as he looks down at me, the shadows from the trees and moon adding to the overall horror of this moment. "You gave yourself to this boy." His toe nudges harder, all around Austin's body as he circles him, a hunter ready to finish off his prey.

I scramble to my knees. "Leave him alone."

"Leave him alone?" Emil's laughter is low and humorless. I make it a two feet before his eyes transfer from me to Austin. "You move and I kill him."

His left hand shifts, pulling back the coat he's wearing and revealing a weapon. I can't see a gun against his dark clothing, but I know there must be one.

I fall back. "What do you want?"

"I told you I would find you, Cassandra."

Yes. He did, and somehow I'd convinced myself he wouldn't. Stupid. So very stupid. Is there oxygen here? I can't breathe. My palms press against my chest. *Breathe, Cassie. Breathe. Figure this out.*

I'm still gasping for air, and a plan, when Emil steps before of me. He squats, and I force myself to remain still.

"Cassandra, my love. Why did you leave me?" His voice is haunting. The heavy accent tinged with hurt and anger. A fingertip touches my cheek, wiping at the never-ending parade of tears marching down my face.

He leans closer. "I love you," he whispers, rubbing his cheek against mine. He murmurs the words over and over, his hand caressing at my jawline while his nose skims under my ear. I remain immobile—dazed—terror crushing me. Emil inhales sharply and my body tenses. His hand slips to my neck.

"You smell like him." He pulls away from my ear, his face inches from mine. "Your lover."

"Emil—" I don't reach for his hand. I know better than to fight. He always wins.

"I took you in, gave you everything you needed, loved you, and this? This is how you repay me." His thumb digs harder into my windpipe.

My eyes bulge, begging him to release me. "You don't love me," I gasp, and he sneers. "You hurt me."

Something flickers across his face. I might think it's regret if I thought he was capable of feeling that emotion. He isn't. He looks like a man capable of ruining the world. His black eyes narrow to slits, the muscles in his jaw flexing as his mouth tightens into a grim line. His hand falls from my neck and he stands swiftly. Too swiftly as he returns to Austin's side.

"I hurt you?" he asks lowly. Then again louder. "I hurt you?" His leg rears back, kicking into Austin's side. "Let me show you the pain I can inflict."

He kicks again and again, and I throw myself at his legs only to be kicked back. I'm crying and trying to scream, but I don't think my voice raises above a garbled plea. I can't get enough air in my lungs to be heard above the heavy thuds of Emil's foot connecting with Austin's body. His leg, his stomach, his face. The abuse wrangles a groan from Austin. His body rolls to the side. Whether it's of its own accord or from the force of the attack, I'm not sure, but he moves. And placing his back the way it is leaves it open to the brutal kick Emil delivers at the base of his spine. My dinner floods my throat.

"Stop. Please, I'll do anything. I'll come with you," I cry, crawling toward Emil once more. I brace for him to kick at me again. "Emil, please leave him be."

Emil is too incensed to hear my words, my fingers rake at his leg, and he drags me behind him as he assaults Austin over and over. He's muttering under his breath with each kick, but none of his words make sense.

"You'll kill me?" Emil shouts over Austin's body. "You want to play protector, Austin Rutledge?"

You'll kill me? What is he talking about?

"Emil. Take her and go." My mother's sharp voice raises above over Emil's rambling.

Of all the things I imagined happening when, or if, I ever saw my mother again—this is not it. Those words—*take her and go*—were not what I expected. She rushes my way, giving Austin and Emil a wide berth as she bends over me. Her hands grabbing at my arm as though she's trying to pull me from the ground. I slap at her, my eyes fastened on Emil as he leans low over Austin.

"I own her," he spits.

Beside me, my mother kicks at my legs, yanking on the arm I keep fighting away from her. "Get up. He will kill you. Get up," she hisses as I sag to the ground.

This is my life. My mother—the one who used me to keep men, who turned the other eye when those men ruined me, who threw me out of her house when I fought fire with fire—she's now giving me to a man who will, in all likelihood, kill me some day.

"Did you ever love me?" I ask her, all my fight gone.

She stops grabbing for me. From the corner of my eye, I see Emil rise, stepping away from Austin. *Good. Come my way, asshole.* I straighten, rising to my feet. A sharp pain sears across my torso. Every breath I take is painful. Did he break a rib when he kicked at me earlier? I don't care as long as I can get them away from Austin. I'll take whatever punishment I have coming. I never should have let him become involved in this.

My mother steps back, her eyes flicking between Emil and me. Her face unreadable.

"Why are you here?" I turn to Emil. "Why is she here?"

Silence.

Emil takes hold of my biceps and pulls me close, his arms slipping around my back. "Are you not happy to see your mother?"

I force myself not to laugh into his chest. I force myself not to punch him, or kick him, or scream. Getting away from Austin, that is my goal. *I've never had much reason to pray or believe in a higher power, but if you're there—please, God, help me. Help Austin.*

My head shakes. "You know I hate her."

"Cassie." Her voice holds a warning, and I turn from Emil to look at her.

"Did you expect something else? I hate you." Emil's arms loosen their hold, and I step closer to her. He follows, not allowing me even an inch of space to run. Not that I would have, not with Austin laying here helpless. "I. Hate. You. What kind of woman are you, what kind of person? The things you did to me."

She laughs. It's a spiteful, ironic laugh. "And look at you now. You've wrapped Emil Cermak around your little finger."

It's my turn to laugh. "You want him back? Take him."

Something like fear flashes across her face. Emil's fingers tighten on my wrist. "Cassandra."

I look between these two despicable people who have used and abused me, and I long to fall to the ground and weep out the misery of my life. "Why can't you let me go?" I ask him, not expecting an answer. To my mother, I implore, "Do you have no decency? You're just going to hand me over to him?"

She shakes her head, almost imperceptibly.

"She has no choice. Do you, Gwen?"

Of course. She bartered for her life. Mine against hers.

I actually smile. This might be the last moments of freedom I will ever have and I smile because I realize my whole life has been nothing but a cruel, sick joke. "Tell me, is he letting you keep the money you stole? What's the going rate on my flesh?"

My heart doesn't crack at the hard look in her eyes as she shrugs. "You wanted him," she says.

No love lost. I knew it, and maybe when I have time to consider this moment, it'll hurt. If I'm honest with myself.

Right now, though, right now the hatred I feel for this woman overwhelms me.

"It was never about him. It was all about you. He wanted me, more than you, and you hated that didn't you? You still hate it." I fight off Emil's grip, attempting to get closer to her. "You hate it so much you don't care what happens to me."

"Oh, Cassie, sweetheart. That's where you're wrong. I never cared what happened to you. You were always a means to an end. You never should have been born."

Yes. This is definitely going to hurt when I look back on it. If I have the chance to look back on it.

I have no response, and Emil doesn't allow me the chance to give her one. He steps around me, dropping my arm at the last moment and wrapping her in an embrace. For one moment, she looks excited, or amazed to find herself there … then there's a jerk of her head, her arms drop, and her jaw opens—dark liquid pouring from her lips.

Blood.

Emil releases her and she collapses to the ground. His hand yanks me into his side before I'm able to muster a scream. Before I'm able to process anything.

"You will walk with me to my car and you will keep your mouth shut. Do you understand?" I'm immobile. "Do you understand, Cassandra, or do I have to end his life as well?"

That threat jolts me. My head bobs automatically.

"Let's go home."

I'm angled enough in Emil's arms that I'm able to see Austin when Emil says that. Home. Home for me will forever be the four walls that comprise his dorm. The room where I made my first move at trust. Where I fell in love with a football player who wanted nothing more than to get to know me. Where I found peace.

I'm still looking at him—my home—my eyes straining to see the rise and fall of his chest, to see some movement, when Emil drags me with him. Walking away from the house party, away from Austin, away from my mother's dead body—to where? I don't know.

AUSTIN

*I blink, setting off a bomb of excruciating pain.
A mirror has exploded within my head,
the shards tearing fissures through my brain matter, chasing the lurking
shadows from my mind.*

"He's waking up. Tell them he's waking up."

A voice like a gunshot speaks from above me. Loud. Jolting. I turn away from the noise, and a click reverberates, filling my ears as a searing slice of pain screams up my neck, shooting into my jaw.

The shadows return, pressing me down, down, down. I gasp.

"Hey, dude, don't move." I feel a sudden pressure on my forehead. "We've called 9-1-1. Stay still."

My mouth fills with sour bile as I attempt blinking again. My eyes won't open, not completely. My vision is reduced to a slit of light. A glowing face. No. A face, lit by the glow of a cell phone, and outlined by the night sky. My mouth opens and nothing comes out. My tongue is thick, coated with the tang of metal. I swallow. Blood?

"Is that—" A feminine voice joins the deeper one above me. She's further away. Standing, maybe? Her gasp is audible. "Ray, that's Austin Rutledge."

Ray's gunshot voice startles me, "Holy—"

Yes. Yes, I'm Austin. What happened? Why won't the words form?

"What about the other—?" the female's voice waivers. There's sniffling. A sharp intake of air. Is she crying? The pressure on my forehead lessens. What did she mean by "the other"? What is "the other"? Answer her question, Ray.

There's a faint whir of sirens in the distance.

"They're almost here. Hang in there, man."

I attempt drawing in a deep breath, wheezing at the pain and lack of oxygen. What is wrong with me? Think, man, think. Where are you?

A scream explodes in my head. A memory.

It's female and blood-curdling.

"Damn it," the words tumble from my lips, blood pooling in my mouth. I twist, spitting out the thick warmth, gagging on it, and on the fear in her scream. Dread coils within my gut.

"You shouldn't move. You could have a spine injury," the wavering female voice advises. Spinal injury?

My mind scrolls through sounds and images in an attempt at figuring things out. There was a scream—*she* screamed, didn't she?

Why can't I remember?

"What do you think happened?" the girl asks Ray. His reply is a low mumble, their voices fading as the sirens become louder as they come closer.

I blink. I have to concentrate to accomplish the simple movement—my forehead wrinkling, my teeth gritting. I have to force it. Each breath is an order, not an act of human nature.

Ray moves out of my line of sight and I focus on the sky. The night is black. No city lights or buildings. It's dark pillows of grey clouds painted against an inky sky with pin prick stars peeking in and out of view.

Red flashing lights break into the haze.

I grip at the cold grass beneath me, my fingers digging into the ground for leverage as I attempt sitting up. It's pointless. Fire burns within my arm, and my shoulder is numb. Do I even have an arm left? I can't feel it, but it's there. I know it is because earlier she was holding onto it. I see it. I see her—laughing up at me, holding my arm, making a joke.

"C-c-c," the gurgled sound barely touches the air beyond my lips as fire and darkness press down on me. Sirens fill the air, much louder now. Doors slam. New voices speak. My eyes slip closed as hands probe. I float between two worlds. Darkness and pain. Darkness fights harder, winning ... except...

Her scream ... her voice.

I jerk awake, but don't move. I'm tied down. Wincing, I force my head to clear. To see. To speak.

"Cassie." Her name is stronger this time. My chest tightens as though my air was cut off.

A face appears before me. "There you are. It's going to be okay, Austin. We're—"

"Cassie." Blood dances over my taste buds as I raise my voice. "Where's Cassie? Where is she?"

The face morphs into a frown, shaking back and forth.

No, don't shake your head at me. Where's Cassie?

My body goes weightless. A gurney. An ambulance. The pieces of the puzzle sort themselves, understanding sinking in. I've woken to a nightmare. I'm being loaded into an ambulance. I'm broken. The police are here. The medics are here.

Cassie?

She's not here.

I blink, forcing my eyes wider—and I vomit as the ambulance doors slam closed. A medic tilts the board I'm attached to sideways as the feeling of movement sets in. The ambulance drives away from the wooded field where my body was found, leaving behind the couple who found me. Leaving behind strobes of red and blue lights.

Leaving behind a black body bag.

I love you. She said the words. Didn't she? I flutter in and out of consciousness. My lips repeating her name each time I come to—a different face, a different frown greeting me. No answers.

Everything fucking hurts. Everything.

♥

"Austin?" West's voice is the first thing I hear over the beeping and clicking of machines. My eyes adjust to the bright light. My hand is squeezed. I squeeze back. "Hey." His face comes into view, hovering over me.

"Cass?" I manage to say her name, my mouth sour with the taste of vomit and blood.

West's eyes flick away, his lips forming a thin line. "The nurses said you could have some water when you woke. Here—" He slips from my immediate view. I turn my head, following him, the small movement sending jolts of pain across the back of my skull.

"Shhiiittt."

"Don't move," West barks, his hand squeezing mine again. "You got a nice crack in the skull, it's going to hurt for a while." He holds a large plastic cup with a long straw over my head. "Wait, let me sit you up a little more."

"Is it … Can I—"

"It's okay, you can move. You think I'd torture you if I wasn't allowed?" There's a dash of forced humor in his voice as he presses the remote, sitting me forward a few inches. "Take a sip."

I do. The first drop of water is painful, the second not much better. By the time I've taken enough sips to rinse some of the foul taste from my mouth I'm exhausted. There are compression bandages around my torso and more swathing on my right arm from my shoulder to my elbow, and IVs and tubes, but other than that I see nothing. No casts, no neck braces. I look at the machines on the opposite side of the bed from West. There's a bag of blood hanging from some contraption. Shit.

West removes the cup from in front of my face.

"What…" I can't finish my question, but West reads my mind.

"Broken ribs, concussion, collapsed lung, loss of blood—"

My eyes go to the IV in my arm. Blood. They are pumping me full of some random stranger's blood. I know they test donations for everything under the sun these days, and I've donated blood myself, but the thought of actually getting someone else's in my body … I never thought I'd need it.

"They said you were lucky. The attacker missed your main arteries, man." His hand rubs across his forehead and into his hair, pushing his already disheveled hair up into mountain peaks, falling every which way. "An inch lower or a few minutes longer and we would have lost you."

I catch the glow of tears filling his eyes a moment before his knuckles sweep over them. An inch. I owe my life to an inch.

"Collapsed lung?" My eyes go back to the machines and tubes attached to my body. I take a small painful breath, as if my air is going to cut off.

"Breathe, Austin. You're okay." His hand reaches for me, but my right side is covered in gauze. "Dad's on his way. You're going to be fine. A few days here. That's all. I'm supposed to let them know when you wake up. They have questions for you." I assume he means the police.

Cassie.

What the hell? I'm sitting here making small talk with my brother, and where is she? What happened, why in the hell hasn't he asked me? He said attacker. Not Emil, but attacker. Shit.

"West, it wasn't a random attacker." The monitor registering my heart rate speeds up. "It was Emil, Cassie's ex."

The door to my room cracks open, three light, but firm raps pulling my eyes from my brother to the entrance. "Mr. Rutledge?" A man enters the room, his face clean of emotion. Definitely a detective judging by his dark slacks and button-up shirt with rolled sleeves. Speak of the devil. He must have the instinct of a bloodhound tracking his kill. "I'm Detective Rush—"

I interrupt him, frantic now for news. "I was attacked by my girlfriend's ex. His name is Emil—Emil—Shit, I don't even know his last name. He's from Vegas." The detective steps closer to the side of my bed, standing opposite West. West, who's looking at me not in shock at this information, but with utter despair on his face. Why? "Where's Cassie?"

"Mr. Rutledge," the detective begins again.

"Austin. Please." I don't know why, at a time like this, I would be correcting a detective on what to call me. I press my fingers to the tender skin of my jaw, feeling the swelling. The more I talk, the more it aches. "Where is she?"

"We don't know." It's West who answers my question, and Detective Rush sends him a stern look. "Sorry, I'll go call Dad and let him know you're awake and see how far away he is." I nod as he leaves the room, closing the door behind him.

"Can you tell me what happened, please?"

The detective's hands slide into his pockets, his eyes watching me intently as he speaks. "We were hoping you could tell us."

"I was knocked out; I don't know what happened. I was with Cassie, and her mother was there, and her ex. He cold-cocked me from behind. I only know it was him because I turned at the last moment before I blacked out. That's it. I woke up in an ambulance." A fuzzy memory comes to mind. A black lump on the ground before the ambulance doors closed. A body bag.

My sight goes hazy. I inhale so sharply at the memory I feel as though my chest is going to explode.

"Is she dead?" Oh, God. Please don't tell me she's dead. Please. Please. Please.

He's quiet for one second too long and my thoughts scream within my head.

This is not the time to draw out the tension in this fucking moment, Detective. This isn't some network show going to commercial break where you leave the significant other hanging on the line for three shitty commercials about beer, detergent, and car insurance.

"Jesus, just tell me," I shout as my head explodes, causing me to gag. I'm reaching for the water pitcher next to my bed and expelling the liquid contents of my stomach before Detective Rush can blink. "There was a body bag—" I manage to prompt him as I spit into the container.

"Yes, there was. It wasn't Cassandra—"

"Cassie," I correct him, hating the sound of her full name. Emil called her that.

"Cassie," he repeats with a nod. "It wasn't her. We believe it was her mother. We're waiting on a positive ID still."

My stomach muscles bunch and coil as I clench my eyes. This is all a nightmare. I'll open my eyes and I'll be back in my dorm with Cassie in my bed.

"Austin, I need more information from you. Anything you can tell us."

I open my eyes, but I'm not on campus. I'm still in the hospital.

Detective Rush is still standing before me—removing a notepad from his pocket. And Cassie is still missing.

I give him every last piece of information I can on her life, her mother, and Cassie's ex. A murderer. Cassie was kidnapped by a murderer. And I'm hooked up to wires and machines, an inch from having lost my life. I've never felt so damn helpless.

CASSIE

*I look at my hands, at the sleeve of my sweater;
they're covered in Austin's blood.
And I've got bigger things to worry about right now ...*

The knife used to kill my mother sits in the console five inches from my body.

The man who killed her sits twelve inches from my body.

The knife rattles at each pothole, bump, and crack in the asphalt—the metal stained with my mother's drying blood.

The man never utters a word. Her blood still colors the edges of his thumb and pointer finger, the ones that gripped the knife when it plunged into her back, or her neck. I'm really not sure what happened—I didn't see it.

But I saw the way her chin thrust forward as her head jerked up. I saw the blood pour from her lips. I saw the woman I hated—who hated me—sink to the winter-hardened ground with a distinct thud I will never forget. Never.

Then I walked away from her. With him.

The man who murdered my mother before my eyes.

The man who beat me, raped me, searched for me for over a year, and harassed me. I walked away with him. Without a fight.

No. I did it for Austin. Emil wanted to kill him. He would have, probably meant to, but she stopped him. My mother yelled at him, telling him to take me and go. She cracked the spell his anger had over him. For my sake or for Austin's? I'll never know.

"She can never hurt you again, Cassandra. She cannot come between us again." His hand, his bloody, murdering hand pinches my upper leg.

I bob my head in response, looking out the window at the street lights blurring as we speed past them. The voice of years gone by crawls into my head. *Run for it, Cassie.* My mind seeks that place years of abuse taught it to go. *Run for the deep, black pit of nothingness where they can't hurt you. Where their words, their looks, their touches won't destroy you.*

I clench my eyes tightly, coaxing my lungs to breathe deep, steady inhales and exhales, and I see it. Emil's finger tracing circles up my thigh disappears. The oh-so-wrong scent in the vehicle, the tang of blood and sweat disappears. I see nothing, I feel nothing, I fear nothing ... except, there in the corner. There's movement in the back, in the darkness of my mind, and my legs take me toward it. I find myself reaching for what I cannot see. What I know is there. A room. Four walls. One bed. One large chair, a television, a bookshelf, and a fuzzy blue blanket. One ridiculous poster affixed to a white painted brick wall. One voice that says my name. He calls me. Cass. Elmer. Annie. Little one.

I open my eyes, launching myself back to the present. To the car with the knife, with the murderer, with my body—fully capable of fighting my way out of this. So I plan. I plan for the moment when I will jump from this car, or grab the steering wheel, or throw the gear shift into park. But I start with making him angry.

"Do you know who he is?" I ask, my eyes surveying our location. An empty highway at one in the morning. Not ideal. "Austin?" I clarify.

The hand resting on my thigh snaps to attention, whacking me in the mouth. My tongue passes over my bottom lip, the familiar taste of blood greeting me like an old friend.

"You do not say that name. He is dead to you."

I laugh, my lips stinging as they stretch wide. "He is a star football player at A&M, Emil. His dad played professionally. His brothers, you ask? Also superstars." I chuckle as I point this out. A scared, nervous laughter born of stress and shock. "The whole damn state of Texas knows who they are. Do you really think you're going to get away?"

"Yes." The calm in his tone is unnerving. I push further.

"Do you think he's going to let you take me without a fight? He loves me." Emil's grip tightens on the steering wheel, his blood-freckled knuckles turning white. I shift closer to the passenger door in an attempt to minimize the impact his fist will make if it flies toward my face once again.

"Did you hear me? Austin is in love with me, and I'm in love with him."

I've scarcely braced myself for the fist colliding with my chest. He threw it across the car, a battering ram breaking down a wall, and I collapse in on myself. I should have known better. The car swerves toward the shoulder of the highway as the same fist seizes my hair, yanking me toward the center console.

"What did I say?" he asks pointedly.

"Will you kill me, too?" I gasp. I must have a death wish.

"There are worse things than death, Cassandra." We've rolled to a near stop, the car off kilter as it straddles the gravel shoulder and asphalt of the highway. He jerks my head up, his shadowed eyes meeting mine. "Don't make me hurt you."

He releases my hair and I sit up as his fist connects with my temple and the world goes black.

♥

Highway 6. I catch the road marker when I wake.

"I'll make you love me again, Cassandra." His breathing is quick and shallow, like he's been running for hours.

"Again? I didn't love you before. I used you. I was a little girl playing a game I didn't understand."

"No, you loved me, and I didn't appreciate you. I allowed Gwen to blackmail me into keeping you secret. Into hiding what we have." What?

"You're mistaken; she didn't know I was with you once she kicked me out." Did she?

Emil laughs, his eyes flicking all over the place now. The rearview mirror, the side windows, behind us, in front of us. He's nervous.

"She knew. She knew from day one. I had to pay her off to keep her quiet. More than once. Of course, I let her think she was the one who owned my heart. She didn't care as long as I kept her in the lifestyle she wanted. The blood-sucking whore."

"You killed her, Emil. You murdered her and left her body where I'm sure she's been found already." I pray someone from the party ventures through the park and comes across Austin and my mother tonight. I gambled on just that the moment I walked away. I gambled on West and Jules showing up and seeing Austin's car and knowing we were around. I gambled on college kids at a party realizing something was wrong. Please let the gamble pay off.

Emil laughs under his breath. "It's not the first time, love. It's under control."

Not the first time? What kind of monster did my mother allow into her life? My life?

My fingers curl around the door handle. There's no way to hit the lock without Emil knowing. Then, even if I opened the door, I'd be jumping out of a moving vehicle. I press my forehead to the glass, my eyes focusing on the road. Is jumping to almost certain death now better than what awaits me?

"Please, let me go," I whisper, my breath fogging up the glass.

His answer is final. "Never."

AUSTIN

I'm in pain, I'm alone, and I'm scared,
The only thing I can do is talk to God.
You took away my mom,
please don't take away Cass.

She's been alone with Emil for hours now.

There's an APB out on them. Though no one knows what they're driving. If they're even on the highway. If they're even driving at all. No one knows where they went. No one knows anything.

Every person who knows us is out driving around town, searching.

Every person who loves her—Jules, Jess, Katie, Jeff— is in shock upon hearing the story, provided by West, about the shy girl who went into hiding on A&M's campus to get away from an abusive ex who stalked her.

My family and friends are doing what they can, searching for Cassie, as I lay in bed, fighting with the nurses about taking meds that will make me drowsy. I beg them to allow me to remain awake. They beg me to get rest because I won't heal without it.

It's nearly 3:30 in the morning when my father rushes into my hospital room, his face haggard.

"Austin?" He rushes to my side.

I'm so damn tired, my brain is barely functioning and I hurt all over, and one look at my dad has me breaking down like a baby.

"Dad," I reach for his shirt as he leans over me. Pulling him closer, my safety blanket during this waking nightmare. "What if he hurts her? What if I lose her?"

God, I can't imagine it. My life without Cassie. In October I'd resigned myself to never having a chance. In December, I'd considered the possibilities, a touch of Rutledge optimism sparking to life within me when she stopped me to apologize for the way she blew me off. A month ago, I fell in love with the girl who allowed herself to open up and let me in.

And now I know. This moment, this thought of maybe never looking into her eyes again, never hearing her Elmer laugh, or touching the crinkle in her forehead—this moment confirms what I already suspected. I can't live without her. I'm so fucking head over heels in love with this girl, I can't think straight. She never gave me a choice. Love never gave us a choice. And now I'm afraid Emil won't give us a chance.

CASSIE

At the first sign of blue lights in the distance, Emil doesn't panic.
They could be going anywhere, answering any call.
The second set of lights don't faze him either.
It's the third and the fourth, coming from both directions—north and south—
that do it.

I sit straighter, tugging at my seatbelt, bringing it snug against my chest as his foot presses on the gas. The lights draw closer and the speedometer creeps higher. Sixty … Seventy … Eighty. My feet push into the floorboard, looking for the passenger side brake that isn't there.

"Emil, turn yourself in. If you run, they will never stop looking for us. For you." I touch his arm as I search for my most persuasive tone. "Just pull over. For me, please. I'm scared."

Our speed holds steady as one hand drops from the steering wheel, grasping at mine. He presses my fingertips to his lips. I can feel the sheen of sweat peppering his upper lip. His quick breaths blow across my hand. "I won't let them hurt you," he promises.

He's demented. He's lost all concept of reality, his obsession with me leading him, and me, down a one-way street to destruction. He likes games. He found a thrill in playing dangerously; sneaking into my room to steal a kiss when my mother wasn't looking, teasing me to near release and then walking away. Games. So I play along.

Reaching for his cheek, my fingers stroke tenderly. I hold back the urge to scratch his eyes out as I turn toward him in my seat. "No, I'm scared for *you*. I don't want them to hurt *you*."

The engine quiets. We slow.

His face leans into my palm. "I want to taste you. I wanted to take you far away from everything and spend my days and nights—"

Use that! Use his desire against him. "Take me now. Stop the car and touch me, kiss me." My hand goes to his thigh, slipping over his crotch. He's already hard, the adrenaline of danger stoking the fire within him. "We'll go in together, Emil. I'll tell them it was self-defense," I lie.

A smile crosses his face.

We stop, not on the shoulder as I expected, but in the middle of the highway—like some car chase they would show on the news. The entire highway—the grass in the median, the trees surrounding this stretch of road—all of it is lit up in blue and red. A damn helicopter floats overhead.

The moment he slams the car into park, he slings his seat back and he's dragging me half out of my seat, forcing himself on my mouth. *One or two kisses. I can suffer through that to get away.* A hand shoves its way up my shirt, tearing at my bra until his sweaty palm touches my naked skin. His tongue forces itself against mine.

"I own you," he says into my mouth, his teeth biting at my lip, my tongue. "I will always own you."

We shift, his body looming over mine as he rises from his seat, his hand leaving my breast and reaching for the recline button on the side of the seat. I slide backward. Scooting up, I try remaining in a seated position as his hand clamps against my neck.

Outside, a voice speaks to us from a speaker system. They say his name. They warn him. Emil ignores them, his teeth gnashing together as his free hand moves lower, making quick work of the button and zipper on my jeans. I whimper, no longer able to shelve my fear at what he is doing.

"You little actress. Do you think I trust you?" The elbow on the arm at my neck jabs into my breast, pinning me against my seat. "You ran from me. You allowed another man to touch you, to taste you. I heard you, Cassandra. You let that boy fuck you with his mouth and his fingers. With his body. You enjoyed it. You betrayed me." Spittle from his rage sprays my face as he presses closer.

I jerk to the right, but move nowhere. "You're right. I did enjoy it. Every single time he came inside of me, I enjoyed it. And every single time you touched me, I wanted to kill myself."

Emil laughs through his nose, a rumbling coming from deep in his throat. "I will be the last man to ever taste you." His hand delves down the front of my jeans. "I will be the one to own you, forever."

Reality hits me as my airway is taken away. His hand is a belt around my neck, tightening notch by notch. I'm going to die. I'm going to die with Emil laying claim to me.

No! I fight, my legs kicking. My nails scratch at his hands, at his face. My attempts do nothing. I might as well be throwing feathers at a wall for all the good it's doing. My chest burns as my lungs beg for air. My vision wavers, bright flashes of light mixing with rogue waves of black. *Not like this, not when I've just started living.* My body bucks at his hand intimately violating me, my thighs trying to close, but the movement only helps him. I jerk at the pain between my legs, in my chest, at my neck.

Closing my eyes, I picture brown eyes, a gorgeous smile, and a baseball cap. I picture the guy who leaned against a bookshelf watching me way back on the third day of school. I picture the guy who hovered over me, chasing away the demons of my past when his body joined with mine.

I picture all of those things and I lift my hands in surrender, my fingers brushing against the headliner as Emil grips my neck tighter, pushing me into the seat.

I don't know why I want to look into the eyes of the man who kills me, but I do. I want to remember what he looks like so if I see him in the afterworld I will never be fooled by the suave face he showed me when I was barely sixteen years old and filled with a fiery jealousy over what he offered my mother.

I open my eyes to find Emil crying.

Crying as he adjusts his grip around my neck, the movement allowing the slightest gasp of air into my lungs before he blocks it out again. Crying as his forceful hand slips out of my body and up over my chest until he's touching my cheek. Crying as he promises me forever, as his eyes catch a movement outside the car window, as his jaw drops, as glass shatters across the interior of the vehicle and a bullet—making its mark centimeters to the left of the middle of his smooth, tan forehead—propels him across the car.

AUSTIN

I hear two things:
Cassie telling me she loves me as her body clenches mine,
and Cassie's bloodcurdling scream as Emil knocks me out.
I wake in a cold sweat...

"Dad?" My father's entering my dimly lit room, the only light coming from a table lamp.

"A call came in. They've tracked a car up Highway 6. They think it's them, but that's all I've been told."

I rub my forehead, forcing myself to remain calm. "How far? Is she okay?"

I see the same helplessness I feel inside as it flashes across his face. "Austin, they aren't in jurisdiction so they're waiting on news. They're a few hours northwest."

The door opens, an officer who West said was assigned security duty outside my room pokes his head in. "Another call came in. Two victims are being transported to Stephenville. She's alive."

"She's alive?" I repeat, unsure I heard him correctly. My body hurts too much to do more than make fists. The officer nods, a reassuring smile popping up. "She's alive," the words pour from my mouth in a heavy exhale.

"How long until she'll be back here? What is she, like, four or five hours away? What happens now?" Tears of relief burn my eyes as a siege of questions hit me.

"Austin, bud, one thing at a time." Dad holds his hand up. He moves to the end of my bed, his hand resting on my blanket-covered foot, one of the only spots not sore right now.

Repeating my questions and some of his own, he grills the officer for the normal protocol in a case such as this one. According to Officer Anderson, Cassie will be held and questioned in Stephenville where they were apprehended. She'll be held there for the next several hours at least, not including time for medical attention she might need. The officers there will question her about what happened here while things are still fresh in her mind.

"Do you want me to go to her?" my father asks the moment Officer Anderson leaves the room.

"Would you?" I rub the bandages along my ribs carefully. I'm not leaving the hospital for a week according to the doctors and nurses. "I don't want her to be alone."

"Of course. It's a few hours. You get some rest and I'll call you as soon as I get there. I'll send Carson back in, he went to grab me coffee."

"Thanks, Dad."

Moving to the head of my bed, he leans over me and hugs me as carefully as he can. My fist grabs at the front of his shirt as my throat closes up.

"Can you tell her I love her and that I'm sorry?" I can't stop the tears as they start flowing again.

His palm taps against my cheek, a little knocking of some sense. That's what he used to call it when we were little. "You didn't do anything, Austin. This isn't your fault."

I shake my head despite the pain it causes. "You're wrong. I'm the one who baited Emil into finding her. I gave him my name, like an idiot. A few clicks on the internet and he would have found my name, found our school. He found her because of me. This is all on me."

CASSIE

*I can't tell which dark stains on my skin belong to me,
which belong to Emil,
and which belong to Austin.*

I close my eyes, then immediately open them. The scenes playing behind my closed lids are ones I'd rather not witness again.

"How are you doing?" asks Detective Crane, a female cop, the only cop they've sent into this room since the interrogations finished. She sets a cup with steam rising from it on the table in front of me.

My hands reach for it, my frozen fingers sighing as the heat thaws them. "No one will tell me about my boyfriend."

"There are a lot of questions needing to be answered here. We're getting close." It's a canned answer. I've seen enough procedural television shows to know when the cops are stalling.

"Questions about what? I've told you everything." Sitting straighter, I stare at the middle-aged detective. "I want to go home. I want to see Austin. Is he okay? Is he alive?"

The officer wets her lips, her head shaking, but she doesn't answer my questions.

"Why can't you tell me anything?"

It's been hours. I know my mother is dead—that was the first order of business with the police once I was examined at the hospital. I know Emil is dead—that one I saw with my own two eyes. I don't know where Austin is or what happened once I walked away from his broken body at the park.

"There are some concerns. I promise we will get things straightened out soon."

There's a commotion outside the small room we're in; shadowed figures walk by the blinds, and I hold my breath as the door pushes open. I'm tired of being questioned, especially by the suits who showed up as part of a larger investigation into Emil Cermak's illegal business dealings in Las Vegas.

"If we could just—"

A body walks through the door with a face so blessedly familiar, although older than the one I love, staring back at me. He walks straight to me, his face stern as he holds up a hand and looks at the two detectives who follow behind him.

"Cassie, sweetie?" Mr. Rutledge says my name as he crouches down beside my chair. "Honey, are you alright?"

Love and concern shine through his eyes, and I nearly collapse into his arms, nodding and bursting into tears.

"Austin?"

His hand presses against my head, holding me against his strong chest. "He's fine. He's worried sick about you, though. He wanted me to tell you he loves you."

He's fine. He's fine. He's fine.

"Mr. Rutledge," one of the detective says.

I'm coaxed to my feet as Austin's dad stands, still holding me.

"Are you charging her with something?" He's not playing around. His voice is filled with authority.

"No, sir, but we—"

"Then she's done here. She's answered all the questions she is going to without a lawyer present. She's been through enough tonight, and I'm going to get her home to the people who love her."

One of the detectives argues, but Detective Crane speaks up over him. "Let her go, Pete."

After a moment, we're walking out of the interrogation room and down a hallway.

"The Vegas guys are going to need to speak with her again," Crane says behind us.

"Fine, they know where to find us. I'll have her lawyer call the station within the hour and you can set up whatever you, or they, need."

"That'll work. Cassandra?" Detective Crane says my name, and Mr. Rutledge stops walking. I look up from beneath the strong arm he has holding me into his side. She gives me an encouraging smile. "You're a tough girl, you're going to be okay."

I nod. I'm going home to my friends and Austin. My family. Yeah, I'm going to be fine.

♥

I fall asleep within moments of climbing into Mr. Rutledge's truck and wake only when the engine turns off. I expect to see the hospital in College Station, but find we're sitting in the driveway to the boys' shared house off campus.

"Why are we here?" I ask, unbuckling my seatbelt and stretching my neck. Four hours slumped over did my already aching body no favors.

He removes the keys from the ignition and opens the door, allowing the frigid early morning air into the toasty cab. "I figured you could use a shower before we go to the hospital."

"No." I shake my head as he climbs out of the truck. "I need to see Austin," I call after him, shoving the door open as he walks around to my side. "I can shower later. Please, take me to the hospital."

"He's sleeping, Cassie. Carson has kept me updated all night. He's doing well and getting rest. Let's get you cleaned up and then we will go right over." I refuse to step out of the vehicle, so Mr. Rutledge braces his hands in the door opening and leans in. "Sweetheart, my son is worried sick about you. I've seen Austin break down twice in his life—when his mother died and last night. Even as a little kid he was the tough one. He's always been the one to brush off disappointment and fear by using humor and a hefty dose of cockiness."

He holds his hand out for me. "If he sees you like this, he will go crazy. He already blames himself for what happened. I'd rather he not see this." His eyes scan down my hair and face.

"I'm a mess, aren't I?" Although the hospital gave me scrubs when they took my clothing for evidence, I'm still covered in blood. My hands are streaked with red. My wrists and arms still covered from where Austin's blood soaked through my sweater. My neck and face itch from beneath Emil's dried blood.

I'm covered in the blood of the man who I've been running from for almost two years. I swallow hard, my hand shaking as I cover my mouth. "He's dead."

"He can't hurt you ever again," Mr. Rutledge assures me, his voice cracking.

I take his hand, allowing him to lead me into the house. The house where I fell in love with Austin, even if I didn't want to admit it at the time.

"Let me find you something in Mindy's things to wear."

"Thank you." I toe my shoes off at the door. "Wait, no. Austin's room. He has sweats I can wear."

"Of course," he agrees with a small smile.

In a trance, I walk to the bathroom, starting the shower and turning the water as hot as I can stand it. Mr. Rutledge delivers me some clothing and I shut the door, looking in the mirror for the first time. My face is marbled black and blue with bruises, cuts, and blood. The glass from the car window sprayed across my skin, luckily doing only superficial damage. My neck is ringed with purple. The ends of my hair are dyed with blood.

I step into the shower, the water draining pink as I clean myself. I scrub between my legs where Emil touched me. The water and soap sting the scratches he made along my tender skin, but I don't stop.

I cry the entire time. I cry and cry and cry until I sink to the floor, the shower wand in hand, and cry some more.

When I'm done, I dress. I braid my hair back, slip on the same boots of Mindy's I used the day Austin and I built our snowman, and I climb back into Mr. Rutledge's car and head for the hospital. And Austin.

AUSTIN

*The hospital has to be the worst place to sleep.
I've slept in cars, tents, on the floor of an airport.
Hospital? This shit sucks.*

Nurses come in every other hour to change drips, check my temperature, verify my oxygen levels, and poke around. Apparently having a collapsed lung is a pretty big deal. I'm sure I'd be freaked out about it if I wasn't going out of my mind waiting on Dad and Cass to get here.

A nurse wakes me, once again, and I open my blurry eyes to see the object of all my worry standing by the door to my room, her hands partially covering her face. Tears flow down her cheeks, unchecked as she watches the nurse messing with my machines and taking notes.

"If you don't bring your ass over here right now I'm going to hurt myself climbing out of this bed to get to you." Her eyes snap to my face, a hiccup of a gasp releasing as she sees I'm awake.

Her mouth forms my name, although no sound comes out. Then she's touching my face and leaning over me, her cheek pressed against mine. The nurse in the room continues working.

"How long have you been here?"

She moves back so I can see her. "Fifteen minutes." Her soft fingertips graze over my sore jaw. "I'm so sorry," she cries, her mouth pressing to mine.

The kiss isn't enough, it's just a peck. My hand gingerly goes to the back of her neck, forcing her back to my lips. "Don't you dare apologize to me again."

Our mouths join. I kiss her gently, over and over, just lightly brushing my starving lips against hers. Her hair is damp against my hand, and she smells like me, like my soap.

The third person in the room clears her throat. "I need to check your chest tube and then I can leave you two alone," my nurse says.

"Chest..." Cassie drags herself away from me, her brows furrowed as she looks me over. "A chest tube?"

"It's pretty standard in cases like mine. It'll come out in a few days."

The nurse comes around to my right and Cassie steps back. I watch her face as the nurse pulls back the tape from the gauze covering both the tube entry and the place where Emil sliced my arm open.

"Looking good." Her hands probe the area, causing a slight discomfort now that my pain meds are wearing off. "The biggest concern at this point is infection, Austin. That's why we're pumping you full of antibiotics."

"What about his ribs? They're broken, right?" Cassie asks, her face contorted with a look of pain.

"They should heal just fine." The nurse pats my arm. "I'll let you two have some time. Breakfast should be here in about an hour."

"Thanks."

She stops next to Cassie, setting a hand on her shoulder. "If you're careful, you can climb up next to him on the left side there," she says with a smile before leaving the room and shutting the door behind her.

We stare at each other. My eyes soak up every inch of her. Her face is bruised and cut up, but she seems okay. She's wearing my clothing, something I'm more than happy about, and Mindy's boots. Dad obviously brought her by the house, which explains her damp hair and the smell of my body wash.

"You heard the nurse," I tap the small empty space to the left of me. "Get up here with me."

She shakes her head, biting her thumb nail. "I don't want to hurt you."

"Cass, get over here," I warn lovingly.

"How do you not hate me? How does your father not hate me? Look at you. You could have died because of me."

"Don't—" Does she not see how badly her guilt hurts me?

"Don't what?"

"Don't play that game again. This isn't your fault. None of it is. Just like the things that happened to you growing up weren't." She stands firm in her denial, her face self-deprecating. "Let me hold you, please."

She moves closer to the bed, her eyes roving over the machines and my body with each step. "Cassie, I called Emil. I threatened him and told him my name. It's my fault he found you." She inhales through her nose, confusion marring her face. "It was when we were in Tyler. Remember when you told me he was still calling you?"

"Yeah." She barely whispers the word.

"That night, after you fell asleep, I took your phone and checked it. I just wanted to know how often he was calling. Even after everything you told me about him, I didn't think he was dangerous. I just assumed he was messing with you, so I checked your texts. That's what set me off. The things he said. I was dialing his number before I could think twice. I figured if he knew you weren't alone anymore he would back off. I thought he was preying on you because he could."

"Oh, Austin," she sighs.

"I told him to come after me," I laugh lightly. "I called what I thought was his bluff. Obviously, it wasn't."

"I should have told you how dangerous he really was."

"Was?" Past tense. I hold my breath.

Cassie moves to my side and tugs back the white blankets. "He's dead," she says softly, as though she's sharing a secret.

Those two words send an avalanche of mixed emotions through me. On one hand, the prick can never hurt Cass again. I have my justice, and she has hers. But on the other, I look at her pale, drawn face and I wonder what she went through. What happened? What did she see? How will this affect her going forward?

I pat the bed, attempting to scoot over, but the movement is too painful. "I have plenty of room," she assures me as she climbs in.

Her legs press up against mine as she sidles up to my side, wrapping an arm around my bicep and resting her head on my shoulder. Her palm settles gently over the hand I have resting on my stomach.

"Is this okay? Am I hurting you?" she asks, kissing my shoulder.

"This is perfect. Don't you dare move," I tell her, and she nods, her hips arching closer to my side. "Do you want to talk about it?"

She exhales heavily, and I wait for an answer. "Eventually," she breathes after a moment.

"Okay. There's no rush, I'm not going anywhere."

"I'm not either, Austin." She tilts her head up, her tired eyes searching mine. "I meant it last night when I told you I wasn't running. I did think about it once I realized those flowers had to be from him, but I realized I could never leave you."

"I was going crazy thinking about it, Cass. I didn't know what you knew. I didn't want to scare you, but I was so damn worried you would walk away without telling me."

She shifts, pushing herself up so we're face to face. "I wanted to. I should have because it could have saved you from this." She touches my arm and chest. "My mom and Emil are dead because I didn't run.

"Don't try to deny it," she says with a determined look toward me when I start to argue. "I could have prevented what happened tonight a long time ago. I should have gone to the police. I should have filed reports a long time ago, but I was too scared. Running seemed like the best answer. Then I met you and I fell in love with you, and I allowed myself to hope he'd just give up. I knew better, and I still put you in jeopardy. I'm sorry."

"No regrets. Ever."

"Ever?" she asks with a wary lift of her brow.

"Not when it comes to you, Elmer."

"I love you."

I smile. I have this faint memory of her saying those very words after we made love last night, before her mom and Emil showed up, but now I know she said it, and I'm over the moon. Screw broken ribs and lungs and concussions—I've found the girl I'm going to love for the rest of my life.

We're sitting in my hospital room two days later: Dad, Carson, Mindy, West, Jules, and Cassie are talking about her interviews at the police station today. I'm pissed as hell that I couldn't be with her, but at least Dad was. As was the lawyer, a longtime family friend, he hired for her.

Cass sits on the edge of my bed, her hand wrapped tightly in mine as she and Dad take turns answering our questions.

"The guy on campus who was following me is one of Emil's men. They pulled him in for questioning this morning. I guess he was keeping tabs on me for Emil."

"But why? Why would he wait for three weeks before coming after you?" West asks. Everyone in this room was filled in on most of the truth to Cassie's story. They think her mother kicked her out and Emil offered her a place to stay. They know she was abused by him, they know her childhood wasn't pleasant, but we've left out the details for now. My dad and I are the only two who know everything. She opened up to him when he joined us that first day after we were reunited.

"Apparently, he was waiting on my mom. She knew things about his business dealings that he couldn't have out there. So he used me as leverage to get her to come back. If she helped him get to me, he'd let her go." Cassie shakes her head. "Or something like that. It doesn't make much sense since he knew where I was. I think he was banking on me going with him to save her, but he knew I hated her. That would have been a strange risk for him to take. There must be more to it all, but we'll never know now."

So many unanswered questions now that the two people with all the answers are both dead.

"Bo is concerned about Emil's partners. That's the most important issue for this family right now," Dad says, causing my stomach to sink.

"What are you talking about?" I ask him, my eyes going to Cassie, who's not looking at me. When they returned, she didn't say anything to make me think there were any problems left.

"The man was a medium-sized player in a much larger game. There are people who may come looking for their own answers to what happened if they're worried about their own asses." Dad looks around the room.

"We've kept your name out of the police reports for your own protection, Austin, but Cassie was already known to some of his men. Her mother was well-known by the men he worked with, too."

"Is this like the mob or something?" Jules asks.

"I suppose you could call it that." Dad nods, and Cassie's head tilts away from the others as he continues. "The detectives working in Vegas are monitoring chatter about Emil, and so far there haven't been any tears shed for the guy. Someone is always waiting in the wings to rake in the last guy's money."

"So we wait and hopefully it'll all blow over and no one will come looking for Cassie?" Carson asks, his eyes meeting mine.

"They suggested I go into hiding for a while," Cassie says softly, not looking up.

If anyone else says anything it's drowned out by my own shout of disbelief. "Tell them to go screw themselves."

Cassie's eyes close before she shifts my way. "Austin."

"No. You're not running away anymore. The man is dead. Your mother is dead. You get to have a life now, Cass."

"They're not saying I have to give up my life."

"Like hell they aren't," I growl, flinching at the tightness it causes in my chest.

Dad stands and my gaze snaps to him. "Can you leave us?" I look at my brothers and Mindy and Jules. "All of you?"

When they've shut the door behind them, Cassie slides off the bed. "Austin, this isn't just about me. If I stay here and someone comes looking for me, they could come after you or anyone in your family. Jess and Katie, too. Anyone I love could be in harm's way."

I push myself up. Damn it! I want to punch something right now. "You're not running."

"It wouldn't be forever—"

"You're not running," I continue as she crosses her arms over her chest. "It seems to me like the only real issue here is your identity. They don't know you, right?"

"I never met anyone other than a few bodyguards. There was that pool party when I was barely sixteen, but I didn't speak with anyone there," she confirms.

"Fine. So we change your name and you stay low for a few months. If anything comes up we can discuss going into hiding at that point."

"We?" She cocks her head. "You're safe from all this, you know."

"You're cute, you know that?" I shift, tucking my leg under me and crooking my finger at her until she sits next to me. Taking her fingers in mine, I bring them to my lips. "Sweetie, we're a package deal. If you're not safe, I'll be with you."

"No. You're not doing that. You're not giving up football and school and your family to follow me."

"If the detectives tell me you have to, I will." She attempts to stand, but I gently yank her back. "You're my family too, Cass. I'll happily give up the other stuff to be with you."

"If your dad and brothers could hear you now."

I smile. I know exactly what they would think, and I know exactly what I want. "They would tell me to protect my wife."

She chokes. "Your wife?"

"Marry me?"

"Are you crazy?"

"You need a name change, and I need you by my side forever. I'm not crazy, I'm in love."

She pulls her hand from mine, covering her face. "Oh, God. Oh, God," she mutters in a low voice, rubbing at her forehead and pushing her fingers through her hair. "This isn't a joke, Austin."

"You're right, it isn't. I just asked you to marry me. Do you see me laughing?" My hands move to her hips and back, turning her toward me as I pull her between my legs the best I can on the bed.

"This isn't how it works."

"What? Love? Marriage?" Her utterly confused face looks at me like I've grown a second head. "Cassie, I love you. I knew you were the one the first time I spoke to you. There isn't a perfect formula for relationships that we have to follow. Hell, my aunt and uncle were engaged and married within three months, and they've been married for over twenty years."

She snorts and returns to muttering.

"Keep invoking God's name, Cass. I'm sure we're gonna need his help over the next fifty or so years."

Her head swings my way and I wink. "You're crazy."

"Yep." I take her face into my hands and lean in until we're inches apart. "Want to marry a crazy man?"

Her hands cover mine. "Austin."

"Say yes."

"What if this hadn't happened? What if Emil hadn't shown up?"

"But he did." I'm not talking in hypotheticals; it won't help my case right now. "And this is where we are."

"Exactly. If he hadn't shown up, you wouldn't be asking me to marry you. You wouldn't be worried about protecting me right now. You would be worried about school and football and the next time you're going to get laid."

I ignore her arguments. "Do you love me?" She tries to argue, so I ask again. "Do you love me?"

"Yes," she breathes in exasperation. "Yes, I love you."

"Good. I love you too." I kiss the tip of her nose as she smirks. "And since you want to speak in hypotheticals, let's play this out. Forget the events of Friday and Saturday morning. We go on with our lives, we date, I play football, I finish school, I get laid—by you—a lot over the next year. You know what happens then? I ask you to marry me. Or I get my masters, we keep dating, and I ask you to marry me when you graduate. Or I consider playing pro, I get picked up by some team, and I still ask you to marry me.

"Don't you see, Cass? Every scenario of my life works out to my asking you to marry me. The only thing I don't know is what your answer will be."

"Yes you do," Cassie whispers, her eyes filling with tears.

My chest tightens. "I do?"

"Yes," she nods. "Yes, I'll marry you, if you're sure."

"I'm so sure." I'm kissing and answering her at the same time.

She jerks away. "And only if your dad approves," she says seriously.

"Sweetie, I'm twenty-two. Technically, I don't need his approval."

"Yes, we do. If everyone thinks we're crazy, I want you to listen to them. Promise me you will."

"Fine, I promise." I do because I know they'll agree. They love Cassie, and they know me well enough to know this isn't some stupid whim.

"Holy shit, Cass. We're getting married!" I laugh.
"If you're family approves," she inserts once again.
"We're getting married!" I repeat, kissing her.

TWO WEEKS LATER

CASSIE

When I was a little girl, I didn't dream of my wedding day.

I didn't dream of a prince coming to rescue me.

I didn't envision that guy who would love me for the rest of my life.

Nope. I didn't do any of those things until I met Austin.

Austin Rutledge changed my life, and today he's changing my last name.

AUSTIN

Eight weeks ago, I watched my older brother marry the love of his life, never considering I'd be doing the same thing today.

"Hey, man, the girls are ready." West pokes his head into the room followed by Carson.

"Cass is ready?" I adjust my tie for the fifteenth time.

"There's a problem when the bride is ready before the groom." Carson leans against my dresser, watching me. "You ready for this?"

I look at my brothers. The two guys who have been in my life every step of the way. They didn't balk or question us when Cassie and I sat them down and told them we wanted to get married. They bought into the idea from the beginning.

"Totally ready."

I walk into the living room to find my bride, waiting for me alone. She's dressed in a simple cream dress with long, lace sleeves and a fitted knee-length skirt.

"You are gorgeous," I tell her, taking in the soft, flowing curls falling over her shoulder.

"What, this old thing?" She grins, flitting from side to side. "It's just a dress."

"No way," I move closer, mindful of the promise I made to her last night that we wouldn't kiss again until we said I do. "This is the dress you're going to marry me in. I'm not sure if you'll ever be more beautiful to me."

"You haven't seen what Jess bought me to wear tonight," she teases.

"Oh, really?"

"Mm-hmmm." The smile never leaves her face.

"Remind me to thank her after the ceremony."

The doors down the hallway open as our family and friends make their way to the living room, obviously deciding we've had enough time alone.

"You two have an appointment at the courthouse, let's get going." Dad claps his hands, herding everyone toward the door.

We step around the boxes cluttering the foyer thanks to Mindy and Carson speeding up their home search and securing a move-in ready home they'll be moving into this weekend while Cass and I have a two-night weekend honeymoon in Dallas. It's not much, but thanks to my doctor's permission—finally!—I don't plan on leaving the bed.

"Hey, West, you know what just occurred to me?" I chuckle, taking Cassie's hand as we step out into the cold.

West turns around, curious. "What's that?"

"You're still not getting the master bedroom."

His face falls. "Damn it. Hey, Jules, you want to get married?" he calls out, and Jules, Jess, and Katie turn toward him in tandem.

"Ask me again in a few years," she winks. Jeff punches West in the forearm as everyone bursts into laughter.

"I knew y'all were competitive, but damn, proposing marriage just to get the master bedroom is a little much don't you think?" Jess teases.

"It's a really great bedroom," Mindy laughs while Carson nods his head in agreement.

Cassie leans into my side. "Don't worry, I'd marry you even if we had to live in the dorms."

"And give West the satisfaction of having the biggest room? No way," I point out with no shame. She gives me the same look my mother did when I didn't play fair with my little brother as a kid, and I grin in response. I kiss her knuckles, my eyes never leaving her glowing face. "Sorry, little one, it's a Rutledge thing."

"And this is what I'm marrying into?"

"Right?" I tease, my eyes innocent and wide. "You won the lottery, Cass."

Full blown Elmer laughter erupts from her red lips, warming every inch of my body the same way her touch does. That is the laughter I plan on falling asleep to every night and waking up to every morning.

Hell yeah, I'm the one who won the freakin' lottery.

THE FREAKIN' END!

EXCERPT - UNTIL WE CRASH

If Austin is your introduction to the Rutledge boys please consider picking up the beginning of this series, *From The Wreckage,* and learn how Jules, West, and Austin end up where they are in *After The Fall.*

Did you love Jess? Fast forward a few years and check out her super sexy story *Until We Crash!* Here's a peek…

SYNOPSIS

Carter Cooper: Big Man on Campus at Rossview High turned football star at Oregon until injuries sidelined him.

Jessica Womick: Rossview High cheerleader turned carefree A&M coed until family issues send her home for the summer.

He's found a new direction for his future;
She's become the caretaker to a drunk.

These are not the directions they planned on taking, but when their paths reunite, they can neither deny their attraction nor their mutual need for distraction.

Finding joy in the struggle is rarely easy, and when Jess's world tumbles into the unrecognizable, Carter sets out to prove that not everyone in her life will fail her.

JESS

There's a strangling bitterness that creeps into my bruised and suffocating soul at having to save him over and over. It takes the shape of an impenetrable wall, adding height and depth with every bailout. After ten years, it's an unmovable tower. No matter, I stretch to the tips of my aching toes and claw to the top—hoping *this* is the last time. This time he'll notice how hard I'm climbing for him, and he'll wise up. He never does. I rescue him, and when I'm done, I'm alone and bitter and hopeless. My battered heart cries out; I'm trying to fix him. Will anyone help fix me?

The question plays across my mind the way an inclement weather warning scrolls over my favorite television show—at the most inopportune time. I should be on a beach or at the lake with friends. Nope, I'm wandering into the land of beer and desperation for the umpteenth time. I enter, squinting and adjusting to the feeble lighting as the aroma hits my nose. Hell, bottle the stench and I'd own the perfume of every bar I've dragged Dad out of over the years. On the opposite side of the chipped red doors, the sunshine is abundant on this early June afternoon. Within these walls, is another world. There are no windows reminding patrons what they're missing on the other side; there are only dusty fixtures hanging over scratched wooden tables and dank walls. Unlike the bars around A&M's

campus, the music flowing out of this jukebox is old-school country—a little Tammy Wynette "Stand by your Man." How poetic.

This is my summer vacation—returning to Rossview and following around a man who cannot pull his shit together. Ten to one, I'll lose the one job I found because he's unable to hack sobriety for an hour, forget the time it requires to work an entire shift.

"He's in the corner, darlin'." Eddie waves from behind the bar.

Yea, we're on a first-name basis. There are a handful of bars in Rossview, and Dad is intimate with them all. "You could refuse him service, Eddie."

"And have a repeat of last year's incident?" Eddie sniffs. "Sorry, he pays, he drinks."

Maintaining a grown man's sobriety is not the responsibility of Eddie or any other bar owner. My head shakes with disappointment as I offer up thanks.

"You called, so that's something," I say, steering toward the lump of a human hunched over a glass of amber liquid.

Dad.

My shoes suction to the floor with each step. Another lovely trait Dad's favorite haunts have in common. Sticky floors, sticky air, and—come sundown—sticky morals. At this hour, though, the television in the corner flickers in and out, re-airing a football game as Tammy's song ends and Hank comes to life. Yep, there *is* a tear in my beer, Hank.

Weary faces turn my way, and I tug at my skimpy work uniform. I'm a college girl and former cheerleader—I'm comfortable showing my body off, but the twenty steps across this bar put me on display. The mid-afternoon drinkers are factory workers coming off the first shift. They stop by with their buddies, have a beer, and return to their wives and kids before repeating the process. The life is one I understand well—unchanging and straightforward—but today they've won a free show with their liquor: Jessica Womick and her curves.

"What an exhibitionist. Like her mother." Even if unsaid, I imagine the thoughts run through the mind of every man present.

I near the corner and Dad's bent form. "Dad?" I struggle for a smooth voice.

He grunts into the table.

"Dad?" I inch in. A second unintelligible grunt greets me. Sweat dampens the small of my back as I poke his rounded shoulder. "Dad, time to go."

He lifts his head, and unfocused eyes stare past me. "Jess?"

Maintaining an even tone and treating him like an adult is difficult as I hunch at his side and say, "Let's go."

When I was a child, he was a vibrant hulk of a man with thick, dark hair and smiling eyes. He would throw me on his shoulders and parade me around our hometown. He was a man who was proud of himself and the life he'd built. He worked for his girls—for Mom and me. Things changed. We moved to Rossview, and the factory underwent layoffs. They cut hours and brought in automation. Money became tight, and our home became loud.

The hulk disappeared. The pride fell. The daily grind of a life filled with backbreaking work chipped at him, but Mom's betrayal left the husk of a man I see today.

He straightens in the chair and wraps one hand around his liquid savior while extending the other toward me. "I needed fresh air." His words slur as he pats my head.

I manage a sympathetic pat of my own. Offering compassion is challenging after years of excuses. Impossible when his right hand lifts toward his lips for another drink.

"Stop, Dad. Come on." I reach for his glass.

My attempt is in vain. He blocks my arm while angling himself toward the wall and tossing the last shot of whatever poison he's drowning in today back in one gulp. The worst part of his drinking? He's an alcohol whore. He throws down anything he gets his hands on. Whatever sends him to the place of incoherence the fastest is his new best friend. His empty glass hits the table with a thud. With nothing left to guzzle, he stands on wobbly legs and throws a hand out as if saying, 'After you.' It's the second-worst part of his drinking. He's a happy drunk for the most part. Hell, he doesn't even fight when I cut him off nowadays.

Eddie offers his assistance as I stumble to the door under Dad's weight, but I refuse. This is a familiar rodeo, pal. I'm adept at the job. I release my hold on his side and sling my arm around him, digging my keys from my waistband as we exit. He wanders with the change in my grip.

"Dad"—the keys fall to the gravel drive as Dad ricochets off a parked pickup truck like a pinball— "my car. The red one," I say through gritted teeth, kicking the keys.

"Red?" he mutters. "Red. Red. Red."

Settling him into my vehicle is a two-person job, and by the time he's buckled in and I've closed the passenger door, my boobs swim in sweat. I inhale a deep breath and lean my hip against the car. He isn't three-sheets-to-the-wind wasted today, which is a good thing. When Eddie called with the news of Dad's arrival, he said he'd serve whatever Dad's measly dollars could afford. Eddie could tell Dad drank before he arrived. This means he bought alcohol at the grocery store, consumed it, and returned, where they likely refused him for being impaired. It wouldn't be the first time.

A dense thump against the car window prods me into action. I round the vehicle and climb in, giving Dad a cursory glance before I crank the engine. He's leaning against the glass, eyes closed, body slack. Great, he passed out. Heading home should be uneventful.

***

The drive from Rossview's bars to the ranch-style house we moved into the summer before my freshman year of high school is minimal. The proximity is what keeps Dad knee-deep in liquor. I suppose I'm grateful he doesn't drive drunk, but his having easy access to alcohol derails my cause. Driving to the back of the house, I park nearest to the door as I can get. Our neighbors are at work, but it's summer, and people talk. All I need is one kid getting an eyeful of me chaperoning Dad from my beat-up Acura to the front door, and the do-gooders will arrive in swarms. The Womick name is a permanent fixture in the rumor mill these days. I've been at work for three days, and the looks of pity from my new co-workers have already started.

I shift into park and cut the engine. "Dad? We're home."

His even breaths are soft, and I lean my head against the headrest with a sigh. The sun is on a mission to incinerate the earth, or I'd roll down the windows and let him sleep this off. His waking up in a pool of his sweat would be a daughter's justice. The thought is fleeting. I need the car to return to work, and as angry as I am with him, finding the strength to hate him and stop taking care of him isn't happening. Not today.

CARTER

"Hey," her muffled voice says as she nudges at my calf with the toe of her shoe. I yank out my earbuds and roll out from beneath the chassis of the pickup I've screwed around with all afternoon. "Coach Dolino called."

"And?" I spare her a glance. Her hands land on her hips as she peers at me, an impression of our mother's glare on her face. Damn, she's good. She's like an angry giant hovering over me. Unhappy with that image, I level the playing field by sitting up. The wrench resting on my stomach clatters to the garage floor, and she retreats a step.

"Carter."

"Cha-a-ase." I mimic her resigned tone while holding her glare. She is the only person who manages to string my name out that way. As usual, the first fold goes to Chase, and I smirk. A small victory for the big brother.

"Whatever." She huffs, her eyes rolling as they tend to do whenever she speaks with me. "Why do I bother with you?"

I chuckle at her red-faced glowering and lift a brow. Good question. Why does she bother with me? Why does Coach? Why do Mom and Dad? I'd ask, but no matter the line of shit they feed me, nothing changes. What's done is done.

"How is this place so quiet?" I change the topic while leaning sideways for a glimpse of the clock Chase is blocking while lording over me. "Wait, it's after five? Did the guys head out without telling me?" I straddle the creeper and push to my feet. The awkward movement sends a knife-like slash of pain from my right knee down my leg, and I hiss at the jolt. Chase observes my clumsy maneuvering with pursed lips, but she's smart and keeps her big mouth shut.

She ignores my question until I'm on two feet and stretching toward the ceiling, trying my damnedest to cover my discomfort. "The twins are hanging about, and Owen's in the office on the phone."

"Huh, okay." My spine pops and cracks as I work the kinks out and survey the shop, taking in our current projects, "the rent," as Owen prefers to call them. They are the jobs we do to keep the garage cash flow positive. The work we suffer through so we can afford our passion—restoring and customizing cars.

The Chevy I'm installing a lift kit on appears to be the last unfinished job of the day. The twins' customized WRX sits in her bay shiny and ready for her owner to drool over in the morning—a day in advance. A win since fast turnaround time is vital for repeat business.

"Where's the Z Owen was working on?" I ask Chase while walking toward the office.

"Finished. He's on the phone with the paint shop."

How did those three finish their shit without me noticing? Metal clinks behind me, and I check over my shoulder and find Chase straightening my workspace. Typical.

"Hey, go on, sis. There's no overtime in your employment contract." I wave my hand like she's a bothersome fly before pushing through the glass doors to the reception area. She shoots me a scowl and continues messing with my tools. I let her be.

Owen's voice floats my way as I walk around Chase's desk and down the short hallway to our one office. "Yeah, Meteor Gray Metallic"—he hums in agreement with whatever is said on the other end of the line—"it'll look sharp. Yup, I'll drive her over if you're willing to hang for twenty."

I prop my shoulder against the doorframe.

"Hey, man," he says when his call ends.

"Did I lose consciousness? How the hell did you three finish your jobs before me?"

Owen scratches his jaw and declines in his chair. "Beats me, you had the pansy job today."

"The pansy job?" Installing a lift kit sounds simple, but there are a million things to consider when jacking up a truck beyond factory build. I sink into the chair opposite Owen's desk and prop my boots on the edge. "You know damn well it takes a long time to re-gear and get a vehicle ready for lift. Shit is tedious as hell. I'd work on wing and hood installs all day every day."

"Yeah, yeah, stop picking the short stick, and you'll stop landing the pain in the ass jobs." Owen shifts through the piles on his desk. Finding a notepad, he jots notes before ripping off the sheet and standing. "I'm gonna drive the Z over to Ace. You about done? We're grabbing drinks and dinner at Bleachers."

I consider the job. "Sure, I'll meet you in an hour."

♥

Chase lingers in my workspace when I return to the garage. "What's up?" I ask. She damn well has opinions to share or questions to ask if she's hanging around.

Her gaze falls to the ground as she shrugs. Three years have passed, but she resembles the naive girl I left when I headed off to college at Oregon more than the college freshman she'll be in the fall. My kid sister, who coaxed me into hiring her for a summer job at the garage over working at Mom's boutique. Her reasoning for the request remains unclear, but I have a good idea why.

Snatching a screwdriver from the table, I speak over my shoulder. "You don't need to keep me company, Chase, go hang out with your friends."

She releases a little laugh. "Why would I want to hang out with my friends when you're this pleasant?"

I ignore her jibe and go to work, adjusting the truck's headlights, re-aiming them toward the ground to compensate for the new height. Without asking, Chase dims the garage lights while I verify I have the headlights right. I squat and nudge the housing one final time before replacing the covers.

"Did you take something for the pain?" My head snaps at Chase's question. She cocks hers to the side. "You're wincing."

"I'm tired."

"Bullshit." She grabs the other headlight cover and screws it on for me. "Your surgery was only eight weeks ago, you're pushing it."

"C'mon, Chase." I toss my screwdriver on the table. "If I wanted to hear nagging, I'd have stayed living at home."

"Who's nagging?"

"You are." I turn and trip over the creeper I left hanging out beneath the truck, and my repaired knee protests at the odd movement as I stumble. "Dammit." I hiss and catch my weight against the hood. Chase's worried gasp burns my ears as curses fly from my mouth.

Dropping my head on the truck, I inhale. "I'm done."

Chase touches my shoulder. "Carter?" Her concerned tone has my body folding in on itself.

"I'll take something, okay?" I hate my weakness.

Her footsteps echo through the dim garage as she walks toward the office, where she stashed my painkillers in hopes I'll pop them when needed. I push to my forearms and watch her through the glass door. She's my self-appointed savior. *That* is why she's working at the shop. Chase loved hanging out in the garage with Owen and me growing up. She loves the smell of rubber and grease, but she took a job with Mom at the boutique once she was fifteen. Chase hung around while I was home after my first injury last year, but her daily life remained unaltered. When I returned after the second surgery this past April, my sister dropped everything. The final weeks and weekends of Chase's senior year, she kept me company by watching every action movie available. She drove me to therapy without asking about my feelings. She let me vent without casting judgment over my decisions. Chase was present. She *is* present. My pain in the ass baby sister, hell-bent on saving me from the depression my family, friends, and coaches fear will creep in.

She returns with a water bottle and a giant pill. "I'm roasting a chicken for dinner tonight. Come eat with us."

She's aware tonight is Bleachers' night: Thursday night baseball, sports trivia, and beer.

"No drinking on pain meds," Chase says after I swallow my pill. I curse under my breath. "C'mon, Mom and Dad will be happy to see your grumpy face. You need to stop by; they miss seeing you."

During my first two years of college, they were lucky to see me a few hours a month. Since my injury, we have weekly visits. I stretch my neck and think.

I could hang out with the guys without drinking, but my knee aches and sitting on my ass and doing nothing sounds appealing.

"Fine, but you're running interference. No talk about school, football, or my future."

Judging by her eager agreement, I've ignored my family since moving out of the house last month.

Want more? *Until We Crash* is available to buy or read for FREE on Kindle Unlimited.

ACKNOWLEDGMENTS

I'm always so very grateful to the people who support me through the book process and life:

My husband and kids deal with me forgetting laundry, dinner, carpool, emails—how they put up with me I'll never know!

My amazing crew of readers, bloggers, and friends on Facebook and 'in real life' keep me sane and make this solitary life a little less solitary and a lot more lifelike.

My PR agent, Rick Miles and the crew at Red Coat PR—You're the best pimps ever. Thank you for your advice and for making me look good.

My Literary Agent, Italia Gandolfo, and Gandolfo Helin Literary Management—Your fire is contagious. Here's to the future!

Special thanks to one of my favorite readers, **Jenine Anderson**, for helping justify Austin's hate of mushrooms. 'They squeak' ;)

The professionals who backed me up on After The Fall:

My editor, Samantha—Thank you for not quitting on me when I gave you a stressful deadline! You help make all of my ideas shine brighter!

My cover team—

- Starla, of Designs by Starla, thank you for creating a beautiful design for Austin as well as all of the other From The Wreckage novels.

- Regina Wamba of Mae I Design, thank you for your beautiful photography.

Printed in Great Britain
by Amazon